The Cookbook Collector

Allegra Goodman is the author of six novels, including *Kaaterskill Falls* – a finalist for the National Book Award. Her novel *Intuition* was shortlisted for the Wellcome Trust Book Prize, and longlisted for the Orange Prize 2009. She lives with her family in Cambridge, Massachusetts.

Also by Allegra Goodman:

The Other Side of the Island

Intuition

Paradise Park

Kaaterskill Falls

The Family Markowitz

Total Immersion

The Cookbook Collector

ALLEGRA GOODMAN

Atlantic Books
LONDON

First published in the United States in 2010 by The Dial Press,
an imprint of The Random House Publishing Group, a division of
Random House, Inc., New York.

This trade paperback edition first published in Great Britain in 2011
by Atlantic Books, an imprint of Atlantic Books Ltd.

1 3 5 7 9 10 8 6 4 2

A CIP catalogue record for this book is available from the British Library.

ISBN: 978 1 84887 539 5

Printed in Sweden by ScandBook AB

Atlantic Books
An imprint of Atlantic Books Ltd
Ormond House
26–27 Boswell Street
London WC1N 3JZ
www.atlantic-books.co.uk

To Irene Skolnick and Susan Kamil
colleagues, friends, believers

I can live no longer by thinking.

AS YOU LIKE IT, v.ii.50

Contents

CONTENTS

PART ONE

Friends and Family

Fall 1999

1

Rain at last. Much-needed rain, the weathermen called it. Rain drummed the little houses skyrocketing in value in Cupertino and Sunnyvale. Much-needed rain darkened the red tile roofs of Stanford, and puddled Palo Alto's leafy streets. On the coast, the waves were molten silver, rising and melting in the September storm. Bridges levitated, and San Francisco floated like a hidden fortress in the mist. Rain flattened the impatiens edging corporate lawns, and Silicon Valley shimmered. The world was bountiful, the markets buoyant. Reflecting pools brimmed to overflowing, and already the tawny hills looked greener. Like money, the rain came in a rush, enveloping the Bay, delighting forecasters, exceeding expectations, charging the air.

Two sisters met for dinner in the downpour. Emily had driven up from Mountain View to Berkeley in rush-hour traffic. Jess just biked over from her apartment. Emily carried an umbrella. Jess hadn't bothered.

"Look at you," said Emily.

"Mmm." Jess brushed the raindrops from her face. "I like it." University Avenue's stucco and glass storefronts were streaming. Runoff whooshed into the storm drains at her feet.

"You're getting soaked."

Jess swung her bike helmet by the straps. "I'm hydrating."

"Like a frog?"

"You don't have to be amphibian to hydrate through your skin."

"Get under the umbrella!"

Jess had a theory about everything, but her ideas changed from day to day. It was hard for Emily to remember whether her sister was primarily feminist or environmentalist, vegan or vegetarian. Did she eat fish, or nothing with a face? Uncertain, Emily let Jess choose the restaurant when they went out to dinner.

The two of them nibbled samosas at Udupi Palace, and Emily said, "I'm sorry I kept rescheduling."

"That's okay." It was two weeks past Jess's twenty-third birthday, and the restaurant with its paper place mats looked small and plain for a palace, but Jess didn't mind.

"Veritech has been insane," Emily explained, "and Jonathan was here. . . ."

"Oh, Jonathan was here," Jess echoed in a teasing voice. "What did you do with Jonathan?" She often took this tone about Emily's boyfriend. The longer the relationship went on, the more serious it seemed, the more she teased. Jess didn't like him.

"He was just here very briefly on his way to L.A.," Emily said. "The last couple of weeks have been—"

Jess interrupted, "I've been insane too."

"Really?" Emily realized she sounded too surprised and added, "Doing what?"

"I'm taking the Berkeley, Locke, Hume seminar, and logic, and philosophy of language. . . ." Jess paused to sip her mango *lassi*. "And working and leafleting."

"Again?"

"For Save the Trees. And I'm also taking Latin. I think I might be as busy as you."

Emily laughed. "No." She was five years older and five times busier. While Jess studied philosophy at Cal, Emily was CEO of a major data-storage start-up.

"We're filing," Emily explained.

"I know," Jess said in a long-suffering voice.

Jess was the only person in the world bored by the IPO, and Emily loved that about her. "I got you a present."

"Really? Where is it?"

"You'll see. It's in the car. I thought we could take it back to your place so you can try it on."

"Oh," Jess said cheerfully, which meant, "I don't mind that you got me clothes again."

"You wanted something else," Emily fretted.

"No, I didn't."

"You did."

"No! Nothing specific. Maybe a horse. Or a houseboat. That would be nice. And a photographic memory for verb tables."

"Why are you taking Latin, anyway?"

"Language requirement," Jess said.

"But you know French."

"I don't *really* know French, and I need an ancient language too."

Emily shook her head. "That program seems like such a long haul."

"Compared to going public after two and a half years? It's true."

The sisters' voices were almost identical, laughing mezzos tuned in childhood to the same pitch and timbre. To the ear, they were twins; to the eye, nothing alike. Emily was tall and slender with her hair cropped short. She wore a pinstriped shirt, elegant slacks, tiny, expensive glasses. She was an MBA, not a programmer, and it showed. Magnified by her glasses, her hazel eyes were clever, guarded, and also extremely beautiful. Her features were delicate, her fingers long and tapered. She scarcely allowed her back to touch her chair, while Jess curled up with her legs tucked under her. Jess was small and whimsical. Her face and mouth were wider than Emily's, her cheeks rounder, her eyes greener and more generous. She had more of the sun and sea in her, more freckles, more gold in her brown hair. She would smile at anyone, and laugh and joke and sing. She wore jeans and sweaters from Mars Mercantile, and her hair . . . who knew when she'd cut it last? She just pushed the long curls off her face.

Jess leaned forward, elbow on the table, and rested her head on her hand. "So, Emily," she said. "What's it like being rich?"

Emily began to speak and then caught herself. "I don't know," she answered truthfully. "I haven't tried it yet."

They hoisted Jess's bike into Emily's car and drove to Durant with the hatchback open. "Look at that," Emily said. She'd lucked into a legal parking space.

Jess lived at the edge of campus, where fraternities sprang up in every style, from Tudor to painted gingerbread. To the north, the university rose into the hills. John Galen Howard's elegant bell tower overlooked eucalyptus groves and rushing streams, the faculty club built like a timbered hunting lodge, the painted warnings to cyclists on the cement steps: DISMOUNT. To the south, Jess's neighborhood boasted the best burrito in the city and the best hot dog in the known universe, Pegasus Books with its used fantasy and science fiction novels, People's Park, where bearded sojourners held congress at the picnic tables. Amoeba Music, Moe's, Shakespeare & Co. Buskers playing tom-toms, sidewalk vendors selling incense and tie-dyed socks. Students, tourists, dealers, greasy spoons of many nations.

Jess's building was Old Hollywood–hacienda style: stucco, red tile, and wrought iron. Sconces lit the entryway, where the mailboxes were set into the wall. Jess paused, looking for her mail key. "Oh, well," she said.

An elderly neighbor climbed the steps. "Hey, Mrs. Gibbs, how are you?" said Jess, unlocking and holding the door open. "Do you remember my sister, Emily?"

"We have not had the pleasure." Mrs. Gibbs was a petite black woman with freckles on her nose, and she wore a white nurse's uniform under her black raincoat. White dress, white stockings, green rubber boots. Mrs. Gibbs placed her hand on Emily's head. "May you always be a blessing."

"That was strange," Emily whispered as Jess led the way up the stairs.

"She's a friend."

"What do you mean, 'friend'?" Jess tended to collect people. She was friendly to a fault. She went through little fascinations, and easily fancied herself in love. "Do you actually know that woman?" Emily's voice echoed in the stairwell. "Does she usually put her hands on people's heads?"

Jess held open the door to her apartment, a real find, despite the rattling pipes and cracked tile in the bathroom. Eleven-foot ceilings, plasterwork like buttercream, closets deep enough to sublet. "She's lived in the building for, like, thirty years," said Jess, as if that explained everything.

Her roommates Theresa and Roland lolled on the couch watching *Wuthering Heights* on *Masterpiece Theatre*. Theresa was studying comparative literature and writing a dissertation that had something to do with migration, borders, and margins. She'd grown up in Honolulu but couldn't swim. Roland was lanky and wore pleated pants and a dress shirt and gold-rimmed glasses; he worked as a receptionist in the dean's office.

"Hey," said Jess.

Roland held up a warning finger. "Shh."

Jess led her sister into her bedroom. The walls were lined with overloaded Barnes & Noble folding birch bookcases. Piles of sweaters and Save the Trees leaflets filled a papasan chair. A battered wood table from the street served as desk for an ancient IBM desktop computer. On the wall hung a framed Ansel Adams poster, the black-and-white image of a glistening oak coated and crackling with ice. On her bulletin board, Jess had pinned photos of their father, Richard, and his wife, Heidi, and their little girls, Lily and Maya.

"Maybe you should dry off before you try on the . . ." Emily was rummaging in her shopping bag as Jess peeled off her socks and her damp sweater. "I have something else in here for you." She produced a thick prospectus.

"Initial Public Offering for Veritech Corporation, Sunnyvale," Jess read off the cover.

"Right. You should read all of that. And also these." Emily handed Jess a wad of papers. "This is our Friends and Family offering. You fill this out and send a check here." She pointed to an address.

"Why?"

"You're eligible to buy one hundred shares at eighteen dollars a share. So you need to mail in a check for eighteen hundred dollars."

Jess grinned in disbelief. "Eighteen hundred dollars?"

"No, no, no, you have to do this," Emily said. "After the IPO, the price will go through the roof. Daddy's buying. Aunt Joan is buying. . . ."

"Maybe they can buy some for me too."

"No, this is important. Stop thinking like a student."

"I am a student."

"Just leave that aside for the moment, okay? Follow the directions. You'll do really, really well."

"How do you know?"

"Have you heard of Priceline?"

"No."

"Sycamore Networks?"

Jess shook her head as Emily rattled off the names of companies that had gone public in 1999. The start-ups had opened at sixteen dollars, thirty-eight dollars, and were now selling for hundreds of dollars a share. "Just read the material, and mail the check. . . ."

"But I don't have eighteen hundred dollars," Jess reminded her sister.

"So borrow."

"All right, will you lend me eighteen hundred dollars?"

Emily lost patience. "If you'd just temporarily give up your aversion to money . . ."

"I don't have an aversion to money," Jess said. "I don't have any. There's a big difference."

"I don't think you understand what I'm giving you," said Emily. "I get only ten on my Friends and Family list."

"So it's sort of an honor," said Jess.

"It's sort of an opportunity. Please don't lose this stuff. You have ten days to take care of this. Just follow through, okay?"

"If you insist." Emily's bossiness brought out the diva in Jess.

"Promise."

"Promise," Jess said. After which she couldn't help asking, "Do I still have to try on the clothes?"

"Here's the blouse, and the jacket. Here's the skirt." Emily straightened the blanket on Jess's unmade bed and sat on top.

The skirt was short, the jacket snug, and they were woven in a rust and

orange tweed. The blouse was caramel silk with a strange lacquered finish, not just caramel but caramelized. Jess gazed for a moment at the
three pieces. Then she stripped off the rest of her clothes and plunged in.

"Oh, they're perfect," said Emily. "They fit perfectly. Do you have a
mirror?"

"Just in the bathroom."

"Here, brush your hair and tie it back. Or put it up. Go take a look."

Jess padded off to the bathroom and peeked at herself in the mirror,
where she saw her own bemused face, more freckled than she remembered. The tweed jacket and the silk blouse reminded her of a game she
and Emily had played when they were little. They called themselves
Dress-Up Ladies and teetered through the house on high heels. Sometimes Emily would wear a satin evening gown, and pretend she was a
bride. Then Jess would be the flower girl, with scarves tied around her
waist. That was before their father gave away their mother's clothes.

"Can you see?" Emily called from the bedroom.

"It's really nice," Jess called back.

"It's a Vivienne Tam suit," said Emily when Jess returned.

"Thank you. I could tell by the . . . label." Jess sat down cautiously on
her desk chair. Comically, experimentally, she tried crossing her legs.

"You hate it," Emily said.

"No! It's really very pretty." Jess was already undressing.

"Just say you'll wear it once."

"I'll wear it to your IPO." Jess pulled on a giant T-shirt and sweatpants.

"You aren't going to the IPO. It's not a wedding."

"Okay, I'll wear it to your wedding." Jess flopped onto the bed. "Don't
you miss him?"

"We're used to it."

"I never would be," Jess declared, and added silently, Never in a million years. She would never deny herself the one she loved, or make excuses for him either. She'd never say, It's complicated, or We have to be
patient. Love was not patient. Love was not kind. It didn't keep; it
couldn't wait. Not in her experience. Certainly not in her imagination.

"What did Dad and Heidi get you?" Emily asked.

"Just the tickets home for Thanksgiving. And they sent me pictures from the kids. See—Lily wrote her name, and a rainbow." Jess spread their half sisters' drawings over the bed. "I think these scribbles are from Maya. And I have Mom's letter here somewhere. . . ."

Their mother, Gillian, had passed away when Emily was ten and Jess was only five. Fighting breast cancer, suffering from long treatments, alternately hoping and despairing as the disease recurred, Gillian had cast about for ways to look after her daughters when she was gone. She'd then learned that some patients wrote letters to their children for their birthdays. Jess and Emily each had a set of sealed envelopes.

Jess pulled her letter from a stack of notebooks on the floor. "It's short." The letters got shorter and shorter. Reading them was hard, like watching their mother run out of air.

"*Dear Jessie,*" Emily read aloud as she smoothed the creased paper, "*I am trying to imagine you as a young lady, when all I see is a five-year-old girl waving her little legs in the air—that's the sign that you're tired. I imagine you with your hair untangled. Your sister tried to brush your hair this morning and you wouldn't let her. I wish you would.*" Emily paused a moment, sat up straighter on the bed and continued. "*Surely by now you are embarking on a profession. If you have not yet embarked, please do!*"

"Ahem," said Emily.

"I have embarked!" Jess protested. "A doctoral program is embarking."

"She means working."

"Philosophy is work. And I also have a job." By this, Jess meant her part-time job at Yorick's, the rare-book store on Channing where she did her reading in the afternoons.

"*I don't mean a job—*" Emily read, and then stopped short. "She knew what you were going to say."

Jess giggled, because Emily treated the letters like such oracles.

"*I don't mean a job. I am talking about a career, and a vocation. George Eliot wrote 'that things are not so ill with you and me as they might have been, is half owing to the number who lived faithfully a hidden life'—but that was more than one hundred years ago. I'm hoping that you and your sister will set your sights a little higher.*" A little higher, Emily thought, as she placed the letter on the bed, and yet Gillian had been a mother, no more, no less.

Would she have done more if she had lived? Much more? Or just a little? Jess was sorting through her mail on the floor. "You aren't even listening," Emily accused her.

"Yes, I am. Things are not so ill with you and me."

"You never take these letters seriously."

"I do! Of course I do. I've read them all—lots of times."

Emily was shocked. "All of them? Up to the end?"

"Yeah, I read them all at once when I was twelve."

"You did not!" Emily had always looked forward to her birthday letters and missed them now. Gillian had only written them up to age twenty-five. "That's just wrong."

"Why? She never said you have to wait for your birthday every year."

"But that was the intent!"

Jess considered this. "Maybe. I just opened all of mine at once. Then I got into Dad's computer and opened the WordPerfect files."

"Why would you do something like that?" The idea was foreign to Emily. Not only dishonorable, but self-defeating, like peeking to see how a book ends. "Didn't you feel bad?"

"No. Yours were better than mine, anyway."

"You read *mine*?"

"They were more interesting," Jess confessed cheerfully.

"Jess."

"Well, you were older, so she knew you better."

"I'm sorry," said Emily.

"Sorry that you're older?" Jess hit her sister with a pillow. "Why are you so sad tonight?"

"I'm not sad," Emily retorted, but she was; she was. Birthdays saddened her. She missed their mother, and she did miss Jonathan, although she wouldn't talk about it. He had his own start-up on the East Coast and they didn't see each other enough. Of course Jess knew that. She knew what Emily kept hidden, and so their time together was difficult, and also sweet.

Jess found what she was looking for on the floor, a photo of Lily and Maya in red and green plaid nightgowns. "Look at this."

Emily examined the picture. "Have you noticed how Heidi likes

Christmas colors?" she asked Jess. "It's like she celebrates Christmas all year round."

"Mmm." Jess loved her sister most when she was catty. Emily was so disciplined, as a rule. Jess waited for those occasions when Emily said an unkind word. There was nothing cozier than talking about their father and his house in Canaan, Mass.—the house where they had not grown up. Nothing sweeter than wondering how Heidi got their father to go running—about which they felt the same way—pleased and also secretly a little angry, because he had never felt the need to exercise before. They discussed the cuteness of their half sisters, aged three and one; they never forgot to speak of this, but they reverted quickly to Heidi and how she didn't cook. On the one hand, they were supposed to fly east for Thanksgiving, and on the other hand, they would be eating at a restaurant.

"It's the worst of both worlds," said Emily. "Guilt without home cooking."

"I think I'd be afraid of Heidi in the kitchen," said Jess, and Emily could not stop laughing. It was as if all their talk before, about the IPO and the birthday letters and the suit had been a prelude to this—the real conversation about their father and the family, all new people: Heidi and the little girls. Jacinta, the live-out nanny, who kept house and took care of dinner, but unfortunately took off weekends. Elmo, the new goldfish, who had arrived without the children's knowledge after the first Elmo went belly-up. Richard was new too, someone who changed diapers.

They talked until almost midnight. Then Emily said she should be going, but the rain fell outside and thrummed the streets, and it was so warm in Jess's room that she stayed a little longer, and longer still, until she began to forget about driving back across the Bay to Mountain View. The rain poured down, and she and Jess kept whispering until sleepily, half-dreaming, they began to talk about the old days, the vanished time when their mother was alive. Emily remembered better than Jess, but when Jess was with Emily, she remembered too. Their mother had white hands, long tapered fingers, and when she kneaded dough, her wedding ring clinked against the bowl. She was always singing softly as she played the piano with her white hands. She accompanied Emily's dance recitals and she could play anything, but Chopin was the one that Gillian loved.

She played Chopin every night, and when she turned the pages, she wasn't really looking at the music. She knew the saddest Waltzes by heart. The saddest were the ones that she knew best, and she would play at bedtime, so falling asleep was like drifting off in autumn forests filled with golden leaves.

2

Yorick's Used and Rare Books had a small storefront on Channing but a deep interior shaded by tall bookcases crammed with history, poetry, theology, antiquated anthologies. There was no open wall space to hang the framed prints for sale, so Hogarth's scenes of lust, pride, and debauchery leaned rakishly against piles of novels, folk tales, and literary theory. In the back room these piles were so tall and dusty that they took on a geological air, rising like stalagmites. Jess often felt her workplace was a secret mine or quarry where she could pry crystals from crevices and sweep precious jewels straight off the floor.

As she tended crowded shelves, she opened one volume and then another, turning pages on the history of gardens, perusing Edna St. Vincent Millay: *We were very tired, we were very merry, / We had gone back and forth all night on the ferry* . . . dipping into Gibbon: *The decline of Rome was the natural and inevitable effect of immoderate greatness. Prosperity ripened the principle of decay* . . . and old translations of *Grimm's Fairy Tales: They walked the whole day over meadows, fields, and stony places. And when it rained, the little sister said, "Heaven and our hearts are weeping together. . . ."*

During her first days at Yorick's, the bell had startled Jess when a customer arrived, and she'd been reluctant to stop reading. Then the shop owner, George Friedman, had reminded Jess that he paid her to help others, not simply to help herself to books. He didn't have to tell Jess twice. Now she engaged every customer she had the pleasure to meet. She greeted and advised, volunteering opinions literary, philosophical, or poetic. George rued the day.

Jess had a look about her—an unsettling blend of innocence and pedantry. She fixed her gray-green eyes upon the customers and said, "You like Henry James? *Really?*" as if she couldn't quite believe it. Or she'd warn the purchaser of a multivolume history of domestic life in Victorian England, "You know, this is a history of women's work based almost exclusively on male sources."

"It's a free country," George called out from the back room. Or sometimes, sotto voce, behind the counter, "Just ring up the damn books."

She came in three afternoons a week, and while he'd hoped those would be times he could absent himself, George didn't like leaving Jess alone to chase away the odd shopper who came in off the street. True, Yorick's was more of a project than a business, but he planned to break even one of these years. Jess had to be watched. She was well read, opinionated, unconcerned with profit. Also George liked watching her.

He was old money, a Microsoft millionaire now returned to Berkeley where he'd gone to college in the seventies, majoring in physics with a minor in psychotropics. He had worked in the Excel group when a long-haired physicist was not so uncommon, and Bill Gates still lived in a conventionally pretty house with a computer on the kitchen counter. Microsoft had been feisty in George's day, competing for market share. By the time he left, the place was expanding geometrically, so that construction crews and moving trucks and summer interns swarmed the Redmond campus. Podlike buildings multiplied around the shallow pool known as Lake Bill. Theme cafeterias sprang up with different cuisines in each. The company picnic began to look like a county fair, except that the band playing was Chicago, flown in for the occasion.

As share prices soared, George's friends had bought cars. They began with sports cars, and then they bought vintage cars, and finally, they bought kits and built custom cars from scratch. Then George's friends bought houses on Lake Washington. They bought small houses, and then bigger houses, and then they renovated those houses and commissioned furniture: sculptural dining tables and beds and rocking chairs in bird's-eye maple. They collected glass, and bought Chihulys by the dozen. They retired and purchased boats and traveled, and some started little companies and foundations of their own, and others flew to cooking classes in Tuscany and hosted fund-raisers for Bill Clinton. Along the way, they married and divorced, raised children, and came out, not necessarily in that order.

Like his friends, George retired, traveled, and donated to worthy causes. But he was eccentric as well. He was a reader, an autodidact with such a love for Great Books that he scarcely passed anymore for a Berkeley liberal. Strange to say, but at this time in his life George would have had a happier conversation with Berkeley, the philosopher, than with most of his old Berkeley friends.

He bought a Maybeck house in the hills and looked down upon the city he'd once loved. Previously antiwar, at thirty-nine his new concern was privacy. He grew suspicious—his friends said paranoid—of technology, and refused to use e-mail or cell phones. He feared government control of information and identity, and loathed the colonizing forces of big business as well. He became a benefactor of the Free Software Foundation, boycotted the very products with which he'd made his fortune, and called Microsoft the Evil Empire, although he still owned stock. In the eye of the Internet storm, George sought the treasures of the predigital age. He wanted pages he could turn, and records he could spin. Eschewing virtual reality, he collected old typewriters and dictionaries and hand-drawn maps. He began acquiring rare books and opened Yorick's.

The store was really an excuse to buy, but George ran it like a business. He was a shrewd, competitive dealer, and rarely fell in love with his own stock. He never sold or traded from his personal library, which was small, select, and static, but when it came to Yorick's, George was a glutton and a libertine. Once he claimed ownership and the first flush of happiness faded, he would part with just about anything for the right price. A first edition of Thomas Bewick's 1797 *History of British Birds* flew into

Yorick's and then out again in weeks. George treasured a copy of *My Bondage and My Freedom* inscribed by Frederick Douglass to the woman who bought his freedom, but he sold the volume to a small bright-eyed Stanford professor. He might have considered donating some of his acquisitions to deserving libraries, but he preferred playing the open market, and spurned research institutions. More than once at auctions, he broke librarians' hearts, only to flip his purchases to other private dealers.

Perhaps George was too attuned to profit. Or perhaps he was just fickle, and could not give himself fully to possessing lovely things. Presumably if he had gone into therapy he'd have learned the answer to these and other questions. Old girlfriends seemed to find the notion irresistible, but he was the independent, rumpled sort, and refused ironing out. Some found his refusal irresistible as well.

Yorick's was not always the kind of adventure George wanted. Good help proved elusive. Graduate students, budding novelists, future screenwriters, manic-depressive book thieves—he'd seen them all. With a kind of gallows humor he had printed up a questionnaire that he distributed to those seeking employment. When Jess had turned up, inquiring about a part-time job, he showed her the dark crammed store, the thicket of history, philosophy, and literary criticism in the center, fiction all along the walls and trailing into the back room where random stacks cluttered the floor. Then he returned to his desk and handed her his printed list of questions.

"Could I borrow a pen?" Jess asked, after digging in her backpack and turning up a handful of change and a warped chocolate bar. She was young. She had the clear-eyed beauty of a girl who still believed that, as they used to say, she could be anything she wanted to be. Of course she would not consider herself a girl. The word was offensive, but she had a girl's body, delicate shoulders, and fine arms, and like a girl, she had no idea how fresh she looked.

George handed Jess a black ballpoint, and she took the questionnaire and filled it out right on the other side of his desk. He tried not to stare, although she was leaning over. Casting his eyes down, he resisted the impulse to turn up the sleeve covering her writing hand.

When Jess finished, she returned the questionnaire and waited, expecting George to read her answers right away. He ignored her. When she hovered longer he said, "Give me a couple of days and I'll call you."

But he read the completed questionnaire as soon as she left.

1. Full name: *Jessamine Elizabeth Bach*
2. Are you a convicted felon? *No*
3. Are you an unconvicted felon? *Not to my knowledge*
4. Are you currently taking or dealing illegal drugs? *No*
5. Are you sure? *Pretty sure*
6. Circle one. A bookstore is: a meeting place, a mating place, a research room, a library, or a STORE, as the name suggests. *Store for convicted felons?*
7. Circle one. It's acceptable to wear earphones or use cell phones or notebook computers at work: rarely, sometimes, if I am day-trading, NEVER. *Own none of the above*
8. Circle one. It's acceptable to take money from the register: rarely, sometimes, if I really need to pay my dealer, NEVER. *Wow, sounds like you've been burned. Sorry!*
9. Short answer: No more than three sentences, please. Why do you want to work here? *I want to work here because I really need the money for day-trading (just kidding). I love books and am well qualified to talk about them if you need someone knowledgeable. You have a great philosophy section, and as I mentioned, I am a grad student in philosophy.*
10. Why in your opinion is this store named Yorick's? *Hmm. I think this is a trick question. You want us to say because of "Alas, poor Yorick" in "Hamlet," but I can tell from looking at you that you are one of those guys who reads "Tristram Shandy" over and over again, so I'm guessing you named the store after Parson Yorick in the novel.*

George read this last answer twice. The phrase *one of those guys* chafed. Was she saying he was simply an esoteric type? He fancied himself original, and he was miffed, or thought maybe he should be, for although he had a sense of humor, he exercised it primarily at others' expense. He found Jess a little flip, but she seemed sane, an unlikely arsonist. She'd do.

She often came late, but when she set to work, Jess straightened out pile after pile of books, shelving them alphabetically from Aquinas to Wittgenstein. She cut up cardboard boxes and crafted dividers to separate Aristotle from Bacon, Kant from Kierkegaard, and taped up little signs printed with a laundry marker: ACHTUNG! *If you are looking for philosophers of the Frankfurt School, please visit our Social Theory section.* She shelved all histories of utopian communities together, volumes on Oneida and the Shakers and Fourierism, and she created a separate section titled "Polar Exploration" for books on Martin Frobisher, Admiral Byrd, and Shackleton. Sometimes she disappeared. He'd find her kneeling on the floor, poring over *The Letters of Sir Walter Scott,* or *The Lives of the Lord Chancellors,* or leafing through a tome on Japanese monetary policy. Once he nearly tripped over her. She'd crouched down with a history of Byzantine hymnology balanced on a bottom shelf.

"Oh, I didn't see you."

"Sorry." She scrambled to her feet. "I was trying to figure out whether to shelve this in Religion or Music."

"I wonder if it's worth having sections for just two or three books," said George, as he passed into the other room.

She took this as criticism and called after him, "Maybe some of the sections are small now, but they could grow."

Later, she appeared at his desk and said, "I know the sections help."

"The main ones are useful."

"Well, if you think they're useful, you could thank me." He said nothing and she added, "Gratitude is important."

"I agree." He turned back to the package he was opening.

He liked provoking her, just a little. Caught between polite dignity and anger, Jess was very cute. This was despicable on his part; she should probably sue him. He was male and he was straight; two strikes against him right there. And he was unmarried, although not for lack of trying. Admittedly, all the trying had been on the part of his girlfriends. George had always wanted to get married—but not to them! Until quite recently he'd begun each relationship hoping that at last he'd found the one that he was looking for. He had heard the other narrative—the one women told—about the story of a man who moves on restlessly, seeking pleasure, shutting his eyes to the life he might have shared, but George knew differently. In his mind he tried again and again to marry; he kept looking, but all he found was neurosis and neediness. He had lived for two years with a woman named Andrea who suffered from depression. Later he'd been involved with an anthropologist who threatened suicide when he broke up with her. And then there was Margaret. Generally he avoided thinking about her. He almost never spoke of her, even to himself. Frayed by long experience with the angry other sex, George preferred to keep his distance, especially if he liked a woman. He knew that everything he said or did could be used against him.

She hurried in one day, out of breath. "Sorry I'm late. I just finished reading *An Enquiry Concerning Human Understanding.*"

"Is it such a page-turner?"

"Actually, yes, once you get into it. . . ."

"I've always thought that Hume is overrated."

She stared at him in astonishment and then realized that he was making fun of her. "When I told that lady I thought Henry James was overrated, I just meant his later work."

"Good to know," said George.

Jess stood for a moment with her hands on her hips, then turned on her heels and disappeared into Fiction.

He could see that she had something on her mind, because at the end of the day she began hovering again. She had a way of turning up behind his desk, as if she wanted to see what he was reading. He found it irritating when she appeared suddenly like that, even though he did the same to her. He buried his book under papers and auction catalogs and spun his old swivel chair around.

"Yes, Jessamine?"

"I was wondering something."

"Does it have to do with money?"

His directness startled her. "My sister's company is going public, and I can buy one hundred shares at eighteen dollars each, so I need eighteen hundred dollars." Jess said it all in a rush. "I was wondering if you could kind of give me my future paychecks in advance. And then I'd pay you back."

"Do I know you'd still be working for me?"

Jess nodded solemnly.

"Really? Then you'd be my longest-lasting employee."

"Oh, I could pay you back right away because the shares are going way up."

"What's the company?"

"It's Veritech."

"Veritech! That's your sister?"

"Yeah, she's the CEO."

"She could just give you the money herself."

"She wants me to stop thinking like a student."

He suppressed a smile and said nothing.

"So will you?"

"No," George said slowly. "I think your parents would be a better bet."

She shook her head.

"Well, you don't want to ask, but they're the ones to do it."

"Eighteen hundred is less than the complete Ruskin," Jess blurted out. "You want two thousand for that."

"The Ruskin is thirty-seven volumes in morocco," George said.

"So?"

"Just ask your mom and dad."

She frowned.

"Here, I'll show you." George unlocked his glass-fronted bookcase and took down the first volume and handed it to her.

Her fingers couldn't help caressing the red leather, as he knew they would. Unconsciously, she lifted the book to her face and brushed it against her cheek.

"Ruskin's worth two thousand, don't you think?"

"No," said Jess. "I don't like him," and she returned the book.

———

"I think I'm going to make Yorick's by appointment only," George told his friend Nick Eberhart that Sunday at Nick's house, a Craftsman Style extravaganza. Nick was younger than George, and taller. When he started to lose his hair he had shaved his head so that he had a sleek and streamlined look. He had left Microsoft some years after George and amused himself with designing and selling screen savers: fish that appeared to swim across the computer monitor, shooting stars, flying toasters with tiny wings. After the flying toasters became the subject of a contentious lawsuit with another screen-saver company, Nick gave up the business and began dabbling as a private investor. He built his house a few blocks away from George's place and became a model citizen, serving on the neighborhood council. A couple of times a week, he and George went running in Tilden Park.

"It's cute the way you call it running," said Nick's wife, Julia, and she laughed as she went searching for Nick's knee braces. Julia was a curiosity to George. Ten years younger than Nick, she was blond, athletic, green-eyed. A Jewish girl from Malibu.

George remembered the housewives of his youth. His own mother, Shirley, for example. She and her friends had raised the children and looked after their husbands. They'd volunteered in the schools, maintained the social fabric of the neighborhood. Remembered birthdays, planned parties, kept track of what belonged to whom and who belonged to which. Long before George heard of feminism, his mother had taught him the plight of women. Shirley had been unusually direct, Midwestern.

"I have bad news." George remembered his mother's matter-of-fact voice as he sat with his sister at the kitchen table after school. He was eight, his sister, Susan, six. "Robbie's mother is in the hospital."

"Why?" Susan asked, while George remembered that Robbie had not come to school that day.

"Well, she collapsed."

"Doing what?" George asked.

"Doing everything." Shirley poured the children cups of milk.

"But how did she collapse?" asked George.

"She got depressed."

"Why?"

Susan didn't understand; she was too young, but what Shirley said next shocked George more than anything he'd heard in his whole childhood—far more than his father's so-called facts of life. "The truth is, it's exhausting to take care of other people."

He thought he was dreaming in the yellow kitchen. The floor shifted under his feet. That was how it felt to suspect for the first time that *he* might be other people.

But there was Julia, returning triumphant with the black knee braces, and kissing Nick good-bye. She did not look depressed at all, this latter-day housewife with the MBA and the beautiful two-year-old son, Henry.

As Nick drove up Wildcat Canyon Road, George said, "The problem with a brick-and-mortar store is dealing with people all the time."

Nick glanced at George as he powered up the hill in his SUV. "I thought that was the *point* of the store."

"I don't really like people," said George. "I think I'd rather just work as a private dealer and have done with it. If I could get decent help, it would be different."

"The new one quit on you?"

"I'm sure she will. They don't even give notice; they just leave. It's tedious. I'm tired of it."

"You get tired easily," Nick pointed out.

"No, I don't." Nick missed the point. George didn't tire, he was constantly disappointed. Dissatisfied. He was always looking for the next thing. He had the mind of a researcher, restlessly turning corners, seeking out new questions. But he was not a researcher; he was simply rich.

Nick parked at Inspiration Point with its view of hills and reservoirs like winding rivers far below.

"I don't like kids," George grumbled.

"You're great with kids," Nick countered with a new father's evangelism. "Henry loves you."

"No, I mean the kids who work for me. I don't like dealing with them. I'm supposed to be, you know, employer, confessor, personal banker. It's ridiculous. And they're so ignorant. God."

"You're talking about the new one." A little of the old Nick came through here, a smile, as if to say, You bring her up a lot, when of course George had only mentioned Jess once, or possibly twice, in passing.

"All of them," he said doggedly, and Nick knew, even as they walked up to the trailhead and stretched and started jogging up the Ridge Trail with its canyon views, that George was in one of his apocalyptic moods, half bemused, half horrified. Pedantic. Of course Nick had heard George fume before about the end of Western Civilization, the death of books, the literary tradition either forgotten or maligned. Unfortunately, George didn't quietly despair about these matters; he wrote letters on the subject and served on the board of something called the Seneca Foundation that opposed bilingual education in the schools. George was always reading, not just voraciously, but systematically, the way scientists read, the way technocrats read when they decide to take a position on Western Civilization. Plato first, then Aristotle, Augustine, Aquinas—chronologically, George had built his portfolio of great books. Years ago, he'd read Jack Kerouac and Allen Ginsberg and Thomas Pynchon. Now he pored over Dante and Herodotus. He'd become one of those people who felt he had to defend Shakespeare. He had not aged gracefully. "They're all ignorant," George said. "The new one actually reads, but only to pass judgment. This is the way kids learn today. Someone told them how you feel is more important than what you know, and so they think accusations are ideas. This is political correctness run amok."

Nick picked up the pace, hoping to outrun George's rant. He passed a man walking a brown and white beagle, and an elderly couple in straw hats.

"What was it Jess said today . . . ?" George panted, trying to keep up. "Ruskin is a dogmatic, self-indulgent, sexually repressed misogynist with an edifice complex."

Nick smiled. "Sounds just like you."

Was he dogmatic? George asked himself as he drove home on switchbacks between trees, Bay views, and sky. Maybe, but only for good cause. Self-indulgent? Only sometimes, and at least he admitted to the fault. He should get some credit for that. Sexually repressed? No, easily bored. Misogynist? He took a hairpin turn. Hardly. He loved women!

George pulled off Buena Vista onto Wildwood, then parked halfway over the curb and collected his mail. *Edifice complex* hit close to home. George adored his house, and as Nick could attest, he had become obsessed with its restoration. He'd spent years and more money than he cared to admit. Still, even here, he pleaded innocent. Obsession, yes. Self-indulgence, no. The restoration was about Bernard Maybeck, not George Friedman. He was just a steward to Maybeck's vision. The research he and his designers had done, the ceramic tile, the salvaged wood, the light fixtures, and the hardware had been a labor of love, not ego. He had been patient, looking for the perfect door hinges. He had allowed his shingles to weather naturally, enduring months when his Californian beauty looked like a molting bird, until at last the cedar darkened and his wisteria came into its own.

Walking under a wooden trellis built like a Shinto torii, he climbed two flights of winding outdoor stairs, past eucalyptus, oak, and pine. Tree house and temple, George's home seemed bigger inside than outside. Tossing his mail onto a table, he switched on lights so that his great beamed living room glowed bloodred and deepest green and glinting gold. The fireplace was manorial. The square staircase turned and turned again in the entryway, and all the way up, George could view his framed collection of antique maps. Early novels filled his personal library, first editions of Austen, Defoe, Fielding, Smollett. American poets, almost all signed. He owned a copy of Edna St. Vincent Millay's *The Harp-Weaver* inscribed to her lover George Dillon: *To my darling George.* A signed copy of Sandburg's *The People, Yes* as well as Frost, Cummings, Ezra Pound. He collected first editions of dystopian satires: *Gulliver's Travels, Animal Farm, 1984, Brave New World, Erewhon.* His dictionaries were magnificent, all English and American. First editions of *Webster's,* first fascicles of the *OED,* and, most precious, a 1765 *Dictionary of the English Language* that had belonged to Mrs. Thrale.

Oak tables displayed platoons of typewriters: downstrike typewriters, upstrike typewriters, vintage World War I typewriters, turn-of-the-century typewriters—a 1901 Armstrong, a Densmore 1, a brass 1881

Hamilton Automatic, even an 1877 Sholes & Glidden in its case—each perfect in its kind, primed and polished so the metal shone.

He scarcely glanced at any of these things, but he needed them nonetheless. The collections illustrated each of George's interests in turn, from vintage machines, to poetry, to maps; just as fish give way to bears, and bears to beaked birds' heads on carved totem poles. Some kept journals. Some raised children. George told his life history with objects. His boyish treasures and pirate games now took the form of Northwest explorers' charts. His childhood superheroes metamorphosed into a complete run of Classic Comics, sealed in archival sleeves in the glass cabinets of his butler's pantry. The gold evenings of his youth he stored up in Ridge, Heitz, and Grgich, his California wines.

In the kitchen he minced shallots with his good Japanese knife. He poured himself a glass of Chateau Montelena Chardonnay, and admired its deep almond hue. Liquid possibly too good for cooking, but he used it anyway, poaching the sole with shallots in the wine and butter. He set a place in the dining room, poured another glass of the Chard, and ate his dinner. He was nothing if not civilized.

And yet, he was dissatisfied. The fish tasted bland, the Chard too buttery. Over time, his appetites had changed. He had been young, of course, like everybody else. He had loved a girl and she had hurt him, as first girlfriends did, and he had recovered and avenged himself, more or less, on all the others—although he never considered his behavior vengeful. In his youth his desires had been simple: to drink, to smoke, to screw, and to hang out with his friends, none of whom were women. He inhaled women too quickly, devouring what he most admired: their salt-sweet taste, their arch and sway. In that experimental age—George's teens and twenties, America's seventies—he took what he wanted, running girls and nights together in a haze of pot and alcohol.

Death shook George. His younger sister overdosed, and he lost his taste for the so-called counterculture. As he approached thirty he took stock—considering the women he had seduced, the drugs he had abused—and a new desire consumed him: to live better, or at least less self-indulgently, to give more, to start a family. The resolutions were heartfelt, the results were mixed. He lived with one woman and then an-

other, and willed himself to fall in love, but he did not, and so he grew
more solitary, even as he hungered for companionship. He mourned that
no one in the world was right for him, even as his girlfriends branded him
an opportunist and a libertine. In the worst of these love-storms, he applied himself in penance to his dissertation, and finished in record time.
He had no interest in academia and scarcely remembered why he'd begun
studying thermal dynamics in the first place. Therefore, he took the job
at Microsoft and drove north to Seattle, where he worked long days
building Excel. Yearning for substance apart from his share price, which
was always rising, inexorably rising, he began to read. Reading, he began
to buy.

From the beginning, he had expensive taste. A copy of *The Whale*, later
known as *Moby-Dick*, inscribed by Melville to Nathaniel Hawthorne. The
first self-published poetry that Robert Frost pressed into his sweetheart's
hand. An 1831 Audubon with its black-eyed birds poised to fly, beating
their plumed wings against the page. He dealt with ordinary books, of
course, but only rarities excited him. Pushing forty, George was hard to
please, and difficult to surprise. He had established bulwarks of skepti-
cism against disappointment. And yet he hungered for the beautiful, and
the authentic—those volumes and experiences impossible to duplicate.
How sad, he thought, that desire found new objects but did not abate,
that when it came to longing there was no end.

3

Although Jess was antimaterialistic, she thought about money all the time. Independent-minded, she was insolvent. There was her graduate stipend, of course—enough to keep her in brown rice and sprouts—and, fortunately, the job at Yorick's, but none of this sufficed.

Not this time, she told herself. Not this time, as if she were still a child. And she put off calling her father from one day to the next. She lay awake at night trying to figure out how to raise the Friends and Family funds without falling back upon the patriarchy.

Even when she didn't ask for help, conversations with her computer-scientist father were difficult. Jess had not followed Emily to MIT, but matriculated at Brandeis instead. Nor had she studied applied math like her sister, but declared philosophy her major. If she had pursued analytic philosophy, logic, even linguistics, her father might have understood, but Jess avoided these areas, and spent college contemplating Plato's dialogs, Renaissance humanism, and the philosophes, abandoning the future, as her father saw it, and consigning herself to the dead languages and footnotes of the past.

If Richard disapproved of philosophy as a major, he liked it even less as a doctoral program, and often asked Jess what she intended to do with her degree, and where she thought she would find a job. These questions offended Jess and also bored her; they were so transparent. Her father had a new family, and he would be paying for college yet again when he was old. "Have you considered how you will support yourself?" he inquired, but what Jess heard was, "My resources are not infinite." She was not about to ask for an extra eighteen hundred dollars and listen to him carry on about her "theoretical phase."

She wished Emily hadn't told her about the Friends and Family offering. Money had never interested her before, and now she wanted it. If she had the Veritech money she wouldn't have to worry about the overdraft on her bank account or wonder how she would make ends meet over the summer between TAships. She *did* think like a student. That's what she was.

Of course Jess had never wanted wealth, but the idea of a little money entranced her. Suppose her hundred shares at eighteen dollars became one hundred shares at one hundred dollars. She would have ten grand. As she drifted off to sleep, she dreamed her eighteen hundred shares were growing like Jack's beanstalk outside her window. Ten thousand dollars, one hundred thousand dollars—enough to live on and to give away! In her dreams the money climbed from seed to vine. Emily's company would work its magic. All Jess needed was a handful of beans.

She tried to borrow from her roommates, but Theresa was broke and Roland skeptical. He read the Veritech prospectus and pointed out, "It says here the company doesn't make a profit."

"I don't think that matters," Jess said. "Hardly any companies make profits these days."

"Really?"

"I mean, not yet."

"And it says this is a high-risk investment."

"But it's Emily's company. It's not high-risk," said Jess.

Roland shook his head. "Call me old-fashioned." He returned the prospectus.

"I'd pay you right back."

"But you can't be sure the stock will go up."

"Why do *you* have to be my roommate?" Jess demanded, half-laughing. "Why do I get the only person in the entire country who doubts Veritech is going way up?"

"I don't doubt," said Roland loftily, "I suspend judgment. Socially liberal, fiscally conservative, baby."

Jess's ten days were almost over. Still, she didn't mention the Friends and Family offering when she spoke to her father on the phone.

"Everything's okay?" Richard asked.

"Yup, how are you?"

"We're all fine. Heidi had a paper deadline this week. Lily had an ear infection."

"Oh, poor Lily."

"She's fine," said Richard, after which Jess spoke to the three-year-old on the phone.

"One potato, two potato, three potato *four*, five potato, six potato, eleven potato *more*, five potato, six potato, seven potato eight . . ."

After several minutes, Jess asked, "Could I talk to Dad?"

"Hello, this is Blue Bear. Hello. Come to my house." Blue Bear's voice sounded like a balloon running out of air. "A, B, C, D, E, F, G, H, I, J, K, elemenopee," Blue Bear chanted faster and faster. Lily began giggling. "QRSTUVWXYandZ. ABCDEFGQRSTelemenopee."

"Could I talk to your daddy?" Jess asked again, but Blue Bear hung up, and Richard didn't call her back.

"I can't believe you haven't taken care of it," Emily scolded on the phone. "What are you waiting for?"

"Well . . ." She could hear Emily typing in the background, multitasking as usual.

"It's not very difficult," Emily said.

"I don't have eighteen hundred dollars."

"Didn't you call Dad? All you have to do is ask him nicely."

Now Jess saw what Emily wanted. She wanted Jess to talk sweetly to her father, after which he would help her, and they would get along again. Emily was a firm believer in getting along, no matter what, and seemed to think if you behaved considerately, real feeling followed. But how could affection bloom in rocky soil? What were words without love? Only dust. Jess could not live in such a xeriscape.

"You did call him," Emily said.

"Of course."

"And did you ask him?"

"Well . . . not yet."

If only George had written her a check. He was so rich; he must be to own a store like Yorick's. And he had heard of Veritech. He understood about technology and knew she'd pay him back immediately. But he had to say no. He loved saying no.

He was strange and self-absorbed. He asked questions and then wandered away before he heard the answers. Then when Jess asked a question of her own or tried to start a conversation, he interrupted.

"I've read some Trollope—" she would begin.

"And you were offended by the foxhunting?" George broke in.

"I see no reason," she mused, "that books are more expensive because of who owned them. It's—"

"The way things work," George cut her off.

He was attractive and he knew it, but he pretended he had no idea. Therefore he was both vain and disingenuous. Tall, or so he seemed to Jess, he looked Italian with his dark skin and dark eyes. Very old—again, from Jess's point of view—where anyone past thirty harked back to another era altogether. Despite his years, George had a powerful body, a broad chest, a face of light and shade, a glint of humor even in his frown. When he wasn't lobbing his sarcastic comments, he seemed scholarly and peaceful, like a Renaissance St. Jerome at work in his cave of books. All he needed was a skull on his desk and a lion at his sandaled feet. He wore T-shirts, jeans, rimless reading glasses, sometimes tweed jackets. He had the deep didactic voice of a man who had smoked for years and then suddenly quit and now hated smokers everywhere. He never watched television, and he never tired of telling people so. But the most pretentious thing about him was his long hair. With his chestnut locks threaded gray, he was a fly caught in amber, the product and exemplar of a lost world.

"I'm working on the money," Jess told her sister. "Could I just explain?"

"There's nothing to explain." Emily's voice was tense. "You know what you have to do. Take care of it."

Later, waiting for her laundry in the basement, Jess weighed her choices: angering Emily, or asking Richard. *Take care of it.* Easy for Emily to say. Financially independent Emily got along beautifully with Richard. Ah, Marx was right about so many things—especially the moral superiority money afforded.

Perched atop a churning washing machine, she heard the clank of metal. Had she left her keys in her jeans pocket? A handful of coins? She wished her grandfather were still alive and she could call him. She had been close to her father's father.

Mrs. Gibbs wheeled in her laundry. She pushed it in a little cart with her detergent on top.

"Good evening." Mrs. Gibbs produced a change purse segmented with compartments for each kind of coin. Extracting quarters, she began lining them up in the slots of the machine opposite Jess. "How are you?" Mrs. Gibbs inquired as she loaded her whites.

"I'm okay," said Jess.

Mrs. Gibbs shot Jess a penetrating look.

"I'm fine."

"Fine sitting down here all alone?"

"I was just thinking."

"Fine isn't good," said Mrs. Gibbs. "Fine isn't right."

"I'm okay. My sister is annoyed with me. I said I'd do something and I can't."

"Breaking a promise," Mrs. Gibbs intoned.

"No!"

"Mmm," said Mrs. Gibbs and suddenly all the machines around Jess seemed to hum with disapproval.

"I'll figure it out."

"Mmm."

"I'm not depressed or anything," Jess reassured her neighbor.

"Have you tried prayer?" Mrs. Gibbs reached up to clasp Jess's hands in her own.

"Mrs. Gibbs," said Jess.

"Put your hands together."

"This is just a small thing," said Jess. "It's not a matter of life and death. I'm okay."

"Dear Lord," Mrs. Gibbs prayed, "help Jessamine Bach to keep her promise. Help her and guide her to honesty and truth. Keep her in righteousness and do not allow her to fall. And let us say, 'Amen.'"

"Amen," said Jess. "But I'm not about to fall."

"We could all fall at any moment," Mrs. Gibbs said. "Remember that."

"It's just a little money thing. . . ."

"There are no little money things," Mrs. Gibbs said darkly.

"No, no, let me explain." Jess told the story of Emily's IPO and the Friends and Family deadline. Mrs. Gibbs listened in silence. At one point she closed her eyes, and Jess wondered if her neighbor was praying again silently, or simply appalled at how trivial Jess's conundrum was.

"I have no money to lend you," said Mrs. Gibbs at last.

"Oh, I wasn't hinting!"

"But I will speak to my rabbi and see if he knows what to do."

Jess hopped off her washer in surprise. "Your rabbi?"

Mrs. Gibbs gazed at Jess calmly. "Don't you know, honey, that I am a Jew?"

"You're kidding," Jess blurted out.

"It's not the color of your skin, but the feeling in your heart," Mrs. Gibbs said.

"You're right." Abashed, Jess leaned against a washer. "I'm half Jewish," she volunteered. "My mother was Jewish."

Mrs. Gibbs nodded. "I'm a Jew by choice."

"How did you choose?"

"I didn't," said Mrs. Gibbs, "the good Lord chose me."

"Really?"

"Mm-hmm."

"But how did you . . . how did He . . . ?"

"Many years ago when I first moved to this town, I was at my Bible study reading Deuteronomy 7:6: *For thou art an holy people . . . the Lord thy God hath chosen thee to be a special people. . . .* Just as we read that verse, the good Lord spoke to me and said, *Who is the chosen? Who are the ones going to the Promised Land?*

"*That would be the Jews,* I answered.

"*Correct,* He said. *Why then are you not among them, if they are the holy people?*

"I told my Bible study about this conversation, and they prayed for me. However, they could not point to the text and deny that the chosen are the Jews. After many weeks and arguments, I took my Bible with me to the Berkeley Bialystok Center."

Reentering her apartment with her clean clothes piled high in her laundry basket, Jess found Theresa studying for orals at the table.

"Mrs. Gibbs is a Jew," said Jess.

"Yeah, right," said Theresa, scarcely looking up from her Kristeva.

"Seriously."

"Has she offered to debate the merits of Jesus Christ with you?" Theresa asked.

"No."

"Has she asked you to come with her to Bible study?"

"No. She wants me to meet her rabbi."

Now Theresa shut her book. "Do not go anywhere with that woman."

"Why?"

"Look, I grew up with evangelicals," said Theresa. "I understand them. Mrs. Gibbs wants to steal your soul. I'm serious. Stay the hell away from her. You'll end up dropping out of school, marrying some holy roller, and becoming a Jehovah's Witness in the Philippines."

"I think you might be a little prejudiced," said Jess, and she began telling Mrs. Gibbs's story.

"Where have you been?" Theresa interrupted. "That is a standard conversion narrative. Listen to me. I grew up with these people. I wasn't allowed to date 'til I was sixteen. Then I only dated Christians. Then I took a vow of abstinence. I had to spend my weekends saving souls door-to-door. You have no idea."

"But you escaped," Jess pointed out. "You aren't evangelical now."

"Ha. You never really escape," Theresa shot back. "You're naïve if you think you can." And she spoke from long experience growing up in Honolulu where her strong-willed father had not allowed her to get a driver's license. She spoke remembering her mother's thousand prayers, offered up on every occasion, even for the family dog, a toy terrier who sat up front in the car and panted in the tropical heat. But Jess had never seen the little dog with its pink tongue, and she had never met Theresa's parents.

"I'm not naïve," Jess said.

"Didn't I see you give money to Crazy Al on Telegraph? Didn't you say you got your cards read, quote unquote, for fun?"

"Not for fun. As a thought experiment, and by the way, the guy knows his 'Prufrock.'"

"You have something about you that attracts fanatics," said Theresa. "You have this way of letting them in. It's dangerous. It's like you're blowing some kind of high-pitched dog whistle: Take me, take me. . . ."

4

The Bialystok rabbi of Berkeley, known affectionately as the Berkinstoker, had come west from Brooklyn fifteen years before with his wife and baby. The family had grown, as had Rabbi Helfgott. He'd gained a few pounds with each of his wife's pregnancies, and after the birth of their tenth child, he was a substantial man indeed. He wore the traditional garb of the Bialystoker sect: black frock coat and black gabardine trousers, a white dress shirt, and, when he went out, a broad-brimmed black hat. Burly, bearded, and gregarious, he was a familiar sight near campus, and Jess remembered him well from Sproul Plaza where she leafleted for Save the Trees. She had often seen the rabbi marching through the crowds with leaflets of his own for anyone who looked Jewish. He'd even approached Jess once and suggested, "Why don't we trade? I'll take yours, and you take mine." She had offered him a leaflet titled "Arcata Arboricide" and he'd handed her a glossy brochure titled "Do a Mitzvah Today." Then the rabbi had gestured broadly toward the bare white London plane trees lining the plaza. "You light Shabbes candles, and I will save a tree. . . ." Jess remembered all this as she walked with Mrs. Gibbs to Dana Street, and she wondered if the rabbi would remember too.

The morning was sunny but cool. Mrs. Gibbs wore a white cardigan over her white clothes. Jess pulled up her jacket hood and gazed at a message chalked on the pavement in front of I. B.'s Hoagies & Cheesesteaks:

HASTE MAKES WASTE

IT IS ILLEGAL

TO LOITER, REST, OR BE

POOR AND HOMELESS

IN BERKELEY

THANK YOU CITY COUNCIL

Jess wondered about the author of this message, with its internal rhyme and sorrowful enjambment. She imagined a poet of the streets, chalking up his anger and despair with untaught eloquence, tracing lines of exclusion, sorrowing at telephone poles with a thousand silver staples where police had ripped off and discarded notices and poetry under the rubric "Post no bills." Why not post? Jess thought indignantly. Why was freedom of speech limited to sanctioned bulletin boards? She imagined chalk covering the pavement from Durant to Telegraph. *It is illegal to loiter, rest, or be poor. . . .*

Mrs. Gibbs stopped at the door of a brown Victorian garlanded with rambling roses, ramshackle porches, and metal fire escapes. As soon as Mrs. Gibbs rang the bell, Jess felt a prickle of unease.

The door opened wide, revealing Rabbi Nachum Helfgott. He didn't just smile. He beamed. His eyes crinkled up so that they looked like the tiny black seeds of his round bearded face. "I remember you!" he exclaimed in exactly the tone of a Jehovah's Witness who'd spotted Jess years before in San Francisco Airport and cried out to her, *There you are!*

"I remember you too," Jess replied.

"Really?" Rabbi Helfgott looked genuinely surprised and modest, as though there were many rotund rabbis in black suits and hats walking through Berkeley. "Did you by any chance light candles?"

Jess shook her head. "Did you save a tree?"

"I planted one! My wife and I planted one. Do you see this tree here?" He pointed to a bushy silver-barked tree near the corner of the house. "This is an apricot tree! This is what they tell us."

"Oh, now I feel bad about the candles!" Jess exclaimed.

"It's okay. It's all right. Every Shabbes is a new opportunity. Every week the world begins again. Come in, come in." Rabbi Helfgott seemed to enjoy doubling phrases. He was such an expansive man he spoke in twins. "Tell me your name once again."

"Rabbi, this is Jessamine Bach," said Mrs. Gibbs.

"Ah, Bach like the musician," said the rabbi. "Very nice. Where are you from?"

"I grew up in Newton," said Jess, "but now my father lives in Canaan, Mass."

"Canaan! My brother-in-law lives there! My wife's sister and her family. Who is your father?"

Jess pictured a Bialystoker rabbi in full regalia descending on her father and his Korean wife. "He's not Jewish," she answered instead of answering.

The front and back parlors of the house had been converted into a synagogue with EXIT signs over the doors to satisfy the fire code. A warren of hallways and little rooms and creaky carpeted stairs surrounded these parlors. Through one door, Jess saw a restaurant-style kitchen with banks of cabinets, freezers, and refrigerators. "The house was once an ashram before we came here," Rabbi Helfgott explained when he saw Jess staring. "*Baruch* Hashem, we were already equipped to feed a hundred."

The rabbi ushered Jess into an office piled high with papers and computer equipment. Jess looked back, expecting Mrs. Gibbs to join them, but her neighbor had taken the little book she always carried in her purse and stood by the window praying silently.

"My mother was the Jewish one," Jess volunteered.

The rabbi nodded. He was a true evangelist, although he only sought out Jewish souls. His goal was to return Jews to themselves. "Where is she from?"

"She's dead," said Jess.

The rabbi bowed his head, and recast the question gently. "Where was she from?"

"London," Jess said.

"Really! My wife is from London! What was her name?"

"Gillian Bach," said Jess.

"Sit, sit," the rabbi said, even as he mused. "Gillian Bach. I don't know the family."

Jess sat on an old swivel chair, and the rabbi heaved himself into a larger version behind his desk. There were at least two other swivel chairs of different sizes in the office, and Jess wondered for a moment whether the rabbi kept outgrowing them.

"Mrs. Gibbs tells us you're a student. What do you study?"

"Philosophy," said Jess.

"Philosophy! Very interesting. I myself have a personal interest in philosophy, particularly Jewish philosophy. You have perhaps heard of our *Tashma*?"

She shook her head.

"This is a very great work, covering everything."

"Everything!"

"God. Evil, but especially Humanity, the Soul. The Messiah. In other words, the big philosophical questions, the biggest questions, including the biggest one of all."

"And what's that?" Jess asked.

The Messianic rabbi didn't hesitate. "Ah, the biggest question in Jewish philosophy is very simple: *When?*"

Jess couldn't help smiling at this summation, and seizing the opportunity, the rabbi swiveled in his chair and reached behind him for a thick black book with page edges marbled in striking pink and purple. "This *Tashma* is translated into English with a commentary. Would you like to borrow it for a while?"

"Sure," said Jess, but that felt disingenuous, so she added, "I might not get to it right away. I'm kind of swamped reading for class."

"And what reading is that?"

"Hume," said Jess. "David Hume."

"David Hume. This is the kind of name that in my own field I wonder whether such a David was possibly Jewish."

"Scottish," said Jess.

The rabbi lifted a finger. "The Jewish community in Scotland is very nice."

Jess hesitated. Then she said, "I don't think he believed in God."

"There's the proof!" exclaimed Rabbi Helfgott. "It is a very interesting fact that many of the most famous goys, particularly philosophers, when you scratch the surface turn out to be Jews. Hume in the past could be Hamish. Hyman. Even Halberstam. There are many possibilities. Names are very important, very mystical in their significance. Your name, Jessamine, is very unique, very interesting. Do you have a Hebrew name?"

Jess shook her head.

"Many, many people who come to see us enjoy a Hebrew name, which we can find for them. It's a simple matter that for many people is profound."

On the wall behind the rabbi, a bulletin board displayed snapshots of babies, boys and girls, children of all ages. Above the bulletin board hung a large portrait of a white-bearded man.

"The Bialystoker Rebbe," said Rabbi Helfgott. "You know what a *tsadek* is? A *tsadek* is a saint. However, the Rebbe is not only a saint. He is also a genius. He has spirituality and intellect in equal measures. How many of us can say that? When he saw this thing, the Internet, did he say, 'I am now eighty-six years old; I have no interest in computers'? No. He said, 'With technology the whole wide world is now interconnected. *Baruch* Hashem, this is a miracle. A network of computers makes it possible for souls to transmit Torah everywhere.' He also said: 'There are no coincidences.' It is not by chance that you and I live in such a time as this. People ask every day, 'Why was I put on earth?' As if there is perhaps one reason. The truth is there are too many reasons to count, and each reason and each soul connects to every other. I see in my own life that this is true. Is it an accident that Mrs. Gibbs came here to us, even though she was not a Jew? Is it by chance that she lives in the same building as you? And that you yourself are involved in the Internet?"

"I'm not involved at all," Jess corrected him. "My sister is the one who—"

Rabbi Helfgott was unconcerned. "Everybody is a link. Do you understand?"

Jess nodded, suppressing laughter. There were many evangelicals in Berkeley. Moonies and druggies, hairless Hare Krishnas chanting in their flowing robes. Men in suits distributing little green Gospels. Prophets in sandwich boards preaching the end of days. Jess had seen all these, but she had never spoken at length to a religious guru, and despite Theresa's warnings, she enjoyed it.

"Let me explain," said Rabbi Helfgott. "After Torah, computers are my first love. Even in yeshiva as a boy, I wanted only to learn about these machines. Why? Because I loved the thought of them. Because of their power to change the world. Because of their memory. They take drudgery and make mincemeat of the most tiresome tasks. Some young boys in Brooklyn love baseball and some love candy. I personally loved to learn computer manuals and programming languages. Naturally this was only my hobby. When I grew older, I created the first Bialystok Web page, and I have continued as the webmaster ever since. When it was time for me to become an emissary, I asked the Rebbe, 'Please, send me to San Jose to be the *shaliach* there. This is the center for computers. This is where the lights of truth and learning will transmit instantly to all the nations.'

"The Rebbe said, 'Nachum, I am not sending you to San Jose. I am sending Mindel there instead.'"

Mindel? I thought. He knows nothing about computers. He does not care at all about technology. But I did not argue with my Rebbe. He knew more than I did.

"'For you,' said the Rebbe, 'I am sending you to Berkeley.' The Rebbe knew me better than I knew myself. When Mrs. Gibbs came to tell me about you and your investment, I understood." Rabbi Helfgott opened his desk drawer and took out a long checkbook.

Was this a mistake? Jess thought. Probably. The office door was open. She could walk away, but she did not.

"Eighteen hundred dollars," said Rabbi Helfgott, writing carefully. "This is a very special number. Each Hebrew letter corresponds to a number. Ten is *yud*, eight is *chet*. Together those letters make the word *chai:* life. Eighteen hundred is one hundred times *chai*. A very nice number which is also a round number."

Jess watched, fascinated, as Helfgott ripped the check out of his checkbook.

"I follow the market each day," the rabbi said. "I myself even trade a little in shares. I have some Apple. I have some Cisco. I bought Cross-roads Systems at nineteen. I know from technology stocks. Veritech is the one that everybody wants."

Jess started back, surprised. "You want me to give you some of my shares?"

"No, no, no." The Rabbi raised his hands. "The loan is free. Just return the eighteen hundred after the IPO. If you want to give me anything more, then you decide however to repay me. Give to *tzedakah*—a gift to charity. Give to the Bialystok Center. Or give nothing. This is an invest-ment. You are investing in Veritech. And I am investing in you."

5

Everyone expected Emily to take care and take charge. It had always been this way. When her mother was sick, she'd filled out her own permission slips for school. When Jess signed up to bring home the kindergarten rabbit for the weekend, Emily took care of it. *Look at Emily taking care of her sister,* her New Jersey aunts said to one another after the memorial service. There were no relatives from England. Her English grandparents had died before Emily was born, but the New Jersey aunts were full of admiration. *What an angel. Look how good she is,* her father's sisters said. Emily knew she was not an angel, but the more she doubted, the better she behaved.

At work she was the peacemaker. She wasn't just the chief executive officer of the company; she was the adult when her partners behaved like children. Admittedly her colleagues were young. Alex Zaslovsky, Veritech's chief technology officer, was just twenty-two. He had come to America at fifteen, and still spoke with a slight Russian accent. He'd been a math prodigy and skipped several years of school. He'd also been late to grow, so that even now he had a slight frame. He had black eyes, long lashes, a thatch of thick brown hair. He'd heard a secretary whispering about him at Kleiner Perkins Caufield & Byers. "How old is that one?

Twelve?" He turned on her and gave her the finger right before his presentation to the board.

"Alex!" Emily whispered, and Milton Leong, the company's twenty-five-year-old CFO, turned red with suppressed laughter. She appreciated Alex's mind, and Milton's sense of humor—his jovial personality set the tone for a company profiled in the *San Jose Mercury News* as "the most happy start-up." But there were times when the two of them tried her patience. In a young industry, Alex and Milton acted their age.

This was the story they told about Veritech's beginnings: Once upon a time, back in '96 when Alex and Milton were grad students, they stayed up late finishing a paper, and they decided to order takeout. They started shuffling menus, and just as they settled on Thai food and began debating between Shrimp Delight and Shrimp in Love, a new paradigm for large-scale data storage and retrieval came to them. Each cache of data should have a take-out menu.

"Very funny," Milton said, but Alex wasn't joking. They met Emily, who saw the potential of a new data-storage paradigm, which was ingenious and elegant, and she drafted a business plan. Within months, Alex developed V.0, Milton found the first clients, and Emily organized the company.

The true story of Veritech's beginnings was complex and technical, and had more to do with the paper Alex and Milton had been writing than the collection of take-out menus. They had not debated which sort of shrimp to order, because Alex was allergic to shellfish. Nor had they simply met up with Emily. She had come to them looking for an infrastructure project. But it was the business with the take-out menus that reporters fixed on. A take-out menu with numbered specials was something every interviewer could visualize, an endearing symbol for a couple of brilliant students brainstorming late at night. Veritech's goal was to become the biggest Web-based data-storage company in the world, but its origin myth was all fun and games, as if once upon a time some guys got together and said, "We've got enough talent here. Let's put on a show!"

There had been freedom in the early days, a sense of unlimited possibility, but with each new round of funding, Alex and Milton and Emily felt more constrained. They had to answer to VCs on their board, particularly to the forty-one-year-old Bruno, with his fair hair and sunburned brow. Bruno was Swiss, and he had worked at Xerox and at Apple before moving to Sirius Venture Partners. He cycled competitively, stayed late, and woke early to shoot out e-mails to everyone, "trying," as Milton put it, "to give us marching orders for the day." As they filed for their blockbuster IPO, Bruno's pronouncements and e-mail warnings intensified. "Sensitive time! Remember, we are making an important transition which requires the utmost care. There will be many visitors in the building. Please be discreet in elevators and public spaces."

Of course everyone down to the secretaries knew that this was a sensitive time. Emily had braced herself for arrogance and gloating, a sense of entitlement at the company, but in fact, the ethos was the opposite— one of indebtedness to investors, to underwriters, to the world. With floodgates of cash about to open, everyone felt enormous pressure to produce the next new thing. Veritech stored data for more than one hundred corporate clients, ranging from monumental Microsoft to newcomers like Bluefly, but on the eve of the IPO, Emily began to understand what no one wanted to admit: at the moment, Veritech's real customers were their underwriters, their true audience the analysts poised to examine the company from head to toe, and ultimately Veritech's true product had nothing to do with data storage. What Veritech offered the public was its stupendous expectations.

"We need a new idea every week," Alex complained.

And Emily said, "Well, yes." And then, more thoughtfully, "A new idea is practically built into our share price."

Alex did not enjoy this comment, but he was willing to hear it from Emily. He respected her more than anyone. He was also in love with her. He stammered when he spoke to her. At times he couldn't even look at her. This was awkward, given the amount of time they spent working together, and the tension they both felt. The public offering weighed heavily on Alex, even as he conceived one new idea after another—his latest, the prototype for an electronic-surveillance service.

He presented the concept at an early breakfast in Veritech's rooftop lunchroom, a place with a stainless steel outdoor kitchen and round tables shaded by market umbrellas. Charlie, the tall blond company chef from L.A., was whipping up omelets for Emily, Alex, Milton, and Bruno when Alex announced, "I have a plan for something called electronic finger-printing. This will track every time someone touches data and record who touches it, as well as when and where. The records will be kept in a log for every data-store. . . ."

"Cool," said Milton.

"Cool?"

"What did you want me to say?"

"Something better," Alex said.

Picky, picky, thought Charlie behind the stove as he flipped Alex's omelet—plain with no cheese, no sautéed mushrooms, no roasted peppers.

"Okay, how would this be different from tools we already have?" asked Milton. "We can do all that when we collaborate on projects."

"This tool is not for collaborators," Alex said.

"Who is it for then?" asked Emily.

"People who want to check security. For example, managers who want to check on their employees."

"So managers could use fingerprinting without employees' knowledge?"

"Absolutely."

"Do you see a problem with this?" Bruno asked.

"No."

"When it comes to privacy and human rights?" Bruno prompted.

"No."

"Born in the USSR," Milton teased.

"Meaning?" Alex demanded.

"This is like a Soviet-style app you're coming up with here."

Alex took his finished omelet to the table.

"Seriously," Milton said, following him, "this kind of surveillance idea sounds kind of Cold War, don't you think?"

The four settled at a round table shaded by a green umbrella, and Charlie cleaned his griddle and thought about his future restaurant.

"A surveillance idea is therefore . . . out of date?" Alex challenged Milton.

"Well, yeah," Milton said, "since the Cold War ended, like, ten years ago."

"And what makes you think it ended?"

"You guys," Bruno said. "We are in storage, not security. Are you suggesting that we expand into an entirely new area?"

"Let me show you what electronic fingerprinting can do," Alex said.

"I'm not interested in what it does in general. I'm interested in what it can do for us."

This was the kind of thinking that enraged Alex. "He doesn't get it," Alex fumed to Emily, right in front of Bruno. "He doesn't have the capability to understand."

"My capabilities are fine," snapped Bruno. "But let's pretend that I'm the rest of the world and I have no use for what you're selling me."

"I'm not selling anything. I'm inventing. You don't know the difference." Alex spoke louder than he had intended, and Miguel, the cleanup engineer, as he was called, looked up, even as he kept wiping tables.

"Alex," said Emily.

He glared at her, as if to say, Don't you Alex me. "I'm going to work." He marched down the stairs.

"No, wait." Emily hurried after him into the top-floor lounge they called the Playroom, a space furnished with sagging couches, Foosball, pool, and Ping-Pong tables. "Don't go."

"What do you mean, 'Don't go'? Am I a child for you to order me around?" Alex demanded

"Oh, stop and listen to me," said Emily. "You have got to get hold of yourself. Don't let other people get under your skin like that. You're so smart. Be smart about people too. Be generous when you come to the table with something new."

"I'm not interested in speaking to Bruno about this," said Alex.

"But you've got to. You've got to speak to all three of us. That's how it works," said Emily. "Go back up there and start over."

"No. He should apologize to me."

"Look, there's only one way to get things done, which is to stop taking offense and explain yourself." She was determined to get through to him, her difficult, prodigious CTO. "I won't let them interrupt."

"No one can stop Bruno and his twenty-million-dollar financing from interrupting me."

"I can," Emily promised.

"I told you, I'm not interested."

"Just tell me. Come on." She knew he wanted to explain his idea. She sensed his excitement, along with his pride. In fact, her voice charmed him, as much as her earnest advice.

He picked up a paddle and began bouncing a Ping-Pong ball up and down on its flat surface. Tap-tapping over and over, he explained a plan for data monitoring so audacious and innovative that Emily knew if Veritech did not pursue it, others would.

"There are still ethical questions," she pointed out. "And strategic questions. Bruno's right to ask if we want to go into the security business right now."

Alex kept his eye on the ball. "Storage and security go hand in hand."

"This would be a different kind of security," Emily mused. "Almost forensic."

"Exactly."

"Almost like spying," she said. "We'd have to think hard about that."

"We can think while we build," said Alex.

"No. Think first and then build," Emily countered. "Is the prototype working yet?"

Ah, the fundamental question. "We broke it this morning," Alex admitted. "But the idea is there."

She nodded, half entranced with his scheme. Bold, broad-ranging, category-busting. "The idea is fantastic."

Alex bounced the Ping-Pong ball too hard, and it popped off the edge of his paddle, but he was quick and made the save. "Work with me, then."

She wanted to. She wanted to give him free rein, but prudence prevented her. Her instinct was to distrust his instincts.

"You need to present this idea formally to the Board."

"We'll see," said Alex.

"Say you will, or I'll do it for you."

He bristled. "You aren't presenting anything for me."

She turned away, then, so he couldn't see her smile. He was arrogant, but she'd manage him. His idea had so much potential!

As she took the stairs down to the third floor, her imagination leaped ahead. If Alex let go of his surveillance model, his techniques could be employed in new, more sensitive search engines. His idea of fingerprinting could have applications for passwords. What if Veritech went into password verification? Yes! She would name Alex's new password authentication system Verify. Emily stopped on the stairs and almost laughed. Deliberate in everything she said and did in public, she had a passion for new schemes.

She hoped she could talk seriously to Alex that weekend. The day before the IPO, she was hosting Sunday brunch, an event that impressed Jess as very formal and old-school.

"You have such a sense of propriety!" said Jess, who'd come early to help shop and set up.

"It's not propriety," Emily replied, as they browsed the melons at the Farmers' Market in Stanford Shopping Center. "It's just . . ."

"What?"

"Doing the right thing at the right time."

"There you go," said Jess. "That's what propriety is. You don't even realize you're doing it. You're a throwback."

"To what?"

Jess considered this. Hi-tech at work, Emily was paradoxically old-fashioned in her life. She didn't even own a television. "The nineteenth century," Jess concluded. "No. Eighteenth. You can be eighteenth. I'll be nineteenth."

"I never pictured you as a Victorian."

"No, *early* nineteenth century," said Jess, who had always been a stickler when it came to imaginary games and books. The Blue Fairy, not Tinker Bell. Lucy, not Susan. Jo, not Amy. Austen, not the Brontës.

"Focus." Emily considered the bins of cantaloupes and casabas.

"Let's buy one of everything," said Jess.

"That's too much."

"You can afford it! You're going to be a millionaire tomorrow."

"Shh. No, I'm not." Still, Emily's heart fluttered. Even with the six-month lockup, even with the volatile market, she had three million shares of Veritech.

Jess gazed at the apples arranged in all their colors: russet, blushing pink, freckled gold. She cast her eyes over heaps of pumpkins, bins of tomatoes cut from the vine, pale gooseberries with crumpled leaves. "You could buy a farm."

"Why would I do that?"

"To be healthy," said Jess.

Emily shook her head. "I don't think I'd be a very good farmer."

"You could have other people farm your farm for you," said Jess. "And you could just eat all the good things."

Emily laughed. "That's what we're doing here at the Farmers' Market. We're paying farmers to farm for us. You've just invented agriculture."

"Yes, but you could have your own farm and go out there and breathe the fresh air and touch the fresh earth."

"I think that's called a vacation," said Emily.

"Oh, you're too boring to be rich," Jess said. "And I would be so talented!"

"You took care of those Friends and Family forms, right?"

"Yes, yes, yes," said Jess.

"And Dad was fine with the loan, wasn't he?"

"I told you I took care of it," Jess said airily.

Alex arrived first with sunflowers so big that Emily didn't have a vase for them. "They're beautiful," she said as he thrust the huge paper-wrapped bouquet into her arms. "Hmm." The blossoms were velvety black fringed with gold, their stems thick and rough, their leaves like little limbs. You couldn't trim such flowers with a scissors.

Emily lined up the stems on a cutting board and chopped the ends off with a cleaver. "The question is, what should I use for a vase?" Emily was just thinking aloud, but instantly she regretted asking. Alex looked so disappointed, standing in the kitchen doorway. The flowers were too big. They were all wrong. Poor guy. Sunflowers must have looked perfect in the store: prettiest and least symbolic—not like roses, for example.

"Don't worry," Jess reassured Alex in the living room as Milton arrived.

"What can I do? Am I pouring waffle batter?" Milton asked.

"I'm going next door to ask the neighbors for a vase," Jess called out.

"Okay," Emily said. "No, wait, don't do that—the one next door works nights. He works in the ER at Stanford Hospital. Don't knock on his—" But Jess was gone, and here was Emily's assistant, Laura, and her husband, Kevin, and their two little children. They had come straight from church, bearing cinnamon buns.

"I made half with pecans and half without," said Laura. "You can warm them in the oven."

"You're amazing." Emily spoke to Laura, but she was smiling at three-year-old Justin, in his Bermuda shorts and blue plaid shirt and bow tie. One-year-old Meghan, in her yellow gingham sundress, was already heading for the stairs with Kevin close behind. Kevin was a graduate student in accounting. Laura was twenty-six, just three years older than Jess, but there she was with two children. They were so beautiful, blue-eyed like their mother, their hair even blonder than hers.

"They're easy to make," Laura told Emily in the kitchen.

"They don't look easy," Emily said, admiring the giant glossy rolls.

"When I was a kid I had a summer job at Cinnabon," Laura explained. "I took the recipe home and divided it by forty."

"What temperature do you want?"

"Just very low, as low as you can."

"All right, let me see," murmured Emily, fiddling with the controls. She was unfamiliar with her oven.

"You don't want to bake them any more, just keep the glaze gooey. Here, let's put them on the counter." Suddenly Laura looked a little pale.

"Are you all right? Do you want a drink? Do you need to sit down?" Emily asked.

"I'm fine. I'm pregnant again," Laura whispered.

"Really? When are you . . . ?"

"We aren't telling anyone yet. We just found out," said Laura, and almost imperceptibly she sighed.

Emily wanted to talk further, but Milton manned the waffle iron just steps away. "The green light means they're ready, right?" he asked.

"Let me get you a platter." Emily was reaching for one when Jess burst through the door bearing an umbrella stand for the sunflowers.

"Come sit," Emily told Laura. "You too," she called to her sister, who was using the sprayer from the kitchen sink to fill the umbrella stand. "Everybody has to eat a lot of fruit salad."

"Did you get Bruno's halcyon-days e-mail?" Milton asked as they sat down together, eight at the table, counting Meghan in Kevin's lap.

"Bruno's out of town, so now it's open season?" Emily asked lightly.

"I had to look up *halcyon*," said Laura.

"*These are the halcyon days*," Alex declaimed in his best imitation of Bruno. "*But the days are numbered when we can spend as we choose and operate without scrutiny . . .*"

"*With a public offering comes public accountability*," Milton chimed in with his own version of Bruno's German-Swiss accent.

"Move the syrup, hon," Kevin warned Laura, as Meghan's little hand stole across the table.

"He talks too much," Alex said of Bruno.

"That's his job," Milton pointed out.

Alex rolled his eyes.

"Still angry?" Emily murmured.

"Well, how would you feel?"

"I think I'd be a little patient," said Emily. "And wait for my idea to settle in, and see if maybe there were ways to develop it. If there was a different context . . ."

Alex looked at her with his dark eyes. "It's easier to be patient when you have some hope of success."

"He's just got a crush on you," Jess told Emily after the guests had left, "and you're a little mean to him, don't you think?"

Emily tore off plastic wrap to cover the fruit bowl. "How am I mean to Alex?"

"You ignore him."

"I do not."

"You pretend you don't know how he feels."

This was true, but Emily didn't know any other way to behave. She needed to work with Alex.

He thought he loved her, but what did he know? He had finished college at eighteen and founded a company before he could drink legally. To Emily's knowledge, he'd never had a girlfriend. He'd fixed on her the way a hatchling fixes on the first moving thing it sees. He looked at her longingly, helplessly. Watched her as she walked down the hall, e-mailed her logic puzzles he thought she might enjoy, left chocolate on her desk.

"It's strange," Emily said. "It's difficult. It's like having a secret Valentine every day of the week."

Jess knelt down and rearranged the sunflowers in the umbrella stand. "You have to give the guy a little credit."

Emily leaned over the counter to glimpse Jess in the pass-through between kitchen and dining room. "I can't lead him on," she said.

"But he's devoted," Jess murmured. "You have to give him that."

That night, as Emily lay alone in bed, she called Jonathan.

"Are you excited?" he asked her.

"Well . . ."

"Emily!"

"Yes," she whispered. "*Yes*. And nervous."

"Why?"

"So much is happening, and so much is changing."

"Nothing really changes." Jonathan's deep voice was totally assured. This was one of Jonathan's great gifts, the voice of experience even where he had none. His own company was only a little over a year old, but he and his partners were storming the data-security market. They had developed a product called Lockbox, which encoded data and transactions for a growing array of Internet vendors. An image of a tiny treasure chest, the Lockbox logo was beginning to pop up at the bottom of Web pages everywhere.

Fast Company called Jonathan a wunderkind. *Red Herring* dubbed him a tech genius—but there were many tech wunderkinder starting companies. Jonathan was something rare. He was brilliant cryptographically, with a command of every aspect of his company's Internet security products. And he was also an intuitive businessman—fearless, pragmatic, unyielding at the negotiating table where he always got his way. He upended all the stereotypes. He was like a fighting Quaker. A charismatic geek. "The only thing that changes is people's perceptions," Jonathan reasoned. "You just keep on working like you did before."

"Don't you think perceptions are important?"

"No," he said immediately. "Facts are important. Tomorrow everybody's rich. Anyone who has a problem with that is either ungrateful or jealous."

"That's what I'm afraid of."

"Hey, you earned that jealousy! Enjoy it."

"It's complicated," Emily confessed.

"Is Alex giving you a hard time again? Is he making you nervous? Fuck him. Seriously, Emily. You've been working toward this for how long?"

"Three years." She couldn't help laughing at herself. She knew the time frame was absurd.

But Jonathan's background was in computers, not business. He measured companies in dog years. "Now you get to reap the rewards."

"I love you." Emily laughed.

"Tomorrow is going to be amazing." He spoke thinking of his own company as well, his own IPO, a dazzling coming-out party for ISIS in a matter of weeks. "Say it."

"Amazing."

"Repeat after me. Tomorrow is going to be amazing. Incredible. Fucking ridiculous."

It was so good to hear his voice. He said the things she only whispered to herself.

"Tomorrow is going to be historic!"

"Well, every day is history eventually," she teased.

"You know what I mean."

She sighed happily. "I know what you mean."

"So don't be modest. You don't have to be modest with me. Just think what you did! There was nothing in that space and you . . ."

". . . and Alex and Milton . . ."

". . . said: *Let there be Veritech*. And there was Veritech. And it grew and grew. . . ."

Squeezing her eyes shut, she remembered an old film from science class where flowers bloomed in time-lapse photography. Rain drenched the desert and suddenly, petal by petal, second by second, in saturated Technicolor, all the cactus flowers opened.

This will be the final boarding call. . . .

She started from her reverie. "Is that your flight?"

"Yeah, I'm going," said Jonathan.

"Well, hurry."

"Enjoy it," he told her. "And just remember . . ."

"I don't want you to miss your plane."

"When you see the—" His phone cut out as it sometimes did, possibly low battery, possibly call waiting, and he left her wide-awake in bed, with the rush of his voice in her ear.

She was too excited to sleep. She lay on her back in the dark, and her thoughts seemed to fill the room with rustling wings. She thought about her new plan for Alex, the new system she called Verify. She considered her new fortune, the new funds for Veritech, all the opportunities that money could buy: expansion, new hires, charitable giving. How could she fall asleep and dream, when all her dreams were coming true, first thing in the morning?

All her dreams? No, not quite all. She thought of Laura's children. Kevin, holding Meghan on his lap, the trays of cinnamon buns warming in the oven until the white glaze dripped down their sides, warm and gooey to the touch.

Once, Laura had had car trouble and Emily had driven her home.

She'd driven up Palm Drive into the Stanford campus through the winding roads of Escondido Village, where married graduate students lived.

"That's the one," Laura said. "Seventy-six C."

The brown town house glowed with light. Kevin stood at the door, holding Meghan in his arms. "Come in," he said.

When Emily stepped inside, she saw toys everywhere, and baskets of yarn for Laura's knitting. A high chair, a baby swing, stuffed animals on the couch. Kitchen counters covered with clear canisters of flour and sugar, muffin tins, and a standing mixer. A plate of freshly baked corn muffins.

"Would you like one?" Laura asked immediately. "Oh, you probably want a napkin, don't you? Please excuse the mess. Justin!" He must have been under two at the time. "Don't touch. No!"

"No! No!" Justin echoed cheerfully as he stood in his pajamas, pushing the buttons of the stereo.

"He thinks all electronics are called No," Laura said.

"Hey, buddy, can you say hi to Emily?" Kevin asked, and Emily saw how round Justin was. Round tummy, round cheeks and chin.

"Say hello when people are here," Laura said gently.

"Hello, people," Justin said.

Now Emily felt the longing come over her. Brief but intense, a kind of homesickness, a desire to paint herself into Laura's family. It was strange. She knew how hard Laura worked. Laura was her assistant, after all. She knew Laura was exhausted. She could not forget Laura's news and quiet sigh that meant no, not planned. No, not ready. No, we'd never get rid of it, but now? So soon?

She knew she idealized Laura's existence. Still, the night before the IPO, Emily imagined Laura's life. How might she find a piece of that? Not everything. Not so many pregnancies, or so much church, but could she have a bit of Laura's lamp-lit home? Could she divide the fullness of Laura's days by forty?

She got to sleep so late that she had trouble waking. At first all she wanted was to doze in the soft morning light. Then her jitters returned.

She showered, dressed quickly, and drove to Veritech with wet hair, and Starbucks coffee for her breakfast.

Veritech was a three-story building, a former self-storage warehouse of white cinder block with tinted glass windows. The company had already moved twice, and there was talk of new construction. In the meantime, the start-up had gutted the warehouse with the classic contradictory goals of opening up the space and at the same time packing in as many desks as possible. The result was a hollowed-out building with a freight elevator and a web of metal staircases and balconies overlooking a central lounge that Veritech's architect called the Living Room.

Now software engineers swarmed the oversized beanbag chairs. Every Veritecher in town had come to watch the company's debut. There must have been eighty programmers sitting on the floor.

"Take my place," Alex told Emily, and he gave up his spot on one of the couches to kneel on the rug and open his laptop.

"No, that's okay," said Emily. "I'll find a chair."

"Please," said Alex softly, and she smiled and took the seat. He was cute, trying to act chivalrous.

Wild applause. Whoops of delight. Alex was projecting Veritech's newly minted stock symbol, VERI, on a roll-down movie screen.

Stamping feet and whistles at the graph plotting VERI's numbers. Six in the morning. The Nasdaq had just opened in New York, and VERI's price was climbing, scaling jagged peaks from eighteen dollars a share to thirty-six and then eighty-nine. Applause again. Wait. One hundred and three. One hundred and three dollars a share!

Emily held her cup of coffee in two hands and watched Veritech, flying high. Thousands were trading Veritech stock, thousands were paying thousands to buy. A company that had been a couple of rooms and cast-off office furniture was shooting into the stratosphere. Emily knew that Veritech was still a fledgling. She knew her company was not profitable, nowhere near profitable. She knew her start-up floated on millions of dollars of venture capital. She knew all this. She was a sensible young woman. And yet she gazed at the projection on the screen and the numbers were hypnotic. She told herself to look away, but she could not. She felt the first stirrings of a notion strange but compelling: that Veritech's skyrocketing value reflected the company's real worth. Emily had never looked at a graph and felt this way before. Although she enjoyed math, her pulse had never quickened at the sight of numbers. Now her heart was racing. Her creation had a price, and then a better price, and then a new price better still. Each number shone brighter than the one before, and she who had always been so rational watched Veritech's ascent and began to fall in love.

The programmers were cheering like sports fans, like NASA officials at a shuttle launch. High fives. Hugs. Emily and Milton told each other how relieved they were. Yes, *relief* was the word that felt permissible. Relief after the long, complicated filing and the brief, torturous delays. All along, Alex had worried that the wave might crest before Veritech arrived. Now here they were in November 1999, and the wave was bigger than any of them had imagined. One hundred nineteen dollars a share. They were on track for listing in the top ten IPOs of the year.

Other emotions remained unspoken. While the group rejoiced in its collective fortune, a private calculus commenced. As one of the three company cofounders, with three million shares, Emily had come into a personal fortune on paper of $357 million. Emily's assistant, Laura, as employee four, owned half a million shares. As of that morning, she had $59.5 million. And so on down the line, for each of Veritech's 156 employees, from the oldest, with over two years' seniority, to the newest, who had signed on to work for options. True, everyone's stock was locked up for six months, after which—who knew? The shares were volatile. Theoretically the whole industry could go up in flames, but on-screen, Veritech continued to rise, breaking new ground, etching a new social order. Newly minted millionaires like company chef, Charlie, gazed with awe and quiet jealousy at Veritech's cofounders, now fabulously wealthy. Newly comfortable Miguel, the cleaning engineer, gazed quietly at Charlie. And Veritech, which had been a team where everybody was so free and easy, first names only, could no longer pretend to be a classless society.

"All right," said Alex, after giant cookies had been delivered and more coffee served. "All right, you guys."

Despite the early hour, the others followed him upstairs to work. No one knew the precise etiquette for becoming wealthy in an instant, but it felt wrong to sit and watch the stock price for more than thirty minutes as a group. From now on the programmers would check Veritech's progress every thirty seconds on their desktops.

PART TWO

Light Trading

❧

Thanksgiving Week 1999

6

George was courting a collection. He wasn't sure how many books there were. One hundred? One thousand? He had seen only two. The seller was secretive. She said she had inherited a collection of rare books from her uncle, and George assumed the volumes had sentimental value. The two she brought George were intriguing. The first, an 1861 Mrs. Beeton, was not rare by any means, but it was in exceptionally good condition. Beeton's *Book of Household Management* was so thick that most copies ended up in three pieces because their bindings didn't hold. This copy was a good little brick with its red leather binding still intact. The second volume the seller brought was much older. The long title began: *The whole duty of a woman, or a guide to the female sex from sixteen to sixty . . .* and included a promise to provide *choice receipts in physick and chirurgery with the whole art of cookery, preserving, candying, beautifying, etc.* The book had been published in London in 1735 and would have been valuable, except that it was so badly worn. The cover was falling off and the pages warped and spotted. The title page was torn.

The Beeton was the sort of book listed in catalogs as a "wonderful gift" for the everyday book lover. It would not tempt a serious collector. George could sell Mrs. Beeton for four or five hundred dollars. He was doubtful about *The whole duty.*

"This one's in rough shape." He showed the volume's wear to the seller, even as he noted hers. She was about his age, but she looked shattered, as though she had never recovered from some early loss. Gray-eyed, sharp-featured, she was tall and pear-shaped. Her long gray hair fell straight past her narrow shoulders to her waist. She might have been a teacher once, or a social worker, but more likely she was a perpetual student, and a case study all her own. Her name was Sandra McClintock, and she wore faded clothes and cowboy boots, and she walked everywhere. She told George she'd only brought him two books because she didn't want to carry any more. He did not believe her. "The cover is ripped," he said. "The pages here are stained. . . ." He turned the leaves deliberately.

Were there others like these? Better? And how were they acquired? He tried to look diffident as he wrote a check, one hundred dollars for the pair.

"Are they all cookbooks?" George asked the seller, but she didn't want to discuss the matter. "Are you interested in an appraisal?"

"Maybe. I might be." She didn't object to the evaluation, but she looked disappointed as she took the check. Clearly she had hoped for more.

George fretted after she left that she would not come back. What if Sandra had something really valuable? He waited three days for her to call, and when she didn't, he phoned, and asked to see her. She did not want him to come to her, and so he invited her to bring more books to the store. Had she contacted another dealer? He knew all the dealers in the area. He would have heard. Was she setting up an auction? He didn't ask.

He wanted Jess to hurry up and fly home for Thanksgiving. He was afraid Sandra might arrive while he was out and leave books with Jess, or even allow Jess to open them and ooh and ahh and say, "Those must be worth a fortune!" This scenario seemed unlikely, given Sandra's cautious approach, but Jess had a way of bounding in at the worst moments. She had asked once, in front of college students with a box of books to sell, why George paid so little for contemporary novels.

"Because they're ephemera," he said.

"All of them? Even Thomas Pynchon?" Jess held up a battered paperback copy of *V.* "Even Saul Bellow? *Humboldt's Gift* for a dollar?"

After he'd bought a stack of novels and chucked the rest and said good-bye to the students, he clapped his hand on Jess's shoulder. "Do you think I want a running commentary on prices? When I want your analysis of the book-buying business, I'll ask you. In the meantime, let's treat this as a store, not a seminar."

She didn't look in the least contrite. "I was talking about literature, not analyzing the book-buying business. And if I were, I wouldn't confuse a seminar with a store. And I wouldn't confuse a store with a folly."

"A folly," he echoed, incredulous, offended.

"A folly like an expensive hobby," she said, assuming he didn't know the term. "A folly like a little miniature ruined castle in a garden."

"'Little miniature' is redundant," he pointed out.

"You know what I mean."

"Yeah, well, I'd like my folly to be a little less expensive, which is why I want you to stop theorizing about my prices in front of customers."

"All right, fine."

Tuesdays and Thursdays were peaceful. George's other assistant, Colm, was discreet, spectacled, a tenth-year graduate student writing on Victorian commonplace books and the art of quotation. Far better for Sandra to meet Colm. He was judgmental too, but indirect.

However, as George feared, Sandra dropped in on a Monday.

"Hello," said Jess. "May I help you?"

Sandra hesitated. "I'm here with a book for George."

"We don't buy books on Mondays," Jess informed her.

"Sandra," cried George, rushing from the back room, "come with me." There was no door between the store's two rooms. Bookcases simply poured through the open passageway. "Watch your step," George warned. The back room was a full step down.

"I was thinking," Jess said, following them, "we should install a ramp here."

George gestured her away.

"We could get one made of plywood, and then if we straightened out the front entrance, we'd be almost wheelchair and stroller accessible."

"Jessamine," said George, and she understood and backed off.

"I have one more book to show you," Sandra told him. "But this is the last one."

"The last one you have?"

"The last one I'll show."

Why is that? George thought with sudden dread. Is she saving the rest for someone else? But he said, "Let's have a look."

She unwrapped a pristine copy of *The Alice B. Toklas Cookbook*. "It's the first British edition—with the recipe." Sandra turned to the page with the title "Toklas' Haschich Fudge."

The original hashish brownies. *Peppercorns, nutmeg, cinnamon, coriander, stone dates, dried figs, shelled almonds, peanuts, . . . A bunch of canibus sativa can be pulverized. This along with the spices should be dusted over the mixed fruit and nuts . . . it should be eaten with care. Two pieces are quite sufficient. . . .*

"True," said George.

"What do you think?" Sandra asked at last.

"It's not perfect." He pointed to the tiniest of tears on the dust jacket, the spots freckling the title page.

"You don't want it?" She needed money.

"I want it." The book was charming. It was very good. Of course he wanted it. But what he really wanted was to see the rest. What sort of trove was this? *The whole duty* and *Alice B. Toklas* cohabiting on the shelves? "I'd be happy to appraise your whole collection," he said once again. "If the other books are in this kind of condition . . ."

Sandra looked grave.

"Even if they're not . . ."

He heard the shop door. He felt a gust, a moment of traffic and chilly winter; heard Jess's voice. "Hey!" A man's voice, a rustling as the door closed again. Sandra and George stood together as before, examining the book, but subtly the climate in the store had changed. Jess was talking to a friend in the other room. He guessed Noah from Save the Trees. Jess had introduced the kid to George several weeks ago, calling him Director of Trees or VP of Tree-Saving, almost as though she were practicing for her parents, as if to say, This young man is not only idealistic, but management material as well. Yes, there he was leaning against a table stacked with books. Tall, wiry Noah with the frayed jeans, holes in the back pockets. He of the long arms and wide brown boyish eyes. Noah who was always touching everything. George tried not to notice. In fact, he refused to look.

"Really? You're so lucky!" Jess trilled to Noah in the other room. "I want to go there."

"You should come with us," Noah said.

George couldn't help imagining Jess sailing away with Noah. Surely they'd sail across the sea on Noah's nonprofit ark. He hoped they would.

Even as he ushered Sandra out, he heard muffled laughter. He couldn't see Jess and Noah anymore, but he sensed them in Medieval History. He knew the sounds of flirting in his store. The rustles and faint scufflings between the shelves, the creak of bookcases leaned upon, the squeak of the rolling step stool.

Jess, he chided silently, does he have to be one of those idiots who lie down in front of logging trucks? Really, now. But of course she had to find a leftie leafleter who shouted, "Would you like to save our forests today? Our trees go back to Biblical times!" to complete strangers on the street.

He had never seen Jess in action at the corner of Bancroft and Telegraph, but he could picture her. "Our trees predate Henry James. They gave their lives for him."

"You're not serious," he heard Noah tell Jess.

"I am," she said. "I'm afraid of heights."

"I can't believe you'd work for Save the Trees and never want to . . . experience them!"

"Can't you experience them from the ground?"

Now he was whispering.

Silence.

"Jess," George called.

No answer—as if to say, Oh, now you want me to come, when you brushed me off before.

He sat at his desk and glared in her general direction. In a moment she appeared in a V-necked sweater and a gauzy Indian skirt, the kind sold in stores called Save Tibet. She didn't look embarrassed, or disheveled, or in the least undone. He couldn't fault her, except that she looked far too happy for such a murky November day. There she stood, radiant. Her eyes were shining. All that from Noah? Had the shaggy tree hugger really cast that kind of spell?

"What is it?" Jess asked him.

"Get back to work, please."

She smiled at him. He'd never asked her to do anything "please" before. She didn't hear that he used the word only for emphasis. "Could I show Noah the Muir?"

"Is he interested?" George spoke in the third person even as Noah materialized behind Jess.

"Of course." Then Jess saw that George meant "interested to buy," and she looked a little disgusted. She liked to think of Yorick's as some sort of rare-book room, a miniature Houghton or Beinecke.

He unlocked the glass case, and Jess took out *The Mountains of California.*

"Cool," said Noah.

"*When I first enjoyed this superb view, one glowing April day,*" Jess read aloud, "*from the summit of the Pacheco Pass, the Central Valley, but little trampled or plowed as yet, was one furred, rich sheet of golden compositae, and the luminous wall of the mountains shone in all its glory. Then it seemed to me the Sierra should be called not the Nevada, or Snowy Range, but the Range of Light.*"

Golden compositae, George thought. How easy it was to forget the mountains, just a drive away.

"And look at this." Jess opened the book and showed Muir's inscription on the flyleaf.

Noah traced Muir's signature with his fingertip. "That's incredible."

"That's fifteen hundred dollars." George took John Muir away from Jess and locked him up again.

Later, after Noah had to run off to work, Jess approached George at his desk. "Could I ask you something?"

"You could."

"If you love books, why don't you like sharing them with other people?"

"I do like sharing them," said George. "I like to exchange them for money, in a transaction economists call making a sale."

"You can hardly stand it when other people look at them."

"Looking is fine. I don't enjoy watching people paw through a signed—"

"You touch your books all the time," Jess protested.

"I wash my hands." He had her there, and he saw her smile, despite herself.

"You're very supercilious," she told him.

You're very pretty, he thought, but he said, "Anything else?"

"Do you like owning books more than reading them?"

He began to answer and then stopped. "You want me to admit that I like owning better, don't you? Then you can tell me that books are about reading, and that words are free."

"No, I'm really asking," she said. "Which do you like better—having or reading?"

"I like reading books I own," he said.

"Does owning improve them?"

"You mean why not go to the library? Look at this *Gulliver's Travels*." He unlocked the glass case again. "This is a 1735 printing. Do you see the ridges here?" He held up the page for her. "This is laid paper. See how beautiful it is?"

"What happened there?" She was looking at the white scar on the back of his right hand.

"Cooking accident," he said.

She couldn't help staring at where the scar disappeared into his shirt cuff. "That must have been some knife."

"Look at this. Do you see the chapter headings?" He showed her the thick black type. "When I read Swift here, I'm reading him in this ink, on this paper, with this book in my hands—and I'm reading him as his contemporaries read him. You think there's something materialistic about collecting books, but really collectors are the last romantics. We're the only ones who still love books as objects."

"That's the question," said Jess. "How do you love them if you're always selling them?"

"I don't sell everything," he said. "You haven't seen my own collection."

"What do you have?"

"First editions. Yeats, Dickinson—all three volumes; Eliot, Pound, Millay . . ." He had noticed the books she read in the store. "Plath. I have *Ariel*—the English edition," he added temptingly. "I also have Elizabeth Bishop."

"I wish I could see them," Jess said.

"You would have to come to my house."

"Are you inviting me?" She must have known this was a loaded question, but she asked without flirtatiousness or self-consciousness, as if to say, I only want to know as a point of information.

Yes, he thought, I'm inviting you, but he did not say yes. He was her employer. She could act with a certain plucky independence, but he would always be the big bad wolf.

"I have a theory about rare books," Jess said. "Here's what I think. Rare books—any books—start to die without readers. The words grow paler and paler."

"Not true," George said. "Unread words don't fade at all."

"I meant metaphorically," said Jess.

"You'd rather see them all in public libraries?"

"Ideally, yes," said Jess.

"I've got a signed *Harp-Weaver.*"

"Really!"

He had to laugh. She was so eager.

She saw that he was in a good mood, and took the opportunity to ask, "Could I put up a poster outside the door?"

"No."

"Wait. You haven't seen it." She hurried to the storeroom where she kept her backpack and brought out a poster, which she unrolled over his desk. Comically, with hands and elbows, she tried to hold down all the corners at once. Failing in the attempt, she weighted them with George's books: *Gulliver's Travels, The Good Earth,* an old thesaurus.

George saw a woodblock print redwood against a cloudless sky. One word in green:

BREATHE

"Sorry." George pushed his books away. The poster rolled up instantly.

"It's a limited edition," Jess said.

"I don't collect propaganda," he told her.

"How is the word *breathe* propaganda? You can't object to breathing."

"I don't object to breathing. I object to being told to breathe."

"There is no agenda here," she said.

"This is Save the Trees warning me that without redwoods I won't breathe much longer. Therefore I should support the cause. I hope this is recycled paper, by the way."

"Of course it is."

"No posters anywhere near my store," said George. "This is a poster-and leaflet-free zone."

"Okay, okay," she said.

"I'll have to add that to my questionnaire: *Are you now or have you ever been involved in an evangelical, Messianic, or environmental cult?*"

"Save the Trees is a registered nonprofit," said Jess.

"Oh, that's all right then," said George. "Yorick's is a nonprofit too."

"And 'Breathe' is actually the title of a poem."

> *Breathe now.*
> *Breathe soon.*
> *Early and often.*
> *Between times.*
> *Before it's*
> *Too late.*

"Sorry." George handed her the rolled-up poster. "No."

"You don't like new poetry?" said Jess.

"I don't like bad poetry," said George, and then with some horror, "You didn't write that, did you?"

She shook her head.

"I'm relieved to hear it."

"I used to write poetry when I was younger," Jess said. She had kept a notebook by her bed, in case some line or image came to her in her dreams, but she had always been a sound sleeper, and no Xanadus or nightingales woke her. She read Coleridge or Keats and felt that they had covered the great subjects so well that she had nothing to add about beauty, or immortality of the soul. "Now I just read."

She spoke cheerfully, without a hint of wistfulness. She was indignant sometimes, but never wistful. Opinionated, but still hopeful in her opinions. Oh, Jess, George thought, no one has hurt you yet.

7

Jess saw that George detested Noah, but she thought nothing of it. George disliked Noah because he disapproved of Noah's cause, and George hated causes, unless they were his own. He seemed to think that other people's efforts to change the world were doomed.

Whenever the tree movement got bad press, George cut out the article for Jess. He was a regular clipping service, convinced that Save the Trees had ties to extremists who spiked redwoods with steel rods. He had no hard evidence, of course, but the news was full of loggers spooked and occasionally injured by some radical's idea of altruism. "I suggest," he told Jess on her last day before Thanksgiving break, "that you look at this discussion of possible links between Save the Trees and the incident in Humboldt County."

"No one at Save the Trees would support spiking," Jess exclaimed, as she glanced at the article from the *San Francisco Chronicle*. "I've been volunteering for three months and I've never heard of anyone in favor of spiking."

"How about people in favor of bankrupting and maiming loggers?"

"The loggers are exploited by Pacific Lumber," Jess said. "They're being used."

"So are you."

Someone else would have taken offense, but Jess wondered how George had become so sour. She reasoned that it had to do with being rich, that George had accrued so much that his life became one long struggle to conserve his property. How strange to live that way, like a snail, inside your own wealth.

And yet she had a little money now and liked it. She owned one hundred shares of Veritech, the hottest stock ever. Jess often checked Veritech's progress on her computer, where she loved to watch the stock price bob and float on the buoyant market. At first, watching made her feel guilty, but she quickly rationalized. The windfall wasn't for herself, or her paltry bank account, or paying bills. She would give her stock to a great cause, or perhaps, if its value rose even higher, to several: the Society for the Prevention of Cruelty to Animals, and Greenpeace, as well as Save the Trees.

"Three months," George said as he was locking up. "I didn't realize Save the Trees had been around that long."

"Are you, like, a neo-con?" Jess asked him.

"No!" George shot back, surprised.

"You're so cynical," said Jess.

George considered this as they stood outside the door. "I've been around the block."

"You're very disapproving," she chided gently. "It's not like I've done anything to you. It's not like I've done anything you mentioned on your questionnaire."

"Not yet."

Six o'clock. A light rain fell, and a pile of blankets stirred in the doorway across the street. As the shops began to close, new salespeople emerged.

Jess didn't seem to notice. "Good night," she said, and tugged the bottom of her jacket.

George wanted to zip her up himself. "Where's your bike?"

"It's in the shop," Jess said. "I'm getting a tune-up."

"I'll give you a ride," he offered.

"No, that's okay, I'm just going to catch the bus . . ."

"The *bus*?"

"It's hardly even dark," she protested as George took her arm and steered her across the street to the garage where he parked his Mercedes.

"You drive this big car all by yourself?" Jess asked, as he unlocked the door for her.

"Yes," George said. "I drive unassisted. Where are we going?"

"Derby Street," she said.

That surprised him. He hadn't pictured her there. Then he realized that she was going to Noah's place.

"A bunch of people live there."

Ah, the Save the Trees Co-op. George glanced at her quickly. He wanted to ask, Do you have any idea who owns this property? Have you checked the nonprofit status of this organization? Have you considered that Save the Trees could be a shell for something else? But she was a grown woman, apparently.

He drove to Derby Street with its big old houses and tall fences and brambly gardens. "Thanks for the ride." Jess dragged her backpack after her. "See you later."

George considered the brown shingled co-op on the corner. A great shambling Californian manse, probably as old as his, maybe even a Maybeck with its picturesque peaked roof and diamond-paned windows. There was a garden too, possibly a double lot. Now he was a little jealous. He saw a cottage peeking out above the slatted fence. Jess turned and waved. She seemed to be waving him away, but he stayed until the door opened.

Jess had never been invited to a party at the Tree House before. Quickly she closed the door behind her. She didn't want to introduce herself with a Mercedes idling in the background.

"Hi. I'm early," Jess apologized to the tiny woman who stood before her.

"Hi. I'm Daisy." The woman wore overalls and she had a buzz cut. She seemed both delicate and fierce and wore a T-shirt with HERE I STAND printed on it.

Jess wondered if Daisy was the woman's real name, or one of those forest names old-timers took in the interest of anonymity and protection.

Names like Butterfly or Gypsy or Shakespeare, evoking expeditions, dangers that had passed, inside jokes from long ago. "Is Noah here?" Jess received no answer as Daisy led her down some stairs and up others, through open fire doors and finally into the depths of the house, where Daisy disappeared to answer her phone.

She had never seen the Tree House at night. Vast and dark, lit with candles for the occasion, the rooms looked magical, the staircase a citadel, with its own strange inglenooks and deep dusty treads. In the fireplace, instead of wood, a great gong and mallet hung from a stand. The rooms were filled with couches and mismatched armchairs, and floor cushions, some with cats, and some without. Living ivy climbed to the ceiling and outlined every aperture. In the candlelight the ivy-framed bay window became a bower, the leafy doorways passages to secret gardens.

"Didn't anyone give you a drink?"

Startled, Jess recognized the founder of Save the Trees. Leon was famous in his world, and famous for his look as well. He was over thirty, wire-thin, with black unruly hair, dark skin, and eyes startlingly blue. His jeans and faded T-shirt hung on his gaunt frame. She saw him on occasion leafleting, but she knew him from Brandeis, where he had been a graduate student briefly, her freshman year. *Knew* was probably too strong a word. She'd had a serious crush on him, but he had never spoken two words to her then, and he didn't seem to recognize her now. She had heard the others talk about him, of course. He was a brilliant organizer, a heartbreaker, supposedly, and also somehow rich. He owned the house and rented it for nothing, a dollar a year, to Save the Trees, as headquarters and training camp and experiment in communal living.

"I'm sorry I'm so early," Jess said, as Leon got her a rum and Coke. "I'm Jess. Noah's friend."

"Oh, good, I'm Noah's friend too," said Leon coolly. "Did he give you the tour?"

"I'm not sure where he is."

"Come take a look."

"This woodwork is incredible," she said as she followed him up the stairs.

"This is all old growth," said Leon. "A lot of trees gave their lives in 1905."

"How did you find this place?"

"Real estate agent," Leon said.

"You just asked for listings of fairy-tale houses?"

Leon smiled.

The second floor had a sweet musty smell of old wood and dust. The air was heavy, almost felted with smoke and dust motes. Hushed.

"This landing here is so big we made it into another room with curtains. It doesn't have a door, but it's got a great view of the garden." Leon pulled open a heavy drape spread over a brass rod and revealed a little room with a window seat the size of a twin bed. Noah and a couple of other guys sat there passing a joint.

"Oh, there you are," said Jess, and everybody laughed except for Leon, who watched her quietly. Forgive me, but he wasn't worth it, Leon seemed to tell her with his eyes. Or was she imagining his response?

Noah stood to greet her, but instinctively Jess stepped back. "I'll be downstairs," she said lightly.

"Don't go." Noah followed her.

The living room was louder on reentry, pulsing with music.

"Let me get you a drink," shouted Noah.

"I have one." Jess raised her glass to show him.

"Okay." He looked slightly nervous standing there, as though unsure if she was really angry. Something was dawning on him, the very thought she'd had upstairs: that they'd only been seeing each other for a few weeks; that their friendship was rather tenuous; that they hadn't spent much time together.

"Do I even know you?" Jess asked suddenly. The question might have been devastating in a quieter room, but Noah couldn't hear.

Comically, he cupped his hand behind his ear.

"You look like an old man asking 'What's that, dear?'" Jess told him.

He couldn't hear that either.

"I'm leaving," Jess mouthed at him.

He tried to take her hand, but she was tired of him and slipped away, escaping to the back of the house, wandering into an old-fashioned kitchen crowded with cooks and hangers-on drinking beer.

"He's got this humanist, class-warfare streak," one of the guys was saying. "It always comes down to 'other species are lesser.'"

A dozen pie shells covered a long scarred table. A small buff woman with a tattoo of the god Shiva on her bicep was pouring quiche filling into each. Jess recognized her from leafleting. Her name was Arminda, and as she poured, she talked to another leafleter, a blond, blue-eyed girl from Idaho who went by Cat.

Arminda was telling Cat, "I had one more conversation with Aisha where I said there are things that are so structural I didn't know if we could repair them."

"And that was it?" asked Cat.

"Well, not exactly. We'd have this post–breakup sex where it was supposed to be the last time, and then the next time was going to be the last time, but I was kind of into the idea of being single, and I thought I might have a straight moment, you know?"

Cat giggled.

"Because there was this guy who was kind of eying me. But then—you know Johanna, right? I had this thing with her, but afterward I felt so bad because she was such a sweetheart. She's so sensitive! How do you tell someone you were just going through this crazy thing and you aren't really interested in that person herself? I was behaving really badly. But that's how I got the stomach flu—probably from Johanna. It was this really, really contagious, really virulent . . ."

Jess eyed the quiches on the table.

"I was trying to break up with Aisha and I was behaving so badly with Johanna, but I had to get everything out of my system," Arminda continued as Jess walked out, feeling strange, and also invisible.

No one acknowledged her as she walked down the hall. She saw couples in the bathroom, but no one looked at her. She didn't recognize anybody. Were the other guests all strangers? That couldn't be, but at the moment she couldn't tell any of them apart. She felt light-headed in the hazy, mazy house. The smell of beer mixed with the cloying smoke upstairs and made her queasy. She stepped out the back door and descended creaky steps for air.

How overgrown the garden was. Picking her way through ferns and banana trees, she almost stepped into a pocket-sized pond choked with lily pads. The Save the Trees office looked like a witch's house in the dark, its peaked roof and walls overhung with ivy. Behind the witch's house, a massive oak filled the sky. No stars pricked this tree's canopy, no moonlight sifted through these leaves, but a swing hung down on ropes so long that, in the dark, Jess scarcely saw where they began. She tugged at one; the rope held, and the wood swing bumped her hip. Shivering, she sat down and tucked her skirt under her legs.

Suddenly Leon appeared behind her. She jumped up.

"You forgot your jacket."

"How did you know it was mine?"

"Wallet in the pocket," he said. "Probably not a great place for it, by the way." He looked amused when she tried to take the jacket from him. It took her a moment to realize that he was holding it for her so that she could slip her arms inside. "Too many friends of friends in there."

"Well, that's what I am," she pointed out. "Or was."

"You and Noah?" Leon asked.

"Is that what he told you?"

Leon hesitated a moment, but only a moment, before he nodded.

"I barely know him." Jess sat down again and pushed off with her feet to start the swing, but the ropes were so long she only swayed a little. She kicked off again.

"Do you want a push?"

"Sure." She hoped that sounded diffident enough, as if to say, Since you're just standing there, you might as well, but she wasn't diffident at all. She lifted off as he pushed gently, hand between her shoulder blades. When she returned to him, he pushed lower on her back. A strange sensation, the brief contact, and then the long downstroke of anticipation. "My sister used to push me," she told him.

"I have sisters."

"Really?"

"Are you surprised?"

She stretched her legs and leaned back to swing higher. Her hair blew over her shoulders. Her skirt came loose and billowed over her knees. He was watching her, and as she rose and fell, she felt his gaze as radiant warmth. Of course she knew all about the male gaze, and she resented being gazed upon, but she was young enough that her resentment was purely theoretical. She was a paper feminist, just as Emily was a paper millionaire.

"You don't look like the kind of person who has sisters," she said.

"What do I look like?"

She thought for a moment as she swung forward. When she returned to him, she said, "An only child."

"Too selfish for siblings?" She was almost horizontal now, leaning back as she held the ropes.

"Way too selfish."

He pushed hard with both hands, and she shot forward, laughing. It felt so good to plunge feetfirst into the night. She felt a rush of air as she vaulted up into the dark branches. Too quickly she sank down again, the ground rose up, and the blood rushed to her head and dizzied her. She dragged her feet to slow herself, but she couldn't stop all at once. Twice, then three times, she braked with her feet, until Leon caught the ropes from behind. He was close enough for her to feel his breath against her hair. "Are you all right?"

"Just tree-sick."

He held her by the shoulders, as if to steady her, but she still felt the garden rushing toward her, and the sickening rush of air.

He touched her collarbone with his fingertips. "I remember you from Brandeis."

"Really? You remember me! Why didn't you say something?"

"I thought I'd wait," he said.

"How do you remember me?"

"I remember you as . . . lovely," he said.

She slipped off the swing to face him, laughing in disbelief—not just that he'd find her lovely, but that he would use such a delicate word.

"I asked people about you."

She shook her head at him and he couldn't help smiling. She was so innocent. Delicious. "Why didn't you ask *me* about me?"

"I was shy," he said, and that was true enough, although his shyness had been situational. He'd been unhappily involved.

"*Shy?*" She remembered him as arrogant, eloquent, and also tough. She'd heard him at a press conference, denouncing violence against the logging industry. He never hesitated at the microphone.

He couldn't resist asking, "Did you start volunteering because you remembered me?"

"Not only shy, but vain!"

The swing hung between them, but he grasped the ropes above her head.

"I was interested in halting systematic deforestation of the planet and petitioning for the ballot proposal to ban clear-cutting in Northern California," she said, ". . . and I did remember you."

"Oh, you did."

"Well, vaguely."

"Only vaguely?"

"Very, very vaguely. Just that you were busy, and you never even looked at me. When I got to Save the Trees you stayed true to type."

"Now I'm a type."

"Well . . ."

They were standing so close their noses almost touched. She looked up at him and wondered how his eyes were so blue and his skin so dark, and how he could be shy and also confident, and most of all, what he was thinking, but she didn't dare ask. And he saw her wondering, and he gazed at her delicate upturned face and felt a sudden tenderness for her, a little pang of responsibility. *I'll never never hurt you,* he promised silently, even as he imagined taking her into the office and locking the door. He spoke with a cautious sincerity he didn't feel. "I know you're dating Noah and I won't interfere with that."

"*Dating* is a relative term."

"Relative to what?"

"It doesn't matter."

"Really?" His lips brushed hers.

"I didn't take offense that you ignored me," she explained, "because what interests me is what you do."

"That's good to know."

"I meant your work." Her mouth grazed his. "I wasn't talking about . . . right now."

At first they kissed so lightly, there was no decision. They kissed the way they might trail their fingers in the water. I'm not really standing here with him, Jess thought, and she kissed him more deeply, just to make sure she wasn't dreaming. She touched the corner of his mouth with the tip of her tongue; she sucked his lower lip and tasted wine, and he was surprised, and also charmed, because he saw that she'd surprised herself. She was so curious. She trembled with curiosity.

They flew apart as two wailing fire engines careened down the street. Flashing lights illuminated the yard.

"That must have been the smoke alarm." Leon stood for a moment, watching as the firemen approached in full regalia—boots, jackets, hats. "Wait here," he told Jess. "Stay by the tree, and I'll send someone to take you home."

"Shouldn't I . . . ?"

"No, I don't want you to come in. Stay here."

Already partiers were streaming out, gathering in the front yard and on the sidewalk. There were hundreds, more than Jess would have thought possible, even in that rambling house. Two police cars pulled up. The hordes spilled onto the sidewalk. Jess stayed in shadow, sheltered by the oak.

Two officers entered and instantly a hush fell over the assembled. Jess could actually hear a pall fall over the blazing Bacchanalian house. It took her a second to realize that what she heard was the plug pulled on the sound system. The cops had stopped the music.

One officer stood on the landing, talking to Leon. "We've got noise ordinances, and we've got more than one complaint." She couldn't hear Leon's reply, but she saw that he was perfectly calm and quiet. "Generally speaking, if we have a smoke alarm on top of a noise situation . . . ," the officer continued loudly and laboriously. "When alcohol is served . . ."

She couldn't catch all the words, but did hear *inebriation* mentioned and *underage*.

Leon interrupted here, objecting.

"Let's put it this way: There are students on and off campus; there have been incidents on and off campus. You think you've got a friendly gathering. . . . In the morning you may find yourself with a situation. By situation, I mean someone dead. This has happened in the past. I don't like to spell it out for you, but that's my job—to spell it out for you."

Through the lit windows of the house, Jess glimpsed the firemen tramping through the rooms. What would they find there? She didn't see Noah in the crowd.

"Okay, let's go," someone ordered Jess. Her breath caught. Irrationally, she thought, They've come looking for me too. Then she recognized Daisy, small, fierce, humorless. "I'm taking you home. You have everything you need?"

Jess fumbled in her jacket pocket for her wallet and her keys. She felt like a child as she followed Daisy out the back gate. Did Leon think she was a child?

Chafing at the errand, Daisy didn't speak as they walked to the car, nor did she move the stacks of leaflets from the passenger seat. Jess heaved the bundles into the backseat. "Does this happen a lot?" she ventured.

Daisy glanced at her for a moment, and for a moment she looked amused. "Yes," she said, "this happens all the time."

8

Jess did not tell Emily that she spent the next day playing with Leon instead of packing, wandering in Muir Woods instead of catching up on laundry. Nor could she say exactly why she almost missed the early-morning flight to Boston. That she had stayed up all night talking to Leon at the Tree House, that they had sat on the window seat, looking out at the garden and talking trees and politics, redwoods at risk and those protected, and some in secret groves, unknown to all but a few climbers and scientists. Trees like living castles in the mist. Leon told Jess, "When you see them you . . ."

"You what?" Jess asked him.

"You feel blessed."

They talked about actions against Pacific Lumber Company. Tree sitting, roadblocking, human chains, using webcams and blogs and Listservs for publicity. "Old technology destroyed the environment," said Leon. "Wouldn't it be cool if new technology restored it?"

And Jess leaned against him, imagining a wireless world, a place without telephone poles, those poor denuded trees turned into sticks, a world where you could see the loggers make their kills online, and click to donate and do something about it. A world of webs and nets instead of boxes, logs, and . . . no, she couldn't quite give up on books.

"I don't think I could stop using paper," she told Leon.

He rubbed her shoulders and his hands slipped underneath her shirt. "People gave up on clay tablets," he pointed out. "They gave up typesetting, and eventually, they'll give up paper too."

"I like to turn the pages," she said.

He laughed softly. "It's all I can do not to turn you."

"All you can do? Really?" She turned to face him, and all at once she saw his delight and his surprise and the sun rising through the window. "Oh, God, I have to get to the airport!"

Leon rushed her home to the apartment for her suitcase, and they sped to the airport in his imported hybrid car, so that she dashed to the gate with just minutes to spare.

"I was worried about you!" Emily exclaimed as they boarded their plane. "I couldn't reach you! I thought something had happened to you! You're getting a cell phone."

"Okay, okay." Jess sank into her window seat. "You could have boarded without me."

Her sister had been struggling with just this possibility, torn between concern for Jess and her longing to see Jonathan. "What kept you so long? Do you really hate seeing Dad that much?" Emily stowed shopping bags of gifts in the overhead compartment and pushed her briefcase neatly under the seat in front of her. "Is that what this is about?"

"No! No, of course not."

"I think it is."

"I promise you," said Jess, "Dad could not have been farther from my mind." She took Hume from her backpack to read in self-defense. The plane began taxiing to the runway, and Jess read the same sentences again and again. *There are mysteries which mere natural and unassisted reason is very unfit to handle.... Happy if she be thence sensible of her temerity ... and ... return, with suitable modesty, to her true and proper province, the examination of common life....* What did this mean? Hume seemed to spell the end of philosophy and the beginning of ... what? Jess sneezed.

Emily offered her a granola bar.

"No, thanks," said Jess.

"Did you eat any breakfast?"

Jess returned to Hume, without answering. She didn't want to talk. She was afraid Emily would notice something different about her. When it came to confidences, Jess would rather hear Emily's secrets than tell her own. This seemed fair, and this seemed right. Jess was the more forgiving of the two.

"You catch colds a lot, don't you?"

Jess started. She'd heard her sister say, "You fall in love a lot, don't you?"

Not so often, not so much for someone my age, Jess protested silently to the page in front of her. How would Hume put it? *Though experience should be our guide*—yes, he always started that way—*and we see mistakes are common at the age of twenty-three, it must be acknowledged that not every youthful feeling begins unworthily and ends in error. If this were the case, mankind would have perished long ago.*

Jess slept and woke, and tried to sleep again, tucking her knees to her chest, straining to rest her head, turning in her seat like a cork in a bottle. The day was over by the time they landed with a thump at Logan, and as the sisters stumbled out, loaded with gifts for Lily and Maya, they saw that they had traded a sunny California afternoon for a misty, messy Boston night. Their father had been circling in his Volvo station wagon, "for twenty minutes," he said, even as he embraced them.

"So good to see you," he murmured to Jess, but after kissing Emily, he stood back and shook his head in amazement at his spectacularly successful daughter—a stance Jess recognized as "My, how you've grown."

Emily sat in front, and Jess struggled to unstrap and move two child-safety seats, so she could squeeze in back. The car was overheated, and the windows were locked. She rested her forehead on the glass and stared out at the crumbling brick buildings advertising steakhouses and bars in chipped paint. Growing up, she hadn't noticed how old and dirty everything looked, but she saw it now. The decrepitude back east!

"Why is there so much traffic?" Jess asked. "Is it the Big Dig?"

"The traffic is entirely random," Richard replied. Tall, gray-haired, clean-shaven, he had a quiet face, a recessive chin, eyes the color of a cloudy sky. He had attended MIT for college and for graduate school, and stayed to teach. On his right hand he wore an MIT insignia ring engraved with a beaver symbolizing industry. "Dad!" Jess burst out once when she was in high school and Richard had told her the drama club was a total waste of time, "of course you think that. You wear a brass rat."

But Richard wore his ring with pride. He considered MIT one of the great places on earth, and he was immensely proud that Emily had attended. As for Jess—what fights they'd had. Richard insisting Jess apply, even though she had no chance, and no interest. Bad enough that he'd forced her to take AP Calculus. That had been humiliating, but her MIT interview had been a joke.

"So," said the kindly Institute alumnus who had volunteered to meet with Jess. "When you were a kid, did you ever blow up chemistry experiments in the basement?"

"No," Jess answered truthfully.

"Chart clouds in the skies?"

"No."

"Take apart the family computer?"

"Never once," said Jess.

Her father used to storm at her, "You have a perfectly good aptitude for math, but you won't apply yourself."

"I'm not good at it!" she'd insisted.

"You're not interested," he'd shot back.

"That too!"

This was after Emily left home, and before Heidi. Sweet-natured and playful when Jess was younger, Richard became a fretful, controlling single parent. Outgoing and confident as a little girl, Jess took to her room to read Yeats and count the days until her high-school graduation. Looking back, she realized that Richard had been counting too. They had both been waiting. For what? For life, for love, for liberty. They'd lived for the future and dreaded it as well, and when they'd battled, they'd fought desperately because they only had each other. They'd known they were the last members of their family.

"What's new?" Emily asked her father.

"Nothing as exciting as your news," Richard said. "I had a grant rejected. Mrs. Weldon died. Her place is on the market."

"The house behind you?" asked Emily.

"It's a double lot. A developer is looking at it."

"Is that bad?" Jess piped up from the backseat.

"It's bad if they build five houses and start a subdivision. There's supposedly a nonprofit looking at the place as well, to start a religious child-care center."

"You could send the girls," Jess said.

Richard didn't answer. He hated anything religious, particularly involving children. A single bumper sticker adorned his car: WHAT SCHOOLS NEED IS A MOMENT OF SCIENCE.

"Just kidding," Jess said

It took almost an hour to reach downtown Canaan, which consisted of a real-estate agency, an ice-cream shop, a dry cleaner's, and a traffic light. South of Main Street, Canaan's winding roads and cul-de-sacs were named for Emerson, Alcott, Thoreau. North of Main, Richard's Colonial stood on Highland. The land here did rise slightly, and for this reason Richard rarely had to use the sump pump in the basement. He had done his homework, and he knew to avoid low-lying Hawthorne, Peabody, and especially Alcott. The town's Transcendentalists traversed a floodplain.

Heidi welcomed the travelers with her finger to her lips, and Jess and Emily tiptoed inside, trying not to slam the screen door and wake the girls.

"Come into the kitchen," Heidi whispered. Meticulous, earnest, Heidi had cut her hair to shoulder length and donned large eyeglasses. There was a solidity about her now that she'd become a mother. She wore black jeans and talked about language acquisition. She collected the children's finger paintings in large artist portfolios.

It went without saying (they never said it) that Heidi was accomplished. Her work in databases was "very interesting" according to Richard, and he would know. Heidi had been his graduate student. There was external evidence as well. Heidi taught at Brown. Her position there had prompted the move to Canaan, halfway between Cambridge and Providence.

"How was your flight?" Heidi asked.

"Fine," said Emily.

"Awful," said Jess.

"She's sick," Emily explained.

Jess thought she caught the aggravation in Heidi's eyes—*Oh, great, now we'll all catch this bug*—before the concerned questions, "Would you like a cup of tea? Do you need cold medicine?"

Richard carried in a load of bags. "You left the car door open," he told Jess.

"I did not. I closed my door." Already, Jess had reverted to her sixteen-year-old self. Amazing.

"Only you were sitting in the backseat," Richard corrected her. "Therefore you left the door open."

"Richard," said Heidi. "What's the difference? It's a door. It doesn't matter."

Late that night Emily lay awake in the guest room. She hadn't seen Jonathan in almost three weeks, and while everyone agreed that she should visit Canaan first, the last night apart was almost unbearable. She could not stop thinking about being with him again. She imagined his hands on her shoulders. "Look how tight you got." He would rub until she relaxed, until her whole body relaxed into his arms. They would kiss playfully at first. . . .

"Emily, are you asleep?" Jess whispered from the other bed.

"Almost."

"Why is it so cold in here?"

"It's not cold at all. It's so warm. It's stuffy."

"I'm shivering," said Jess.

Emily kicked off her covers and got out of bed. "You must have a fever." She felt Jess's forehead. "You're burning! Where do you think Dad keeps the thermometer?"

"It's just a cold," Jess said.

"Wait a second." Emily padded out to the bathroom and returned with medicine and water. "Take these." Jess struggled up in bed to swallow the pills. "Okay, now rest." Emily tucked the blankets around her and sat on the edge of the bed.

Their mother had told Emily quite seriously to watch her sister. She had told Emily in the hospital. Jess wasn't allowed in the room at that point, and Emily was only just old enough. "Look after her," Gillian said. "Do *not* let her jump in the street. You have to watch her. She doesn't pay attention. And remember she can't swim yet, even though she thinks she can. Remind your father about lessons."

"I'm fine," Jess said drowsily. "Go back to bed."

"I will," said Emily, but she stayed. Long after Jess drifted off, Emily sat up thinking on her sister's bed. What would her mother say now, if she had lived to see this year? This wonderful year. *I have embarked,* she told her mother softly. *I have embarked on my career. I have someone,* she told her mother. *I'm in love with Jonathan.* And she wished for some sign that Gillian was listening. She longed for some sense, even the faintest echo, of her mother in the house. But there were no photographs of Gillian on the walls and none of her possessions in the closets. Richard had sold Gillian's piano. He'd offered to ship it out to California, but neither Jess nor Emily played. Emily had quit her lessons at "Streets of Laredo" and Jess only got as far as "The Teddy Bears' Picnic." They had Gillian's jewelry, but she hadn't collected much. She had never liked necklaces or earrings. In fact, she'd never pierced her ears. She'd preferred a rosebush or two for her birthday, or a standing mixer.

"This is very sticky dough," she would tell Emily as she rolled it out. "It's very difficult to work with this dough, because it's so short. You see?" She dusted the rolling pin and board with more flour and rolled briskly, as if to tame the stiff pastry, which she then cut into circles with an over-turned teacup, or filled with honeyed poppy seeds, or spread into a glass pan to bake a cake of luscious prunes, their sweetness undercut with lemon. Nothing too sweet. That was the secret. Gillian said as much to Emily in her "Sixteenth Birthday" letter. *Don't doctor recipes. More is less, and sugar will only get you so far.*

Jess awoke Thanksgiving morning to find Lily holding Blue Bear by the side of her bed.

"Where's my presents?"

"Emily has them." Jess was so woozy with jet lag and cold medicine that she could scarcely open her eyes.

"Can I nail-polish you?"

"What?"

"Can I nail-polish you?"

"No."

"Can I pretend-nail-polish you?"

"Fine." Jess buried her head in her pillow and thrust out both hands for Lily.

"Wait, I have to . . ." Lily scampered off and Jess drifted to sleep again.

A moment later, Jess felt something cool and slippery on her fingernails. Lily was coloring each nail with marker. Jess hoped that this would take a while.

At least Emily had Jonathan. He would swoop down from Cambridge and take Emily away, while Jess was stuck in Canaan for the long weekend. In one of Jess's birthday letters, Gillian had written, *I hope that you'll share whatever comes your way.* It was funny to imagine Gillian writing this so many years ago, thinking about sharing toys and candy, and cutting Black-and-White cookies straight across, so that each half had some chocolate and some vanilla. Jess had no desire to split Jonathan down the middle, except when she was angry with him, but she did envy Emily the excuse to get away.

Downstairs, Emily was already dressed and toasting frozen waffles. Heidi was checking her e-mail at the kitchen table. Richard had gone running.

"Would you like a plate?" Emily asked when Jess plucked a pair of waffles from the toaster.

The house was crammed with toys, particularly plastic toys in a certain shade of pink, a bright bubblegum tint like a contagion in every room. Pink plastic chairs and pink doll strollers, pink easels, and a pink and white miniature kitchen. As Jess nibbled her waffles, she made one of her never-in-a-million-years vows. If and when she had a baby, never in a million years would her daughter touch plastic or play with baby dolls. Jess would not allow pink in her someday house, nor would her little girl wear that color. No! Overalls instead, and green checked shirts. Toy trucks, or, better yet, tiny solar-powered cars.

"Let's go outside," Jess told her little sisters. "Let's get some fresh air."

For the next hour, Jess spotted the girls on their cedar climbing structure, and caught Maya at the bottom of the slide. She hoisted the girls into a pair of baby swings, and struggled to stuff their snowsuited legs through the holes.

"Higher!" squealed Lily, as Jess pushed the girls, one with each hand.

Maya shrieked. Lily's hood flew back, and she threw her head back as well and laughed. The chains were short, and they squeaked. Still, if Jess closed her eyes for a moment, she could remember the long arc of the rope swing, Leon's hand on her back, her own flight into the air.

"Underdog!" screamed Lily.

Jess ducked under the swing to the other side.

The yard faced south, and a thousand twittering sparrows sunned themselves in the boxwood hedge that separated the property from the Weldon place. The huge garden there looked desolate, striped with winter shadows. But *that* was not a shadow. No, that was a man in a dark suit. The developer? He wore a round-brimmed black hat, a white shirt, a black frock coat. Shiny black dress shoes. The little man was trying to look casual, as if he'd just happened by.

"Me! Me!" shrieked Maya.

Jess kept her eyes on the trespasser next door. He knew that she was watching him. He decided to make the best of it and walked right up to the hedge, where he smiled and called, "Good morning!" The sparrows seemed divided about him. Some fluttered up in alarm, and others stayed in the hedge, chirping, as he called out, "How are you?"

"I'm fine," said Jess, examining his face. His eyes were the rare pure blue found in the very young or very old. He had a russet beard and rosy cheeks and wore no gloves. He blew on his hands.

"Hello, let me introduce myself," the man said in a welcoming way, just as if he were standing on his own land. "My name is Rabbi Shimon Zylberfenig, and I am the director of the Bialystok Center of Canaan."

"Good to meet you. I'm Jess."

"And these are your children?"

"My sisters," said Jess. "I'm just visiting."

"Very nice. Where are you from?"

"Berkeley."

"I have family in Berkeley!"

Oh, this was too strange. Jess remembered Rabbi Helfgott. *My brother-in-law lives in Canaan! My wife's sister's husband.*

"Do you know Rabbi Helfgott? My brother-in-law," said Rabbi Zylberfenig with some pride. "A very famous rabbi on the West Coast. You have perhaps heard of him?"

"I met him recently," said Jess.

Rabbi Zylberfenig beamed at her.

"It's a funny coincidence," said Jess.

"There are no coincidences," said Rabbi Zylberfenig quite seriously. "I hope you'll come by us for Shabbes at our center here in Canaan. We are not yet so big and well established, but we are a very warm community, very welcoming. You'll come for dinner?"

Rhythmically, Jess pushed her sisters on the squeaking swings. "I think I'll probably need to stay here."

"Bring the family," Zylberfenig urged her. "We always have room for more. In fact, we are always interested in making room."

"Is that why you're looking at the property there?" Jess asked.

"Only browsing," Zylberfenig said, as though he were standing at a magazine stand and not a boxwood hedge.

The girls were fussing. "Up!" Maya cried, by which she meant "down."

"There are many possibilities," the rabbi said.

Rabbi Zylberfenig's wife was waiting on the other side of the old Weldon place. The rabbi had parked on Pleasant Street, and Chaya was sitting in their van.

"Two acres at least. Beautiful," Shimon said as soon as he returned to Chaya. They sat together and looked out at the white house with its peeling paint. Their little ones slept in car seats in the back. The other four were home.

"I met a very interesting woman from Berkeley," Shimon continued. "She knows Nachum."

"Really?" Chaya was slender, bright-eyed, English. "Is she staying? Did you invite her for Shabbes?"

"Of course."

"She's coming?"

Shimon smiled. "Who knows? I hope. She's visiting her family."

"Invite them too."

"I did. I told her please bring the family." Shimon's eyes were still fixed on the two acres. A pair of giant oaks stood in the front yard. "Just four hundred thousand," he said.

Chaya tsked under her breath. She wondered if the place was over-priced, and if they'd get a variance, and if these neighbors would object to a Bialystok Center. Some did and some did not, and you could never predict. But the big question was, Where would they find the money?

"We would have room for expansion." Shimon started the van and released the emergency brake.

"Renovating that house . . . ," Chaya began.

"We won't renovate. *Im yirtzeh* Hashem, we'll crush it down." As Shimon eased down the hill, a loose apple rolled along the floor of the van.

"This is a small community," Chaya said.

"Even a small community can do great mitzvahs. It is very interesting what a small community may do." He spoke softly, so as not to wake the children. "You'll see."

The Rebbe had sent the Zylberfenigs from Brooklyn as newlyweds to bring Yiddishkeit to Canaan, returning lapsed Jews to their own religion. Now, eleven years and six children later (although they did not count children, because it was bad luck), they had not succeeded as well as their peers in other towns. Chaya's own sister in Berkeley, for example, presided over a large establishment with her husband. This was partly because Berkeley was a city, while Canaan was a town of fewer than twenty thousand inhabitants (although it was better not to count populations either). Berkeley was more affluent than Canaan and overflowing with young college students, many of them Jews, ready and waiting, ripe on the vine. Canaan's Jews were older and well settled and often mistrustful of their own religion.

It was also true that Bialystok emissaries had to fend for themselves. Parents might support *shleichim*, but not Headquarters. Each Bialystok Center had to raise its own money. In his wisdom, the Rebbe adhered to the famous dictum "Every tub on its own bottom." Chaya had married with a little dowry, but that money was gone. He was not a saver, Shimon. He was a spender, and a buyer, and always, every day, expected miracles. "We have students," Shimon reminded her. "We have supporters. We may even someday have angels." He was a pious man, but when he said "angels" he meant in the financial sense. Angels who would buy property for them someday. Shimon was always hopeful, always learning, always thinking, and Chaya respected this, but she found her husband aggravating as well, probably because she was a woman, and had to concern herself with laundry, groceries, and cooking. She was constantly sorting out her children's shoes, performing the countless details of mother and *rebbetzin*, even though the Messiah was due at any moment.

9

On Thanksgiving Day, with the markets closed, the whole world seemed to sigh with satisfaction. Emily was worth half a billion dollars. Jess was a happy thousandaire. They drove to Providence with Richard, Heidi, and the girls to eat dinner at a new restaurant called Sonoma Grille.

"Don't you think it's a little weird to fly back east to eat faux Californian cuisine?" Jess whispered to Emily when they arrived.

"Shh!" Emily glanced toward her father as they sat down at the table. They were six without Jonathan, who had to cancel at the last minute.

"Servers went down this morning," Emily explained, and she tried to sound serene, and she tried to feel patient, but she was neither. All she wanted was to take her father's car and drive to Cambridge. "He has to be there."

"An ISIS crisis." Jess poked Maya with a breadstick.

"It's not a big deal," Emily said. "It's just a little . . ."

She trailed off, sensing Jess watching, waiting for her to admit how she really felt.

"We'll have Thanksgiving tomorrow," Jonathan had promised Emily on the phone.

"I'm sorry about the crash," she said.

"It doesn't matter." His voice was light. He was in great spirits, thrilled that Emily had come, and certain that, within weeks, he would be as rich as she.

Everybody knew prosperity would come, that wealth was imminent. Profits followed prospects. Cash kept rolling in. Chaya accused Shimon on Thanksgiving of thinking money grew on trees, and he told her, "But it does!" Chaya was fretting about children's winter coats, but her husband had a deeper understanding of the age. His own student Barbara, a regular at all his classes, was married to Mel Millstein, the director of Human Resources at ISIS. His own Barbara, who came to services each week, had expressed her wish to share whatever wealth the Internet would bring.

Even now, Barbara was serving Thanksgiving dinner in her little house on Fuller Circle. The tablecloth was harvest gold. The salt and pepper shakers, Pilgrims. Barbara served turkey, sage and onion stuffing, cranberry sauce, sweet potatoes, and corn bread to her grown children, Sam and Annie, and her husband, Mel, the angel who didn't know it. Poor Mel, stubborn Mel, who didn't like to listen to Barbara's stories of the Bialystoker rebbes.

"The third Bialystoker Rebbe is known as the Dreamer," Barbara explained to her family. "When he was a young student, his learning was so brilliant that he levitated above the ground As his knowledge grew, he began floating higher, so that, in time, whenever he opened his mouth, he began to fly upward, lighter than air. His teachers had to keep the windows shut. They were afraid the young man would fly away. . . ."

"Your mother is taking a class in Jewish mysticism," said Mel.

"Cool," Sam said politely.

"What happened to going back to school?" asked Annie.

"Oh, I don't think I have time," Barbara murmured.

"Why not?" Annie had always been ambitious on her mother's behalf.

"Well, there's the house. There's the garden," Barbara said vaguely.

"Mom, it's November," Annie said. "How are you gardening in the winter? And what do you need to do in the house?"

"Quite a lot!" Barbara retorted, thinking of the wet basement.

"You need to get a life." Annie meant this lovingly. She was just thinking aloud.

Barbara plunged the serving spoon deep into the cranberry sauce. "I
have a life."

Barbara seemed at times like a woman having an affair. Mel knew, of
course, that she was not sneaking off to sleep with God, or any of his
messengers, but sometimes it felt that way. She hummed. She was always
humming without noticing, and she had never been a hummer. She
glowed when she talked about services or classes at the Bialystok Center.
A sudden youthfulness suffused her skin. Maybe it was love after all, but
if so, Barbara was in love with the whole Zylberfenig family—the rabbi,
his wife, and all their children, down to the baby. Especially the baby. She
was irrational about these people. They held her in their thrall.

Mel was Jewish, named for his grandfather Mendel. With his dark
eyes, strong nose, and melancholy little mouth shaded by a moustache, he
looked as Jewish as they come. But he was from the nonbelieving branch
of the religion. Superstition scared him. In fact, superstition made him
superstitious. These were strange times. The world seemed on the cusp of
some revelation—or some disaster. The Y2K bug lurked inside the
world's computers like a worm eating the world tree. According to the
CIA, terrorists were out to get everyone on New Year's Eve. Even as Barbara began praying and nailing mezuzahs to door frames throughout the
house, Mel felt that something terrible might befall him. Each mezuzah
case was no larger than Mel's index finger and concealed a scroll inside,
so that no scripture was visible, except for one Hebrew letter, the shape of
a three-tined fork. They were small, these mezuzahs, but they were everywhere, each like a chrysalis, a tiny portent. Lately he lived in dread. What
would become of him? What new belief would open up its wings and
flutter through the house today? Barbara had begun praying morning,
noon, and night. Turning toward the east, she clutched her prayer book
and mumbled words in Hebrew. And she wrote checks. Little checks.
Nothing too crazy, but donations all the same, to the Zylberfenigs, those
mystic Bialystokers of hers.

As he cleared and Barbara washed the Thanksgiving dishes, she said, "I'm sorry I snapped at Annie. I'm happy."

"I know." His voice was bleak.

"I'm thankful, actually, because we're all together."

He nodded, although he and Barbara were alone in the house. The kids had driven off to see their friends.

"We're blessed," said Barbara. She turned off the water in the sink and turned to face him. She was glowing again. Her cheeks were rosy, her eyes bright with the sky. She looked as though she'd just come in from walking on a perfect fall day. "Just think what we can do when we sell our stock."

"Our stock? Who's selling stock?"

"We could *give*," said Barbara.

Suddenly, Mel knew the desire in Barbara's infatuated heart. He took a full step back in shock. Donate *stock*! Mel had assumed that after twenty-eight years of marriage he and his wife had discovered every little quirk and source of irritation—but now this! An entirely new category, like a previously uncharted island or a new species in the rain forest. That was how her suggestion revealed itself to him, a new mammal, a giant three-toed rat, just when naturalists thought they'd seen it all.

"Oh, no. No. That's not going to happen. If and when ISIS goes public—if and when I'm clear to sell my shares—there's no way in hell I'm giving them to those Hasidic lunatics of yours."

"Mel," said Barbara, hurt by his language.

Anger swelled within him. "I am not giving a penny of my money to those holy rollers and their evangelical, superstitious, brainwashing cult. Over my dead body."

"I never said anything!" Barbara protested.

"You don't have to. I know. Don't you think I know what they want out of you? And what you want to do?" And he did know, because after all, he had been married to Barbara half his life. He had met her at Brigham and Women's Hospital where he had worked in payroll and she was just a sweet young nurse. He knew exactly how his wife looked when she hoped for something, or when she wanted something, or when she dreamed. He knew her yearning liquid eyes, her tender mouth. He could read her face, even as she became a stranger to him.

10

By Friday morning, Jess was so homesick for California that she begged Emily, "When Jonathan comes to pick you up, could you take me too?"

Emily looked guilty.

"I'm just kidding!" Jess assured her.

Waiting must have been torture, but Emily hardly let it show. She kept busy, playing Candy Land with the girls, and then helping Heidi sort through boxes in the guest room. Jess avoided these activities. Through the kitchen window, as she washed an apple, Jess saw someone in the garden next door. The rabbi again, in his black coat and hat.

"Dad," she called her father.

"Hold on." His voice was muffled through the door of his home office off the living room.

"He's back." Jess stood outside the door.

"Who?"

"The rabbi looking at the Weldon place."

Now the door opened. "Where?"

They hurried to the window.

There he was. They could see the top half of Rabbi Zylberfenig over the hedge. He was gazing contemplatively at the winter ruins of an overgrown rhododendron, surely thinking something mystical about the dormancy and rebirth of plants.

Richard's eyes narrowed. "He must be the nonprofit with the day-care scheme."

"He didn't seem like a psychopath or anything," Jess ventured.

"Except that he'd like to convert every Jew in sight to flat earth ancestor worship," Richard countered.

Jess couldn't help giggling at that last.

"You think it's funny," Richard said.

"No," she protested.

"These people are opportunists," her father declared. "I know what they did in Sharon, and in Bethel. They infiltrate wherever they can, because you know what they want?"

"The Messiah?"

"Money."

Oh, if Richard had known what Jess had done—borrowing from one of them. Fortunately, her father could not read her mind. "The sole purpose of these centers is to raise money to open more centers," he explained. "These things are viral, as is the religion, which is a cult based on their rabbi, whom they worship."

"Oh, come on, Dad, how do you know what they believe?" asked Jess.

"I know more than you think," her father said.

"Let's say they do worship their rabbi. Aren't they allowed freedom of religion? Or are you like those people theoretically supporting battered-women's shelters—everywhere but your backyard?"

"Don't lecture me about freedom, young lady," said Richard. "These people intend to come in, bringing traffic to a residential neighborhood. They are planning a religious school and propaganda center next to my home. Don't tell me their beliefs are sacrosanct when their *practices* threaten to impact me and my family."

Who was this irate man standing in the kitchen? Who was his family? Not Jess and Emily. He spoke of his new wife and kids, of course. They were young and sweet, but Richard had aged, and his doubts had hardened, along with his beliefs. Jess had asked him once, when she was about ten, whether he'd stopped believing in God when Gillian died.

"No, sweetie," he'd replied. "I wouldn't give up believing because of some event that happened to me. Terrible things happen every day. It would be illogical to give up hope in God because of one death in our family. No. I never believed in the first place. Not before, not after."

At the time, Jess had found his answer comforting. Richard's rationality had always reassured her. If she woke in the night, afraid of thunderstorms, he would sit on the edge of her bed and talk to her about probability and statistics, explaining the low odds that she'd get hit by lightning. She didn't worry about crossing the street, did she? Well, she was far more likely to die that way. He'd also explained that the chances of dying in a plane crash were infinitesimally small, and that Newton enjoyed the lowest crime rate in Massachusetts. Highly unlikely, then, for armed robbers to break into their home at night. Now, however, Jess looked at her father and wondered where his anger came from, and why he sounded so obsessed with people he dismissed, and so threatened by a religion he denied. She herself vacillated when it came to belief. She did not particularly believe in God. Or, rather, she didn't believe in a particular God. Nevertheless, she kept an open mind. She was not a melancholy agnostic, but the optimistic kind. She liked to give God the benefit of the doubt.

"Why don't you go out and talk to him?" Jess asked her father.

"I have nothing to say to that man," Richard replied.

"That's not true," said Jess.

Her father returned to his study.

"I think you have a lot to say," she called after him.

Upstairs, Emily sat on the floor with Heidi, contemplating the open box before her.

"What about your father's *National Geographics*?" Heidi asked. "If we could move those boxes out . . ."

"I love those." Jess stood in the doorway with her mouth full of apple. As soon as Heidi lifted them from the box, Jess recognized the cheerful yellow magazines—a complete set from 1915 to 1970. She'd pored over the maps and photographs, the little Afghan children in native dress, the photos of dunes and deserts, the sweep of sand in black and gray and white.

"If you want them, we can ship them all to you," Heidi said.

"Don't be ridiculous, Jess," said Emily. "Pretty soon you'll see them all online." She looked at Heidi. "Give them to the library," she advised. "Jess doesn't have room."

"I'll make room," Jess protested, but just then the doorbell rang and they heard Jonathan's voice, and Richard's welcoming him, happier than he'd been all afternoon. Of course, Jonathan was just the sort Richard loved: technical and bright and poised to conquer worlds.

Emily ran down to him. Boxes and magazines, even Rabbi Zylberfenig was forgotten. Jonathan was like the cavalry coming over the hill. You couldn't help racing to meet him. Richard grinned. The little girls giggled, and Heidi grew girlish herself, laughing when he told her to send students his way.

"We'll lose a generation of academics if everyone goes to work for you at ISIS," she said.

Everyone laughed at Jonathan's response: "Well, that's okay."

Even Jess, who liked him least, felt Jonathan's extraordinary pull. You wanted to please him, or at least stand back and watch. What was it about him? His sheer energy. His masculinity. He was such a guy: square-shouldered, forthright. He had served in the Marines before college, and there was something military about him still, his hair cropped short, his feet-apart, stand-and-deliver attitude even in conversation. He had the devil in him too, a take-no-prisoners smile. He adored Emily, and when they were together his good looks were touched by humility, his blue eyes softened. When he took her hand, his thumb stroked hers yearningly.

At the barbecue where they'd met, his first words to Emily had been, "I have a huge crush on you."

She'd burst out laughing. Surrounded by men at work, she was used to unspoken admiration, passive aggression, sometimes inappropriate advances. Not this mix of audacity and humor.

He'd added, "I like your company too."

"Was that a pun, or did you mean Veritech?"

He'd shaken his head. "I've never made a pun in my life!"

"Not even unintentionally?"

"I guess that was my first. I was talking about Veritech."

"What do you like about it?"

"Your new indexing system, your partners, your client list. You guys are so cool. You're *ubiquitous*." He said the word with reverence. "You're doing everything I want to do."

After an hour, which felt like three, and a snack of Goldfish crackers in the kitchen with the kids, she and Jonathan made their escape. For a moment in the driveway, Jonathan's Datsun wouldn't start, and Emily began to fret, and Jonathan laughed at her, and when the old car started at last, he drew her toward him and kissed her while the engine idled.

"Just wait," said Jonathan as they drove off. By which he meant, "Wait 'til we get to my place. Wait 'til I have you all alone. Wait 'til this old wreck becomes a yellow Lamborghini." Unlike Emily, Jonathan had no trouble envisioning the toys he'd buy, and the fun he'd have. He knew precisely the canary yellow of his future car, its huge motor and bulbous lights, its doors like wings.

In the meantime, the engine sounded hoarse, and traffic slowed down on the pike. When they finally got to Cambridge, there wasn't time to stop at Jonathan's apartment before dinner with their friends Orion and Molly.

"Let's cancel," Jonathan said.

"We can't just stand them up."

"Why not? I want to," Jonathan protested, his expression frank and boyish, softening his words. "I see Orion every day."

"But I don't," said Emily. "And we never see Molly."

"Nobody does," Jonathan said. Molly was an intern at Beth Israel Deaconess.

"Then this is a rare opportunity." Emily was not above teasing him a little. "Not to be missed."

After looping several times through one-way streets, they parked far from the restaurant, and ended up rushing through Harvard Square on foot. Emily always forgot how cold it got. Her shearling jacket wasn't nearly warm enough, and she was shivering, while Jonathan didn't need a coat, only a sweater, and he gave Emily his knit hat, a gesture both chivalrous and clumsy, as he pulled it down too hard, covering her eyes.

They met Orion and Molly on Brattle Street, and when the four of them entered Casablanca, the sudden warmth fogged Emily's glasses. As she took them off and wiped them, she saw Molly do the same, and the two smiled in solidarity, acquaintances searching for something in common. Orion was the one Emily knew well. He had been Emily's childhood friend when, for several summers, they attended CTY, the Center for Talented Youth at Johns Hopkins. At eleven, twelve, and thirteen, they took courses in physics and advanced geometry along with other children selected nationwide. Emily had studied Greek, and Orion took astronomy. Renaissance children, they lived in dorms with other earnest middle-schoolers blowing through problem sets, practicing violin, gathering several times a week for camp games designated by their counselors as "mandatory fun."

At CTY, Orion had been Emily's first sweetheart, the first boy she walked with hand in hand; and one summer night, her first kiss. They had been standing close, studying each other, a small blond Orion and a slightly taller Emily, each wondering what the other was thinking, and each afraid to ask. They both held still. The moment was delicious, almost unbearable. Emily knew she had to do something. She took off her glasses and held them open at her side. His lips touched hers. So this is kissing, she thought. She couldn't taste anything. It wasn't that kind of kiss. It was the kind that hung in the air, beautiful and abstract, like a theorem to contemplate. The moment afterward was lovely, much sweeter than the kiss itself. They could breathe again.

They corresponded during the school year, mailing handwritten letters—Orion's scrawled on notebook paper, Emily's printed on blue stationery patterned with white clouds. She must have written three letters to his one, and she remembered pointing this out on the phone. She'd been tearful, and he'd grown quiet, and finally he told her that his parents were splitting up. Then she understood, and the understanding was pure

Emily—unselfish insight. She realized that corresponding was too much for him, and pining for each other was a little much as well. "Maybe we should stop," she whispered. "We're only thirteen."

By high school, their romance was well behind them, and in college they settled into occasional e-mail exchanges. He went to graduate school at MIT, and one summer when Emily came east to see her father, Orion introduced her to Jonathan. So she had Orion to thank for that. Orion who was now so tall—much taller than she. He was lanky, broad-shouldered, long-limbed, and although Molly had dressed up in a black wool dress and high-heeled black boots, Orion wore jeans and a sweater with holes at the elbows. Molly was short and round-faced; she had an eager look about her, while Orion always had a faraway look in his gray eyes, as though he'd rather be fishing. He wore his hair long in a ponytail thick as a horse's mane. He had something of the wild horse about him.

"Did you break your finger?" Emily asked Orion as they sat down, women on one side, men on the other.

He glanced down at the splint on his left hand. "Oh, I did that playing Ultimate."

"You still play Frisbee?"

"Of course."

"He's in a league," said Molly.

"I still remember your father's poem about watching you," said Emily.

"She's read all Dad's poetry," Orion told Molly.

"*Boy trumps dog . . . ,*" Emily quoted.

"God. Stop!" Orion laughed. "You don't have to *recite* them."

"I happen to like his work," Emily protested, as Jonathan's ankle rubbed her shin, his leg pressing against hers underneath the table.

They ordered elaborate salads with smoked duck, and pizzas with caramelized figs, small rich entrées. There was a wine list, but none of them knew what to make of it, until Jonathan decided on champagne so they could toast Veritech. He didn't know which kind to get, so he ordered the most expensive bottle listed.

"Very good," the waiter said with a half smile, and Jonathan laughed a little, after the waiter had gone. He had missed the waiter's smirk, and thought him silly. Softly lit, decorated with murals of scenes from the movie *Casablanca,* the restaurant was just a bit precious for Jonathan. On one wall, a sad-eyed Humphrey Bogart watched over them, and tears glistened in Ingrid Bergman's eyes.

"One hundred twenty-two dollars a share," Jonathan boasted to Orion. "As of today—right, Emily?"

She nodded, ducking her head, a little embarrassed that she knew Veritech's price the day after Thanksgiving.

"That's amazing," said Molly, and she looked at Orion as if to say, Really? And could that happen to us too, with ISIS? Orion played with the ragged edge of his sleeve.

"The shares split last week," Jonathan told them, because he knew Emily wouldn't boast.

"That's just sick," Orion said.

Indeed. If Emily could sell just a fraction of her stock, she would be beyond wealthy. Of course, *if* was the operative word. The lockup held until June. The price couldn't rise forever, but when would it fall? How would she pick the right time to sell? A delicate question. She and Alex and Milton avoided the subject. They knew intellectually that they had to sell some stock in the summer, but selling felt like cannibalizing their own offspring. Jonathan was about to discover this, but he didn't understand the feeling yet. It was hard to see over the edge of an IPO.

"Is this all right?" The waiter presented Jonathan with the champagne.

"I should hope so," said Jonathan cheerfully. As the waiter poured him a glass, he added, "Pour for everyone." Then came his toast: "To Veritech, and to the future."

"To infinity and beyond," Orion said.

"Hell, yeah."

"But let's get our products working," Orion murmured.

"Orion, here, is still doing research," Jonathan explained to Emily and Molly. "We're building, and he's busy breaking code."

"I broke Lockbox," Orion confessed.

"How?" Emily blurted out. Lockbox was supposed to be unbreakable, the code impervious. Thousands, millions of Internet shoppers depended on Lockbox to safeguard their transactions. If Lockbox broke—even in the safety of the office—that would be a major setback. A breakdown wouldn't necessarily derail the ISIS IPO, but it might delay it, and a delay these days, even for a few months, was like derailment.

"Better to know now, right?" Orion said.

"It's the new version, 2.0, not the one we've shipped," Jonathan reassured Emily and Molly. "The original Lockbox that everyone is using out there is totally fine."

"What did you do?" Emily asked Orion.

She felt Jonathan tense. He pulled his legs away from hers under the table.

"The new code is buggy," Orion said.

But Jonathan contradicted. "It was ready until you broke it."

"If it was breakable," said Orion, "then obviously it wasn't ready."

"There's testing code and there's fucking with it."

"There's solid work and wishful thinking," Orion said. "You can't tell clients you've got stuff ready when you know it isn't ready."

"I tell them what we *will* have ready, if everybody does his job," said Jonathan.

"I'm talking about reality," said Orion, "not some myth of magical security solutions—"

"Oh, come on, you guys," Emily interrupted.

"Yeah, really," Molly said.

Emily chided, "This is the same debate we have all the time between programmers and marketing. Do you think you're so unusual? We broke something just a couple of weeks ago, and now it's crippled."

"Broke what?" Curiosity trumped aggression. "You're building something new. What are you building?"

"It's not public yet," Emily replied.

"What is it?"

"I can't tell you."

"Yes, you can," Jonathan wheedled.

"Well, I won't."

"We have ways of making you talk," he teased.

"She'll never tell you." Orion spoke lightly, but his words suggested his greater knowledge of Emily, and their older friendship—and once again he angered Jonathan.

"I'm tired of your predictions," Jonathan said quietly.

"You don't have to listen," Orion pointed out. "Usually you don't."

Jonathan was toying with his half-filled champagne flute. The glass looked so delicate in his hand that Emily reached across the table and placed it safely next to hers.

"You didn't have to fight with him," Emily told Jonathan in the car.

"He started it," said Jonathan.

"What difference does it make? You should know better."

They drove up Mass. Ave. with its multicultural holiday lights: shooting stars and stylized dancers. "He's irresponsible," Jonathan declared.

"Why? Because he disagrees with you sometimes?"

"You wouldn't defend him like that if he worked for you."

"How do you know?"

"Oh, I know you."

"Well, I don't attack my friends in restaurants."

"I didn't attack him."

"I thought you were going to break his glass and stab him with it."

"Hire him at Veritech," said Jonathan. "Seriously. We'll pack him up in Bubble Wrap and ship him. We don't want him."

"But you might need him."

"For what? Talking about our products?" Jonathan was indignant again. "Next thing I know, Green Knight comes up with a security system just like ours."

He amazed her. He was all energy, and all competition. She was driven to succeed, but her idea of success was focused, pure, and self-defined. Jonathan's idea was annihilating his rivals. Even now, he wove through traffic, muscling his way into one lane and then another, shaving seconds off the drive to Somerville.

"We're very different," she said.

He smiled. "No, we're not. You just like to pretend we are."

"Why would I pretend?"

"Because you're a girl."

"What do you mean I'm 'a girl'? I talk like a girl? I throw like a girl?"

"Yeah. Exactly. You throw like a girl."

"Take it back."

"No."

"Take it back." She tickled him under his arm, and the car swerved. "Sorry! I'm sorry!"

"You could wait for a red light," he pointed out, but waiting was difficult.

When they got to his apartment, Jonathan left the lights off. His roommates, Jake and Aldwin, were away for the long weekend, leaving their bikes in the living room, a shadowy obstacle course Jonathan didn't bother navigating.

"Now take it back," said Emily, even as he took her in his arms.

He pressed against her in the entryway. "No," he said. "You want to win as much as I do."

"It's not a race."

"You know it is. It's a race to patent first, and ship first, and file first. You and Veritech are already winning, so you pretend you don't compete."

"If I do race at times," she said, "I'm not part of some demolition derby, trying to win at all costs."

She was so beautiful, lecturing in the dark. He unbuttoned her coat and slipped her sweater off. He stroked her slender arms, and lifted her silk camisole, even as she scolded. Her moralizing was sweet, irresistible as words whispered in a foreign language. Her voice caught as he kissed her neck, and his hands traveled down, caressing her breasts, spanning her waist.

"The question is what sort of race you want to run," she said, "and what sort of standards you set for yourself."

He liked the way she tried to finish her thought, even as he took her nipple in his mouth. When he knelt before her, and he pulled off her skirt, and rolled down her thick winter tights, she couldn't talk at all, but sighed as his tongue, hard and wet, pressed into her. She was warm, and she wanted him—her fingers dug into his shoulders. He'd behaved badly at dinner, but she was hungry anyway.

"You're no different from me," he whispered.

Yes, I am, she thought, even then, even at the edge of pleasure. Didn't she believe in him? Of course she did. She wanted to. She longed for him. She ached for him, and when they lay down together on his unmade bed, she wrapped her legs around him. If she laughed at his impatience, she was impatient too.

Later, much later, when they'd had almost enough, he lay on his side, looking at her with his head resting on his arm. He was a direct lover, but he could be tender too.

She turned toward him, and they lay so close that when she spoke, her breath was the same as his. "Here's the difference between us," she said. "I trust my friends."

"Not true! You don't even trust me."

Emily knew he was thinking about Veritech. "That's something else."

"Why?"

She hesitated, and then she said, "Because other people are involved."

"Other people?" he scoffed, and he was right. Where were those other people now? What did they matter? She and Jonathan were a world unto themselves. When he touched her and stroked her face, all the longing of the past weeks eased. Or did it? Even as they kissed, she missed the kiss before, and the one before that. How strange the way every moment contained and at the same time hollowed out the last. She thought she should be satisfied, but she wasn't. Why? Because she could not dissolve herself. She wanted to forget herself with him, and give herself to him. No you don't, she told herself. You don't want to give yourself to any man. But she did. She wanted to belong to him—an antique notion, silvery as Ingrid Bergman's fine features, sad as Bogart's gravel voice.

She embraced him, pressed against him, but even as she throbbed again, Emily's cooler self, observing her entanglement, looked down upon her limbs and his. Her reasonable soul broke in, interrupting at the worst possible, or rather, the best possible, moment to ask: Who is this man? And who are you? Do you love him? Does he love you? And how can you tell? What proof do you have? Only kisses melting into air. Touch forgotten in an instant. Don't you have some better evidence than that?

Yes, she had evidence. She would prove herself to herself. Satisfy his curiosity and confide in him, share her work, her life, her most secret joy.

"I've got Alex working on password authentication," she whispered. "It's a new system called Verify, with a feature called electronic finger-printing." He held still as she told him. He seemed to hold his breath as she explained how the system recorded every user of every piece of data—a graphic history of each touch.

"Stop."

"Did I say too much?"

"Of course not," he said, but his voice was surprised. He'd never imagined she would confide so much in him. He was moved by the gesture. Overwhelmed.

She rested her head on his chest. "Tell me something too."

She heard his heart beat faster. Why? Surprise? Chagrin? He was supposed to be the demanding one, the instigator.

"Tell me what's really wrong with Lockbox."

"What do you mean, 'what's really wrong'?" Jonathan asked softly, defensively.

Oh, she was proving his point. She was like him after all, competitive, even now. No, that wasn't right. She only wanted parity, a fair trade of information. That wasn't right either. All she wanted was to draw him in and hold him close. "What did Orion find?" she pressed. Curious, just like Jonathan. Alert, insatiable as he was. "Tell me."

PART THREE

High Fliers

❧

November and December 1999

11

Information was currency, and Jonathan understood this better than most. After all, his company encrypted Web transactions. Credit-card numbers, personal data, customer preferences—these were valuable, but other bits shimmered as well. Information about rival companies, hints at future trends, insider tips. In graduate school Jonathan had studied cryptography. In business he sold electronic Lockboxes and ChainLinx fence, but in life, his instinct was to trade on secrets, not to keep them. Therefore Emily's information about electronic fingerprinting tempted. Alex's idea was dark and clever, and while Jonathan was not sure exactly how such a scheme would come to market, he sensed its value. He had a strategic mind, and he could already envision a world in which some spied with electronic fingerprinting, and others tried to defend themselves against it with new ISIS products. What if ISIS developed an encryption service of its own? He could almost . . . but he loved Emily, and he would not violate her trust.

He had grown up in Nebraska, where he and his brothers rode the school bus an hour and a half each way. His parents, Dan and Jeannie Tilghman, had been farmers, and raised him to be smart, ambitious, and unsentimental about country life. When it came to living off the land, his mother told him, "Don't even think about it." And when it came to school, she said quite seriously, "You're smarter than anyone there, including the teacher."

By fourth grade Jonathan was working independently, whiling away the hours memorizing digits of pi. In fifth grade he studied bookkeeping on his own. He was known as a math genius, but he was also the fastest runner in his class. He could beat anyone in the sixty-yard dash, even Scott Livingston. In revenge for this, Scott lured him into a game of Crack-the-Whip at recess. Watching his classmates holding hands, tugged by the leader in a snaking line whose tail moved ten times faster than its head, Jonathan was tempted by Courtney Cahill, the girl everybody knew Scott liked. She was freckled, her eyes copper-brown with long lashes, her hair streaked gold from the sun. Jonathan stepped between Scott and Courtney and took her hand, the first girl's hand he'd ever held, and as the line whipped back, he felt her soft palm against his, a rush of delight, and the next moment, an explosion of pain on the side of his face, smack against his nose. Scott had stepped out of line and thrown a roundhouse right. Jonathan fell to the ground with blood gushing from his broken nose. Kids swarmed, girls screamed. The teachers were coming, but Jonathan sprang up and sprinted after Scott all the way across the playground. Heart racing, shirt drenched red, he chased his enemy down, caught him from behind, and slammed him to the hardtop. He punched Scott in the face until he was bleeding on the painted hopscotch squares.

Jonathan returned home with a week's suspension.

"How does the other guy look?" his father asked.

"Bad," said Jonathan.

Then Dan was satisfied.

Jonathan's mother wanted to take him to the doctor, but Dan said he would heal better naturally, and so the break mended on its own, into the bold and busted nose Emily insisted she loved anyway.

He skipped two grades, read Ayn Rand, and planned to go to Harvard and become president of the United States, and make a gazillion dollars. Harvard didn't work out. He hit a speed bump at Woodrow Wilson High, where he was too bright and warlike to get along. He got into trouble in his senior year, a brawl involving alcohol and school property, and he was not allowed to graduate—a fact he enjoyed telling interviewers.

He could have done time in summer school, but he took the GED instead and enlisted, serving in Desert Storm, after which he attended Dartmouth, where he became a rugby player and confined his scuffles to the field. He had not yet explored politics, but the gazillion dollars went without saying. He had enormous confidence. He simply knew what to do. Was this good judgment or the extraordinary financial moment? History had never been his subject.

Investors fought to place large sums in Jonathan's hands. He seemed a new breed, part genius, part industrialist—a game changer—and Jonathan did not disabuse them of this notion. But Emily never looked at him this way; she knew his moods and saw through his stratagems. She understood his business as well, because she'd blazed the trail. Long before ISIS, Jonathan had heard of Emily and Veritech. Back in 1996, when he was still pursuing his Ph.D. at MIT, he caught his first glimpse of her. He had been at Orion's place, and Molly was flipping channels when Emily materialized on television—cool, slender, bright-eyed as she explained to an interviewer why she did not pursue an academic career in computer science.

"*That's* the CEO of Veritech?" Jonathan exclaimed.

"Why are you surprised?" Orion asked. "That's Emily Bach. Who did you think it was?"

"You know her?"

"I've known her forever," Orion said.

"Introduce me," Jonathan said. "I'm serious."

He'd turned back to the screen. She had the longest neck, delicate and white. Just the sight of her stirred him, but what she said next changed his life. She expressed exactly what he was feeling and had not yet put into words.

"I did think about a Ph.D. in computer science, but this is a time in industry where theory and practice are coming together in amazing ways. Yes, there's money, but what really interests me is that private-sector innovation happens faster. You can get more done and on a larger scale and have more impact. With all the start-ups out there, I think this is a time like the Renaissance. Not just one person doing great work, but so many feeding off one another. If you lived then, wouldn't you go out and paint?"

If you lived then . . . ? Jonathan remembered those words when he entered MIT's 50K business-plan competition with Orion, Aldwin, and Jake. *Wouldn't you go out and paint?* The four of them took the T downtown to Filene's Basement and bought cheap suits and bad-ass ties—screaming purple, scaly green like lizard skin. In those nasty clothes they presented and fielded questions from the judges. When they won their 50K seed money—pocket money, really—they drank all night and dropped out of school to found ISIS in the morning.

Jonathan abandoned MIT without a backward glance, foregoing orals, academic conferences, third-floor potlucks, and staid job prospects at Microsoft or PARC or IBM Almaden. Cannily, he convinced his advisor to come along for the ride, naming the eminent cryptographer, Oskar Feuchtwangler, Senior Scientist. As a finishing touch, he proposed stealing Mel Millstein, the best of the computer-science administrative assistants, and naming him Director of Human Resources.

Jake had balked at this idea and suggested that hiring Mel away might alienate the department.

"You were fine with Oskar," Jonathan pointed out.

"He's just taking a leave of absence," said Jake, "and he'll come back. He'll always be around. Once Mel is gone, he's gone. We'd be stealing him."

"It's his choice if he wants to leave," said Jonathan.

Jake shook his head. "Maybe we don't want to burn our bridges." He had always been the most academic of the four cofounders, the most theoretical, as he was also the hairiest, with a wild mop of brown curls and thick unruly eyebrows. Dark-eyed, driven, shy, he was an idea man, a Westinghouse finalist in high school, and a gifted pianist as well, a former student in Juilliard's pre-college division. Lockbox had been built from Jake's algorithms. ChainLinx came about as a series of answers to Jake's questions. The others needed him and his exceptional mind. Technically they were formidable, but Jake was creative. He pointed out, "We might want to go back to school eventually."

Jonathan raised an eyebrow. "What fun would that be?"

He liked a good time. His idea of a corporate Christmas party was paintball. His highest praise, uttered without an ounce of irony: "You guys are animals." His rough edges never failed to impress.

"The guy's a natural," the VCs whispered to one another, and shook their heads at Jonathan. Oh, brave new world that had such creatures in it. And yet he had a thoughtful side; he recognized and pursued excellence in every form, particularly in the shape of Emily. He loved her brilliant, principled mind. Why did she test him then, tempting him with Veritech's secret project? How could she, knowing him as she did? He was not high-minded on his own, and he looked to her to model what his soul might become, once he got exactly what he wanted. When he was rich and eminent, a policy maker and philanthropist, Emily would be his wife and chair the family foundation and they would have daughters delicate like her, and athletic sons like him—and all their children would go to Harvard and major in math and play rugby and take up sailing. This was how Jonathan would live when he lay down his arms and beat his sword into time-shares. But not yet! Emily's behavior baffled him. She had set up a kind of competition, trusting him like that, and demanding a secret from him in return. Did she doubt he loved her? Did she want some expensive proof?

After Thanksgiving, when he met with ISIS CEO Dave, Jonathan kept electronic fingerprinting to himself. This was not difficult. Dave was rich and he was experienced, with his years at IBM and BBN behind him. He was a sport, approximating native dress at ISIS, so that where Jonathan wore jeans, Dave wore khakis, and where Orion wore a Grateful Dead T-shirt, Dave wore an Oxford button-down. Dave knew about marketing and goals and five-year plans, but even in his shirtsleeves, he would always be a suit. Dave just barely understood what ISIS was doing now, and could scarcely intuit coming trends. He had his silver-gray hair styled in a salon and he lived in a Cambridge mansion, a brown Victorian on Highland Ave. That wasn't even his first mansion. His first had been companies ago, along with his first wife and first set of kids. Retro CEO Dave carried a fountain pen. He even played golf. The man was like a car with fins.

Jonathan sat in Dave's office overlooking redbrick Kendall Square. The company was about to go public, but it was newer than Veritech, and in keeping with the accelerating market, its rise had been faster. ISIS had yet to build a leafy campus out in Dedham, or renovate a funky mill. ISIS squeezed into an ordinary flat-pack office building off Broadway, starting with the top floors, and working its way down until the company leased the entire building. Electricians and carpenters had just renovated the first floor, finishing the space as a control center with a bank of monitors displaying Secure Web Traffic across the globe. The control center had a space-age look, part NASA, part flight deck from the Starship *Enterprise*. If the control center was designed to impress visitors, Dave's office was built to reassure them. New hire, designated grown-up, the CEO held court behind an actual mahogany desk with family photographs in frames.

"Where do you see us in five years?" Dave asked, philosophical as always when he sat down with Jonathan.

"Five years?" echoed Jonathan as he fiddled with his BlackBerry. "Let's talk about five weeks from now."

Dave smiled and refrained from asking Jonathan to put his new toy away. At times Dave bridled at Jonathan's manners, but no one could argue with his results. The ISIS client list spoke for itself, and to watch Jonathan pitch ISIS to a new company—the kid could give a clinic. Dave was full of admiration for what he called the growing ISIS family, and often said that he learned more from his young colleagues than they could learn from him. Jonathan readily agreed.

"I want you to take the long view," Dave said.

Jonathan nodded. "After the IPO, I want to see ChainLinx adopted by every Fortune 500 company, and Lockbox standard for every transaction, so no one dares to buy anything on the Web without seeing our logo guaranteeing the site's secure. And I want at least fifty more programmers working on new products. . . ."

"You're thinking about more people," Dave mused in his deliberate way.

"Of course." Jonathan glanced at the smooth-shaven face on the other side of the desk and marveled at the way Dave missed the key words— *new products*, code for fingerprinting, scramblers, all the possibilities in the strange new realm Veritech was poised to enter. Dave didn't even ask.

"We need to have a conversation with Mel," said Dave.

"Okay." Jonathan turned back to his BlackBerry.

Dave marveled at the way Jonathan missed the key word *conversation*. Attached to Mel, possibly even loyal to him for old time's sake, Jonathan didn't realize that *conversation* meant they had to let Mel go.

Yo Mel, Jonathan was texting. Find more people your slowing us down.

"Maybe we could set that up for Monday," Dave suggested.

"I'll be in San Jose," said Jonathan, "but you can meet with him."

"I think it would be good for you to be there."

"I just talked to him," Jonathan reassured Dave. "He knows what to do."

Mel was finding people as fast as he could. He didn't know how to hire faster without pulling programmers off the street. Quality did matter. "I have a process," he told Dave.

"I respect that," Dave assured him.

But Jonathan said, "Just speed the process up."

He had never worked like this before. Résumés haunted his dreams. Aldwin talked about opening two new groups, and Jake demanded more support staff. Suddenly Mel was trying to hire HR people to help with all the hiring. With so much money flowing through ISIS, and so much demand for ISIS services, Mel had become the human bottleneck. "You look frazzled," Barbara told him.

Oh, *frazzled* was not the word. Fragile. Dazzled. Fraggled. He woke in the morning sick with anxiety—certain that at any moment Dave would call him in for the talk. He thought about that meeting constantly: I'm sorry, Mel. It's just not working out; you have not met our expectations. How he dreaded those words—and also longed to hear them. He was in over his head, and far too old. ISIS flew at warp speed, and as for competitors, Odin snapped up prospective hires if Mel so much as blinked. Green Knight and Akamai were always in there hustling for talent, and those were just the local companies. Mostly young and single, the programmers Mel stalked thought nothing of moving to Mountain

View or Berlin or Austin. He suffered from motion sickness every day on his commute—not from the train, from the economy.

And yet . . . and yet, Mel had never been part of something magical before. He had never inhaled the fumes of such success, and although every fiber of his body rebelled against the insane pressure of his job, his soul rejoiced. Thirty years toiling in support services at MIT, but Mel had not been so ordinary after all. He was part of the world other people read about in newspapers. He had been one of those people, reading *The Boston Globe* each morning on the train, and now he was in the *Globe* himself—not mentioned by name, of course, but by association. He had ascended to a realm where companies were named for gods: ISIS, Inktomi, Janus, LOKI. ISIS was already the stuff of legend. "One of the most highly anticipated IPOs of the year" was just twelve days away, and Mel felt like Marco Polo, seeing firsthand what others might have written off as myth.

In the past year, he'd watched in awe as his young bosses auditioned VCs twice their age. One morning Mel arrived at work to find Jonathan scribbling the names of venture capitalists on his whiteboard under the headings "Bozos," "Morons," "Losers," "Sharks." Was this the same kid who had borrowed quarters for the vending machines at the department? There were no vending machines at ISIS. All snacks and drinks were free.

Alas, the faster ISIS grew, the more troublesome Mel's fifty-seven-year-old body became. Nausea, insomnia, diarrhea. At first he blamed the lunches Barbara packed for him. Then he blamed the Middle Eastern food truck that pulled up each day behind the building, but everybody ate there and no one else got sick. He went for tests, and the doctor found nothing. Reluctantly Mel admitted the cause of indigestion was anxiety. As soon as he arrived at this conclusion his stomachaches subsided, and his back went out.

"What did you do to it?" his young coworkers asked him wonderingly.

"Nothing. I did nothing!" he replied.

Of course he remembered the day, the hour, the very second he threw out his back. Tuesday, October 12, 1999. Three forty-five in the afternoon. Sitting at his fifth-floor desk, he had been discussing health plans with a new hire on the phone. Carpenters were snapping cubicles together. Cardboard boxes containing workstations stood stacked against the walls, and all was quiet—except for the whoosh of programmers batting a birdie with badminton rackets.

Mel was finishing the routine medical-benefits conversation when he glanced up and saw an electrician grinning at him from a square hole in the ceiling where he'd popped out the acoustic tile.

"Yoo-hoo," the electrician said.

Mel bristled. Carpenters didn't bother him, nor did the badminton or the unpacking. He almost enjoyed the drag and pop of box cutters slicing cardboard—the long rips crisp and promising, like autumn and fresh school supplies—but he couldn't conduct business with electricians wisecracking from above. "You can't go wrong—they're both terrific," he explained to the new hire, as he gestured at the cable-dangling electrician to disappear. "And we do offer dental." He stood, pulling the receiver with him, but the cord wasn't long enough and his phone slid off the desk. Too quickly, he turned to scoop it up. A prickle, like an electric shock, raked his left side, an agonizing spasm. Pain held him in its vice.

That had been six weeks ago. Now Mel had bad days and worse days. There were mornings he stood on the train, all the way from Canaan to South Station, because sitting was too painful. He took the Red Line to Kendall Square and counted stops. Just get me to Charles / MGH, just get me aboveground, he pleaded silently, trying to bargain with his back. All he had to do was make it until the train emerged from its tunnel to rattle over the bridge. Then he could look out at the icy river and dark trees, the boathouses rosy in the brief winter light. When the train descended again, he held the metal pole and told himself, Only one more stop and then the music, and he would try to hold on until Kendall Square Station where long levers in the wall were wired to chimes hanging between the inbound and outbound tracks. Like a parent trying to appease a child, he would treat himself to a gentle pull of a lever, and listen for the soft chime like temple bells in the midst of rushing trains and chattering students and the buskers playing amplified guitars.

The commute was bad enough. One morning he could not get out of bed. If he lay perfectly still, he felt no pain, but the moment he shifted his weight, his muscles seized up again.

"Barbara," he called out, "I can't move."

She rushed in from the living room.

"You'll have to call and tell them. . . ."

"It's Saturday."

"Oh, good. Thank God." The reprieve relaxed him just a little. He could breathe, and even turn slightly.

"Don't try to get up," Barbara warned.

"I'm not. I can't," he said. He closed his eyes, and she brought his Motrin and a glass of water with a straw.

"Don't move. Relax," she ordered, in what the children used to call her nurse voice. She reverted to crisp professionalism when anyone was hurt or sick. Mel used to tease her that she enjoyed their children's illnesses. "I do not!" she had protested, but he knew she loved a damp, hot, docile child.

He didn't blame her. He'd loved the children that way too, and he missed them. Nostalgia overcame him as he lay pinned, and he longed to see Annie and Sam, not as they were now, but as they had been years ago, before their potential had hardened into the ordinary shell of adulthood.

He had always hoped his children would be extraordinary. Wasn't it nine-year-old Sam who had announced he would be an entomologist? How had he become a government major at Amherst? Annie was out in the Bay Area at the epicenter of the high-tech revolution. She had been so good at math. Why was she teaching kindergarten? Absurd that in late middle age Mel was about to make a fortune. Where were his kids? Couldn't they see that the future belonged to their generation? True to the accelerated business cycle, Mel lay in bed and worried, even while his ISIS shares were still a gleam in his broker's eyes, that his children lacked the initiative to achieve as he had done.

Everyone gave Mel advice. Dave recommended a chiropractor. Jonathan suggested that he hit the gym.

"I think," Barbara said cautiously, "you might want to talk to Rabbi Zylberfenig."

"Zylberfenig! Because he knows so much about back pain?"

"He knows a lot," said Barbara.

"How old is Rabbi Zylberfenig?" Mel demanded.

"He's got six children."

"And what's that supposed to mean?"

"He's older than we were at his age."

Everybody had a guru. Even Sorel Fisher, his newest hire, insisted, "I'll give you the name of my Alexander teacher."

"Alexander teacher? What did he teach you?" Mel asked, wary.

"Nothing," Sorel said, bouncing slightly on the green exercise ball at her desk. She was a twenty-three-year-old programmer from London, a performance artist, and a chanteuse. "He was brilliant. He barely even touched me."

Meanwhile, he had to keep advertising and interviewing and issuing ID cards. Everybody loved the new ones he had ordered. You clipped them to your belt and pulled the card out on an elastic string so that you could swipe and unlock doors or elevators after hours. The new fleeces were a big hit as well. Navy with *ISIS* embroidered in gold. Mel was good with merchandise. Proud, not loud. That was his motto. But the week after Thanksgiving when Dave asked to meet with him "to strategize," Mel understood that this was it.

A small voice inside whispered: Let Dave set you free; your back is breaking from the stress. But no. Mel could not imagine leaving. Not now, before his shares were vested. He didn't want to miss what he knew would be a meteoric flight.

On the day before his appointment with Dave, he took tiny steps to Jonathan's office, traversing what seemed like miles of drab rust-red carpet, raveled at the edges. Mel stopped, clutching the top edge of a cubicle. The pain was worse. After three months, he had come to think of it as *the* pain—not his pain, but a larger, impersonal force. The pain—the way opera singers speak of their instrument, the voice.

"Mel Millstein," chided Sorel as she passed by, "you need to go to Alexander class."

I need to stay employed, thought Mel.

"The trouble with you," said Sorel, "is you're misaligned."

Feet on the desk, *Star Wars* action figures lining the windowsill behind him, Jonathan was typing with his keyboard in his lap. "What's happening?"

Mel hesitated. He had planned what to say, of course, but scripts didn't work with Jonathan—none of the scripts Mel knew.

"I need help hiring," Mel said. "I sense that HR needs restructuring, and I'd like to make that happen sooner rather than later." Now, he added silently.

"Okay," said Jonathan. "What do you want?"

My job, Mel thought. My life. Existence without pain. "Well, I have Zoë and Jessica right now . . . ," he began, "and I'm trying to get . . ."

Jonathan considered his hapless HR director. At the computer-science department, Mel had been the go-to guy, straightening out green cards and foreign visas, grappling with bureaucracy. When Jonathan was jockeying for attention from professors, Mel had actually taken the time to ask, "How are things going?" To say, "Let me check his schedule. Maybe I can get you in." Jonathan did not forget old kindnesses, nor did he forget how little he liked MIT, where cryptography profs favored students more theoretical, more purely mathematical.

He had wanted only the best for Mel when he plucked him from his desk at the department. He'd never intended to kill the poor man.

"Mel," said Jonathan, "you don't need help. You need a better attitude. Put on a happy face! This is not a submarine. This is a big fun start-up with a severe shortage of programmers, and all you need to do is go out there and say, 'Hey you guys, come on over.' Is that hard?"

"There are a lot of other—" Mel began.

"But, no, there aren't. You don't think about them," Jonathan cut him off. "We're better. It's all attitude, man. You're smart and talented, you're meticulous—and you're going to have zillions of dollars next year. Did you forget that?"

Ah, yes. Mel remembered the conversation well. When Jonathan had offered him the job at ISIS, Mel had asked delicately about compensation. "Here's the thing," Jonathan replied, and he spoke in all seriousness. "We're all going to be gazillionaires."

"You know what you're doing—you just have to show your stuff to the prospective hires," Jonathan explained now. "Be cool. Be confident. . . ."

"I don't feel confident," Mel confessed. "I feel that my position here is . . ."

"Is what?"

Mel couldn't find the word. No, he knew the word, but couldn't say it. He had to force himself. "Tenuous."

"Tenuous!" Jonathan looked at him as though he'd begun speaking in another language. "What are you talking about?"

"You know what I'm talking about. Dave wants to meet with me."

Jonathan looked at him almost tenderly. "No one's firing you."

"I'm not so . . . I don't feel so . . . ," Mel spluttered.

Jonathan reassured him. "No one's firing you right before our IPO. That would look terrible!"

"I think Dave has a plan," said Mel.

"Yeah, he's got lots of plans. Don't worry about Dave. I'll deal with him. You just do your job, okay?"

"Okay." He realized that this was Jonathan's way of reaching out. "Thank you."

"Don't thank me. Get out there and kick ass! I want twelve new programmers, and I want you to go out there and hire them with a smile on your face."

"I will," Mel answered, stunned. He tried to smile without moving any other part of his body. He was afraid to jolt his standing equilibrium.

"And I'll tell you a secret," Jonathan added, just as Mel was leaving. "We're going to tell everybody at the end of the day, but I'll tell you first. We've signed Yahoo! for premium ChainLinx protection."

"Yahoo!" Now Mel really was smiling.

"Yeah!" Jonathan swung his feet up on the desk and resumed typing.

Mel returned to his cubicle full of hope. ISIS had Yahoo! in the stable, their biggest client to date. This was huge, and Mel knew first. There was no greater sign of favor.

He stood in the back as Jonathan made his announcement. All the employees in town packed the fifth floor near the windows. Outside, a light snow was falling. Inside, programmers perched atop desks, stood on chairs, and the whole company whooped and cheered.

"This is your work," Aldwin said.

"You guys are super," Dave chimed in.

"You guys are animals!" Jonathan shouted, punching the air, and all the animals roared.

Afterward the programmers milled together talking motorcycles, debating which were fastest and which were overpriced—not that it mattered anymore! They spoke of vacations. A company camping trip in the High Sierra. No, a voyage down the River Nile, a cruise to see the Pyramids. They were about to be gazillionaires. Yahoo! As Mel walked to the T station, he came upon Orion, hatless, walking his bike through heavy snow.

"Hey," Orion said.

"Amazing night," Mel said.

"I guess so," Orion said laconically.

The kid was too young, Mel thought, to appreciate the situation. The snowflakes were wet and heavy, double flakes and triple flakes. Mel could almost touch the zillions in the air.

12

Orion had grown up in his father's poetry, and because Lou Steiner was famous, Orion's younger selves had been published and widely anthologized. Orion, *naked wader, minnow-trader* lived on the page, alongside *the sleeper with the tiny fists*. He didn't take any of this too personally, not even his father's collection, *Star Boy*. Growing up in Vermont, he knew many other poets' children who had been immortalized. When it came to publicity, Orion thought his father's wives and girlfriends had it worse, and he had often wondered how they liked word portraits mentioning birdlike physiques, small breasts, sad eyes. Orion tried to avoid Lou's love poems, because he could put the name to each description, and then afterward he felt as though he'd seen his father's lovers, including his own mother, naked. His father found this amusing, but he was entirely unselfconscious on and off the page.

Lou's fame was riverlike—deep and narrow in some places, then broadening unexpectedly into shallows. His books sold a thousand, maybe twelve hundred copies each, but schoolchildren everywhere studied his villanelle "Where Are the Bees?" His later style, increasingly aphoristic, had inspired critics to call him a new minimalist, and at seventy-five, with his unrepentant hippie politics and eloquent *Forest Cycle,* Lou had become an icon to environmentalists, who printed his verse on T-shirts and posters—usually without permission. Like Matisse cutouts, Steiner's late pared-down poems were all space and edges on the page. The best-known was his found poem, "Tree." One line, which read simply:

Here I stand. I can do no other.

Molly was honest. She said Orion's father scared her. Over the years, Lou had grown shaggy, rambling, slightly unhinged. Orion's mother, Diane, thought perhaps Lou was suffering from early Alzheimer's. The idea frightened Orion, who preferred to think late-night rambles, naps on park benches, and tirades to writing classes were existential rather than neurological symptoms. End-stage poetry. Reading Shakespeare obsessively, drinking heavily, a man like Lou was supposed to turn Lear-like when his hair went white.

As a boy Orion had avoided Lou. Naturally, he'd taken his mother's side in the divorce, and lived with her in run-down farmhouses where they grew tomatoes and trained pea plants up strings to the porch roof. He tried to comfort her by staying out of trouble and entering science fairs. His childhood sweetheart, Emily, had been his mother's sweetheart as well, the daughter she had always hoped for, and even now, so many years later, Diane asked after Emily with a certain wistfulness—although she liked Molly very much. Then Orion felt a twinge of guilt, although he knew it was irrational, because he hated to disappoint his mother, even in imaginary ways. In college, where he might have grown wild, he'd settled in with Molly, and stayed with her.

Orion didn't avoid his father anymore, but spent time with him when he could. As Diane said, "He is your dad, and he isn't getting any younger." Lou was charming in his fashion, his countercultural effusions refreshing now that Orion made his way in the material world. True, his father had recently been called to the dean's office to explain an incident in a poetry workshop when he'd ripped up a student's manuscript, dashing the pieces to the floor and stamping on them "like Rumpelstiltskin" as one witness averred in *The Middlebury Campus*. There was also Lou's troubling history with young women poets, his musettes as Diane called them. But he had slowed down in this regard, and if his clothes were wrinkled and his beard untrimmed, he was an original, and it felt good to have a parent who worked in pencil and called Otter Creek his office. Lou had no idea what ISIS did. He had never owned a computer, and the one time he had met Molly's parents, at Harvard graduation, he'd told them a long dirty joke, to see if they would laugh.

He chortled when his son phoned one bright December Sunday. Orion was explaining that Molly's parents had come up to visit and they were all having brunch that morning. "Who brunches these days?" Lou asked.

"I guess I do," Orion said.

"Brunch when you're old, sleep when you're dead" was Lou's advice.

Orion glanced at the closed bathroom door where Molly was showering. Postcall, she'd come straight from Beth Israel Deaconess and had had no time to rest.

"True story," Lou said. This was how all his jokes began. True meant "Jewish." "Three old ladies in Miami, poolside, brunching at the Fontainebleau. They see someone new: *Velcome, velcome. How are you?* Then one of the old-timers says, *Nu, ve don't have time for small talk. Let's get some things out of the vay. Money? Money you have, or you vouldn't be at the Fontinblow. Granchildren? You got? Show.* She opens up her wallet and, you know, fans out the pictures on the table. *Sex? . . . Vat vas, vas.*"

"You think I'm living like an old lady."

"I leave you to extrapolate."

"You think youth is wasted on the . . ."

"I do like a wasted youth," Lou mused.

Molly emerged in a cloud of steam and began searching for clean clothes. Wrapped in her towel, she glanced at Orion and took in his fisherman sweater, worn to threads at the elbows.

"Why do you like a wasted youth, Dad?"

"Listen, it's like the man with his face pressed against the glass at the Ferrari dealership. If you have to ask . . ."

"I should go," said Orion, as Molly pointed at the clock-radio, but he did not get off the phone. "What are you doing today?"

"I'll be walking at Abbey Pond," Lou replied. "You remember, don't you?"

Of course he did. In springtime Lou used to take little Orion to look for lady's slippers. Double petals hanging from springy stems, flowers rising from mossy, mulchy ground. "I don't think they look like lady's slippers," Lou had told Orion. "I think they look like lady's something else."

"Drive carefully," Orion said. "And take it easy out there."

Molly's cell phone was ringing. Her parents were waiting downstairs to take them to Henrietta's Table.

"The ground's uneven," Orion reminded his father

"Old and infirm as I am," Lou intoned, "it's so crowded in the woods these days that if I fall, I'm sure somebody will find me."

"Can we go?" Molly asked.

"I was just waiting for *you*," Orion replied, and then into the telephone, "bye, Dad."

"Farewell. And good-bye, Molly."

Molly's father was famous too, in an entirely different way. Carl Eisenstat was a physicist, and not the garden-variety kind. He had been in one of Orion's college textbooks as the Eisenstat Principle of something or other. Matter? Motion? Orion could not remember, although it was assumed that he knew which. The Eisenstats assumed many things. The last time they'd come up from Princeton, Carl had announced, "I take it the two of you are planning to get married." Orion had started back, offended that Carl would touch on a matter so private and confusing, but Molly's father pressed on implacably: "And I make that assumption because you've been seeing each other for so long."

Of course they had talked about getting engaged. Orion and Molly had lived together in their apartment off Putnam Avenue for three years. They had a routine; they had a life; they had a lot of stuff. Their third-floor warren opened onto a ramshackle but surprisingly large roof deck where they entertained. They kept a hibachi there, aluminum lawn chairs, and a camping table they had found on the street. On summer nights when friends came up for drinks, they passed around a pair of tweezers for the splinters that split off the sun-warped railings.

Molly's plan had been to get married when Orion finished graduate

school, and he had always liked this idea—keeping marriage at an inde-
terminate distance, along with his degree. At the time, Orion's profes-
sional and financial prospects had been pleasantly vague. Now, however,
they were unavoidably bright. Five months after Orion broke Lockbox,
the system was up and running, or as Jonathan put it, "running better
than ever," and ChainLinx was huge. Projected earnings were shooting
through the roof, and this was not lost on Molly's father. Nothing was.

"You've been getting a lot of press," lanky, white-haired Carl informed
Orion in the buffet line at the restaurant, and Orion ducked his head,
something between a nod and a shrug. Orion, Jonathan, Aldwin, and
Jake had just appeared in *Fortune* magazine under the heading "Tycoons
in Training."

"I liked the photo. I recognized the steps of Building Thirteen." Carl
loaded his plate with lox and whitefish, eggs and sausages.

Orion watched Molly's mother pause wistfully at the waffle station,
and then settle on yogurt, fruit salad, and a bowl of Irish oatmeal. The resemblance between Deborah and Molly was striking: dark eyes, a heart-
shaped face, lovely from the front, less so in profile. Molly had her
mother's slight bump in the nose and tiny chin. They were both petite, but
Deborah was also zaftig, a short, wide gerontologist who wore tunic-
length sweaters and long necklaces—silk cords hung with unusual pen-
dants, a tiny woven bag or a many-hinged locket, a miniature kaleidoscope
bouncing like a buoy on her vast bosom.

"Well, this is nice," said Deborah when they reconvened at the table.

"Tell us about the IPO," said Carl.

How different Molly's father seemed from the man Orion had first
met, almost eight years before. The Eisenstats had driven up to see their
daughter, and she'd brought her new boyfriend to breakfast. On that occasion, he and Molly had shared one side of a booth like brother and sister facing their parents. Orion's wet blond hair had fallen in his eyes, and
Molly's short curls had been damp. They'd looked a little too clean to be
entirely innocent, having just come from Mather House, where they'd
shared a shower, but they sat straight with the seam of the upholstered
booth running up between them. Molly's mother had tried to make conversation, but Professor Eisenstat kept his eyes on Orion, who had tried

not to bolt his food or gulp his juice, or think about the night before, lest some memory of warmth and nakedness flash across his face.

Still, Carl had gazed at him with a grim, penetrating look. "I have a question for you." Carl's voice had been taut and slightly amused, as though he were sharpening cruel ironic skewers and looking forward to running Orion through. "How is it majoring in an auxiliary field?"

"Auxiliary? You mean computer science?" Orion had been so busy guarding against attacks on his character that at first he didn't recognize Carl's scientific gambit as such.

"Right. Auxiliary in that computer science is not a true science in itself, but a handmaid to math, physics, chemistry. . . ."

"I like CS," Orion said stoutly.

"But that's my question," Carl pressed. "What exactly do you like about it?"

Orion paused. "Programming."

"Hmm." Carl sipped his coffee.

Twenty years old, Orion had gazed across the table at Molly's father with a mixture of resentment and misery. He was good at math, of course, but he excelled at building little computer systems piece by piece. Orion had always loved to tinker. He was a puzzle solver, no deep-thinking puzzle maker. He had done well in his CS courses: programming, distributed systems, hardware, algorithms, and graphics, for which he'd rendered a faceted crystal vase filled with water and a single red rose so that it cast an accurate shadow on a wood-grain tabletop. Were these exercises at all important? In Carl's presence he'd felt acutely that computer science lacked a certain—he would never say the word aloud—but, yes, the field lacked a certain majesty.

Now, in the glass and farmhouse restaurant with its baskets and bouquets of chili peppers, Carl seemed thrilled with Orion's programming habit. He actually whipped out that morning's *Boston Globe* and read aloud. *"Asked about his heroes, company cofounder Orion Steiner cites computer pioneer Donald Knuth, and maverick free-software activist Richard Stallman."*

What a strange effect money, or even the idea of money, had on people. Orion could not avoid wealth, or Carl either. How could he put off shopping for a ring? In six months, he could afford any ring or bracelet or necklace; he could afford anything. Orion looked at Carl's smooth, close-shaven cheeks and his hawkish gray eyes and he saw what wealth would mean: not just traveling the world and buying toys, but paying huge complicated taxes and living in a house with Molly forever—not forever in the romantic sense—forever like her parents, with a loud dog and yellowing houseplants. Molly would gain a hundred pounds, and Orion would have to start collecting ugly paintings. They'd have a three-car garage and seven bathrooms, and they would sit around at night and debate whether it was better to time-share or buy planes.

"How many employees are you up to now?" Carl asked.

"I think we're at . . . ," Orion hesitated, distracted by the cell phone in his pocket, buzzing against his leg. "Eighty-three?" he ventured, checking the caller ID. "Ninety-three?" It was Jonathan, but Orion ignored the call.

Deborah focused on Orion with a look of quiet pride. Carl leaned forward, keen and curious. Only their daughter paid no attention. Molly had closed her eyes and left him to entertain her parents' expectations on his own. Exhausted, she was still sitting upright in her chair, but she had fallen fast asleep.

Carl and Deborah were driving home immediately to beat the traffic, and they dropped off Molly and Orion on the way. He helped her up the stairs, and she leaned against the wall as he unlocked the apartment. Then dropping her bag just inside the door, she bolted for the bedroom.

"Wait," Orion said. "Molly?"

Fully clothed, she lunged for the bed and seized her pillow. Gone again.

"Aren't you going to take off your shoes?" Orion tugged at one shoe and then the other. Her legs were dead weights in his hands. He reached around her waist, unbuckled her belt, and unzipped her pants. "Ouch," he murmured. Her belt had cut into her soft stomach and left red marks. He tried to unbutton her blouse, but she clung to the pillow, and he couldn't get it off. "I give up," he said.

The dressertop was strewn with bills and mail, bank statements from Fleet. Orion didn't bother opening them. Despite his huge equity in ISIS, he had, of course, no money to speak of in his account. Molly's damp towel lay in a heap on the floor. She had good reason to avoid inviting her parents up to the apartment.

Orion scanned his e-mail. Seventy new messages, two from Jonathan. Subject: URGENT. Message: Get your butt over here now. His cell phone rang again. He didn't have to look. His bike had a flat, and he knew he should get moving if he was walking to Kendall Square. He stuffed his computer into his backpack.

"Okay, Molly, I'm going." He bent down over her curly head. "Bye."

She turned, her face tender with sleep. When she reached out and wrapped her arms around him, she was warm, her skin smoother than the silky blouse that she was wrinkling. Her eyes opened. Her lips parted, and he was about to kiss her, when suddenly she spoke. "Get milk," she said.

"Where the hell have you been?" It was uncanny, as if Jonathan had been standing in front of the elevator the whole time. He played laser tag like that, appearing suddenly, bearing down on you.

"I was having brunch," Orion said.

"Brunch?" Jonathan echoed, as if he'd never heard the word before. Lou was right, Orion thought. Brunch when you're old.

They were walking through what had recently been the second-floor wilderness of the company. At one time, Jonathan and Orion had played a form of indoor badminton here, but new cubicles had been installed to pack more programmers together. There were private offices here as well, for Aldwin the CFO, and Jonathan the CTO. Jake was the chief programmer. Only Orion wasn't chief of anything. That had been his choice. They'd offered him some sort of vice presidency, but at the time, the whole thing had sounded too ridiculous, like aspiring to Communications Minister of the Duchy of Grand Fenwick. Of course, Orion had been wrong about this. ISIS was a cash-rich powerhouse, no fictional Grand Duchy. The CFO and CTO were, in fact, piloting the company, along with Dave, who was much given to navigational language, along with Mission Statements, foam-core credos posted throughout the building like slogans from Orwell's Ministry of Love. *We are a community. We value excellence. We believe in the capacity of each individual to make a difference.* . . .

Jonathan marched to the conference room, while Orion followed slowly, looking in on the programmers, who were writing Lockbox 2.0. Clarence was typing away, as were Umesh and Nadav, and there was the new girl, Sorel. He was always conscious of her, working among the guys. She was tall, long-limbed, lithe, and kept a guitar under her desk. She wore odd black clothes and she had fair skin and strawberry-blond hair almost as long as his. She had the palest eyes he had ever seen; he wasn't sure of the color—they were like water.

Her first day, Mel Millstein had brought her in and introduced her in his fussy way.

"Let's welcome Sorel Fisher. I'm sure everybody here will do their best to help her feel at home." He'd pulled out a swivel chair. "This is your desk," Mel told Sorel.

"Thanks very much," she said, and Orion had been surprised by her English accent.

"What's your name again?" he'd asked after Mel left.

"Sorel," she said. "Like the plant."

Her accent was wonderful, and her voice as well, which was lower than you would expect, and at the same time a little breathy. Sometimes Orion talked to her, just to get her to say words like *corollary,* which she pronounced with the stress in the middle, a little bump and then a rush of speed at the end: "cor*oll*ary." She glanced at him quizzically now as he passed by.

"I'm going to the conference room," he told her with mock gravity.

"Oh." Sorel suppressed laughter as she turned back to her computer. "I won't be seen talking to you, then."

He knew everyone would see him with Jonathan, however. The conference room cut right into the open-plan programmers' space, and the walls were glass, another of Dave's brilliant ideas.

Jonathan and Aldwin perched atop the oval table with the *Globe* strewn before them.

"I've been getting e-mails all morning from investors," Jonathan informed Orion.

"About what?"

"About this." Jonathan shook the newspaper at Orion.

"You cite Richard Stallman as your hero," Aldwin said.

"I happen to admire Stallman's ideas about sharing information."

"Not now, you don't," said Jonathan. "Not one week before our IPO."

"Are you really that nervous?" Orion asked.

Aldwin folded his hands on his knee. With his baby face and mild manners, his well-groomed curly hair, clean clothes, and matching socks, he seemed, literally, best suited of the founding four for corporate life. Jonathan was the star, but Aldwin was Dave's favorite. Everyone knew that. Of course the idea of Dave's favor was strange, to say the least. The four of them had hired Dave, and at the time, Jonathan had privately conceded Orion's contention that Dave wasn't particularly bright. "You do see that we're in business?" Aldwin asked Orion now.

"ISIS is not the local branch of the Free Software Foundation," Jonathan said.

"You do see how our investors are hoping to make money here?" Aldwin continued.

"Free Software is free as in freedom," Orion retorted. "Not free as in free lunches. I never said I don't want to make money."

"What the hell is wrong with you?" Jonathan exploded. "We are selling a proprietary security system. You are going to reporters, scaring our investors, talking about giving stuff away."

"I never said anything about giving stuff away. I mentioned Richard Stallman's *name*."

"He's a nut case."

"He happens to be a visionary," said Orion, "and I find his questions very interesting. Like, when you think about it, the whole notion of intellectual property is an oxymoron. How can you own something intangible? It's like, you can't own souls, can you?"

"Are you trying to make me angry?" Jonathan asked.

"Maybe you should take your name off our patents," Aldwin suggested.

"I said I admired him. I never said I wanted to *be* him. Jesus." Orion turned away from the CTO and CFO, once his closest friends, and he looked through the glass wall at the programmers in their cubicles. Several guys were crowded around Sorel's desk. Had she got the new high score in Quake III? She was keeping her head down. "I happen to have my own ideas," Orion murmured. "I have my own opinions."

"Your ideas are—occasionally—great," Jonathan told him. "Your opinions suck."

Orion sighed and turned back to listen to the rest of the tirade.

"Aldwin and I have been in Mountain View all week," Jonathan continued. "Jake is still in London. We are taking care of customers and signing partners. We are preparing for the biggest IPO of the year. The three of us have not been home. We have not had brunch. And we do not want to come in here and find that you, with your two million shares, have been . . ."

"Just don't talk to reporters right now," said Aldwin.

"Do not talk to anyone." Jonathan pointed his index finger directly at Orion's chest, but Orion didn't flinch. He had been an athlete too, although his sport was skiing and involved no contact, only swift descents.

"When you get phone calls, refer them to Vicki," said Aldwin. "That's her job."

They were ganging up on Sorel. Orion could see the guys spinning her swivel chair around, forcing her to look at them.

"And another thing . . . ," said Aldwin.

Orion strode out of the conference room. Under his breath he murmured, "Fuck you."

Clarence, Umesh, and Nadav were standing over Sorel.

"Lockbox went down again," Umesh told Orion.

"She crashed the system," Clarence said.

"What—the new version?"

"She checked in buggy code," Umesh said.

"She gets the rubber chicken." Menacingly, Nadav swung the rubber chicken in Sorel's face. It was the sort of plucked rubber chicken you found in joke shops, its limp body yellow and gelatinous.

"Oh, *stop*," said Sorel. She sounded indifferent, almost bored, but Orion could see that she was upset.

"You crash the system," said Clarence, "you get the chicken."

Nadav pitched the rubber bird directly into Sorel's lap.

"Put that chicken nicely on her desk," Orion ordered.

Clarence hesitated for a moment. Orion acted like one of the guys, and now he pulled rank on them.

"Now," Orion said, and he waited until Clarence pitched the chicken onto Sorel's desk. "She's going to debug the code now," Orion announced. "Party's over."

When the little crowd dispersed, Orion pulled up a chair next to Sorel. He watched her long fingers on the keyboard as she scrolled through code on the screen. "I break stuff all the time."

"I know." She smiled.

"So let me help you."

"Aren't you busy?"

Orion thought of Molly sleeping after thirty-six hours at the hospital. He considered Jake in London and Jonathan and Aldwin, who didn't brunch. "Not really."

Slowly, line by line, they combed Lockbox 2.0. He took the workstation next to hers, and they worked in parallel on separate computers. As they searched, they turned up little items and oddities: missing comments, obscure bugs, strange bits of circuitous reasoning, the dust bunnies in the code. Hours passed. They didn't speak, but mumbled to themselves. "What happens when this line executes?"

"And what happens here?"

"What's the value of the variable now?"

They worked until numbers seemed to imprint themselves on Orion's eyes. The chambers of the program drew Orion and Sorel deeper and deeper into the software's formal logic. They counted their steps as they descended into dark passageways. The voices all around grew muffled, the ambient light on the floor began to dim. Orion's phone rang, but he didn't even glance at it.

Night came. Programmers departed, and others took their place. Jonathan and Aldwin were long gone. Still, Orion and Sorel kept hunting underground, watching for errors, listening for rushing water, tapping walls.

"Why are you smiling?" Sorel asked at one point.

"I'm just concentrating," he murmured, half to himself. Then he confessed, "Actually I love doing small repetitive things."

"I don't," she confessed. "I need fresh air."

"You can go home if you're tired," he told her. "I'll finish."

"No. I can't go home. I'm responsible. I'm just going out for a minute."

Suddenly he realized that she was going down alone into the dark. "Wait!" He ran after her. "I'll come down with you."

"No, don't," she said. She stepped into the elevator and as the doors closed she confessed, "I just want to smoke."

How could she smoke? She was so beautiful. He hated that she smoked. While she was gone, he raided the company kitchen for salt-and-vinegar potato chips and jelly beans. He took four cans of black-cherry soda from the fridge, and lined them up on her desk. He wasn't sure why he did that. They looked silly. He brought them to his own desk and kept working. When he heard the elevator bell he kept his head down, pretending he hadn't been waiting for her.

"You like working all night," she said.

"I'm good at it." Orion was showing off a little, but he was also telling the truth. He had an eye for detail, a grasp of the small picture, the obsessive game-playing mind of a superb hacker.

They shared her computer now, and the monitor glowed before them as they found their way back inside the code. They made their way without a map; the program was their map, spreading in rivulets before them. Their hands hovered over the keyboard and overlapped. Her wrists were delicate, her skin fine as rice paper, but he pretended that he didn't notice when their hands brushed. She pretended as well, even when she felt his fingers close reflexively on hers. The task before them made pretense easier, because they had to concentrate. They were like diviners, searching for the source of her mistake.

Suddenly Sorel found the bug. "Stupid, stupid," she groaned. "Over there. I forgot the bounds check."

"Aha!" cried Orion. She had neglected to specify enough memory for the number of items in her piece of the Lockbox system.

"It's not even an interesting mistake," she griped as she typed in proper array bounds. "Wait, why isn't it working now?"

"Be patient." He took over the keyboard.

"No." Gently she pushed his hands away. "Let me."

By the time they got Lockbox up and running, the sun was rising, shining through the floor-to-ceiling windows, drenching East Cambridge in liquid gold.

"Got it." Orion basked for a moment in accomplishment. "We got it back up," he announced to the nearly empty room.

"Cool," somebody said faintly from across the way.

Orion extended his hand to Sorel, and she shook it. He felt joyous, masterful after the all-nighter. "I knew I'd get to the bottom of this."

"*You!*" she said. "Give credit where credit is due."

"You found the bug," he admitted.

"And don't forget that I created the bug too. I created a monster!" She picked up the rubber chicken and told it sweetly, "I'm going to murder you."

"Let's go down to the river and drown it."

"Yes!" She hunted for the black heap that was her coat. As she turned it here and there, trying to figure out which end was up, her pack of cigarettes fell from one of the pockets. She didn't notice.

"I can carry that. . . ." Orion took her guitar. "What kind of . . ." He was about to ask her what kind of music she played, when everything faded. The lights dimmed, the computer monitors darkened. The constant whirring of machines ceased, and only the EXIT signs remained illuminated.

"The control room," Orion said, and they sprinted downstairs to the new ISIS nerve center with its monitors covering the entire wall, illuminating the world in all its time zones. There on that map, green dots indicated servers for the ISIS global security network. At desks in the control room, as at NASA, at least two ISIS programmers monitored the ISIS network at all times.

Clarence and Anand were watching that night, and they saw the power fade, even as Sorel and Orion burst through the door. The over-head lights died, and for a moment only the wall of monitors illuminated the space in wavering blue.

"Are you still online?" Orion asked Clarence.

"The network hung." He typed frantically.

"But what about the generators?" Sorel asked.

"Nothing," Anand said.

For a moment ISIS went dark, and its vast network, all its points of light, disappeared. It was as if the stars themselves had vanished from the sky, the whole fabulously rich ISIS enterprise, the solar system, the galaxy, the entire Milky Way had vaporized. And then power returned. Overhead lights blazed white again. The electronic map glowed, the ISIS security network restored itself onscreen in all its particulars. The soft whirring of the building's myriad machines resumed, replacing harsh silence to reassure the ear.

"Just a brownout," Sorel murmured. Like all brief frights, this one was instantly forgotten.

They walked outside between the half-built laboratories and biotech offices of Kendall Square. Orion carried the guitar as they picked their way around the slushy puddles.

"Did you ever see such ugly code?" Orion asked her.

"Disgusting," Sorel said. "I suppose Jonathan thinks there will be time to straighten out Lockbox later on, but by then everyone will be too rich to care. I know I will."

"Don't say that."

"Don't you want to be fabulously wealthy?" she asked him.

He considered a moment. "I think I'd like to buy my mom a new car. And I'd buy my dad a house. He probably wouldn't stay in it, but . . ."

"Funny, I was thinking just the opposite. I'd buy Mum a car if she promised to leave my dad."

"You don't like your father?"

"Well, he's just my stepdad, really. Why wouldn't yours stay in a house?"

"Oh, my dad's a little bit . . . Sometimes he falls asleep on park benches," Orion said. "He's a professor at Middlebury, but since he doesn't dress that well, sometimes he looks kind of—homeless. Once he fell asleep on a bench, and when he woke up, he found two dollars in his hat."

"Oh, no!" She laughed, and as she looked at him, sidelong, her cheeks were pink in the chilly air, her long hair spilled red-gold over her black cloth coat. She was so tall. He didn't have to bend down to look at her. The light caught in her eyes.

"Wait, stop a minute." They stopped walking, and right there on the sidewalk, he looked into her eyes. "Green."

"Yes, thanks, I knew that."

They hurried on through Central Square, with its piles of dirty snow and flattened cardboard, its closed shops and somnolent bars. The Plough & Stars, the Cantab Lounge, the Middle East.

"Coffee?" Orion asked.

"Absolutely." They bought coffee and donuts at the Store 24 near the Central Square bus stop. Sorel devoured her donut while Orion paid. "Sorry," she said. "They're very small!"

Orion felt an almost overwhelming desire to kiss the corner of Sorel's mouth. He wanted to lick the powdered sugar from her lips. The young cashier in her head scarf startled him with her question: "Anything else?"

They walked all the way down Pleasant Street to the river, icy in the middle, brackish at the edges. Sorel handed the rubber chicken to Orion, who sat on a bench with the coffee cups and guitar. He watched her fumble for her cigarettes.

"Don't you want to throw it?" he asked her.

"I suppose." She was a little distracted, irritated that she hadn't found what she was looking for. Sorel walked right up to the edge of the muddy riverbank and balanced on a wobbly rock.

"You do the honors," Orion encouraged her.

She lifted the rubber chicken like a football and then stopped. "If I get arrested, they'll deport me."

"What do you mean?"

"I'm on a student visa. And I think there's something in there about never throwing chickens in the water."

"I'm sure they meant live chickens," Orion said.

"Oh, that's all right then."

She hurled the rubber chicken into the air, and it sailed for an instant above the water. Then it splashed down and floated, sickly yellow on the surface.

"I'm going to write about you," she called after the chicken. She returned to Orion on the bench, opened her guitar case, and unwrapped her instrument, which she'd swaddled in soft T-shirts. "I got it at a pawnshop. Isn't that sad? It's a bit scarred here, but it's a good traveling instrument." Experimentally she tried some chords, and then launched into song.

> *Ugly little chicken*
> *Where have you gone?*
> *Don't you be pickin'*
> *Where you don't belong.*

He laughed with surprise. Her throaty voice was not English or European, but bluesy African-American. "Those Folkways records," he said, thinking of his dad's LPs. "You listened to them too."

"I listen to *everything*." Leaning back, Sorel felt his arm on the bench, against her shoulders. "Everything American. Do you think that's strange?"

When he looked into her lively eyes, Orion saw the possibilities before him, each spreading outward, the branches of a decision tree. He could answer her. He could keep quiet. He could make some excuse to leave. He could kiss her. He imagined kissing her. "I don't want to go public," he confessed.

She shook her head at him. "Poor you! When the time comes, you'll just have to find the strength." She strummed out a second verse.

> *Rich little chicken*
> *Keep movin' on*

"Stop! I get it!" He pulled her toward him and tickled her.

"No tickling!"

He stopped.

"Hold on." Carefully she put her guitar away, and then she turned to him, and he did kiss her, softly, on the lips.

"Sorry," he said immediately.

"What do you mean?"

"If I surprised you," he said.

"It's all right." She spoke as though she weren't the most lovely girl he'd ever seen. Sensibly, she said, "It's just a kiss."

That was when he began to fall in love with her. He felt a wave of sleepiness, or possibly just contentment, hearing her calm voice, sitting there with her, sharing the illusion that they would remain nothing more than friends.

"What do you really think of ISIS?" Sorel asked him.

"I don't like it as much as I did."

"Just because you were fighting with Jonathan?"

He didn't answer.

"I saw you through the glass," she said. "And I could hear you too."

"Useless conference room."

"I heard you defending the Free Software Foundation and all that."

"I happen to believe in the free exchange of ideas," Orion said. "And the individual's right to privacy and self-expression . . ."

"You can afford to," Sorel pointed out.

"It's not a question of affording to believe something," Orion said.

"Well," said Sorel, "I can't afford to believe quite so *many* things. I'm just a graduate student—supposedly. I used to be, until Mel hired me."

"What were you studying? Computer science?"

"Physics."

"Oh, physics. Molly's father would like you then," he mused.

"Who's Molly's father?"

"Carl Eisenstat."

She sat up straight. "You know Carl Eisenstat?"

There was Molly's father again with Orion in his sights. There was

Carl, sometimes disdainful, sometimes delighted, always examining Orion with his quick hawk's eye.

"The Eisenstat Principle of Viscosity," said Sorel.

"So that's what it's a principle of. I always forget."

"You didn't know?" she asked him, and then, "Who's Molly?"

"My girlfriend." He darted a look at her. Subtly, almost imperceptibly, the space between them had grown. "I guess I should have mentioned her earlier."

"But she didn't come up," Sorel said.

"No."

She smiled and said, "Right. I should get breakfast."

"I'll go with you," he told her.

She shook her head. "Not this time." He thought she was talking about breakfast, but she explained, "I can't see someone who's involved with someone else. I've done that."

"I'm really sorry," Orion said again.

"I was too," she said. "Thanks for all your help. Good-bye, good morning, and all that. You'll have to explain about the rubber chicken."

"It was your idea to drown it," he called after her as she hurried away. "You should be the one to tell them."

She turned and smiled. "I'll say you donated it to the Free Software Foundation. Everyone will understand."

13

"Where's the milk?" Molly asked as soon as Orion arrived home.

"Oh," Orion said.

"I tried to call you."

"I was working all night."

"And what do you think I was doing?"

Coming in from that gold morning, he felt as though he were returning from Italy—from some far country filled with art. The apartment looked sad, neglected. Dark. He yanked on the shade in the bedroom and light poured in to reveal the pile of clean laundry on the bed.

"That's depressing," Molly said.

"I just got home," Orion protested.

"So did I!"

This was their competition—to see who could stay out working longer.

"All I asked you to do was buy milk," Molly said.

"I know. I'll get it."

"And when you go down you could take out the recycling," she said.

"Okay." He settled on the futon in the living room and opened his laptop.

"Now."

"I said I will."

Then she shook her head at him, snatched the recycling bin and carried it downstairs, magazines and plastic bottles trailing behind her.

"I said I'd do it." He followed, picking up after her.

"I'm not interested in waiting until you feel like doing it."

"Molly." He opened the door at the bottom of the stairs, and she ran down the cracked cement steps in front of their building and heaved the bin onto the curb. Too late. The orange Cambridge Public Works recycling truck was driving away.

She didn't say a word, but turned back, tromping the stairs to their apartment with heavy dejected feet. Orion followed her inside with the recycling bin. The city would fine them if they left it out.

"Look, I'm sorry," he called up to her on the stairs.

"Don't talk to me."

"I did the laundry like you asked," he said as they reentered the apartment.

She looked through the open door at the pile of clean rumpled clothes. "Half the laundry."

"All of it!"

She turned on him. "If you don't put it away, that's half the laundry."

There was something grand and ridiculous in this argument, but he knew better than to say so. "We need a wife," he said lightly.

"Good idea. You can give her options." Molly strode into their bedroom, tore off her scrubs, and went to bed. He had never imagined that pulling up the sheets could be so much like slamming a door.

Later, much later, she woke and showered and they ordered pizza and picnicked in the living room, and they talked about hiring Merry Maids to come once a week to clean the apartment, and they agreed to send out their laundry and have it all washed and folded, and they decided to buy a car for Molly to drive to the hospital so that she wouldn't have to take the T at all hours. They didn't have the money yet, but they would in six months. They could solve almost all their problems soon.

———

The next day at ISIS, Orion kept busy writing code, but he could not stay inside it. Numbers no longer printed themselves on his retina. He saw Sorel's face instead, and heard her low voice. Her chicken song. Where was she? Her desk was bare, her cubicle empty. Was she somewhere in the building? Out on the sidewalk smoking? She was such a strange, compelling person, the only one he liked at ISIS. Why, then, had he kissed her under false pretenses? What a stupid thing to do. He sat at his desktop and typed:

`Sorel: How was breakfast?`

He deleted the line.

`Sorel,` he typed, `forgive me if I made you uncomfortable.`

Forgive me? Uncomfortable? He deleted again.

`Sorel, how are you?` Delete.

`Sorel, who are you?` Delete.

`Sorel, you didn't come in today.` Delete. Obviously she knew that.

`Sorel, where are you?` The moment he sent this message, his own words returned to him in his in-box, and for a split second he imagined she was writing back. New message. Subject: Where are you?

But the message wasn't from Sorel, it was the usual ping from Jonathan. Orion was late. The R & D meeting had started. Where are you?

R & D meetings weren't bad—just Orion, Aldwin, Jake, Jonathan, and Oskar, their old advisor, now chief scientist. As students, Orion and his friends had gathered in Oskar's office and worked for results worthy of a paper at STOC or FOCS. Now the aim was new product and patents for the company: more customers, fresh revenue, to build on the upcoming IPO. The stakes were higher now, the goals financial, but meetings with Oskar were the same as always. Four guys in mismatched swivel chairs, vying to impress their difficult-to-please professor.

Oskar did not acknowledge Orion when he bounded in and took his seat in the corner. He continued scribbling on the oversized whiteboard covering his office wall. When Oskar finished, he stood back and everyone gazed at his new model for a secure system. The drawing looked like an exploding star.

"What if you drew these edges together?" Jonathan asked.

"Show me."

Jonathan took a green dry-erase marker and simplified the star.

Oskar shook his head and took the marker out of Jonathan's hand. "This is the flaw. Do you see?"

Orion didn't see, but Jonathan flushed a little where he was standing by the board, and tried to explain himself.

"N-N-N-No." Oskar wagged his finger at Jonathan, shooting him down.

"What if you tried this?" Jake rubbed out half of Jonathan's star with his hand and redrew it in red.

Long pause, as Oskar considered the board, and his students waited for his verdict. Their resident cryptographer was a lively seventy-year-old who had come to America by way of Israel. His eyes were small and gleaming, as was his bald head. He had been married "once upon a time" as he put it, and his son and daughter were both theoretical computer scientists, one at Hebrew University and one at Carnegie Mellon. Oskar's accomplished children were nowhere near as accomplished as he, but Oskar did not lose sleep over this. He was accustomed to his superiority.

He was so much fun, thought Jake. Otherworldly, mused Orion. Egomaniacal, Jonathan protested silently.

Jonathan was slightly out of sorts, annoyed with Orion for coming late, jealous of Jake's easy brilliance. As CTO, Jonathan did the most on a day-to-day basis to build the company. He did the most and cared the most, and yet, in Oskar's office, Jake's ideas were the best. Jake did not work for those ideas; he did not have to travel or negotiate or fight for them. He was original. And Jonathan was smart enough to understand the value of everything Jake said. The businessman he was becoming rejoiced and looked for ways to capitalize on Jake's gifts, but the boy in Jonathan felt differently.

"Don't you think it's good for you to fall short sometimes?" Emily had suggested once, a question sweet and also cutting as she lay folded in his arms.

"No," Jonathan had retorted. "I don't think it's good for me at all."

"This may be possible." Oskar delivered the verdict on Jake's drawing. "This is slightly faster."

"I don't think slightly faster is really what we're after," Jonathan said. "We want more than incremental improvements."

Oskar spread his hands. "What you want," he said, "is not always what you get."

"Then we need a different paradigm," said Jonathan.

"A paradigm is not a dime a dozen," Oskar pointed out.

"I never said it would be easy," Jonathan said. "We need new products, and we need to start developing them now."

"You have a proposal?" Oskar's challenges were all the more potent because they were so gentle, always so bemused. "Tell us!"

And that was the moment of temptation. That was when Jonathan wanted to pull out electronic fingerprinting and say: Look, surveillance is where we should be going. Record every touch on every piece of data, know its security status at every turn. Other companies are starting to pursue this. We need to move into this space too. He knew Oskar would turn toward him, fascinated. He would say, Ah, now this is interesting. And in his pride and his frustration, in the heat of the moment, with Oskar calling his bluff and Jake standing there, and Orion daydreaming in the corner, Jonathan struggled against the impulse to shock them all.

"I see you have not yet decided on your new paradigm," Oskar taunted Jonathan mildly.

"I do have one." It was against Jonathan's nature to turn the other cheek, and yet, once again, he felt Emily near him, and remembered her voice.

"I have to trust you," she'd told him late that night in his apartment. "I have to, if I'm going to love you."

He had never known anyone like her. She made his previous relationships seem trivial. It was her unusual strength, the courage of her convictions that drew him to her. She insisted she was nothing like him, but he understood her differently. He saw himself in Emily—not the man he was now, but the man he could be. Sometimes he rebelled against this solemn feeling; sometimes he didn't want to love her quite so much, and he was secretly, cruelly relieved to leave her in California and return to his less-reflective life apart. He felt unready to give up childish things like rugby and lying and beating the crap out of Green Knight. But he never stopped thinking about her; he never stopped longing for her or anticipating their time together. Being with her was still new for him, her warmth still startling because she was also so reserved. When she kissed him and wrapped her arms around him, she seemed to overcome something in herself, and he knew that he was exceptional in her life as she was in his.

"So when you are ready, please let us know," said Oskar.

"Oh, I will," Jonathan said, and he pretended that his phone was buzzing, and left the room.

He wished his phone really was ringing. He had to speak to Emily, to hear her steady voice.

He closed his office door and dialed. Her phone rang and rang again, and each time it rang he missed her more.

"Hello?" Emily answered at last, surprised.

"Did I wake you?" He looked at his watch. It was only seven thirty in the morning in California.

"No, no," she said sleepily. "I'm up. I'm on the phone with Jess."

"Do you want me to call you back?"

"No, that's okay. I think we're done."

"You're never done," he said.

"She's making me crazy," Emily admitted. "Hold on. . . ." When she got back on the line he heard her sigh.

"Where is she now?"

"You don't want to know," said Emily.

"Where are you now?"

"In bed with my computer. I have to get up."

"No, don't," he said. "Stay there."

"It's getting late."

"I left Oskar's meeting," he blurted out.

"Why? What's wrong?"

"Nothing." He had nothing to confess except a brief opportunistic impulse, and he was not about to upset her by admitting that. The uneasiness he felt required reassurance, not expiation. Perhaps his logic was circular. He followed the circuit nonetheless: He needed Emily to believe in him so that he could believe in himself. Because of this, he did not always tell the whole story about himself, or even about ISIS. That night, when she had pressed him to explain what was wrong with Lockbox, he had lied to her, glossing over the structural problems Orion had discovered, insisting Orion broke the system by willfully abusing code. He lied now, as well. "Nothing's wrong."

"You're not happy."

"I am happy," he contradicted. "We've got Yahoo!"

"I know, but—"

He interrupted, "I miss your voice."

"Just my voice?"

"Not just your voice."

"You have my voice," she pointed out.

He pulled down the shades. "Keep talking. I'll imagine the rest."

"I'm in your arms," she whispered. "I'm kissing you and I can taste the coffee on your tongue."

"And then what?"

"Then what! You tell me."

"I'm kissing your neck," he said. "My hands are around your waist. I'm lifting up your nightgown." He closed his eyes, imagining her slender neck, her skin, her breasts. "Take off your nightgown."

She was quiet.

"Are you?" he whispered after a moment.

She hesitated, and then said, "Yes."

And he was with her, and he began to forget the meeting. "Please," he urged her.

"Will you?"

"Yes," he breathed, and he was not upset anymore. His company was going public within the week. He'd celebrate with her; he could hear her even now. He felt almost, on the verge, soon to be intensely happy. He was no longer lying. What were lies, anyway? Only futures waiting to come true.

14

Harvard Square glowed with artificial candlelight. Damp air misted the glass doors of Brattle Street Florist with its potted azaleas and glossy-leaved gardenias. Cardullo's stocked Dutch licorice and Belgian chocolate, Bendicks mints, Walkers shortbread, Turkish delight. Every shop tempted with earrings and antiquities, evergreens and crimson KitchenAids. But the millennium's end was not altogether jolly. The hungry still hungered, addicts scratched and stole. The season had its somber rites, exams and funerals. Hushed students filed into Houghton Library to view the manuscript of "Ode to Autumn" and puzzle at its wailful choir of loss and consolation.

The market dipped and rose, and rose again, and some speculated that the new economy had limits. It was popular to say, even without believing, that this time might never come again, that it was late in the day. Some said the markets had already peaked, and Wall Street wizards agreed that timing was everything. Therefore, ISIS celebrated its December IPO with equal parts relief and trepidation.

Orion noticed that where there had been banter about boats and cars, bikes and ultralights, now the talk was strictly options and derivatives, wills and trusts. Dave instituted wealth seminars. Lawyers arrived from

Hale and Dorr, and consultants visited to discuss charitable giving. *Shelter* became the byword, replacing *speed.*

Programmers ridiculed the seminars, but they attended anyway in small groups, gathering in the glass-walled conference room to hear account managers from Goldman Sachs hold forth in suits of navy so dark the color could not exist in nature, except possibly in the deepest ocean, where giant squid inked out their predators. These reps from Goldman were all named Josh and Ethan, and they arrived bright-eyed, cuff-linked, trussed in ties of burgundy, and they were thrilled to answer every question, psyched to help out in any way possible, and honestly happy to talk whenever, because most of all they were about having fun and learning and teamwork and making dreams happen—not just short term, but long term, which was very much what they perceived ISIS to be about. They loved innovation, said Ethan. They lived for flexibility, said Josh. When the lockup ended, they couldn't wait to innovate with everybody in the company. They worked with your lawyer and your accountant and your bank, but when it came to strategy, they said, Picture, if you will, myself and my colleagues as the quarterbacks of your team. This above all: They loved to communicate. Communication was the key, as in life, because at the end of the day, it was relationships that mattered. It was all about trust—just knowing that your team was there. Bottom line, that's who they were in private-wealth management—your team, when you were worth ten million or more.

In one of these seminars, especially for the Lockbox group, Orion glanced at Sorel and saw that she was scribbling studiously, or maybe sketching. He leaned past Clarence to look, and she saw him and smiled.

Gradually, without discussions or apologies, the awkwardness between them had subsided. Their night together, or rather their all-nighter, seemed less embarrassing in retrospect, and slowly, over weeks and months, Orion had begun to cultivate Sorel's friendship. At first he tried the smallest gestures, a glance, a word. The briefest exchanges.

"Nice snowstorm."

"Lovely, if you like that kind of thing."

He sent her lines of particularly bad code from the new Lockbox system:

`Did you see?` Orion typed.

`Worst ever,` Sorel replied.

`Trying to solve from back to front.`

`Might not be possible.`

`Fundamental flaws?`

`Yeah.`

`Cracks in foundation?`

`Worse than that.`

`Shaky ground?`

`ORIGINAL SIN.`

☺

A rationing of interactions until they spoke easily again. That was Orion's major goal these days at ISIS. He had refused an executive position, and he had no project to administer.

"Can I see?" he asked her after Josh and Ethan had distributed their heavy white business cards, and taken their leave.

"It's nothing." She showed him the sketch.

"They look like gangsters." He drew his swivel chair a little closer.

"You think?" She'd turned her notebook so that the faint green lines on the page ran vertical, like pinstripes, and then she'd drawn the pair of financial advisors as suits with dollar signs for eyes.

"You could add guns."

She looked skeptically at her drawing. "Could do. But I like to keep my sketches subtle. Either dollar signs *or* guns *or* the Angel of Death." She began to giggle.

"Cancel the guns," Orion said.

"Good. No guns on your financial team. *We're all about listening*"—she imitated Ethan's voice perfectly—"*how do you feel about risk?*"

"How the fuck should I know?" Orion said.

"Are you still planning to buy the house for your dad?"

Orion shrugged. "He doesn't want a house."

"It's hard to know what people want," Sorel mused. "It isn't always obvious."

"That's a good thing," Orion said.

———

He was dreaming about her. He dreamed of touching her, but just as he brushed her slender arms, she slipped away. He listened to her practice her guitar at night when they worked on Lockbox 2.0. "ISIS is my day job," Sorel reasoned. "So if it's night I can compose." And she sat atop the table in the conference room, and experimented with complicated chords.

ISIS, which had been so bleak to him and gray, became the place he might see Sorel. He stayed late and arrived early, locking his bike and running up the stairs as his heart beat hard in anticipation. He sat at his desk and thought of her. Even as he worked, he hoped to see her. He was programming in some kind of infinite recursion, dreaming at ISIS, which was itself a dreamscape, strange, wondrous, and frightening, the tiny company growing into an earthshaking colossus, his friends now executives impatient with him, his girlfriend hurt and angry because he had not yet set a wedding date, her parents rising up in sudden outrage, and on top of all this, his own imagination now transformed and turned about, so that he worked at ISIS but thought constantly of leaving, and slept with Molly but imagined someone else. Her husky voice, her laughter, her red-gold hair, her long legs running up the stairs.

One night, as he and Molly walked through Harvard Square, he saw a tall figure standing on a pedestal in front of Jasmine Sola. An angel dressed in white and painted white from head to toe. Feathery wings rose up behind her and white robes draped her body down to her white feet. Orion had seen these living statues before: angels, brides, cavaliers, standing on their pedestals, never moving, scarcely breathing until passersby dropped money at their feet. Like coin-operated automatons the statues bowed or curtseyed, doffed hats or winked. He had seen them all before, but he stopped in front of this one.

"Come on," Molly said, eager to get to their movie, but Orion couldn't help staring at the angel with her outspread wings.

"Sorel?" he murmured. The ghostly figure did not move. "Is that you?" Molly was puzzled. "Is that who . . . ?"

"It's someone from work."

"From ISIS? Are you sure?"

He wasn't sure. The figure stood so still and seemed so solid, her face layered with thick white greasepaint, her figure heavy in its draperies. Maybe he was just imagining Sorel. He saw her everywhere. Then he caught a red-gold gleam, one loose hair. "It *is* you!" he called up to her.

But Sorel was a Method angel and would not break character. She continued, calm, majestic, unblinking even as children tried to touch her feet, and other buskers covered Simon & Garfunkel in shop doorways. *Hello, darkness, my old friend.* . . . Orion allowed Molly to hurry him away.

"That was you!" he told Sorel on Monday, as soon as she walked in.

"That was art," she said, sliding her guitar underneath her desk.

"Admit it," he said. "You saw me in the Square!"

She laughed. "I admit nothing."

"Why do you do that? Why do you stand out there in the cold? You don't need the money."

She conceded, "I give it away."

"Why do you stand out there so late at night?"

"It's personal. It's intimate."

"It's intimate to disguise yourself and stand out there in a crowd of strangers?"

"Yes. Compared to this place."

He leaned against the gray wall of her cubicle. "What if some guy starts hitting on you? What do you do then?"

A smile played on her lips. "Turn him to stone."

"What if . . . ?"

Sorel gestured toward the neighboring cubicles where Umesh and Clarence were already typing. "Let's get to work, shall we? God knows this poor benighted excuse for a Lockbox needs it."

Were Orion and Sorel the only ones who understood that at any moment Lockbox could come crashing down? Orion was convinced that latent sleeper bugs lurked waiting to hatch inside the code. Of course nothing would happen with normal use, but one day some hacker would pick Lockbox and bring it down—and every company that used the system, every transaction and piece of data would fly out into the world. Orion was sure of this, but Jonathan wouldn't hear it.

"I'll tell you why you're under the impression I don't listen to you," Jonathan had told him the day of the IPO. "You're under that impression because it's true. We're building a company and you're off in your own world. You would rather cling to your theories of the way things should be than put your head down and work."

"What about feasibility?" Orion shot back. "What about truth in advertising?"

"What about loyalty?"

This was after all the cheers and speeches, after ISIS rose to $133 a share and Dave confessed he was getting a little emotional via speaker phone from New York. Orion had buttonholed Jonathan at a table of brownies and precut cantaloupe and sprigs of seedless grapes.

"We need to close down Lockbox and start over."

"You're bringing this up *today*?" Jonathan was amazed.

"When am I supposed to bring it up?"

Then very quietly, with so many people standing all around them, Jonathan said, "Get out of my face."

"I will when I get a straight answer," said Orion. "I think when I raise an issue over days and weeks I deserve some kind of response."

Jonathan shook his head. "No. You don't deserve anything from me. You made a choice. You stepped out of the critical path a year ago. When you leave the team, you don't get to be the referee."

"Who says I left the team? Who says I'm leaving?" Orion demanded. The idea was wonderful when he was alone, but sounded like defeat when he stood facing Jonathan.

"Be very careful," Jonathan told him.

The end of the century, which was also the end of the millennium, ISIS held a New Year's Eve blowout with a caterer, a corporate party planner, and an elaborate conceit: 2000 Leagues Under the Sea @ The New England Aquarium. The waiters dressed in antique diving gear with helmets of copper, nickel, and glass. Secretaries wore slinky dresses, while the programmers donned black sweaters with their jeans. Dave wore black from head to toe: a black suit with a black dress shirt, no tie, like an East Coast

Larry Ellison. Only the fish came as themselves: the prickly puffer fish and blue-striped wrasse, the lumpy grouper and billowy eel. As the party ascended a spiral ramp around their giant tank, armored sea turtles rose from the depths along with undulating rays. Disdainful sharks circled with mouths agape, all needle teeth and pinprick eyes.

On the mezzanine overlooking the open penguin habitat, Sorel's girl band, The Chloroforms, were performing, Sorel out front, all legs and boots, wearing what looked like a cardigan sweater for a dress.

Do androids dream of electric sheep? Sorel sang. *Do technoids scream 'bout mission creep?*

Good night. . . .

Sleep tight. . . .

"Is that Jonathan over there?" Molly asked Orion.

It was hard to see anything in the dark cavernous space. The great illuminated fish tanks cast watery shadows on the walls.

Don't let the bad bugs bite . . . , sang Sorel, and her Amazonian bandmates rocked behind her.

"Wait for me," Orion called to Molly. He wasn't sure what Jonathan would say to her if she approached him all alone. She did not know about Orion's latest run-in with Jonathan. He didn't want to worry her, and then again, the situation was complex. Far easier to suggest that there were tensions at ISIS than to describe them.

He caught up with Molly just in time, and saw that Jonathan was smiling. "Hey," Jonathan said by way of greeting, and he looked past Orion to scan the crowd.

"There you are," said Jonathan, as Emily approached carrying a plate of sushi.

"Hello!" She kissed Orion and Molly. "It's been too long."

She stood at Jonathan's side, slender, elegant in black tailored trousers and a pale silk shirt. Had Orion really introduced these two? They made no sense, unless Orion imagined the old Jonathan, the rambunctious, fun-loving, lay-down-his-life, wake-up-in-the-middle-of-the-night, drive-anywhere-for-his-friends Jonathan. Only Emily and the old Jonathan made sense. Orion had loved him too.

Good night. Sleep tight. Don't let the bad bugs bite. Sorel sang with increasing urgency. *But if they do* . . . Drums throbbed underneath Sorel's husky voice. *Take off your shoe! Take off your shoe!* Bam, bam, bam the drums pounded as Sorel screamed in crescendo. *And beat them! Beat them! Beat them!* . . .

Suddenly the penguins in their arctic habitat began barking to one another. Orion rushed to the concrete barrier and saw that the birds, usually so stoic, had begun diving into the water. Molly came along to look, and while Jonathan didn't bother, Emily joined them, balancing her plate of sushi on the wall.

'Til they're black and BLUE! Sorel howled, releasing her inner Dylan.

"The song is actually scaring the penguins off their rocks." Emily laughed a little, imagining what Jess would say, and how she would worry about the birds' eardrums.

"Maybe if we walk up the ramp it'll be quieter," Molly suggested.

"Okay. Soon," said Orion.

"Meet me up there. I'll try to get us some food." Carefully, Molly began ascending the crowded ramp in her high heels.

"Are you all right?" Emily called out to Orion.

He shook his head.

"What is it?"

Sweet Emily, his dear old friend, first crush, first love—what could he say? The time and place were so absurd, with all those bug-eyed fish swimming past, and the oily penguins swimming below. "Nothing."

But Emily would not take that for an answer, and led him away from the band, past the sushi bar, and raw bar, and the tables serving tapas, to a quieter cove with dark tanks lit by purple phosphorescent fish. "What's going on?"

He hesitated. "I think you know."

"I don't," she told him.

"Yes, you do."

"Not from your perspective."

So of course she did know. That confirmed it. She was only trawling for information. "Do you think it's fair to ask?"

"Wait," she said. "Explain."

She took off her glasses and looked much younger, almost the girl he had once kissed. "Is it true you're leaving ISIS?"

"Is that what Jonathan told you?"

"Were you considering it?" she pressed, and he knew she wanted to know why.

"I'm not leaving."

"Good." She smiled. "I know Jonathan values your opinion."

Orion murmured, "You know he doesn't. He values his own opinion."

"You got along before."

"I'm like everybody else," said Orion. "I get along with Jonathan until I cross him."

"Why do you say that? He likes debate. He likes discussion."

"Why are you the one talking to me then?" He was upsetting her, but he didn't care. "Why are you talking to me instead of him?"

"Because I want to understand. . . ."

"What is there to understand, Emily? Jonathan and I aren't getting along."

"Why not?"

"That's not a fair question, and you know it."

"You look worried."

"What are *you* worried about?" he countered. "Why don't you talk to him?"

She tilted her head slightly, a pensive move that he remembered, along with a slight narrowing of her eyes, as though the world were slightly askew and needed further study. And at that moment Orion realized that she had talked to Jonathan. She had made her inquiries, and whatever he'd said had not satisfied her. Orion wanted to hug her around her shoulders. He wanted to say: I'm worried that Jonathan is a liar. I think he's willing to sacrifice people for products, and trade quality for profits. And above all, he wanted to say: What about you, Emily? How is he treating you? But he couldn't ask her this. Some diffidence or shyness or guilt prevented him, and he only said, "I'm sorry."

"I know he has a temper," Emily told him, "but he feels he's given you a lot."

"Given me!"

She nodded.

Had Jonathan warped Emily as well? Could she care for an ambitious creature like that to the point of admiration? To the vanishing point?

She said, "I'm speaking as your friend."

"No, I don't think so. You're speaking as his friend. And it's beneath you, Emily. It really is. It's wrong of you."

PART FOUR

Best Offer

~

October 2000–January 2001

15

This was a strange time, a fairy-tale time. Mel and Barbara moved into a dream house on Pleasant Street, a mansion developers had built on spec just as Richard Bach had feared, right behind his old Colonial. The Millsteins lived there in twenty-one rooms, and they had central air and central vacuuming and bay windows and marble baths. Barbara tiptoed through her new country kitchen, and Mel drove a black Lexus to see Bobby Bruce, the Alexander teacher, who showed Mel where his posture was indeed misaligned. In all his years, Mel had never known he was off-center, and now with strange synchronicity, he discovered the problem just when he could afford to treat it. By the same token, Dave's temperamental Bentley gave out just as the ISIS lockup ended, and he treated himself to a powder-blue Jaguar.

As it turned out, a windfall came in handy. Aldwin's parents were celebrating their thirty-fifth anniversary, so he rented a villa in the south of France for a family reunion. Sorel's landlord raised the rent, so she moved out and bought a decrepit worker's cottage in East Cambridge that she planned to paint purple and restore as a house cum studio. Orion bought his first car, a silver BMW. Jonathan found Emily a ring.

He took Emily shopping on Newbury Street. They spun through Shreve, Crump & Low with its sapphires and china, Cartier with its square-cut gems and gleaming watches. Brodney Antiques & Jewelry was piled with detritus from every decade: old lamps and dusty tea sets, rows of opera glasses and ugly broaches—gold bees with diamond wings, little frogs with ruby eyes. Emily could not find anything she liked. She looked and looked, and Jonathan got hungry waiting, and they went to lunch at L'Espalier where they sat wedged into a corner table in a room adorned with antique mirrors and crystal chandeliers, and they ate a dandelion salad and the smallest sirloin steak Jonathan had ever seen, along with matchstick potatoes.

"These," Jonathan told Emily, "are exactly the way I always thought matchsticks would taste. Except real matchsticks have sulfur tips, so they're probably better."

Emily laughed. "I think they're good."

He took her hand in his. "I think you need a ring."

"We'll find one eventually."

She spoke in such a patient voice, and the restaurant with its pillows and silk curtains felt like such an overpriced tea party that he rebelled, jumping to his feet. "Wait here. Have some dessert."

"Where are you going?"

"I'll be right back. Get yourself some coffee."

And he returned to Shreve, Crump & Low, and told the first saleswoman he saw, "I'm sorry, I didn't catch your name."

"Prathima," she said in a soft voice.

"So, Prathima, what's the best diamond you have in stock?"

She was really a very small saleslady, delicate and easily affronted in her navy suit. She sat down with Jonathan at a table, as a loan officer might sit down with a client at the bank, and she showed him a chart, and a color portfolio with "Diamonds Are Forever" printed on it, and her voice grew ever softer as she explained the four Cs of diamonds. She pointed to various photographs. "This is our signature series," she whispered, as if she were in church. "Each diamond is inscribed with a—"

He cut her off. "You do sell real diamonds here, right?"

"Of course." Prathima looked offended.

"Okay, could you just bring out the most highly rated diamond you have?"

"In which category?" she asked.

"In all categories." He demonstrated his newfound knowledge, reciting: "Cut, color, carat, clarity."

"Well . . ."

"My fiancée is waiting at L'Espalier," he announced, as another sales associate joined them, and a third called a guard to open the safe. "I don't want any loose gems. I need something ready to go."

When he returned to Emily, she was waiting with a cup of coffee and a crème brûlée. "I saved some for you."

"Mmm."

"It's very sweet," she said, dying of curiosity and at the same time conscious of the other people in the restaurant.

"No, it's not too sweet." He spooned up the dessert. "It's just right." He knew he was keeping her in suspense. His eyes were shining, but he kept a straight face. "It's good."

"Jonathan!"

"Yes, Emily?"

"Did you . . ."

"Did I what?"

She burst out laughing, even as he pulled a velvet box from his pocket. Then the laughter stopped as he opened the box to reveal a ring that cost more than a suburban house in most parts of the country, platinum set with three diamonds, small, flawless, dazzling white. "Oh, they're so beautiful," she whispered.

For a moment he didn't know what to say and hesitated, and she loved his hesitation more than his reply. The hesitation was all him. His reply was heartfelt but conventional. "Not as beautiful as you."

Their visits were brief, their hours islands in a sea of time apart. They wanted to wake up together and spend all day together and fall asleep wrapped in each other's arms. When the markets rose all this seemed possible, but within months the Nasdaq fell back again, and they couldn't leave their posts. By the end of October, Veritech had lost more than half its value. ISIS, which had soared to $133, dipped below sixty and then hovered at thirty. Dave put his private plane on hold. Orion garaged his car on Green Street and continued biking to work from his ratty apartment. There would be time enough for spending when the markets revived. No one wanted to cash out before the next zephyr, the expected gust of buoyant air.

Everyone was waiting, except Mel, who panicked days after he moved into his palatial house. He sold all his stock at thirty-three, a move that angered Jonathan.

"I couldn't sleep at night," Mel confessed. Already he regretted selling as the share price rose again.

"Man," Jonathan said disdainfully. "You're old."

Jess was out of the game as well, but for a different reason. She had donated her shares to Save the Trees. She did not mention this to Emily. Her sister did not approve of Leon.

"You have a way of losing yourself in other people," Emily warned Jess on the phone.

"Don't you think," Jess countered, "that maybe sometimes they lose themselves in me?"

"No," Emily said decidedly. "You're the one at risk. You're the one behaving dangerously."

"You always say that." Jess sat up in Leon's bed, sans Leon, who was in Oregon.

"You're moving in with a guy ten years older than you, and you plan to do—what? Live with him in this amorphous environmental group, which you yourself admit includes other women that he's dated? Where do you think this is going?"

"Stop," Jess said.

"Someone has to ask," said Emily.

"You can ask as much as you like," said Jess.

"And you can't answer."

"And you can't be my mother."

"Just go back and read her letters. Look at what she says about this kind of situation."

"She never wrote about real situations," said Jess.

"Oh, really? Let me show you. Let me bring it up for you. . . ." Emily kept all her birthday letters on her laptop.

"You should know the difference between loving and being in love," Emily

read aloud. *"Loving is calm and good, and being in love is so much better and so much worse. You might—"*

"Do *you* know the difference?" Jess challenged Emily. "Do *you?*"

She hung up and buried her face in Leon's pillow. How did he get by with so little rest? He made her feel lazy and impractical. Her father had tried to make her feel that way. Emily attempted to jolt her awake, but Leon succeeded where they could not. His energy awed and attracted and piqued her as well, because living with him, hiking with him, making love half the night with him, exhausted her. She felt sleepy in contrast to Leon, but she was also sleepy *because* of him. Jess pulled the sheet over her bare body and sat up in bed to contemplate her dirty clothes. She sighed and wrapped herself in a blanket to pad down the hall to the communal bathroom.

When she was with Leon she belonged, but when he was gone, she felt like a stowaway. Strangely, the more time she spent with him, the closer they became, the more difficult her position in the house. Now that she'd moved in, she was no longer a regular leafleter. She was Leon's girlfriend, with all the resentment that entailed. When would he return? When would she see him again? She could forget the others when she was studying the brown flecks in Leon's eyes, his words, soft with surprise, his whisper—You're beautiful—his body, not diffident at all when they were alone, not cool, but heated, trembling.

When she biked to campus, a car swerved and almost hit her. For a moment she caught herself up, and pulled over to the side of the street. Breathing fast, she tried to calm down. Be more careful! she told herself. Wake up! Eat! But she was already late for Aristotle, and she had no time to shop for food. Later, she did pause briefly at the Student Union, but the produce there was coated with some kind of fruit polish. How could she eat another shiny apple? Or a hard little plum? Or those bright-hued, jet-lagged cherry tomatoes? She didn't drink milk. She wouldn't eat a box of Froot Loops. Briefly the plastic bins of candy tempted her. Swedish fish and gummy bears and sour gummy worms—but she knew those treats were full of boiled calf bones: gelatin.

Outside the Union at the bike racks someone called her name. "Jessamine!" a voice sang out, and she turned to see Rabbi Helfgott bearing down on her with fistfuls of brochures. Her heart jumped in surprise and dismay. He was wondering, of course, about his loan. He was about to ask, as he had every right, where his money had gone.

"Good to see you. Good to see you," said Helfgott.

"Rabbi! I'm sorry!" she began.

"Why is that?"

"I have to pay you back."

"I know you will," he told her, and she thought, That makes one of us. She had planned to repay him, but a cash shortfall at Save the Trees had endangered summer operations. Seizing the opportunity, Jess had donated her shares, reserving just a few to repay the rabbi's loan. The trouble was that she had donated the shares at $302. The very week she made the transfer, Veritech released its earnings, just a penny lower than analyst expectations, and the share price plummeted to $150. The six shares she had kept to pay back Rabbi Helfgott had sunk in value, and they would not rise again so she could sell and repay him.

Perhaps Helfgott knew this, because whenever she'd called about paying him he always assured her that he was in no rush. He never pestered, except to invite her to events at his center. A tree planting, a Torah class. She made excuses every time.

Now she stood before him, guilty, swinging her bike helmet by the straps. What kind of person was she to take a rabbi's money and hold on to it as she had? By rights he should be charging interest. "I made a donation," she confessed. "I donated my stock to Save the Trees."

She was amazed at his response. He smiled. "This is a wonderful thing."

"Really? You aren't angry?"

"I myself am very fond of trees," he told her. "I myself have an interest in the ecosystem. Without this system, where would we be? I have spoken many times about this in classes and also festivals. You have perhaps heard of Water Awareness Month? I gave a benediction for this month in Redwood City. We have an expression in Hebrew: Mayim Hayim. 'Water is life.' With water, with sunshine, with the spirit of the Creator comes life and also trees. We have another phrase. Etz Hayim. 'The Tree of Life.' Perhaps you have heard of it? In our tradition the Torah is the Tree of Life. It is very understandable that when you find a tree, particularly one of the majestic redwoods, you would wish to donate your money to that tree. This is your way of saying: I see the Tree of Life, and I will hold on to it."

Jess swallowed hard, moved by the rabbi's words. "I'm going to pay you back as soon as possible."

"Don't pay me. Pay the Bialystok Center of Berkeley," he said. "Then you can write off the donation on your taxes."

"I'll pay you and I'll pay you interest," she resolved.

"No interest," said the rabbi, spreading his hands. "No monetary interest."

"What other kind of interest is there?"

"Ah." The rabbi smiled at her. "I am thinking of a more substantial interest."

"And what's that?"

"I am interested in *you*."

"Me?" Jess asked.

"You have heard the expression 'Time is money,'" said Helfgott. "Some people prefer payment in money. I prefer payment in time."

"What do you mean?"

"Come to us for Shabbes," he told her. "Or come to class, and when you're done coming, *then*"—he drew out the word in a singsong voice— "*thehen* repay the loan."

She was late to work. Half an hour late, forty-five minutes late. George sat at his desk at Yorick's and called Jess's home number, but no one answered. He began to call the Tree House and then hung up.

His old black telephone sat silent on his desk. The boxes he had stacked near European History remained unpacked. She'd quit. That was the most likely scenario. She had decided to leave but hadn't bothered to give notice. That was usually the way with students. She had run off with her boyfriend, an amphibious creature George had met just once in passing at the Farmers' Market, where Jess hailed George from a booth selling root vegetables.

"I want you to meet someone!" she called out in her friendly way. Then she drew Leon from the shadows, as one might draw a dark slug off a lettuce leaf. The boyfriend was a tall Russian, or Armenian perhaps, with slippery black hair and olive skin, and eyes of an unusually pale, druggy shade of blue. The better to see you with, my dear, thought George. "This is Leon," Jess said.

"Hey," said Leon as George extended his hand.

"This is my boss, George," Jess told Leon.

Leon sized up George. "You're the bookseller."

"I am."

"Good for you," said Leon as though George were a child or a student or a dog performing some stupid trick. "What's selling these days?"

George frowned. "Nothing you'd like."

How quickly Jess had traded slacker Noah for sinister Leon. She was now over an hour late, later than she had ever been. Maybe she had not run off with Leon. Maybe she was dead.

He walked to the shop window, which Jess had set up with a display for Shakespeare's birthday. Used paperbacks of the Histories and Comedies framed a leather-bound Complete Works, and a *Tales from Shakespeare* in two volumes, very fine condition, with illustrations by Arthur Rackham. She had opened one volume to display a color plate of barefoot Miranda dancing with fairies on her father's island, but George had vetoed that idea, closing the book to save its spine and protect its colors from the sun.

No one outside even stopped to look. The fine fall weather kept people out of dark little bookstores. He told himself this, although on rainy winter days, he tended toward the other opinion, concluding that few would venture out to browse when they could stay home and order books online or reread books they already possessed. Vanity, vanity. Instantly accessible, infinitely searchable, the Internet precluded physical transactions, so that there was little point to keeping a bookshop, even in Berkeley. Moments of discovery in the store were sweet but all too rare:

the reunion of a customer with the long-sought *Zen and the Art of Motor-cycle Maintenance,* the discovery of Linus Pauling's copy of *On the Origin of Species.* Why live for such occasions? He only felt lonelier afterward.

He pushed away those melancholy thoughts and looked ahead to dinner. He had invited Nick, and his friend Raj as well. He had his own dissolute companions—or by the end of the night he'd make them so. There would be no wives or girlfriends, only good food and drink, George's favorite kind of evening. Why, then, was Jess late today? She was holding him up. He had planned to leave early so that he could pick up dessert (he didn't bake) and begin cooking.

The bell rang, and as the shop door opened, George backed away from the window lest he seem anxious. Surprised, he recognized the woman who walked in: not Jess, but Sandra.

"Welcome," he said, noting her cloth bag. She had come just twice over the past nine months, and each time she had brought an ordinary book. A first-edition *Fannie Farmer,* and an old *Mastering the Art of French Cooking.* He had offered only ten dollars for the last, and she had left Yorick's in a huff. Then he concluded that, when it came to her uncle's estate, Sandra had already sold him the crown jewels, such as they were. "Another cookbook for me?"

"No." She pushed her long hair back over her shoulders, a gesture surprisingly young for a woman so gray.

"May I help you find something?"

"No." She stood quite still before him. "What I would like," she said, and she spoke with precision, "is to take you to the house."

"To your house!"

"My uncle's house," she amended. "The house he left me. I'm interested in an appraisal."

Why now? he thought. And why him? Did she want a second opinion? Or was he the first? Just how desperate was she?

"Some of the books are valuable."

Let me be the judge of that, he thought.

"Some are unique."

"How many are there?"

"Currently," she said, "eight hundred and seventy-three."

The number startled him, because it was bigger than he expected, and more exact.

"Sorting out that many will take time."

"That's just it; time is of the essence," she told him. "Would it be possible for you to come this afternoon?"

With some humor, he considered his empty store. "Sure."

"I'll show you."

"I'd have to lock up," he said. Jess should have been there to cover for him.

He stuck a Post-it on the glass shop door. "Back in an hour."

Then he dashed off instructions for Jess, who had a key. He took his fountain pen and covered a note card quickly with his small tight cursive:

J.—I assume you're writing a new theory of moral sentiments or testifying against Pacific Lumber. In either case, the books have not been shelved. Take care of that and break down the boxes!—G.

They took George's car, because Sandra didn't drive, and they drove through Elmwood with its beetle-browed old bungalows. Towering hedges of eugenia nearly obscured Sandra's home from Russell Street. Her uncle must have bought the place for about a dollar, thought George, as he picked his way through a jungle of ornamental plum, live oak, and Australian tea trees, trailing their branches luxuriantly. There were figs and lemons, roses and giant rhododendrons, all overrun with thorny blackberry canes.

"Watch out for the cat," Sandra told George as he followed her up peeling steps to the front porch.

She gestured for George to step in close behind her as she unlocked the door. Like a furry missile, the black-and-gray cat launched himself, trying to escape outdoors. George blocked him with his legs. Sandra scooped him up in her arms. "Down, Geoffrey," she ordered, as if chastising a dog, and she dumped the animal onto a couch draped in dark green slipcovers. Geoffrey jumped onto the back of this well-protected piece of furniture and glared at her with furrowed brow and narrowed eyes.

The living room was stuffed with armchairs, end tables and book-cases, stacks of magazines and yellowed newspapers. Empty antique birdcages filled the front bay window. Abandoned pagodas. Flanking the dining table, open cabinets displayed bowls and goblets of dusty ruby-colored cut glass. A phalanx of botanical engravings adorned the walls. No bright tulips or orchids here. The engravings were all pale green and gray, portraying and anatomizing moss and lichens. Odd choices, George thought. Geoffrey purred, and instinctively, as he leaned over the green couch for a closer look, George touched the cat's soft fur.

"He bites," said Sandra.

Too late. George gasped as the cat nipped his finger.

"I warned you." Sandra's voice rose.

The wound looked like two pinpricks, the puncture marks of a tiny vampire.

"I told you. I said watch out for the cat. He's a very . . ."

She disappeared into the next room, and George followed her into a kitchen that smelled of bananas and wheat germ and rotting plums. The paint on the cabinets was chipped, the countertops stacked with dishes and small New Age appliances: rice cooker, yogurt maker, fruit dehydra-tor. Little cacti lined the windowsills. Prickly cacti, hairy cacti; spiky, round, bulbous, hostile little plants of every kind.

"He was my uncle's cat," Sandra explained. "He was abused when he was younger. My uncle found him and took him in, and then when my uncle passed . . ."

Ignoring this sob story, George marched to the sink.

"He felt abandoned," Sandra said.

George turned on the tap and a cloud of fruit flies rose from the drain. Disgusted, he held his finger under the running water.

"Let me get you some iodine," said Sandra. "Let me . . ." Her voice trailed off again. "You do still want to see the books?"

"That's what I'm here for."

She had turned her back to open the kitchen cabinets. For a moment he thought she was searching for the iodine, and then he saw them. Leather-bound, cloth-bound, quartos and folios, books of every size. The cabinets were stacked with books. Not a dish or cup in sight. Only books.

Sandra bent and opened the lower cabinets. Not a single pot or pan. Just books. She stood on a chair to reach the cabinet above the refrigerator. Books there as well.

George stepped away from the sink without noticing that he had left the water running. Injury forgotten, he gazed in awe. He leaned against the counter and stared at bindings of hooped leather, red morocco, black and gold. Sandra opened a drawer, and there lay *Le Livre de Cuisine*. She opened the drawer below and he took out *The Accomplisht Cook: or, The Art and Mystery of Cookery*. He opened the book at random: *Section XIII: The First Section for dressing of fish, Shewing divers ways, and the most excellent, for dressing Carps, either Boiled, Stewed, Broiled, Roasted, or Baked, &c.* He had never tried to roast a carp. *Take a live carp, draw and wash it, and take away the gall, and milt, or spawn; then make a pudding with some grated manchet, some almond-paste, cream, currans, grated nutmeg, raw yolks of eggs, sugar, caraway-seed candied, or any peel, some lemon and salt, then make a stiff pudding and . . .* The cook in him wanted to read on, but the collector was distracted by the array in cabinets beneath, above, below.

Where should he begin? How could he approach, let alone assess a trove like this? Books like these would take a specialist, a Lowenstein or Wheaton. The sheer numbers were overwhelming. The antiquity. And the strangeness of it all, the perversity of substituting cookbooks for utensils, domestic treatises for pots and pans, words for cups, recipes for spoons and spatulas and cutlery. Still cradling *The Accomplisht Cook,* George tried to comprehend the open cabinets and drawers before him. He did not make a sound until Sandra opened the oven. Then a cry escaped. Books piled even here, arrayed in boxes on cookie sheets! The collector had converted oven racks to stacks.

"Where did he find these?" George murmured to Sandra.

She shook her head. "After the War," she said, "when he was young. But he kept them in boxes until he retired, and then slowly he unpacked them, and shelved them here. He didn't cook."

George knelt before the open oven. He slid the top rack out partway and took a flat box in his two hands, keeping it level, as one might support a cake. "Oh, my God," he murmured. Inside the box lay *La Cuisine Classique,* volume two, bound in worn red morocco.

He opened the book, and scraps of paper fluttered to the floor.
"What's this?"

The book was stuffed with folded notebook paper, even index cards,
the precious volume interleaved with notes. George looked up at Sandra
in alarm. "These aren't acid-free. You see this?" He held up a note card
covered with black writing. "The acid in this card will eat your book alive.
This has to go."

Notes and even newspaper clippings. The nineteenth-century volume
was stuffed with what looked like shopping lists and pages torn from address books, thin typing paper brittle with age. Black ink leached onto the
title page.

"You don't keep folios like this," he told Sandra. "Not in ovens! Look
at this." The collector's block printing stained recipes for aspic, and
smudged an engraved illustration of eight desserts, including *pralinées
aux fruit* and *abricots à la Portugaise.* What had the man been thinking?
Notes in permanent black ink pressed between these pages? He pulled
out a folded article from *The New York Times.* An obituary for Samuel
Chamberlain.

"He asked me to keep everything," Sandra said.

George wasn't listening. "Do you see this? A paper clip!" The silver
wire clipped several scraps of paper to a recipe for *petites meringues à
l'ananas.* George pulled it off, and showed Sandra the rusty impression
left behind. "This is criminal."

The paper clip upset him most of all. And there were others. A rare
cookbook with lavish illustrations required lavish care. What George saw
here were pages stained and crimped. "Have you opened these?" George
demanded.

She shook her head.

"Have you seen their condition?"

"I try not to . . . I don't want to crack the bindings," she said.

He did not believe her. Who could resist cracking books like these?
He wanted to open them right now, one after another on the kitchen
table. He wanted to shuck these books like oysters in their shells.

"He asked me to keep the collection together," she said.

George caressed a quarto bound in brown leather, hooped at the spine, secured with a gold clasp curiously wrought with scalloped, spiraling designs, engraved initials *CWM,* and the date 1735. Inside the book a title page printed in prickly gothic letters: *Das Brandenburgiche Koch-Buch.* Oh, glorious. The frontispiece depicted men and maidservants dressing fowl, and roasting meat over a roaring fire. Through a stone archway the lady of the house watched over all, raising her right index finger to instruct the staff. She held a great key in her other hand. The key to the house? To the spices? To cookery itself? In a reverie, George turned the page—and discovered folded typing paper.

He exploded. "You cannot stuff a book like this. Do you understand?"

"These are my uncle's notes."

"He was not a scholar," George said, for he could not imagine a scholar imposing his notes on books like these.

"Yes, he was. He was a lichenologist." She watched as George unfolded the brittle piece of typing paper. "He was very well known—in his field," she added anxiously. "His name was Tom McClintock. He held the Bancroft Chair in . . ."

But George was lost in the thicket of McClintock's words—poetry cross-referenced with recipes: *I prithee, let me bring thee where crabs grow (iii crabbes and oysters) / And I with my long nails will dig thee pignuts, / Show thee a jay's nest and instruct thee how / To snare the nimble marmoset; / I'll bring thee to clustering filberts (xiii iellyes, puddings, other made-Dishes) . . .*

"He taught at Cal for almost forty years," Sandra said.

George had found another paper, covered with hand-printed lines—part love poem, part recipe, part threat: *. . . snare you, dress you, cut you with the bone still in. Mince you small with suit and marrow, take sweet Creame, yolkes of Eggs, a few Razins of the Sun . . .* An ink drawing illustrated these lines. A nude woman lying on a tablecloth. She lay on her side, all line and tapered leg, head resting on her hand. The drawing was expressive, despite its small scale. The subtlest marks indicated the arch of her foot, her brow, her full breasts.

"What have we here?" George asked, even as Sandra snatched the paper from his hands and folded it again.

"My uncle was a very scholarly, modest . . . ," Sandra began.

"And what was he doing with these books?"

"I don't know," she whispered in reply.

And George wanted the collection then. He wanted it, notes and all, to read and puzzle over. He wanted days and weeks with these rare books and their strange apparatus, the notes and drawings of their collector. He would satisfy his curiosity. But first, "I'll need to bring in an antiquarian. I have a friend—"

The front door rattled and Sandra jumped, hand on her heart.

"What was that?"

"Only the mailman," she said. "He frightened me."

George looked warily at her. She was far too nervous, far too gray—ashen-faced, really—wide-eyed, shaken.

"I'm afraid," Sandra said.

Oh, God, thought George, but he asked, "What are you afraid of?"

She mulled the question. "I'm afraid in general."

"Afraid of selling?"

"I need to sell, but I'm afraid of him."

"Your uncle's gone," George reminded her.

"Yes, I know," said Sandra, but her voice trembled. "He's dead, and I'm going to betray him."

Red-letter day! He had heard from other dealers about triumphs at swap meets, or, as his friend Raj dubbed such adventures, Victories at Flea. He had heard of Alcott family papers in a New England barn, and a hand-drawn map of Arabia by T. E. Lawrence tucked underneath the endpapers of Lawrence's eighteenth-century Josephus. These were tales of the trade, but he had never contributed a legend of his own.

Sandra was a strange one. She had her apprehensions and her guilt, but George had never seen conscience-stricken sellers turn from good hard cash. He would make an offer to light up her gray eyes and make her feel almost young again. He felt euphoric. He would open his 1974 Martha's Vineyard that night. Best of all his cabernets, the one he had been saving. He jingled his keys as he returned to Yorick's. He could almost taste the deep red, lush Heitz.

He saw that his Post-it had disappeared. Turning the key, he found the glass door unlocked, and stepped inside to find Jess, reading at his desk. Her hair was falling in her eyes, and she wore a wrinkled linen dress too big for her; she wore all her clothes that way—loose, voluminous—and then while working, she would push up her sleeves, revealing her forearms.

"Long time, no see," George sang out, taking his 1892 *Leaves of Grass* from Jess's hands. "You found my note?"

"I did." She snatched up the utility knife.

"You haven't even opened the boxes."

"I was just about to!"

"As soon as you finished 'Song of Myself'? That's all right, don't bother."

"Don't bother? What do you mean?" She looked up at him as she often did, all innocence, bright-eyed, polite—until she could determine if he was really angry with her or only bluffing. "Why are you so happy?" She squinted, examining him closely, and then smiled, triumphant. "You bought something!"

He thought of telling her about the books. For just a moment he considered confiding in her, but he was superstitious until he closed a deal. "I didn't buy anything."

"Really?" She leaned back in his desk chair.

"Careful."

She sat up straight, all business with four chair legs on the floor. "I'll shelve the books. Just let me take care of it."

"Jess," he said, "you had all afternoon to take care of it. It's four o'clock, I'm closing early, and now you've missed your chance."

Four o'clock. Her day had been so long that she couldn't remember its beginning. She had been running since she woke up, and she was exhausted, the afternoon a blur of missed lunch, talking to the rabbi, sitting with Professor Sakamaki for almost two hours to discuss her Kant paper with its problems "in argumentation, structure, and style." She had made a huge effort to get to the store.

Now George shooed her away with his hands. "Go home."

"Don't you want to know why I'm late?"

He was honest. "No, not really."

"My professor wants me to take an Incomplete. He says my Kant paper is really two different papers and I have to separate them. And I already have an Incomplete in Philosophy of Language, and I have another . . . thing."

"A . . . thing?" George couldn't tell whether she was serious or not. "What do you mean?"

"It's just a thing," Jess said.

Instantly George thought of Leon. Instinctively, he suspected her self-absorbed, voracious lover. George was old enough to read a whole story in Leon's face—the charismatic opportunist alighting in Berkeley, the pseudo-intellectual, the rebel with an environmental cause, masking his appetites with altruism. But of course Jess could not interpret Leon as George did. She couldn't even read George. She had no idea how George delighted in her funny ways, or watched her through the window as she stood outside, finishing an apple or nibbling sunflower seeds. She did not register his glances, his quick inventory of her clothes, his pleasure in her face and wrists. She did not know his heart.

"Why are you looking at me like that?" she asked playfully, and then he changed his mind about her, as he often did, and decided that in fact she read him pretty well, and knew more than she let on.

"I was just trying to assess the nature of the problem," George said. "Legal trouble?"

"No."

"Mortal danger?"

"No, of course not."

"Oh."

"Oh?" she echoed

"Well, what would you like me to say?"

"Generally speaking," she told him, "if you hear someone is not in mortal danger, you should say 'good.'"

He laughed. "Get out of here. Go home. I have people coming for dinner."

"You can go. I'll lock up."

Then he understood. She wanted to finish reading his very-good-condition-with-only-slight-foxing Whitman. "You want to sit here alone with *Leaves of Grass,* don't you? *Smile O voluptuous cool-breath'd earth!*" he read aloud. *"Earth of the slumbering and liquid trees!* I'd like to see a liquid tree."

"If we keep on the way we're going, you aren't going to see any kind of trees," Jess said.

Despite his good mood—perhaps because of it—George refused to let this comment pass. "You know," he said, "you worry too much about forests."

"You can't worry too much," Jess replied immediately.

George snapped Whitman shut. "You go out there on weekends, confronting angry loggers, and risk your life for redwoods, but are you, personally, going to save them? Do you think that by saving a few trees here, you'll have the slightest effect on the global environmental problem?"

"Yes," said Jess, "because of what we'll prove to everyone."

George smiled. "Who's everyone? Just other comfortably well-off tree savers like you."

"How am I comfortably well-off?" Jess asked.

"This environmental theater of yours has limited impact."

She looked miserable for a moment, but George did not let up. "Look, I'm older than you are, and I know a few things about . . ." He was going to say, Types like Leon, but he said, "Organizations like Save the Trees. These are businesses-slash-cults started by refugees from the East Coast who come out here to graft their radical-chic plan onto some unsuspecting western species like the spotted owl, or the coastal redwood, or the Berkeley grad student. Ultimately their goals are self-serving. The money they collect supports their lifestyle. The signatures they gather justify a pyramid scheme. I sign on and then I get five friends to sign, and soon I've got a thousand friends supporting my incursions in the old-growth forests, where I do what? Hope someone will photograph me shouting down some logger? What's the plan? And where are all the donations and the signatures going? Save the Trees is a self-sustaining public-relations firm. It's not substantive or effective. It's not real."

"As opposed to your rare-book store?" Jess countered. "What's yours is real, and what's mine must be imaginary?"

"How is Save the Trees yours?" George asked her, and now he was quite serious. "In what way does it belong to you? You belong to it. Those people are taking advantage of you."

"You know nothing about Save the Trees. If you want to know about it, come visit, and I'll show you around myself."

"No, thank you," he said without a moment's hesitation.

"You have to admit, then, that you prefer your prejudices to actual knowledge. You don't really know anything."

"I know you're sitting in my chair," George said.

That startled her. She had forgotten. When she sprang to her feet, he knew he'd hurt her. She took the utility knife and silently began slitting open boxes.

That night cooking, he regretted his words and his proprietary tone, his lecture on environmental politics. Again and again as he sautéed portobello mushrooms, he remembered how Jess looked at him when she jumped out of his desk chair. A glance both angry and reproachful. All the light in the room had drained away, her joy yielding to his pedantry. I'm sorry, he told Jess. Forgive me. And he imagined her forgiving him. He dreamed of that even as he stood there at the stove and watched the mushrooms softening. To be honest he had always dreamed of Jess— a girl so open and unself-conscious, so free. He had always imagined her. He lifted the pan and covered the Aga burner with its special lid.

Enameled deepest, darkest green, a Craftsman color to match the tile backsplashes, the Aga oven was one of George's few concessions to modernity, along with a dishwasher hidden inside a lower cabinet and a Sub-Zero refrigerator concealed behind a wall. Preservationist that he was, George had studied old photographs to re-create his kitchen's 1933 layout with two open cupboards for dishes, scant counter space, and just one sink. No downdraft grill, no appliance hutches, no microwave, no island, only an oak table. George's kitchen was all air and light, with arched windows soaring almost sixteen feet to a peaked roof supported by trussed beams. Californian and medieval, the room was chapel-like, its woods ranging from gold to claret, its floorboards aged, its honed soapstone counters silky to the touch, luscious black when wet.

He opened the first bottle of the evening, a crisp Soave by way of appetizer, and as he sipped, he parboiled new potatoes, blanched green beans, reduced the sauce for the béarnaise. He had learned his way in the kitchen from an old girlfriend, flame-haired, dark-eyed Margaret. She had been thirty, he'd been twenty-nine. She'd worked at Chez Panisse, and she taught George the mysteries of meat and fish, how to fillet a trout, and the best way to braise lamb and steam artichokes. She had explained the varieties of mushrooms and their uses, demonstrated the gentle stirring of risotto, how to select a perfect ripe tomato, and when to buy a peach. Margaret had taught him about wine as well. She had a discerning palate and a way with words, so that she could articulate the most elusive undertones. "Tobacco," she would say, and that was it exactly. "Dried cherries." And she was always right. She had prepared fantastic meals, feasts for all their friends in a student apartment with just two working burners. At the end of the night, exhausted and exhilarated, she and George would fall asleep with the scent of cinnamon or lemongrass or cardamom clinging to their hair and clothes. Yes, Margaret had been beautiful, talented, and wild as well. Fair to say that George had been scarred by the relationship. Like the vein on a leaf, his scar traveled from his right thumb all the way up his forearm, where Margaret had scored him in a fury with her paring knife.

"You're too selfish to marry anyone," Margaret told George when she left. And, of course, as soon as she said these words, she was exactly right.

He had tried to prove her wrong. He had always imagined sharing this kitchen and this view out over the Bay and through the Golden Gate. The lights below like tiny jewels, the sky past sunset, more silver than gray, clouds like a pearl silk dress in a ter Borch painting. Endlessly he had searched for his love, and when he couldn't find her, he looked for signs, traces of her beauty in books and maps. He surrounded himself with talismans and reliquaries, but he never stopped desiring the one he couldn't find. Superstitious heart: He began to see her reflected in impossibilities—the Rackham illustration of Miranda dancing, Jess's delighted laughter. The one he couldn't find became the one he couldn't have.

"Close your eyes," he told Jess in his dream, and he would lead her to these windows and stand behind her, hands on her shoulders. Unconsciously, he closed his own eyes as he stood there at the stove.

The doorbell. A surprise and a relief. "It's unlocked!" he called, and Nick appeared in fresh pressed clothes, a plum-colored shirt, Italian shoes.

"You look good." George poured him a glass.

"What do you mean?"

He meant that Nick looked entirely different away from Julia, free from the kid. "You look yourself," George said.

Nick sat at the kitchen table, and George set before him dishes of olives and pickled eggplants the size of grapes, a platter of French bread, a saucer of sea salt. "How is everybody? How go the renovations?"

"Behind schedule."

"Your kitchen couldn't take as long as mine," George said, by way of encouragement.

"Yes, well, you weren't trying to live in the house with a small child."

"True," George said. "I planned that well." He liked to flaunt his freedom once in a while, even as Nick flaunted his domestic bliss. They were each a little jealous, and like brothers they provoked each other.

"I noticed someone stole your hood ornament again," Nick said.

This was a sore point. "It's happening while I'm at Yorick's. I pay to park in a garage, and they're supposed to have security cameras."

"Must be an inside job," said Nick. "You should buy a screw top you can take with you."

"Either that or I should start biking again and give up driving altogether." By biking, George meant motorcycles, and he knew full well that when it came to motorbikes, Nick was not allowed.

"You're too old," Nick said. "But how about—" he disappeared into the front hallway where he had left his backpack and returned with a bottle wrapped in white rice paper— "this." It was a 1970 Chateau Latour.

"Nick!"

"You're welcome."

"We'll drink your Latour along with my Heitz."

"Oh, good," said Raj as soon as he walked in and saw Nick's bottle.

Perfect, George thought. Raj was carrying a 1975 Chateau Petrus, peer and rival to the Latour.

Small, dark, and handsome, Raj wore shades of black and gray. His glasses were gold-rimmed, his hair parted on the side. His body was slight, and his eyes unusually large and beautiful. He had been an academic once, and then a lawyer, but at the moment he spent most of his time wrangling with an unreliable Bentley, two Westies, and a rich ex-boyfriend. He lived in a cottage in Palo Alto, the pocket-sized guesthouse of a larger estate where, as he put it, he worked at home, buying, trading, and selling rare books.

"We're going to have a competition," George explained from the stove where he was searing tournedos of beef. "Nick's Latour versus your Petrus. And both against my Heitz."

When George decanted the Latour, the friends watched with some solemnity, each anticipating the taste to come. The two French wines which promised greatness. The luscious Californian, from a year they knew to be exceptional.

"A toast," Raj insisted.

"Well," George began, "the markets are down. . . ."

"For the moment," Nick said.

"Bush and Gore are neck and neck."

"Not an attractive image," said Raj.

"I don't think we can toast necks." George fingered his glass. He knew what he would be toasting secretly. His great new find.

"What, then? Or whom?" Raj asked pointedly.

"I don't have a whom," George said.

"I'm relieved to hear that."

"Why?"

"Because you get so boring, darling," Raj confided. "Love does not become you."

"To old friends, then." Nick raised his glass.

The wines were great, and better by the minute, even as the drinkers softened. Just as wines opened at the table, so the friends' thirst changed. Their tongues were not so keen, but curled, delighted, as the wines deepened. Nick's Latour was a classic Bordeaux, perfumed with black currant and cedar, perfectly balanced, never overpowering, too genteel to call attention to itself, but too splendid to ignore. Raj's Petrus, like Raj himself, more flamboyant, flashier, riper, ravishing the tongue. And then the Californian, which was in some ways richest, and in others most ethereal. George was sure the scent was eucalyptus in this Heitz, the flavor creamy with just a touch of mint, so that he could imagine the groves of silvery trees. The Heitz was smooth and silky, meltingly soft, perhaps best suited to George's tournedos, seared outside, succulent and pink within, juices running, mixing with the young potatoes and tangy green beans crisp enough to snap.

They finished dinner with lemon sorbet garnished with fresh mint, and carried their glasses and their bottles into the enormous living room where they sat on George's monumental chairs, built like heartwood thrones. George lit a fire, and as the three friends watched the flames in the great fireplace, Nick became dreamier, Raj more argumentative, and as for George, he found himself discoursing on every subject—from books to cars to the economy to the school shootings in Columbine.

"Kids are numb," George said. "They live in a simulated world, a gaming cyber world, and they lose the distinction between the virtual and the real. They want to feel. This is a fin de siècle problem."

"I disagree," said Raj. "It's a First World problem. Americans, Japanese, Koreans live a virtual life because they can afford a violent simulated world. In other countries the real is quite real. All too real. If you walk through Calcutta, the real will find you, and chase you down the street and try to kill you or steal from you or both."

"Granted," George said, a little miffed. Generally an unrepentant aesthete, Raj turned political and brought up India when you least expected it. "But I'm making a different point. Violence isn't just a matter of impaired judgment. It comes from sensory deprivation."

"This is First World deprivation that you're talking about," said Raj. "Boredom, anomie, et cetera. Other people can only aspire to that sort of spiritual bankruptcy." He smiled rakishly. "I know I do."

"Even now?" asked Nick.

"Of course. Having achieved a certain level of comfort, I look for more, whenever possible." Raj took a long sip of the Latour.

"Then you're never content," said Nick.

"If I have the luxury to choose, then I prefer the chase; I like pursuit better than so-called fulfillment. Everybody does."

Nick shook his head. "Not true."

"You're no exception," Raj insisted. "You love risk. It's an erotic pleasure."

"It is not."

"Look at your positions in Veritech and Inktomi. Look at you playing with Angelfire. It's just gambling, and gambling is just like risky sex."

"You forget," Nick told Raj, "that I'm actually interested in new technology. I'm not a thrill seeker. I'm investing in the information revolution."

Raj held out his glass for George to refill. "Violence is luxury, and in America the revolution comes with a prospectus and a public offering."

"Do you really think we're all so decadent?" asked George.

Raj cast his eyes over the enormous room with its bookcases like upended treasure chests, its massive beams, its woods glowing in the firelight and resonating with the crackling logs so that the whole house seemed cello-like. "We've got an acquisitive gene. We want and want, and there's no way around it."

"I think you're discounting the nature of discovery," George said. "You forget that some aesthetic experiences satisfy. This wine, for example." He held up his glass. "This Petrus is an end in itself. I want nothing more than to taste this wine." He grasped the thick edge of his armrest. "This chair. This oak is solid. There are objects sufficient in themselves, and experiences which are complete. There is such a thing as excellence, and I do know it when I see it, and when I find it I am fulfilled. I don't want to keep on hunting endlessly. If I'm restless, that's not because I want to be or because I can't help it. I'm not chronically dissatisfied; I've been disappointed. There's a difference. When I discover something beautiful and right and rare, I'm happy. I'm content. I am . . ."

"What did you discover that's so beautiful and right and rare?" asked clever Raj.

"You'll be jealous," George demurred, savoring his secret. "Consumed with jealousy."

"Try me."

"I'm not going to tell you."

"Animal, vegetable, or mineral?" asked Nick.

George thought of the recipes for trout and leeks, the descriptions of sea salt. "All of the above." How he delighted in puzzling his friends. How he loved secrecy. Childishly, tipsily, he enjoyed his secret so much that he could not keep it any longer. "I've discovered a cookbook collection. A great one. You can come with me to the owner's house and look. You can touch them if you like, but you can't have them. I made her promise."

"Who is she?" Nick asked. "Is she a whom?"

"She is not a whom; she is a witch, and she lives in a little house crammed with crap, and a cat named Geoffrey."

At which Raj began to sing in a light tenor: *For I will consider my cat Jeoffry. / For he is the servant of the living God duly and daily serving him . . ."*

"These are the most important books I've ever found directly," George told Nick. "I have never unearthed anything like this on my own. It's like opening an ancient Egyptian tomb and stumbling upon a gold sarcophagus. . . ."

"*. . . at the first glance of the glory of God in the East he worships in his way,*" Raj continued, for he had been a choral singer at Cambridge. "*For this is done by wreathing his body seven times round with elegant quickness. . . .*"

"I said I'd keep the books together. She wants a private sale."

Raj broke off singing. "The books are good. They're wonderful. Strange about the oven, but nothing's burnt."

"You saw them!"

"Yes, of course." Raj's eyes sparkled. He was so pleased with himself. "I saw them several weeks ago."

Now George set down his glass of wine, and his evanescent joy burst and dissipated all at once. "Sandra showed them to you first."

"Why wouldn't she?" Raj asked.

"She never told me that."

Raj shrugged.

"And you never told me either."

"That wouldn't have been like me," Raj pointed out.

"Did you offer?"

"I'm considering," Raj said.

"She promised me," George repeated.

"What, exactly, did she promise? Did she say she would accept your unknown offer?"

"Did she accept yours?"

"She said she would consider it."

This was maddening. George should have written Sandra a check right there. But for what amount? What was the collection worth? More than he could spend lightly. More than Raj could afford without selling off some volumes. What was the value of those books? A complicated question. Value to whom? To the dead collector who had valued privacy? To Sandra, who needed cash? To some aesthetic ideal of excellence and rarity? Honor, fear, shame, jealousy, all those factors came into play, even as George told himself that value was simply what the market would bear. "I am seriously interested," said George, "and I believe she is seriously interested in selling to me."

"We'll see," Raj replied.

"What do you mean, 'we'll see'?"

"As I said," Raj told Nick. "He's boring when he falls in love."

It was late, past one, when Nick and Raj departed, and George began to clear the table and wash the wineglasses one by one, turning them under the running water, rubbing his fingers inside their rims. Oh, he regretted showing his hand. He rued sounding so excited before his friend and rival. Raj would never make a mistake like that, but then Raj had been a dealer longer. Sly and witty, Raj needed money, and he was brilliant, while George, who had much deeper pockets, still thought like an amateur.

The trick was not to fall in love at all. Better to pursue unfeelingly, play the market, and enjoy the chase. Better to look dispassionately at these city lights.

He poured out the last drop of the Petrus and wished earnestly that he were less earnest. He hated his sincerity, and resolved to give it up. As Raj said, it did not become him. Yes, George could be heartless on occasion. He could bargain with the best of them. Sarcasm, light banter, a cynical veneer—he could manage that, but Raj and Nick saw through him. Selfishness was one thing, but George was sentimental too. That was unforgivable. Scratch the surface and he was all enthusiasm, like the Heitz, strongest at the beginning against the French, but lacking structure in the end.

Sentimentally, he thought of Jess. Irrationally, he imagined her. Sadly, he despaired of having her. But this was not a question of pursuit. Raj would laugh at him, and Nick would look askance. His fantasies were nurturing, not predatory. If he could have Jess, he would feed her. Laughable, antique, confusingly paternal, he longed to nourish her with clementines, and pears in season, fresh whole-wheat bread and butter, wild strawberries, comté cheese, fresh figs and oily Marcona almonds, tender yellow beets. He would sear red meat, if she would let him, and grill spring lamb. Cut the thorns off artichokes and dip the leaves in fresh aioli, poach her fish—thick Dover sole in wine and shallots—julienne potatoes, and roast a whole chicken with lemon slices under the skin. He would serve a salad of heirloom tomatoes and fresh mozzarella and just-picked basil. Serve her and watch her savor dinner, pour for her, and watch her drink. That would be enough for him. To find her plums in season, and perfect nectarines, velvet apricots, dark succulent duck. To bring her all these things and watch her eat.

16

"Jess," said George as she taped clear plastic covers on a complete set of P. G. Wodehouse, "can I trust you?"

She looked up from the work table, an old metal desk in the back room. "What kind of question is that?"

"I mean, can I trust you to keep a poker face if I bring you into someone's house?"

"Whose house? Is it Sandra?" she asked immediately. "Does she really have a collection to show you?"

"You wouldn't talk about how amazing it was, would you? You wouldn't gush?"

"I would never gush!" Jess protested.

"I might need your help when I go to the house, but only if you're quiet. It's a difficult situation. She's skittish."

Jess nodded.

"She keeps postponing the date. We've got a competitor as well. At least one. It's going to be tricky to evaluate her books, and we'll have limited time. What do you think? Could you come to her house for three days straight, if necessary?"

"What are the books like?"

"The most amazing I have ever seen in a private home," George said.

Her eyes widened.

"But that's not to be repeated."

"I know, I know."

"Would you be available at short notice?"

"Of course." Jess had never before heard George speak this way. She liked the urgency in his voice.

Working at the store, she had become a connoisseur of sorts, someone who knew the difference between a first printing and a latter-day edition. She had come to appreciate white rag paper and color plates with tissue over them and marbled endpapers and gilt titles. Once, she had insisted that content was all that mattered. Now form began to matter too, and her eye delighted in elegant type, and her hand loved thick creamy pages. She treasured what was old and handmade, and began to enjoy early editions more than new. George had influenced her this way, not so much by what he said, but by example. His passion and his knowledge inspired her. When he acquired a new book, he called her over. "Jess, come quick!" Sensing her interest, he explained what made the volume scarce and fine. At those moments, she wished she could work longer hours at Yorick's. The trouble was that she had so little time.

She knew that she was overextended, but she couldn't help herself. Student, tree lover, citizen of the Earth, she was busier than ever as she raced through Berkeley on her bicycle, and stood on street corners with petitions. She was a blithe spirit, and increasingly a hungry one. Vegan, but not always strict. She never ate meat or tuna fish or honey harvested from indentured bees, but sometimes she craved eggs, and cheese, and even butter, and she bought herself a croissant or ate a slice of whole-wheat pizza, or a whole box of saltine crackers which she ate in bed, one by one, so that they dissolved on her tongue like the heavenly host. She felt bad afterward, and her guilt mixed with missing Leon.

A year ago, she and Leon had been inseparable. They had driven north to Humboldt County, and camped near ancient roots where he held her in his arms and whispered he would make a climber of her, show her the ropes. He promised he would rappel with her into redwood crowns that swayed and creaked like floating islands in the sky, rich ecosystems unto themselves, of lichen and lungwort and insects, and even miniature trees, bursting forth like Athenas full grown from the Creator's brow. If only Jess had overcome her fear of heights to join Leon up there. If only she were not afraid, she might have been with him, and lived *in* the trees—not merely for them, or under them. Alas, the very thought of climbing made her ill. Her heart and mind longed to glide into the air, but she could not overcome her fear. Leon had tired of cajoling her to try on a harness and practice on the old oak in the Tree House yard. Impatient, he reminded her that even children could climb trees this size. Then Jess steeled herself. She said she would, but at the last minute, her stolid feet refused to leave the ground.

On weekends Leon began driving north to tree-sit in Wood Rose Glen. He scaled a redwood the Savers called Galadriel, and spent nights in her lovely branches. Jess envied that beautiful redwood, and all the people in it, although she pretended that she didn't, and went to dinner at the Bialystok house, and sometimes attended mysticism class where she sat with Mrs. Gibbs and listened to Rabbi Helfgott hold forth on God's laws, which were numerous, and His designs, which were intricate. She enjoyed the company on a Friday night. Fellow students, Israelis, tourists, Russians, sad-eyed runaways, a panoply of souls.

Jess didn't eat, but she loved to listen to the Friday-night blessings over candles, wine, and bread, and the singing, especially the wordless tunes called *niggunim,* which Mrs. Gibbs hummed and Jess sang in chorus with the others at the table. While she did not believe in mystic Judaism, she enjoyed its tropes and songs and angels. The Tree House felt chilly without Leon. At the Bialystok house, the rabbi and his wife, Freyda, welcomed her as an honored guest.

One wet December night, Freyda Helfgott sat with Jess at dinner and introduced her to her sister Chaya Zylberfenig, who was visiting from Canaan.

"This is Jess!" Freyda told Chaya. "She is one of our best singers. And she is a philosopher."

"Really?" said Chaya, and she looked at Jess with her shrewd dark eyes.

"Well, I'm not really a philosopher yet," Jess demurred.

"You look like a Gould," said Chaya.

Freyda cocked her head and looked Jess up and down. "Do you think so?"

"What's a Gould?" Jess asked, thinking that perhaps Chaya was talking about some mystic sect.

"Freyda and I are Goulds," Chaya said warmly. "A Gould is one of us."

Jess knew the Tree Savers did not feel quite the same about her, although she tried to pull her weight. While Leon was away, no one looked overjoyed to see her, or saved a place for her at the kitchen table. No one moved a car to help her park in the communal driveway when Jess returned that night, driving her sister's car. Emily was back east for the holidays, and she had left her new Audi for Jess to use.

After Friday night dinner, Jess had to drive several blocks before she found a space. Just her luck. As soon as she parked, it began to rain. She ran to the Tree House in a downpour.

Once inside, she pulled off her shoes, left them on the rubber mat, and ran all the way upstairs in her wet socks. She was hoping Leon had come home, but when she opened the door, the room was just as she had left it, bed unmade, desk strewn with unfinished problem sets for logic class, and a badly tangled Hegel paper in notes and drafts. Chilled, she took off her dripping clothes and hunted in the closet for dry sweatpants and a warm sweater.

She picked up her Fichte reader and her Hegel and her reading notes, and turned once more to her term paper on "being for self." She was staying in Berkeley for winter break so that she could take care of her Incompletes. But the work was lonely, and she paced the room and thought of Leon. Sometimes late at night he slipped into bed with her, and she turned and wrapped her arms around him, and he pulled off her T-shirt and slid on top of her to take his first rough kiss. And then sometimes she woke and realized that she had been dreaming, and she was still alone. She did not expect to be with her boyfriend all the time. She had always known he was a traveler and a politico, and she admired him for it, but she missed him, even as she wondered why she needed companionship so much.

This is a mistake, she thought as she took *Phenomenology of Spirit* into bed. The book made her sleepy at her desk. Under the covers she didn't have a chance.

What was it about Hegel that got her down? His sentences bristling with bony definitions? His arguments disguised as systems of the universe? He was everything Jess had come to loathe in her philosophy classes: stentorian about the world, but somehow alien from it. She had come to philosophy reading Plato's dialogs, and now she found herself waist-deep in inner monologs about the Self. Was there a future for her in this marshy field? Or did she like forests too much? And leafleting? And living? She propped her head on the pillow and alternately read and dozed, and dreamed that Emily asked her in Hegelian fashion: *What is now?*

Now is night, Jess answered.

What is this? Emily inquired, pointing to a lonesome pine.

This is a tree, said Jess.

If I turn around the tree vanishes, said Emily.

Now is still now, said Jess. *This is still this. Here is still here.*

How do you know?

Cautiously Jess said, *Because I'm still me.*

Really? Emily pressed. *Are you sure?*

When Jess opened her eyes and saw the blue morning light, she wasn't sure at all. She could not remember what Hegel said about consciousness; she could not even remember her own dream. All she knew was that she had to drive to San Francisco to pick up Emily from the airport.

Later she recalled forebodings, an inner certainty that something bad had happened, but in fact she felt no inkling until she discovered that Emily's car was not where she had parked it. She was sure she'd left it on the right side of Derby. Anxious, she walked up and down. Then, more anxious still, she crossed the street and walked up and down again, calling softly under her breath, "Car, car, where are you?" as though she were out looking for a cat. Had she really been so stupid? Had she really lost Emily's new car?

She ran back to the Tree House and burst into the kitchen where a bunch of Tree Savers were eating oatmeal. "Where do you call if you think your car was towed?"

Daisy looked up from her bowl. "Maybe it wasn't towed. Maybe somebody stole it."

"No!" Jess gasped. "But it's Emily's Audi!"

"Not anymore," said Daisy.

"Take a breath," a Tree Saver named Siddhartha suggested.

"Have some oatmeal," Noah offered, and he tried to serve her from the pot on the stove.

"I can't! I can't have oatmeal. I have to pick her up from the airport!" Jess rushed outside and hopped on her bike for the BART station. On the platform a flautist in patchwork pants was playing a husky, breathy "Killing Me Softly with His Song," but Jess scarcely noticed.

Emily, I have bad news. Emily, something bad happened. Emily, I'm sorry. Jess rehearsed all the way to the airport on the rattling train, until the woman sitting next to her changed seats.

"I'm sorry I'm late." Jess ran toward Emily at the baggage claim. "I'm sorry. . . . I'm so sorry."

"What happened?"

"Well . . . ," Jess began, and suddenly she thought it would be better to tell the news outside, and she started walking.

"Are you all right?" Emily followed her through the automatic glass doors.

"I'm fine," said Jess. "Except . . ."

"Jess!" Emily stopped suddenly on the walkway and her rolling suit-case stopped with her, like a well-trained dog. "Tell me what's wrong."

"I'm fine."

Emily sighed with relief. "Okay. Let's see." She studied the signs. "Ground transportation. Central parking. Short-term parking."

"Um, we won't need to . . . We don't have to go in there," Jess said.

"Where did you park?" Emily asked.

"Well—I didn't, because—I'm so sorry. I'm pretty sure someone stole your car."

"Really?"

Jess nodded miserably. "Right off Derby Street."

"Did you call the police?"

"Oh, God, I didn't think of that! I was afraid I wouldn't get here in time, so I just rushed to catch the train."

Emily shook her head at Jess.

That did it. The gesture of disbelief, with its suggestion of great forbearance. Jess burst into tears right there in front of the United Airlines terminal. "I had a feeling when I woke up this morning," she sobbed. "I just had a feeling something was wrong, and then . . ."

"Jess"—Emily unzipped the outer pocket of her rolling bag and produced a travel package of tissues—"come with me." Emily wheeled her obedient suitcase back into the airport.

"Where are you going?"

"To rent a car," said Emily.

"But what will you . . . ? How will you . . . ?"

"Please stop crying," Emily begged her sister. "I have insurance. It's just a car. It doesn't matter. I'll buy a new one." And Jess recalled that her sister was worth more than $100 million. Emily never acted spoiled or materialistic—not in the ways you would expect, but at times like these the money showed.

"Who are you calling?" Jess asked.

"Laura."

"On Saturday morning?"

"Hi, Laura. How are you? Really?" She smiled. "Listen, could you call the police and also Commerce Insurance about my car? We think it was stolen last night in Berkeley. I know!"

"I need an assistant," Jess said after Emily got off the phone.

"Why?" said Emily. "You have me."

Do I? Jess thought. Emily could give her money, but Jess's asking would have meant explaining how she'd donated her stock to Save the Trees. Emily could give advice as well about school, and Leon, and life in general, but none of the advice was what she wanted to hear.

She felt like an item on Emily's to-do list: (1) fly to Banff with Jonathan; (2) establish Veritech Foundation to promote math education in underserved communities; (3) ask Jess what she's doing with her life.

More like a fabulous old aunt than a sister, Emily began to pick up Jess every couple of weeks and take her to brunch at Greens, where she plied Jess with French toast, and Jess abstained and ordered blueberries with nothing on them. Then they would walk along the Presidio walls, with the wind whipping their hair, and they would gaze out at the ocean, and Emily would ask earnestly, "Are you sure you really want to be with Leon?"

Or Jess would sleep over at Emily's condo, and they would drive together to the White Lotus in San Jose for vegan Southeast Asian food. Coconut soup, summer rolls with peanut sauce, mock squid lo mein, mushroom hot pot, and no-dairy flan for dessert. And Emily would say, "Are you sure you want to be in grad school if you've taken so many Incompletes?"

She had met Leon one day when she came to visit Jess at the Tree House, and her response had been about what Jess expected. "Totally inappropriate! What is he—forty? *Who* is he? Do you even know?" And she had taken the extraordinary step of assuming Jess's share of the rent at her old apartment on Durant, simply because she could not bear the thought of Jess living in the Tree House.

"It's a waste of money, keeping that empty room for me," Jess told Emily.

"You need a home away from him," her sister said. "You need somewhere to go."

Jess had begun to dread these conversations. Generally, Emily's Outings, as Jess began calling them, coincided with weekends Jonathan had canceled a visit, and Jess was not above pointing this out. "You only want to see me when you can't see him," she complained on the phone one January night.

"That's not fair," Emily said.

"You mean that's not nice of me to say."

"That too."

Undaunted, Emily asked, "Do you want to go to the city on Sunday?"

"I have to work." Jess sat cross-legged on the floor with her Logic text in front of her. George needed extra hours. Classes were beginning on Wednesday, and she still had Incompletes in Hegel, and Logic, and last year's Incomplete in Philosophy of Language. She was in danger of losing her meager fellowship.

"We could go to Muir Woods."

Jess hesitated. "I would," she said, "but all you want to do is lecture me."

"I don't."

"Right, you don't want to, but you think you have to," Jess said.

"We could drive the new car."

Jess felt a pang of guilt about the old one.

"I'd like to go," said Emily.

"Don't tell me you've never been to Muir Woods before," said Jess.

"Never with you."

"You have to promise you won't have an agenda."

"No agenda," said Emily.

"And no hectoring!"

"How is hectoring different from lecturing?"

"It's louder."

Jess carried a volume of Robert Frost when Emily picked her up.

"What's that for?" Emily drove her new Audi along the coast, and the ocean rose and dipped in the sun.

"To read. To meditate!" Jess said blithely, and she thought, To avoid hectoring if necessary.

"Okay," Emily said, bemused and, sensing Jess's unsaid reason, a little hurt.

"The woods are lovely, dark, and deep," Jess intoned as they took the path down from the parking lot. She had imagined finding a spot to read and meditate, leaving Emily to walk alone for half an hour, but the trees were so tall, and the light filtering down so green that she forgot her stratagem, and her troubles as well. The saplings here were three hundred years old, their bark still purple, their branches supple, foliage feathery in the gloaming. They rose up together with their ancestors, millennia-old redwoods outlasting storms, regenerating after lightning, sending forth new spires from blasted crowns. What did Hegel matter when it came to

old-growth? Who cared about world-historical individuals? Not the sala-manders or the moss. Not the redwoods, which were prehistoric. Poten-tially posthistoric too.

Jess closed her eyes to inhale the forest with its scents of earth and pine. "Couldn't the Veritech Foundation be for forests?" Jess asked.

"No."

"Why not?"

"Because our mission is math education."

"But without trees there would be no math," Jess said. "Let alone math education. Without trees we'd suffocate—literally and figuratively."

"How do you suffocate figuratively?"

"You box yourself into received ideas, so you can't breathe. You can't even see where you are and you just . . . die from lack of perspective. Did you know that tribal peoples aren't even nearsighted? Nearsightedness is a result of reading and staring at computer screens."

Emily took off her glasses and gazed up at the blurry canopy. When she slipped her glasses on again, she much preferred the finer view. She saw the fertile detail all around her, the spores speckling the underside of ferns, the pinecones extending from every branch, pine needles drifting down and carpeting the mossy ground. Fecund, furrowed, teeming with new life—even the fallen trees blossomed forth with lichen and rich moss and ferns. Every rock and stump turned moist and rich, every broken place gave birth. Each crevice a fresh opening, each plant a possibility, putting forth its little hook or eye.

"You see?" said Jess. "And this place is tame. Up north you feel like an ant looking up at a blade of grass."

"I'm not sure I'd want to feel like an ant."

"Why not? Don't you like to feel small sometimes?"

"No," Emily said honestly.

"I do. I like it. I prefer feeling insignificant," said Jess.

"I don't believe that."

"I didn't say *worthless*, I said *insignificant*, as in the grand scheme of things."

"But why?"

"Because humans have such a complex. We're so self-involved. You have to get out to a place like this to remember how small humanity really is."

And Jess was right. Numbers didn't matter here. Money didn't count, and all the words and glances, the quick exchanges that built or tore down reputations had no meaning in this place. The air was moist. Fallen leaves, spreading branches, and crisscrossing roots wicked water, so that the trees seemed to drink the misty air.

Jess said, "All your worries fade away, because . . ."

Emily finished her thought. "The trees put everything in perspective."

"Right. It's like your soul achieves its focal distance."

The word *soul* startled Emily from her reverie. She turned on Jess. "You're dropping out of school, aren't you?"

"No—I never said that! I might take the semester off, just so I can catch up. And we've got a major appraisal coming up at Yorick's. . . ."

"Jess . . ."

"I was actually making a serious point."

"And I was asking a serious question."

"I'm not talking about graduate school. I'm talking about how you can come out here and know your place in the universe."

"And what would that be?"

"Very small. Very tangential," Jess said cheerfully.

"You're so bright," said Emily.

"I thought we said no hectoring."

"It's not hectoring—it's my . . . I just want you to do well."

"I would rather be well than do well," Jess said beatifically, and laughed at her sister's yelp of frustration.

"You actually seek out platitudes."

"I only do it to annoy."

"But you believe that stuff."

"Yeah, that's the disturbing part, isn't it?" Jess said wickedly.

Emily folded her arms across her chest. *"When are you going to embark on a career?"*

"Don't you think," Jess asked, with just the slightest edge in her voice, "that you have enough career for both of us?"

"I worry about you."

"Well, I worry about *you*," Jess countered. "You're in this crazy industry where people eat each other alive. No, wait"—she stopped Emily from interrupting—"it's in all the newspapers and the chat groups. Microsoft taking out Netscape. Veritech suing Janus."

"You heard about that?" Frankly, Emily was surprised to hear that Jess followed any news at all.

"Yeah, I read this whole article—did you see it? *Anything you can do I can do better: Janus takes on the storage sector. Veritech fights back.* It's online, on *The Motley Fool.*"

"You read *The Motley Fool?*"

"Doesn't everybody?" Jess asked. "Actually," she confessed, "Dad sent me the link. Are you really suing Janus for eighty million dollars? Isn't that, like, an expensive thing to do?"

"It's just part of doing business," said Emily, affecting a calm she didn't feel. Lawsuits, particularly the big one against Janus, were a huge drag on Veritech's finances and corporate energy. "We can afford the legal fees, if that's what you're worried about."

"That's not what I mean. There you are, getting and spending, and you're with this guy who's in the thick of it—but you're not really with him, because he's so careerist he won't come out here to be with you."

Emily started walking, brisk and purposeful, as though they had to complete the trail loop. "I don't think you should bring boyfriends into this. I don't think you should talk about Jonathan—who actually works—when you're with someone with no visible source of income or direction. . . ."

"Direction! Leon travels for his beliefs. Jonathan travels for his share price. There's a difference, don't you think? Leon has a cause. Jonathan is just another greedy, techno-freak gazillionaire."

They waited on a wooden bridge for a Japanese family taking pictures. A couple sauntered along, with hands in each other's back pockets. A small girl, only three or four years old, sprinted past in a green hooded sweater, and her little feet beat against the wood planks as she raced away, to hide, to fly. Her parents called after her nervously, "Wait for us, honey. Not so fast!" Now Emily stood perfectly still, and she said nothing, and Jess knew by her silence that she was truly angry.

"You worry about me," Jess ventured nervously, "so why can't I worry about you?"

Emily said nothing.

"You know Mom would have hated both of them," Jess cajoled.

"She would have hated Leon," Emily said, with feeling. "She would have despised him."

"She'd have hated Jonathan too."

"How do you know that? You don't know that."

"Find someone musical," Jess quoted, for she was not above citing Gillian's letters in a pinch, and she knew Jonathan could not carry a tune. *"Find someone giving. Find someone who will sacrifice for you."*

"You do look at the letters," Emily said.

"Every once in a while."

"And what do you think?"

Jess watched a thick, yellow banana slug squirm at her feet. "I think, probably, we aren't turning out the way that she intended."

"You could change that."

"*I* could? How about you?"

"I'm going to marry him."

"You keep saying that." Jess glanced at Emily's sparkling ring. "Do you have a date?"

Emily shook her head. "I can't—"

"Good for you!"

"Shh!"

Jess couldn't help smiling at the way Emily shushed her, even in front of trees.

"I meant we can't set a date right now." Neither she nor Jonathan could move cross-country yet. Not at this moment in their companies' young lives. "We're not ready."

"This is true," said Jess. "This is more than true. Jonathan will never be ready for you."

"You don't know him."

"I know enough. I've known him for three years! And I told you— I read about him in the papers, taking down Green Knight. . . ."

"The stuff in the papers isn't true."

"Couldn't you just meet someone else?" Jess asked winsomely.

"You know, Jess," Emily exploded, "I'm supposed to sit by while you drop out of school and move in with your tree lover, and it seems to me that, for someone who demands so much unconditional support, you are strangely judgmental. You stand here talking about the natural world, and how humanity is insignificant, and then you have the nerve to tell me what to do. How do *you* intend to change your life? Just what exactly is your plan?"

Jess thought for a moment. "All right," she said. "You be my witness."

With a sinking feeling Emily watched her sister place her right hand on Robert Frost. "This year," Jess vowed, "I swear I will overcome my fear of climbing."

"Oh, no."

"Oh, yes. I swear on . . ." Jess opened her book at random and looked inside. "I swear on a dimpled spider, fat and white, that I will climb this year."

"That's not what I meant, and you know it."

"This year," Jess said, "I'm going to climb Galadriel."

"You need a job," Emily told her.

"I have a job."

"You need a regular income. And health insurance! What if something happens to you? What if, for example, you fall out of a redwood?"

"I'd just die," said Jess dramatically, "so I wouldn't need medical care." When she saw the look on Emily's face she amended. "Sorry."

"Please don't face your fears."

"I want to." Jess looked up at the forest canopy.

"Jess, I'm serious. You're making a huge mistake. You're afraid of heights for a reason. You of all people should not be climbing in Wood Rose Glen. And don't think you're going to impress Leon."

"This has nothing to do with him!" Jess retorted. "This is just for me."

"Oh, God."

"It might sound New Ageist, but I don't want to live like a coward on the ground."

"I don't want you to crack your head open."

"Since when are you so risk averse?" Jess asked. "Wasn't coming out to California a risk? Wasn't founding Veritech a risk?"

"I never risked my life," said Emily.

"Okay, granted, technically you risk other people's money, but you put your life into the company, right? You invest yourself. Isn't that true? In Veritech, in the stock market, in Jonathan."

Emily looked at Jess as if to say: Where do you come from? Her analogies were so fanciful. "Yes, I'm sure every choice involves some kind of risk—but tree climbing is life-and-death."

Jess stood on the wood bridge and saw birds flying in the forest light. She saw herself flying upward, ascending to the treetops in the clouds.

But Emily interrupted, "You fall from a tree like this, that's it. You don't get another chance."

"And don't you think you can die too?" Jess countered. "Don't you think your decisions are life-and-death too?"

17

Emily did not treat business decisions as life-and-death. If she was nervous, she didn't let it show. She worked with cool confidence and inspired everyone around her. Her success inspired her employees to start dotcoms of their own. Even Charlie, the company chef, launched his own restaurant, and flush with stock, Laura's husband dropped out of his accounting program.

Laura was a little anxious when Kevin left school, and jittery as well about purchasing a two-million-dollar fixer-upper in Los Altos.

"We always said that you would teach accounting," Laura reminded her husband at their wood-grain kitchen table in Escondido Village. "That's why we came here."

"I don't like accounting," Kevin confessed.

Laura set down her mug of herbal tea. "You never said that before."

"I couldn't afford to say it before."

Laura knit her brow. She had a gentle manner, and her sweet voice belied her reservations. "I'm just not sure we should change all our plans so quickly."

"What plans? Our plans were to have a family and be happy," Kevin said. "We have the family, and now we have a chance to build a house and spend time with the kids. We're going to have a swimming pool, teach the kids to swim. You'll have a dream kitchen!"

"I don't need a fancy kitchen." She glanced at her cluttered counters.

"Don't you want more space?"

"I'd be happy with a regular kitchen with more space, not a—"

"But you deserve one. You're amazing, Laura. Just think what you could do with counter space and pull-out pantries, and you could have a whole baking station with a marble inset. . . ."

Laura smiled ruefully. "Stop watching those kitchen shows."

"We've had this amazing luck," said Kevin. "Don't be afraid to do something with it."

"But it just seems . . ." She couldn't help feeling that their ship had come in rather suddenly. Laura had taken the job at Veritech only to pay the bills while Kevin was in school, but working for Emily had proved more interesting than Laura had ever dreamed. How mysterious life was. Laura and Kevin still looked like the couple in their wedding pictures, those young sweethearts who could not afford floral arrangements and decorated the tables at their reception with autumn leaves, but now, they were interviewing architects. Kevin clipped pictures from magazines and talked about a kitchen opening out onto the garden, an airy light-filled space with double ovens and a breakfast bar. "It just seems like this will cost a fortune," Laura said.

"But we have a fortune," he reminded her.

"I'm afraid . . ."

"Afraid of what?"

"I'm worried about spoiling the children," Laura said. "I want them to do chores."

"Definitely. Everybody pitches in," said Kevin.

"I would like a better kitchen," Laura admitted, "but I want everything else to stay the same."

Laura's kind of constancy was Emily's goal at Veritech. Level-headed optimism. Veritech's products were essential, its culture young and happy, liberal in all the right ways—open, green, fun-loving, civic-minded; its people were building a corporation not only great, but good. Idealistic, and entirely invested in her creation, Emily believed this. After all, she had named Veritech to soar above the rest—to merge technology with truth.

Her concerns for Jess were real, but she went to work in high spirits, thrilled with Veritech's price, its promise, its purchase on the future. She loved her job; she loved her colleagues. Even Alex had calmed down, working in his intense and solitary way on his own project.

When Alex presented his new work on fingerprinting to the board, Emily had settled into her cushioned chair, expecting the full flowering of her password-authentication idea. No one was more surprised than she when Alex unveiled his unadulterated electronic-surveillance plans.

He had spent six months on his prototype, a surveillance tool designed to record every time a user touched a cache of data, and to follow the user's movements through the cache without his or her knowledge. A "lookup" function identified the user, a "markup" function linked the user's searches and retrievals to those of others, and the whole system was so devious and paranoid that Emily interrupted him in the boardroom. "What happened to Verify? What happened to the password applications?"

And Milton chimed in, "Have you considered privacy at all?"

"Remember," said Bruno, "we are like a strongbox, a safety-deposit box. We want to be as private as a Swiss bank account for our customers. We don't want to sell the keys."

Alex stood before them with the last slide of his PowerPoint presentation hovering on the wall, and nervously he clicked his laser pointer on and off, pointing the red light at the floor. "Look, a parking garage has security cameras. What if every car inside had its own security camera too, and when I took out my car I knew who had parked next to me, and who tried to hot-wire me, and who maybe dented me?"

"You're talking about spyware, aren't you?" said Emily. "You're talking about bundling our storage services with spyware. That's not what we discussed. That's not—"

"That's not what you wanted?" Alex shot back, and she felt his anger and his disdain. Who did she think she was? He was the artist here.

"You are suggesting we live with little cameras everywhere," said Bruno.

Tight-lipped, Alex looked at Emily. He seemed to her at once bashful and arrogant. "It's fair to everyone," he said, "if everyone is watching."

"It can't be legal," Emily told him. "And if it is legal, then it shouldn't be."

"That's what Martin's for," said Alex, referring to the company's in-house counsel.

"No," murmured Emily, furious. "No. We won't pursue this."

"We won't pursue this?" Alex cried in disbelief. His Russian accent flared, along with his temper. "Just like that? You liked the idea before. You were the one suggesting I develop it." He snapped his laptop shut.

"We discussed how you would develop it," said Emily. "We agreed that you would have free rein. You ignored everything I said, and you went off and did exactly what you wanted."

"I don't work for you, Emily," Alex declared as Milton and Bruno looked on.

"Yes, but I thought that you were working with me!"

"You don't design my projects," Alex said.

"You lied to me! You agreed to do something that—"

"I never lied to you."

"You told me you were working on a plan you had no intention of following. And it's a dangerous plan. It's a bad plan. It's not where we want to go."

"Why is that?" Alex demanded. "Because you're prejudiced! You think the storage business should be warm and friendly, right? We should sell people what they want to hear." His eyelashes were so long that they brushed against the lenses of his glasses. He was twenty-three years old. "This product doesn't make you feel good—is that what you're telling me?"

"Let's take some time," Bruno told them, and in the heat of battle they turned on him together, surprised at the interruption.

The war waged all that day and the next. Alex told Emily that she did not understand his project's potential and thought she could dilute his ideas into some trivial password application. He said she did not care about innovation. He said that she masked her subjective opinions in ethical language, but she only did it to get her way. Finally, he stood in the parking lot next to his glossy black BMW, and he accused her of trying to manipulate him.

He stood close to her, too close. "You like my ideas when you think you can control them. When I express myself, you reject my projects out of hand."

"I thought we were on the same page," Emily said.

"You mean your page?"

"You said everything was going so well."

"It *was* going well. Now you want to pull the plug on nine months' work!"

"Could you stop blaming me for just a moment?" she retorted. "Could you just step back and consider what I'm saying?"

But he would not step back. "What you're saying is totally defensive," he told her. "You want to protect what Veritech has, and you won't try anything new. Meanwhile the market is changing and you lag behind. We're leaders now. Do you think that will last? Not if you're afraid of innovation."

"I'm not afraid of innovation," she told him. "But we have to think about our direction."

His face reddened. "Our direction means we're going somewhere."

"I don't understand why you won't listen to me," she said.

"What? Do as you say? Obey you? Did you think you could manage me? Was that your idea? Why don't you listen to me, for once? Or do you think I'm too young?"

Emily spoke quietly, although she didn't feel quiet. "I thought I'd found a framework for you to pursue your work in keeping with Veritech's goals."

"I'm not interested in your frameworks, or your goals." Alex clicked his BMW keys, and she saw the lights flash on and the driver's seat adjust and the convertible top fold back like origami.

"Where are you going?"

"I'm leaving." Alex got in the car and slammed the door.

"What do you mean?"

"I'm leaving Veritech."

"Wait—"

"I'm tired of waiting." He gunned his engine.

"Contractually, the work you do here stays here," she reminded him. "Remember that."

Like an angry teenager—no backward look, no seat belt, Alex roared away. If Emily could not contain him, he would take his brilliant, conspiratorial ideas elsewhere.

That was the frightening part—his dark imagination. Alex was so smart and irresponsible. It was obvious to Emily that bundling spyware with storage services was morally wrong. Why was that not obvious to him? It was obvious to her that she had encouraged his research, but never endorsed electronic fingerprinting as a product. Why then did he accuse her of leading him on? He was always projecting past the simple truth, sending her flowers, for example, after a Veritech party, where she made the mistake of dancing with him. But he'd behaved better the past few months. He had not e-mailed her excessively, or waited for her in the halls. She'd thought he was over his infatuation. Now, she sensed the situation was much worse. His voice, his stance, his eyes were threatening. What if he drove back again and found her? He had never hurt her, but for the first time, she began to feel that he might. The parking lot was well lit, and full of cars, but what had she been doing, fighting with him there, alone? She retreated to her Audi, and locked the doors.

She checked the time and dialed Jonathan on her cell. It was just after ten at night back east. "Hi," she said, "it's me."

"Hold on," he said. "Let me get inside my office."

"I told Alex we weren't going forward with fingerprinting."

He didn't answer for a moment.

"Are you there? Jonathan?"

"Yeah, I'm here," he said.

"I feel terrible," she said.

"Why? What did he do to you?" Jonathan asked sharply.

"He didn't do anything specifically to me. He said he's leaving."

"Good."

"I don't know."

"What do you mean you 'don't know'?"

"I don't know if I can let him go. It would be such a loss," she said. "A tremendous loss."

"What—the fingerprinting stuff?"

"No. I mean Alex. The surveillance project is all wrong for us."

"Okay." Jonathan wasn't just relieved. He was delighted, liberated from the weight of Emily's proprietary secret. He had been so careful for so long, and now he felt that electronic fingerprinting was practically in the public domain. "Forget fingerprinting, and tell Alex to fuck off and die."

She laughed a little. "Oh," she said, "I wish it were that easy."

"It can be," Jonathan told her.

"I wouldn't let him have his way," said Emily.

"Of course not."

"And he absolutely could not accept my point of view."

"Sweetie, he's a shark. He's not going to change course, ever. Why are you surprised?"

She was surprised because she was Emily, and she did not share Jonathan's frank assessment of coworkers as losers, whiners, bozos, sharks. No, she imagined people were rational and courteous, as she was, and when they proved otherwise, she assumed that she could influence them to become that way. Dangerous thinking. When she was truthful, she expected to hear the truth. Reasonable, she expected reasonable behavior in return. She was young, inventive, fantastically successful. She trusted in the world, believing in poetic justice—that good ideas blossomed and bore fruit, while dangerous schemes were meant to wither on the vine. She had passions and petty jealousies like everybody else, but she was possessed of a serene rationality. At three, she had listened while her mother sang "Greensleeves" in the dark, and she'd asked: "Why are you singing 'Greensleeves' when my nightgown is blue?" Then Gillian had changed the song to "Bluesleeves," and Emily had drifted off. Those songs were over now, Gillian long gone. Despite this loss—because of it—Emily was still that girl, seeking consonance and symmetry, logic, light.

18

"What's that noise?" George asked.

"I have no idea." Jess strained her ears to hear an odd trilling in the distance.

"Is that a cell phone?"

"Oh, it must be mine." Jess jumped up. "Sorry." She tripped over Sandra's cat, and he snarled in outrage as she ran to the entryway where she and George and Colm had left their coats and bags. The outside pocket of her backpack glowed. "Hello? Hello? Hi, Emily. No, I didn't lose it. I forgot I had it." She held the phone too tightly and it beeped. "Could I call you later? I'm working. . . . Yes. It's a huge project and we're on deadline! Why are you laughing? Do you think I'm joking?" Jess looked back at the pair of camping tables George had set up in the living room. The tables were piled with folios and quartos arranged by language and by century. Colm was carrying in more books from the kitchen. "Seriously, I can't talk," Jess said. "I'll call you later."

They had just two more days to appraise the cookbooks. Colm and Jess were carrying and sorting, and George was typing in titles on his laptop. Conditions were difficult. Sandra hovered. Colm was allergic to the cat. They couldn't wear shoes in the house, so they padded around in thick socks. In January Sandra seemed to skimp on heat. Colm wore a vest over his button-down shirt, and a tweed jacket on top of that. George wore a thick black pullover, and Jess a giant brown cardigan with a red knit hat pulled down over her ears. George had to suppress a smile the first time he saw the hat.

"What?" Jess demanded.

"Nothing." George tried not to look at her.

They worked long hours like a sequestered jury, deliberating at the tables with copious evidence before them. There were eighteenth-century German cookbooks with fold-out diagrams of table settings, plates and platters arrayed like planets, little dishes orbiting larger courses. There were cookbooks small enough to fit in the palm of the hand, and others gargantuan, so that George used special foam book cradles to hold them open and protect their bindings. To assess these volumes was to consider tastes both delicate and omnivorous, to view exquisite illustrations like the French engravings of dessert spoons, or grotesque—like the plate in *Le Livre Cuisinaire* of *tête de veau en tortue,* a savory tart garnished with red crustaceans, a still life with claws and tentacles and beady eyes. The task would have been daunting even without the collector's bookmarks, notes, and clippings; his menus on scrap paper, where he drew up imaginary feasts with inky thumbnails of partridges and steaming puddings: *Pudding boiled, pudding of cream, pudding quaking, pudding shaking* . . . Often as the collector wrote, his firm hand grew tremulous. His print would wobble, and his notes burst into erotopoetic menus, as recitative lifts into song:

First course:
Rabbits

Second:
Cockles

Third:
Loin of Veal

Fourth:
Quails

Fifth:

Sparrows

Sixth:

Jellies

When her loose gown did from her shoulders fall
And she me caught in her arms long and small,
And therewithal so sweetly did me kiss,
And softly said, "Dear heart, how like you this?"

"He knew his Wyatt." Colm leaned back in his chair, pushed his wire-rimmed glasses up, ran his hand through his thick brown hair. Young fogey that he was, nearly British after his long studies of English literary history, he flushed red in patches on his Shropshire-lad cheeks, and fanned himself with one of George's auction catalogs.

"Did you see this?" Jess plucked a small sheaf of notes from *The Accomplisht Cook*. The papers bookmarked a passage titled "To dress Tortoise." *Cast off the head, feet, and tail, and boil it in water, wine, and salt, being boil'd pull the shell asunder, and pick the meat from the skins, and the gall from the liver, save the eggs whole if a female, and stew the eggs, meat and liver in a dish with some grated nutmeg, a little sweet herbs minced small, and some sweet butter* . . . "He went to town with this one." Jess read the collector's notes under her breath. "*To begin with, Turtle soup, / to sail with, Turtle soup . . . / to dine on mince, and slices of quince, / to eat with a runcible spoon* . . . What is a runcible spoon anyway?" She unfolded the collector's notes to see his drawing. "That's not a spoon! That's more of a . . . hmm . . ."

"Focus," George admonished as he examined Anna Wecker's tiny 1679 *Neu, Köstlich, und nutzliches Koch-buch*. Worms had drilled through the later chapters, and the title page was much worn, but George marveled at the gorgeous typeface, so feminine, capitals all curves.

They had to hurry, but the longer they looked, the more convinced they became that they were holding treasures in their hands, and the more convinced they became, the harder it was to evaluate the books. The recipes entranced, and the collector's notes distracted. They could not stop peeking at McClintock's black-ink menus and thumbnail sketches.

"Jess!" George told her. "Put that back."

She took a last look at the turtle-soup drawings, replaced them, and turned to another treasure, a fragile American quarto titled *The Art of Cookery Made Plain and Easy*, by "A Lady." The book fell open in her hands to "Chap. XV.: Of Making Cakes &c." *To Ice a great Cake*, Jess read, *Take the whites of twenty-four eggs* . . . and even as she read, new sketches fluttered onto her lap. A woman's arm, a torso, three different drawings of a pair of legs. Legs crossed, legs spread, legs pressed close together—each study small, but revealing—tendrils of pubic hair, pointed toes—all drafted with a naturalist's attention.

"I wonder who she was."

"That's Hannah Glasse," George said after a quick search online. "And watch the binding please."

"I didn't mean the author." Jess folded the little nudes away again.

"Oh, my God," George gasped. "This is a signed *Mrs. Fisher*."

Jess leaned over the table to view the book he held open in his hands. The book was slender, the pages smooth and unspotted, with clear simple type. Recipes for *Sweet Pickle Pears, Sweet Pickle Prunes, Sweet Watermelon Rind Pickle, Onion Pickles*.

Colm shook his head. "I think you've got to bring somebody in."

For once they could speak freely. Sandra was tending the front yard—at least for the moment. She never stepped outside for long, and when she did, hacking back the blackberry canes, she didn't venture far. Through the window they could see her in her old straw hat.

George told Colm, "If we bring in a specialist, we risk another rival." He'd informed Sandra that he knew Raj was looking at the books, and he'd tried to find out who else she had invited in, but she only turned away.

"You could get a scholar and pay him up front as a consultant and he doesn't get to bid," said Colm.

"It wouldn't work that way."

Colm whipped out his handkerchief and blew his nose. "I think you'd get a more accurate estimate—maybe lower than what we would come up with."

"Maybe higher." George turned back to the reference books and catalogs in front of him. "I just don't know what Raj is offering," he murmured. "If I had a . . ."

His voice faded as Jess returned to the kitchen for another stack. How strange the disemboweled room looked with its cabinets open, emptied of their treasures. A skin-deep kitchen, cupboards bare, while the countertops remained cluttered with cheap cookware, spotted bananas, coupons, receipts, bills. A calligraphed card lay open next to the toaster.

"Come in here! You have to see this."

"Don't tell me you found another Gouffé," Colm called back.

"No, it's really strange."

"Could you just bring it out?" George didn't want to stop typing.

But she was afraid to pick up the card. Dramatically, she thought: What if Sandra caught her prying? What if Jess's fingerprints were on it? "No, you have to come here."

Reluctantly, Colm came in. He stood with Jess and the two of them gazed at the card. "George . . . ," Colm called in a weary voice, "you'd better have a look."

Evidently unworried about fingerprints, George picked up the card and read it twice.

A DONATION TO THE GAY AND LESBIAN LEGAL ALLIANCE

HAS BEEN MADE

IN HONOR OF SANDRA MCCLINTOCK

BY

RAJEEV CHANDRA

"Raj!" George was amazed at his ingenious friend.

"I didn't know Sandra was gay," Jess said.

The three of them stared at the card in George's hand. "I don't know what she is," George said at last.

"Maybe we should find out," Colm suggested.

"We aren't even half done."

"Why isn't Raj sorting?" Jess asked.

"I'm sure he's seen everything," George said nervously.

"How do you know?"

Because that would be just like Raj, George thought, to assess everything in advance and on his own time and then make his own preemptive offer. "He's very experienced," George said. "And very clever."

"He knows Sandra," Jess said. Softly, Geoffrey slipped into the room. On little cat feet, he sprang onto the kitchen counter. Unconsciously, Jess lowered her voice in front of the cat. "What have we found out about her?"

"I know enough," George said. "She needs money. She wants to play me against Raj for the best price. She claims she's afraid to sell the books. She's nuts."

"That's not the way to think about it," Jess said. "You've got everything backward."

"Oh, really?"

"This strategy of assessing books is wrong."

"And what would you suggest, Jess?" George inquired.

"Hmm," Jess said, delaying her answer just a moment, for the simple reason that she enjoyed seeing George exasperated. "I would suggest that instead of focusing on the collection, you think about the owner."

"The lichenologist."

"No, I mean Sandra. She's the one you should assess. You need to figure out what she really wants."

"Money," said George.

"That would be easy," Jess said. "I don't think it's purely money that she's after. I think she wants to tell someone her story."

"Oh, God," said George.

"She wants to be heard."

"Obviously, Raj has been listening." Colm replaced the calligraphed card on the counter.

"But she's looking for the best listener."

"I hope you're wrong," said George, "because hearing this woman's superstitious, delusional . . ."

"How do you know that she's delusional?" Jess asked him.

"I don't have patience," George said.

"Don't you want this collection?" Jess pressed. "Isn't that why we're here?"

They heard Sandra at the door, and rushed back to their places.

Sandra did not say hello. Well aware they had been whispering, she set her hat atop the bookcase full of cut glass and marched upstairs into—her bedroom? Her study? They heard her shut the door.

Jess and Colm looked at each other. Jess mouthed to George, "Go talk to her."

George shook his head and put his finger to his lips.

You're making a mistake, she scribbled on a note card. They all looked at Sandra's closed door. Something was up, Jess thought. One of them would have to speak to Sandra. One of them had to learn the thing Raj had already discovered: her history, her crisis, her fantasy.

George tried to keep working but he stopped, hands hovering above the keyboard.

Colm took off his glasses. He had to sneeze, but he could not. Then he had to sneeze again. He saw cat hair everywhere. "Send her," he said, and he meant Jess. "Send her."

It was one thing to theorize about Sandra, and quite another to climb the creaky blond wood stairs and face her closed door. "Sandra," Jess called softly, but she heard no sound.

She descended the stairs halfway and looked back. Colm pantomimed his suggestion to knock again.

Up she went. "Sandra," Jess called, knocking louder.

"It's unlocked," Sandra said, and Jess let herself in, shutting the door behind her.

The study was so tight that when Sandra turned around in her swivel chair, she almost ran over Jess's toes. The room was slanted, tucked under the heavy angled roof of the house; its single window, large and low, looking out on the riotous garden; the desk, rough boards, built under the window. The walls were lined with scientific journals. *The Lichenologist, International Journal of Mycology and Lichenology, Proceedings of the Inter-*

national Symposium on Moss and Liverwort. A framed black-and-white photo stood on one shelf. A serious and homely looking man in wire-rimmed glasses.

Sandra was wearing a long flowing batik dress, but her posture was schoolmarmish as she sat up paying bills, stamping and addressing envelopes; her mouth tight, puckered in concentration. Jess had a fleeting memory—or was it her imagination? The image of her mother sewing, with her mouth tight, full of pins.

"What is it?" Sandra asked, glancing up.

Jess took off her knit hat and held it in her hands. "Your cookbooks are the most beautiful I've ever seen."

"Have you seen a lot of cookbooks?"

"They're the most beautiful *books* I've ever seen," Jess amended. "I just want to assure you that we are treating them with respect. And we realize that they have sentimental value."

"They don't have sentimental value for *me*," Sandra said, and she turned back to her bills.

"Oh!" Jess could not conceal her surprise. "I'm sorry."

"What are you sorry for?"

"I misread you," Jess said. "I thought you were upset."

"I am upset." Sandra's voice caught. "I'm upset about my daughter. I'm upset about my uncle. I'm upset about the situation."

Jess might have escaped then into the other room. Perhaps she should have, but she could hear the desperation in Sandra's voice.

She knelt down level with Sandra. "What is the situation?"

"I promised my uncle I wouldn't sell."

"Do you think maybe he would understand?"

Sandra thought about this. "No," she said. "He was in the hospital. He weighed nothing. He had no children. He was ninety-three years old. He was very clear. He said, 'Sandra, you're my only niece. I'm leaving you the house. Do anything you want with it, but don't sell the books.'"

"Wow," said Jess.

Sandra nodded grimly, appreciating Jess's awestruck response. "He said, 'Promise me that you'll take care of them.'"

"But did you have any idea?"

"No!"

"Didn't you come over to the house to see them? Didn't you ever see them in the kitchen?"

"I lived in Oakland. He lived here, and he was reclusive. We weren't close. I came twice, and both times he offered me iced tea. He never invited me inside his kitchen. He wouldn't even let me clear away my glass."

"When he said don't sell the books, you thought he meant this stuff?" Jess pointed to the study bookcases.

"Of course."

"How can you make a promise when you don't know exactly what you're promising?"

Sandra closed her eyes. "That's what I tell myself. That's what I keep telling myself. I'm afraid of him."

Jess nodded. Instinctively, she understood what George did not. That as far as Sandra was concerned, Tom McClintock still hovered in the house.

"I believe in past lives," Sandra explained, and she opened her gray eyes. "I lived before."

Like a girl in a labyrinth, Jess tried to follow. "Really?"

"I believe we've all lived before, and will again."

Someone else might have laughed, or cringed, or backed away. Jess asked, "What were you?"

"A Russian princess," Sandra said quite seriously. "In the days of the Tsars."

Which Tsar? Jess wondered, but thought it best not to inquire. She knew the kind of Russian princess Sandra meant: the kind who wore silk and velvet and danced in palaces and rode in sleighs through fairy-tale snows in the early pages of Tolstoy's novels, until narrowly escaping execution at the hands of the Bolsheviks. "What will you be next?"

"That's what frightens me," said Sandra. "Every life hinges on the one before. And what I do now will shape . . ."

"I understand," said Jess. Emily would have asked: Why is it that those of us who were serfs in some past life never remember the experience? But Jess thought: How dreadful to feel that guilt accrues like debt from this world to the next.

"Do you think your uncle is living a new life?"

Sandra nodded.

Jess looked at the photograph on the desk. Unsmiling, weak-chinned, the lichenologist seemed to peer out at the world from behind his glasses. "And do you think he's sort of—watching you?"

She closed her eyes again.

"And you'll join him there—and then maybe he'll punish you?"

She closed her eyes tighter.

"You had no idea what he was giving you," Jess said. "How could you have any idea what these books are worth?"

Sandra's eyes popped open. "How much *are* they worth?" she asked, and Jess felt a prick of fear; she felt the difficulty of her position, for Sandra was no longer keening and mystical.

"We'll have to finish the appraisal," Jess said cautiously, "and then George will make the offer."

"I don't like him," Sandra said in a low voice. "I don't think I can trust him."

"You can," Jess assured her. "He may come off as impatient or arrogant at times, but he's a good man."

"Why do you say that?"

"I've worked for him more than a year."

"And what do you know about him?" Sandra asked.

Jess considered the question. "He's old-fashioned," she said at last. "He has a sense of history. If he had a past life, he would have been a gentleman—even though he acts so adversarial. He loves books more than anything in the world."

"But will he keep the collection intact?"

"I think so."

"Will he promise?"

Jess thought about the books George flipped regularly, the Whitman he had sold within days of acquisition, the small collection of early twentieth-century poets he had bought from a dealer in Marin and quickly dispersed. "You'll have to talk to him," Jess said.

"I don't like talking to him," said Sandra. "I don't want to sell these books. Do you understand? They're private. They are my uncle's past life."

"Then maybe he doesn't need them anymore?" Jess ventured.

Sandra bristled, and instantly Jess saw her mistake. In Sandra's mind everything was necessary. Every artifact counted in some grand celestial tally.

"I don't want to sell them. I would never sell them for myself. My daughter needs money."

For a moment Jess wondered whether this daughter was real. Perhaps she was imaginary too? A past daughter? But she followed Sandra down this passageway as well. She chose to believe her. "What's wrong?" she asked. "What's happened to her?"

"She's losing her children," Sandra said.

"What do you mean? Divorce?"

"Leslie raised them, but her partner is the biological mother."

So Leslie is the one Raj meant to honor, Jess thought.

"You have no idea what it's like," said Sandra.

"I don't," Jess admitted humbly.

"Leslie was the one who cared for them. She was the one who woke with them and fed them, and pushed them in the stroller to the playground every day. She was the stay-at-home mother. She dedicated her life to those boys. They're all she's got, and her ex took them to New Jersey."

That's why she needs money. Legal fees, Jess thought.

"I'm worried," Sandra said. "I can't sleep at night. My daughter hasn't seen her children in over a year. And I'm afraid . . ." Here, her voice broke entirely. "They're only five and three. I'm sure they don't remember her."

Jess answered gently. "You never know what children can remember. I lost my mother when I was five, but I still remember her. I think I remember her sewing, and I remember standing on a chair and baking with her. And also . . ." Jess searched for another memory she could put into words, some event she might produce, although most of her memories were flickers: light and shadow, hedges along the sidewalk, her mother's white hands pulling her away when she tried to lick—what was it?—a fence? She loved the tang of metal. The ladder to the slide?

"You're missing the point," said Sandra.

Again Jess felt that this was a test, and it was no ordinary exam: not a test of what Jess knew, but of what Sandra believed. "Your situation is more complicated than your uncle could have imagined," said Jess. "You wouldn't be selling for a profit. You'd sell to pay your lawyers. In that case, don't you think that he'd approve?"

Sandra searched Jess's face.

"I don't know Raj. I don't know what Raj would do with these books, but George appreciates them. He'll study them—and so will I, and so will Colm. We're not just collectors. We're readers."

Sandra nodded.

Emboldened, Jess continued, "And wherever your uncle is, he'll understand, because the point is, children shouldn't have to remember their mother."

Then tears started in Sandra's eyes. All the tension seemed to leave her body, and she sighed, a drawn-out sigh. "Yes," she said, and then, almost a sob, "Yes. That's true."

When Sandra opened the study door, George and Colm started up. Colm raised his eyebrows questioningly; George searched her face, anxious for the verdict. Jess didn't say a word in front of Sandra. She couldn't gloat. She pressed her lips together, trying not to smile. Oh, she'd done well—and George and Colm didn't even know it yet. There they were, waiting in suspense. She bit her lip, determined to keep a poker face, but her cheeks began to dimple anyway. She'd passed the test: She'd got Sandra's Sphinxian riddle right. Princess in the morning. Bitter in the afternoon. Grandma in the evening. What am I? Lonely.

Eager, mystified, George looked at Jess, and she met his gaze. Who knew that Jess, who was such a terrible salesman, would be a brilliant buyer? Jess hadn't known herself—but here she was, victorious. Didn't you think that I'd win her over? Jess asked George with her eyes. Didn't you think that I could win these books for you?

PART FIVE

Free Fall

～

March through August 2001

19

The markets swooned. Like a beautiful diver, the Nasdaq bounced three times into the air and flipped, somersaulting on the way down. Tech stocks once priced at two hundred, and then seventy-three, and then twenty-one, now sold for less than two dollars a share. Companies valued in the billions were worth just millions, and with a blood rush, investors thought, So this is gravity, this is free fall. This is what the end feels like, ripping through water. But the end was not the end. There were still more ends to come.

Looking back, analysts could predict the crash. They spoke of weak fundamentals, softening in the tech sector, reckless speculation. But who can measure appetite, or predict the limits of desire? Who can chart love's parabola, from acquaintance to infatuation to estrangement? Multiply by millions buying and selling. Small exits accrued into a great migration, darkening the sun. So many hearts beat rapidly together, so many investors rose up calling to one another as they took flight, that it seemed there were no buyers left, except the day traders screaming obscenities on message boards, scavenging and wheeling like gulls.

Rabbi Helfgott was one such day trader, although he did not post on message boards. Waking before dawn to log in as the markets opened in New York, he made a few dollars, even as the crash wiped out his portfolio. He blinked sometimes and shook his head, as his investments melted away. Veritech at two, Janus at a dollar fifty, ISIS at seventy-five cents. Nevertheless, he remained hopeful. He had a sanguine nature, prayed three times a day, and believed the Messianic age was imminent. Therefore, he was better prepared than most for market turbulence.

He himself had read some economics. In fact he had read *The Wealth of Nations,* a book Jessamine had recommended, and he saw in Adam Smith a very Jewish form of Providence. What was the invisible hand Smith always spoke about, but the hand of God? What was a correction, but the Creator's recalibration of the world? Had he studied physics in college, Helfgott might have learned that what goes up comes down. But the rabbi had not attended college, only seminary, where he learned that what comes down, must rise again. Applying this principle, he believed that what the markets destroyed they would, God willing, speedily restore, and this belief sustained him, as did the knowledge that he owned the Bialystok Center of Berkeley free and clear. Many years before, he had saved the life of a young man, an addict in the ashram occupying the building, and the boy's grateful father had purchased the property and then sold it to the rabbi for a dollar. Now the young man was married, living in New Jersey, and a father himself! Such was the marvelous circularity of exchanges. Such, with God's help, was the world's hopeful trend, difficult in the short term, but in the long run beautiful.

Others were not so philosophical. When ISIS hit a new low of seventy—not seventy dollars, but seventy *cents*—Jonathan took the debasement personally. His high-flying company was about to be delisted, too small to register on the Nasdaq stock exchange. He knew that ISIS would come roaring back. He knew because he would make it happen. In the meantime—well, he hated meantimes.

Sleepless, he paced his Somerville apartment. His roommates had moved on, but Jonathan still lived there and he hated that too. He hated the stasis, the stalemate developing between him and Emily. Although he and Emily had set the date for their October wedding, they had not bought a house, nor had she left Veritech. She was rolling out a new product. She was setting up a research group for Alex—an unfathomable idea—rewarding Alex for his bad behavior. Twice, three times, she post-poned her move east, and then she pushed the wedding off as well.

She said she missed him. At the end of every visit her eyes filled with tears—but she returned to California anyway, and somehow she re-mained patient. Where did this excessive patience come from? Did she still have reservations? She had told him in her sweet teacherly way that now she was ready—*they* were ready—to be engaged, but he had no idea what she meant by readiness. *Waiting, taking time, becoming ready*—this was the vocabulary women used to divert attention from what they wanted. And what did women want? The same thing men did—only slower.

What would it be like to live without this level of intense anticipation? Like ancient nobles he and Emily waged wars and signed treaties, con-vening privy councils in their separate conference rooms. What would it be like when Emily abdicated to live with him full-time? Would she? Could she?

Hard times. He kicked an empty soda can across the bare floor. Thirty million invested at Goldman Sachs seemed a paltry sum, a pittance, next to the hundreds of millions he had once possessed on paper. What Jonathan had was nothing next to what he wanted. Prisoner of his enor-mous expectations, he paced the floor, plotting to reclaim what might have been.

Friday when the markets closed, ISIS had climbed a penny to seventy-one cents. Then Jonathan called a company meeting in the newly renovated lobby. Over one hundred Cambridge employees sat on the gray carpet, while oldsters like Dave sat in swivel chairs, and Jonathan, Orion, Aldwin, and Jake stood together in the center, all four of them in town at once, like a rock band reuniting without instruments, four accustomed to mosh pits of celebration, now gazing out at anxious upturned faces.

Shakespeare's Henry rallied his troops at Agincourt: *If we are mark'd to die, we are enow / To do our country loss, and if to live, / the fewer men, the greater share of honour.* At a later date, George Washington tried to mol-lify his mutinous men: . . . *let me entreat you, Gentlemen, . . . to rely on the plighted faith of your Country, and place a full confidence in the purity of the intentions of Congress.* Now Jonathan took the floor. "Okay, guys, listen up. There's share price and there's reality. Prices go up and they go down. There is a certain amount of randomness built into the system, a certain amount of envy and media shit, a certain amount of stuff happening in the market as a whole that for better or worse reflects on us. But the reality is our products, our services, and our customers. That's what you have to wake up and think about every single day. Excellence, accountability, and the bottom line. We did not establish ISIS as some fly-by-night dot-com."

"Yeah!" the programmers cheered.

"We established ISIS for the long haul, and we will be here for the long haul."

"YEAH!" they cheered louder.

"You guys are not involved in a low-rent operation."

"No kidding," Aldwin said under his breath. The lease on the Kendall Square building cost almost two million a month, and he was looking for cheaper space.

"Stand up," Jonathan ordered his people. "Everybody stand up." Programmers and secretaries, marketing team and legal counsel all scrambled to their feet and scrummed together around their bold, ruddy-faced captain. "You guys are not geeks for hire," Jonathan announced. "You didn't come looking for a quick buck. You came to *build* something. You came to change the way the world does *business*. You guys are the best."

"Whoooo!"

"You kick ass!" Jonathan shouted.

"Yesss!"

"You guys are *animals*!" This last unleashed such a frenzy that Jonathan couldn't see Sorel pushing through the crowd. She had been on shift in the control center. And because everyone else was at the meeting, she alone, gazing at the bank of monitors, had seen the first signs of trouble in the ISIS security network. A single white dot representing a data center in Shanghai turned emergency red.

"Security breach!" Sorel cried, but even as she spoke, another dot turned red as well, and then all the dots around it until, like a plague, hundreds of white points all across the digital Earth broke out in red, a contagion spreading through thousands of ISIS data centers from Beijing to Baltimore.

She worked her way through the crowd, but she could not get close to the front. Only Orion saw her. He caught her eye and mouthed, "What's wrong?"

She shouted, "Lockbox is down. Lockbox is broken." But the screams and cheers continued, drowning her out, resolving into call and response.

"Who's the best?" Jonathan shouted.

"We're the best!"

"Who's the rest?"

"Fuck the rest!"

Orion pushed his way to Jonathan. He told Jonathan softly, underneath the rising noise of the crowd, "Lockbox is broken."

Jonathan didn't hear him.

Orion cupped his hands and repeated directly into Jonathan's ear, "Lockbox is broken."

The blood drained from Jonathan's face. His jaw tightened. He held up his hand for quiet and the roar died down. "All right!" he said. His voice was grim, but only Orion and Sorel knew why. The others heard grim satisfaction as he bellowed, "Back to work!"

What new hell was this? Hackers had targeted Lockbox and found the tiny chinks Orion had identified long ago. Those chinks were now fissures compromising the security system. Alarms were sounding all through ISIS as programmers, product testers, and Customer Care struggled to make Lockbox safe again. Clients were panicking, and every hour, the public-relations crisis grew.

For two days and two nights, the ISIS team struggled to make Lockbox right. Projects went on hold. Travel plans were canceled. A programmer sat at every computer, a Customer Care counselor manned every phone. The tide of empty soda cans was rising.

Orion and the Lockbox team were working as fast as they could, but the break was bad, and the news spread everywhere, from *The Wall Street Journal* to *The Motley Fool*. At the end of the second night, Dave broke precedent and made an executive decision. ISIS was recalling Lockbox. All Lockbox customers were being upgraded automatically for no charge to ChainLinx.

"No!" Jonathan cried out at the emergency board meeting. Even now he hated to admit that Lockbox was flawed.

"We've almost got it up again," said Jake.

But Dave shook his head, as if to say, Boys, boys. "Sometimes," he said, "you have to look at the big picture. You have to think about our customers, our reputation, and our weakening position. We aren't talking about saving Lockbox anymore. We're talking about saving ISIS."

Exhausted, Orion rested his head on his arms right there on the table. Bitterly, he thought of the old fights. If Jonathan had listened to him . . . If Jonathan had not been in such a rush . . . He looked up at Jonathan across the table. What were the chances that Jonathan would apologize? What were the chances he would show the slightest regret?

Nil. Jonathan didn't even glance at Orion as he swept out of the glass-walled conference room.

But there was no point thinking about that now, when there was so much to do. There was the conversion of every Lockbox account to ChainLinx. There were phone calls. There were press releases. All through the hallways, up and down the stairwells, ISIS hummed with new activity. Even as the programmers gave up their nighttime vigil, the morning reinforcements arrived. Support staff trooped into the building with their cups of coffee, and Mel Millstein showed up at the quaint hour of nine. As Orion walked out into the hall and headed downstairs, he felt relief. The worst had happened, Lockbox was history. Now ISIS could rebuild. His resentment faded, and he felt pride instead, a strange pride at this resilient organism, this company of so many different parts and people—a society of its own, a world unto itself, a little planet against the hostile universe. He knew how Jonathan felt. Let the markets fall, let the siege begin, ISIS would outlast all comers, hackers, analysts, and doubters. Jonathan's faith never wavered, and Orion began to feel partisan too.

"He's very sure of himself, isn't he?" Sorel said of Jonathan.

Orion was giving her a lift on his bicycle. She perched on the seat and he walked the bike, one hand on the frame, the other on the handlebars. Gently he wheeled her along, as a knight might lead a maiden on a palfrey.

"Well, he has a right to be," Orion said.

"Are you defending his mistake?" The afternoon was sunny and might have been warm, if not for the brisk March wind that blew her skirt over her knees. She was wearing her long loose coat, and the black satin lining showed at the bottom, because her hem was down. She'd strapped on her guitar like a backpack. Her red-gold hair spilled over her shoulders. "He's insufferable."

"He gets results."

"Not in this market."

"If anyone can get the job done, it's Jonathan," Orion said.

"Oh, please! You sound like his henchman."

"His henchman? No."

She wondered, "Are you succumbing to some sort of Stockholm syndrome where you start identifying with your oppressor?"

"How is Jonathan my oppressor?" Orion protested. "He's my colleague—and my old friend."

She looked down on him for that. He could see the expression on her face, a kind of disdain coming over her. In her mind, Jonathan was the enemy.

"What's wrong with working with people?" he asked defensively.

"Hmm. I liked you better before when you were more . . . disaffected. You were more original then."

They were walking through Cambridgeport, where the streets were down to their last piles of ash-gray snow. The trees were bare, but the clapboard houses colorful, painted purple with teal trim, or ochre and bloodred, or lavender, or puce, and the yards were filled with art as well as cars—scrap-metal cats and penguins—ceramic pots bristling with fierce crocuses. They had been working day and night, troubleshooting Chain-Linx to take on the massive new customer load.

"What day is it?" Orion asked as they arrived at her place.

"Monday," she said. "No, I think Tuesday."

Molly was on call. "I wish I could . . . come in."

She shook her head. "Thanks for the lift." She hopped off the bicycle in front of her ramshackle worker's cottage. She'd done some work on it, but the house was still a work in progress. Wood supports propped up the porch. "Go home to bed."

But he kissed her instead. Arms inside her unbuttoned coat, he found the gap between her skirt and soft wool sweater. She was so long and slender—sleek like the girl-women in his father's poems, her breasts like buds under his fingers. She didn't push him away. He felt the hollow inside her hip bone, and her shoulder blades were like folded wings.

"Don't you want me to?" he whispered.

"No," she said longingly, "not at all."

"Not at all! Don't overstate your case."

"It's a good case," said Sorel. "It's a strong case."

"A Lockbox?"

"Right. Except that you can't hack your way inside."

"I wouldn't," he said, but even as he released her, even as he watched her unlock her door, he longed to solve this puzzle, and find a way to her encrypted heart.

20

When the market sank, Bruno sent an e-mail about riding out the storm. Emily kept working without complaint, but a little furrow appeared between her eyes, a subtle wrinkle, not a worry line, but a mark of concentration. The stock price fell to forty on Tuesday, then to thirty-three on Wednesday, and finally hit a new low of sixteen on Thursday, and everyone was shocked, because there was no good reason for the steep decline, and yet the price was falling all the same.

On the upswing, every Veritech employee felt masterful. Now those masters felt like leaves tossed in unexpected storms. Laura read *Winnie-the-Pooh* at bedtime to her children in her unfinished house, and as she read about Pooh's tumble through the branches of the oak tree, she held the baby, Katie, in her lap, and she thought: This is exactly what it's like to lose half your net worth in three days.

"Oh, help!" said Pooh, as he dropped ten feet onto the branch below him.

"If only I hadn't—" he said, as he bounced twenty feet on to the next branch.

"You see what I meant to do . . ."

"Of course it was rather—" he admitted as he slithered very quickly through the next six branches. . . .

"More!" demanded Meghan from the bottom bunk.

And Justin sat up in the top bunk and said, "Why are you stopping, Mommy?"

And Katie pulled Laura's hair.

But Laura could not help pausing to consider how well A. A. Milne described the falling sensation, the surprise and sudden thumps as one lost economic altitude, and began to wonder whether renovating in Los Altos was such a good idea, and then, whether private school made sense, and finally, whether leasing a car might be more prudent than paying cash.

Kevin told Laura, "We can't panic. It would be terrible to sell all the stock we have left."

"What do you mean, 'the stock we have left'?" Laura asked him.

"We lost some," he admitted as he helped her hook up the rolling dishwasher to the sink in their temporary kitchen.

"How do you lose stock?" Laura asked him.

He didn't answer immediately.

"Kevin?"

"I borrowed on margin to pay the contractor," he said.

"You what?"

"I didn't want to sell, because I knew Veritech was going back up."

She turned on him. "Can you hear what's wrong with that?" she demanded. "Can you even hear?"

"I guessed wrong," Kevin said.

"No, that's not what I meant, Kevin James Miller. What's wrong is that you didn't ask *me*. What were you thinking, borrowing against my stock?"

"It was our stock. And I'm sorry, Laura."

"I earned it," she declared. "It was mine, and, yes, I made it ours. But it was never *yours* to do what you wanted. It was never yours to decide about without consulting me."

"You never showed any interest in handling the money," Kevin pointed out.

She had never been so angry. "You never *asked*."

"Do you think you could have given me better advice? Whenever I asked about investments in the past, you trusted my judgment."

Laura stood before him in their plywood makeshift kitchen, and she said, "Maybe I have a little more sense than you do. Or if I don't, then maybe we'd make our mistakes together."

"We've still got stock," he soothed her. "Up 'til now, we've been very, very lucky."

She folded her arms across her chest. "Don't you ever gamble with my hard-earned luck again."

"I said I was sorry!"

"Because if you do, I'll leave you," she warned him, and she was half serious. "I'll take the children and start a company of my own."

He wasn't sure quite how to take this. She had a sweet, soft voice; a patient, forgiving nature. She played the flute. "I always said you could start a bakery." He tried to steer the conversation back to calmer waters. "You could sell your lemon—"

"I could sell truth serum," she told him.

"Laura! I keep telling you—I'm sorry. I didn't think—"

"You didn't think I'd *care?*"

She cared enormously. Everybody did, but like all watched pots, the market would not boil.

At this moment George chose to buy. He bought Cisco at bargain-basement prices. He purchased IBM and Apple. And he paid cash for Tom McClintock's cookbooks. He wrote a check for just under half a million dollars, exactly the money Sandra needed for her daughter's legal fight.

Clever George. He knew the books were worth much more, and he unpacked them with guilt and pleasure, turning pages with sumptuous color plates, unfolding the collector's notes, strange and brittle as pressed flowers. What rare and secret treasures, historical and also private. Not just a collection, but a reliquary. George had pulled off a bibliophile's Louisiana Purchase, or rather, Jess had pulled off the deal for him.

His spring party, therefore, was mostly in Jess's honor, although he did not advertise this. He presented the gathering as a viewing of the McClintock cookbooks, which he had installed in special cases in his great room.

The glass-fronted bookcases were quartersawn oak and built quite low, underneath his west windows. Atop the bookcases he had built illuminated glass display cases—the kind he had seen at the Huntington Library—so that on occasion he could show off certain volumes. For the party he had set up a little display of women's cookbooks: the Brandenburg, the Salzburg, *The Compleat Housewife. American Cookery. A New Present for A Servant-Maid,* the expanded 1771 edition of Eliza Haywood's 1743 handbook.

The cabinetry was exquisite, book-matched for George's precious books. He did not fault his architect and carpenter for assuming the party was to celebrate their months of work. Sandra was coming, of course, along with her daughter, and George expected Nick and Julia, and antiquarian colleagues and Microsoft friends. Gracious in defeat, and hinting impishly at a purchase of his own, Raj accepted George's invitation. Colm would be there. Colm had unpacked and installed the cookbooks. By the time the bookcases were ready, Jess had been traveling up north to chain herself to trees, to demonstrate in scenes George tried not to think about. Colm had done the work, but Jess was the one George thought about. She was the one he planned for. She had never been to the house, and he walked through the rooms, trying to imagine her impressions. He thought of her when he chose his champagne. He imagined her nibbling the strawberries he bought at the Farmers' Market. She did eat strawberries, didn't she? He prepared platters of cheese and biscuits, grapes, fresh figs, poached quince. He hired a pastry chef to bake lighter, smaller versions of the old recipes: bite-sized tarts, tiny crème brûlées. George's housekeeper, Concepcion, climbed a painter's ladder to dust the great beams, and then descended to polish the vintage typewriters. George hoped Jess understood that this party was for her. He imagined lifting his glass to thank her—if he could manage without sounding like a complete idiot.

"Bring friends—bring your sister if you like," he had told her on the phone.

"I think her boyfriend is going to be in town," said Jess.

"Bring your boyfriend then," he said. "I mean her boyfriend." He felt strangely tongue-tied. He had been extremely nervous, and he knew it showed, but he tried not to think about that. He tried to concentrate on what he could control: the party, the glass display cases lit with LEDs. Over six months he had built a proper home for McClintock's collection. These rare volumes would never see the inside of a cupboard, cutlery drawer, or oven again.

He had planned the party for early evening, and as his guests drifted in, the last sunlight sifted through the windows and danced across the floor. The musicians had already arrived with guitar and flute, and they were playing "Greensleeves" sweetly, a little too sweetly.

Concepcion grinned. "You getting married, George?"

"How about something livelier?" George told the guitarist, who obliged with Leo Brouwer.

So to the strains of Cuban music, George welcomed his guests and graciously accepted their congratulations on the collection, the cabinets, the house, the champagne, the sunset, and all the while he kept his eyes on the front door.

Sandra arrived in a long Guatemalan patchwork skirt. She wore a black shirt and silver jewelry, and she was almost beautiful with her long gray hair down her back. Nothing like her small tattooed daughter in a wife-beater tank top. What was that inked between her shoulder blades? A bar code, or a word? And if it was a word, partly exposed, what was it? *Redemption?* Or *Reinvention?* Raj came in with them, and George realized that the three had driven up together.

"Yes, I drove," Raj said cheerfully as the two women admired the display cases. "That was the least I could do."

"Still courting?" George asked. You never knew with Raj.

"I've bought the engravings," Raj whispered. "I bought all McClintock's framed engravings right off the walls for a hundred dollars apiece."

"Which engravings?"

"The lichens over the couch. They're originals from *Flora Danica*—pre-1800, hand-colored."

If only the cat hadn't bitten George, just as he'd leaned in for a closer look!

"They're from the botanical atlas that was supposed to include plates of every plant in Denmark. These are the engravings Prince Frederick ordered copied on china for Catherine the Great. Every piece was supposed to bear an exact copy of a different plant from the collection. I'm getting them reframed. . . ."

"The least you could do," George said wryly. Once bitten, twice shy. He had not ventured near McClintock's odd art again, although now, of course, he wished he had. The cookbooks were the real prize, and he knew it was churlish to begrudge Raj his find, but the competitor in him sulked. It took three glasses of champagne and two major compliments from his antiquarian friends to shake his pique.

The first compliment began to mollify him: "I have never heard of a private collection like this in Berkeley."

The second delighted him: "There may be cookbooks here that no one has seen."

All the dealers admired and envied George's acquisition, and that potent mix set the party buzzing, just as tiny stinging bubbles enlivened the champagne. No toast, George decided. No need to congratulate himself. He spoke to Sandra and showed her the humidity sensors he had installed in the bookcases, and he spoke to Nick and Julia, just as Julia's cell phone began ringing.

"It's Henry," she told Nick. "He says he doesn't want his babysitter anymore. He wants to know when we're coming home." She turned back to her phone. "Why don't you use the other bathroom, sweetie?"

And George kept circulating, and watched Raj flirt with Colm, who looked flustered and spoke rapidly about his dissertation. "The excerpt," said Colm, "becomes a genre of its own."

Raj smiled. "Yes, but is that genre at all interesting—on its own?"

Colm looked offended.

The sun was low, the sunset draining away, and George thought, This is the moment in Virginia Woolf where somebody lights the lamps. The golden light slipping into the Bay, the guests absorbed in conversation. George walked among them and he adjusted the lights, and while he turned the dimmers, he saw a tall woman enter the room with a square-shouldered blond athlete—and he realized that this was Emily and her boyfriend, both dressed in open blazers, as though they were going to a yacht club, and then he saw Leon with his long glossy black hair and his jeans and untucked white dress shirt. Had Jess told him to wear that? She was the last inside the door and seemed to look everywhere at once. Unconsciously she clasped her hands behind her, as though stepping into a museum. She wore a sleeveless shift, less a dress than a slip of gray silk so wrinkled it must have been the style. Approaching his bookshelves, she examined the titles, one after another. The famous Millay and the Plath, all the cloth-bound poetry.

"You can open them if you like," he said.

That would have been enough for him, watching Jess open his books. Meeting her accomplished sister.

"Your house is lovely," Emily said.

"Amazing!" exclaimed Jonathan. "Who's your architect?"

"Bernard Maybeck," George said.

"You should hire him for Veritech, when you guys move," Jonathan told Emily. "Seriously."

George couldn't help smiling. The desserts were superb, the champagne subtly teasing, like a word on the tip of the tongue—*methodological, perspicacious*—the word that comes to you, playfully, when you think you have forgotten. *Palimpsest. Irreversibility. Inamorata.*

He would have been perfectly happy, if not for Leon. Why was it that the youngest, most innocent-looking women consorted with the creepiest men? Their boyfriends were not boys or friends at all, but shadowy familiars: bears, wolfhounds, panthers.

Leon cast an appraising eye over George's collections, and bent down to look inside the display cabinets.

"Be careful," Jess warned. She had indeed asked Leon to wear the white shirt, and she was a little nervous about bringing him to George's house—not so much that he would break something, but that he would be bored, and therefore rude. She knew instinctively that Leon and George would bring out the worst in each other. Here it was, happening already.

"Elbows off the glass," George said.

Leon did not apologize, but straightened up, smiled, and shrugged carelessly as if to say, What are you, a fag?

And George looked at Leon, and he thought, Have you really been with Jess a year and a half? And he imagined smashing Leon's toothy mouth. But he tried, instead, to act the gracious host, and asked with only the slightest hint of mockery in his voice, "How are the trees?"

"The trees are well," Leon answered, matching George's satirical tone perfectly.

"You've been up north?"

"We've been everywhere," said Leon.

"Success?" asked George.

"We've had good discussions," Leon said smoothly. "Success is up to Sacramento."

"So you don't win your victories in the forest, but on the ground."

Leon glanced at Jess as he said, "Nothing with trees happens on the ground."

Jess traced the smooth edge of the display case with her finger. Despite her resolution in Muir Woods, despite her weeks up north with Leon, she had not overcome her fear of climbing.

"I'll get you some champagne," Leon offered Jess in a gentler voice.

"No, thank you."

George searched Jess's downcast face as Leon ambled to the bar. He wished he could talk to her alone; take her into a different room without seeming obvious.

"Are you all right?" George asked. That startled her, and he regretted the question. Too intimate. Too concerned. "Could I get you some strawberries?" he amended.

She shook her head and kept gazing at the rare cookbooks under glass.

"Please let me get you some."

"Please?" She teased gently. "Have you started saying please to me?"

"A rare slip," he said. "But I did buy the strawberries for you."

"Why?"

Because I love you, he thought. "Because I owe you," he said.

"You don't owe me anything," she replied in her easy way.

"You know I do. You got me these books." His voice was low. "You made the deal, Jess."

"True," she conceded with a smile.

"Would you like to work on them?"

"Work on them how?"

"We need a descriptive catalog, for one thing. We have to sort the notes and store them separately with records of the page numbers where they were found. Colm started, but I need him at the store, and he's got his dissertation. I was wondering if you would like to try."

He opened the glass display case and took out the palm-sized 1814 *American Cookery*. The binding had cracked, and he held the book as if it were a fledgling with a broken wing.

"*Independence Cake,*" Jess read over George's shoulder. "*Twenty pounds flour, fifteen pounds sugar, ten pounds butter, four dozen eggs, one quart wine, one quart brandy . . .*" She laughed softly. "Was this for the Founding Fathers reunion?" She turned the next several pages and found a black-ink drawing on a slip of typing paper, a nude woman holding a round fruit to her mouth. Jess plucked it out and read the collector's tiny caption: "*Do I dare to eat a peach?*"

"Will you?" George asked, closing the book and placing it atop the cabinet.

"Maybe," Jess said lightly. "Do you have any?"

"No peaches."

"Oh, well. I can't ruin this dress, anyway."

Words he took as permission to look openly at her. The fabric of her dress, gray and wrinkled at first glance, was really silver. No one else would wear fabric like that, rustling with every breath.

"It's Emily's," she said, disproving his idea immediately. She had borrowed the dress from her sister, although Emily thought it was too long on her.

"Will you take the job? Please?"

"Hmm." Pensive, with just a touch of humor, she said, "I don't think I like that word from you."

"I'd pay you more," George told her. Only half-joking, he declared, "I'd make you curator."

"Oh, a title," said Jess.

Why are you hesitating now? he thought. What have you been doing for the past six weeks? He had scarcely seen her at the store. Across the room, George's friends were clustering at the dessert table like bees. Raj and Colm were discussing William Blake, while Jonathan was holding forth to Nick about how the Nasdaq would rise again. Stealthily, Leon walked among them. George assumed he was casing the joint. George should check Leon's pockets before he left. Search him and then show Jess the content of her boyfriend's character. After which George could comfort Jess, and then . . . he didn't know what happened next.

Jess said, "I want to know who she was."

"What do you mean?" George asked.

"The collector's lover."

"Why do you assume he had a lover?"

"Well, because—because look." Jess held up the nude. "You've got the evidence right here."

"You're missing the point," George told her. "She wasn't his lover. That was why he wrote all the notes and drew the pictures." He took the drawing from her, and his fingers brushed hers. She looked up at him, clear-eyed. *Perspicacious.* She understands, he thought. She knows.

But in the next moment she drew back her hand. "Actually, I think I *would* like a drink."

As he showed her the way to the bar, he finished his thought under his breath, murmuring, "He didn't have her, so he drew her instead."

21

Jonathan was calm when ISIS rose to nine, and still confident when the shares retreated to five fifty. Those who whined and fretted only irritated him. Scared-straight venture capitalists did not impress him now any more than they had back in 1998 when they pleaded with Jonathan to take their cash. Where did they get their ideas about the new economy? From magazines? He did not bother reading publications like *Fast Company*, or *Wired*, or *Forbes*. So-called business cycles bored him. The news, whether paper or electronic, meant little as far as Jonathan was concerned. The news was already old. Weekly, daily, hourly, anything called news was already archival.

He understood that in this world there were news reporters and news makers, investors and innovators. Watchers and world beaters. In each case he took the active role. He did not know economic theory; he knew computers. He did not meditate on trends; he eyed the future. And so, at George's party, when he talked to Nick, he spoke with perfect equanimity. "The strong survive, man," he told Nick, and by *strong* he meant "Those with new technology."

While Emily saw falling share price as a sad decay, a postlapsarian decline from larger, rounder numbers, Jonathan came to view the fall as opportunity. "Buy now," he told anyone who asked, and he began to buy back shares himself, convinced of his company's resilience.

In April when ISIS sank to four, Jonathan called a meeting. Dave, Aldwin, Oskar, and Jake gathered in Oskar's office.

"Where's Orion?" Jonathan asked.

"I'm not sure he came in today," said Jake.

"No, I saw him," said Aldwin, just as Orion walked through the door and took his seat in the corner.

"Okay," said Jonathan, and then paused as Orion opened his cream soda. "Let me tell you what's happening."

"Cisco bought us," Orion said, and for a second everybody froze in shock. "Just kidding."

No one laughed.

"Anyone else want to take a guess?" Jonathan asked icily. Nobody spoke, so he continued. "It's time for a paradigm shift. We are going to develop a new security product for electronic fingerprinting of every view and touch on a piece of data. We're going to call this service Fast-Tracking, and we'll sell it to every security client."

"How would this work?" Dave asked.

"Look, with ChainLinx we encrypt transactions to safeguard the purchaser. Fast-Tracking is really a data-protection and surveillance tool for the vendor." He stepped up to the board and began to draw the new scheme in green ink.

What did Eli Whitney feel when he arrived in America with plans for the cotton gin? What were Francis Cabot Lowell's emotions when, from memory alone, he built a scale model of the Cartwright weaving machine? Elation? Mastery mixed with trepidation? Jonathan felt entirely himself as he played his card, the secret Emily had revealed to him eighteen months before. He was not copying detailed plans, but developing his own. Nor was he attempting to replicate an existing project at Veritech—for Emily had told him in no uncertain terms that electronic fingerprinting was a project that she would not pursue. Ever since that conversation, Jonathan had plotted his own course—a new product for ISIS, a new initiative for programmers, and, most important, a breakthrough to present to analysts and shareholders.

During the Industrial Revolution, memorizing machine parts might have been essential. In this Computational Era, the concept alone, the whispered idea, launched a thousand chips. Jonathan's mind was quick and infinitely flexible, his timing uncanny, his presentation transformative as he made over electronic fingerprinting into new market share. He was not mathematically creative like Jake or Oskar, but he had an acquisitive intelligence, and when he appropriated an idea, he improved it, until his own version not only surpassed, but obliterated its source. Indeed, he no longer recalled electronic fingerprinting except with nostalgia, as he remembered other conversations with Emily, her head on his chest, her bare back under his hand, her thigh against his thigh. Her puzzling confidence became a gift. Her revelation shifted in his mind to inspiration. And Emily herself—he worshipped her. She was his muse. If he did not tell her about this meeting, if he neglected to mention his new plan for ISIS—Well, soon he planned to tell her this and everything.

Emily had promised to leave Veritech in June. She and Jonathan talked endlessly about finding an apartment in Cambridge, or simply buying a house. They had a real estate agent, and no price limit. Therefore Jonathan felt just right as he diagrammed his new Fast-Tracking system on the whiteboard. At last he was getting to the crux of the matter—the new technology that ISIS needed. He loved Emily, and he thanked her silently, although he did not mention her name in his visionary presentation. There was no need. There was no time. Oh, life was sweet.

Dazzled, the others watched Jonathan unveil his new plans. Always a little slow, Dave asked about the legal and ethical implications of the idea, while Jake and Oskar leapfrogged ahead with technical questions.

"Now this is interesting," Oskar said, bestowing his highest praise.

As for Orion, he felt hopeful for the first time in months. Instead of lecturing about release dates, and talking up ISIS products, Jonathan was presenting new ideas. Instead of trying to shut down criticism, he was encouraging debate. In the past he'd sacrificed quality for speed and talked incessantly about market share. Now he proposed building a new system from scratch. Orion saw the plan opening, blossoming like fireworks trailing sparks and smoke in the night sky. They would tag and trace every touch on every piece of data, capture and collect what had been ephemeral. What possibilities for research! What challenges for new analysis! He understood the idea immediately, and the scribbles on the whiteboard were not scribbles to him, but poetry. The design Jonathan unveiled was that elegant.

Aldwin asked, "How will we staff this? Start a new group?"

"Yeah," said Jonathan. "But we'll keep the project confidential. No analyst or investor input! And we need somebody to spearhead it."

"I will!" Orion surprised himself with his alacrity. "I'd like to," he amended.

Jonathan smiled. It was not his fault that his smile looked so mischievous, that his blue eyes sparkled and the corners of his mouth curled as though anticipating some particularly delicious meal. He had always known his old friend would come around. Turn away long enough, and people think you have forgotten them entirely. Show your displeasure, and first they hate you, and then they despair, and finally, scarcely acknowledging it to themselves, they miss you. Change the game again, to see if they follow. The best ones can. The smart ones always do.

"You would have to leave what's left of the Lockbox group," Jonathan told Orion. "Would you be willing to do that?"

God, yes, Orion thought. "Definitely," he said aloud.

"Maybe we could work something out," Jonathan said. "I think that you'd be great."

Such faith in him! For long months Orion's efforts had been ad hoc, troubleshooting substandard code. But to start up this new Fast-Tracking venture, to head his own group, design and build a system to his own standards—to work with autonomy! The idea thrilled him. Orion was moved by Jonathan's trust, and his gesture to restore their friendship. Jonathan had not given up on him; Jonathan still saw him as one of the founders.

"You would report directly to me," Jonathan told Orion, "so I can keep an eye on you."

Orion chose to take this as a compliment. He took this, as intended, as a formal job offer, and he nodded in agreement. He accepted.

Perhaps in the old days, men built their reputations, and then their fortunes. Orion had made his fortune first. He had not designed algo-rithms like Oskar and Jake, or established administrative systems like Dave and Aldwin, or sold Lockbox and ChainLinx to the first clients as Jonathan had, flying all night to charm his way into Disney and CNN when he was still a graduate student with one suit. Too diffident, too dreamy, too cautious, too much a programmer, Orion was worth over twenty million dollars even in this depressed market, but he had not been well employed. He did not sit on the executive board. He was not vice president of anything. Heading a new group, he would step up. He had a chance to justify his wealth, to prove that his success was more than acci-dental, to become a self-made man.

`Meet me downstairs`, Orion e-mailed Sorel as soon as he returned to his desk.

"I'm right here." She was standing behind him, watching him type.

"What happened?" she asked him as they waited for the elevator.

"Shh!"

She looked at him questioningly. *"What?"*

"You won't believe this . . . ," he told her in the elevator, but just then someone else joined them. Somebody from Marketing, ALOK on his badge. Orion could not keep track of the new hires anymore, nor did these recruits know him. Could they have any idea, for example, that Orion had named their company over beers in Somerville so many months ago? Jonathan said then that he wanted some kind of acronym for "Internet Security System," and Orion had remembered his fourth-grade unit on Egyptians and his report on Isis—baker, spinner, weaver, daughter of the Earth and sky. This new guy, Alok, had no idea. There were no historical inscriptions at ISIS, no steles recording early triumphs. No hieroglyphs with bird-headed vulture capitalists and the four founders arrayed like boy kings on the elevator's smooth gray walls.

The doors parted, and Orion ushered Sorel through the lobby with its mobile of oblong mirrors, and its revolving doors of thick, rubber-edged glass.

Into the fresh spring air they hurried, away from ISIS. Sorel thought he wanted to buy lunch at the deli at One Kendall Square, but Orion saw too many ISIS worshippers there. He ushered her into the furniture store Pompanoosuc Mills, vast and airy, filled with handcrafted Shaker furniture—or rather the kind of furniture Shakers would have built if they had softened on celibacy and simplicity and fashioned bunk beds and glass-fronted china cabinets.

Sorel followed him to the back of the store where they admitted to the saleswoman that they were just looking, that they would indeed let her know if they had any questions about woods or pricing, and settled down together, pulling up two spindle-backed chairs to a cherry dining-room table.

Orion said, "Jonathan's got a new plan."

"He needs one."

"Just listen!" Orion watched her face as he told her. He watched the way she sucked her lower lip, appreciating the new scheme immediately, savoring the news.

"You must be joking!"

"Wait. There's more. I'm going to be the team leader of the Fast-Track group."

"*You?*"

"What's wrong with me?" He was a little offended. "Don't you think I can?"

"Of course you can. I just wonder why Jonathan likes you now."

"I think . . . it's just . . . we go way back," Orion struggled to explain. "I think when you go that far back with someone, the friendship never disappears completely, and sometimes, eventually, the relationship regenerates."

"Like a starfish growing a new arm," said Sorel.

"Don't you think sometimes it works that way?"

"I don't trust him, I'm afraid."

"You don't know him as well as I do," said Orion.

"That's why I'm in a better position to judge."

"You're a cynic," he said.

"Probably."

"I think with some people you have shared a history, and it's very deep."

"He says one kind word. You turn to mush."

"Kind word? He's giving me this huge new project."

"The project sounds brilliant—if you can pull it off." Sorel tilted her chair back. "I'm afraid he's setting you up."

"No," Orion said. "He wouldn't do that. This new group is real, and he wants me to run it. He's finally found a way to use me."

"That's just it."

"Sorel!" He turned on her in exasperation.

"Sorry."

"You would make a good spy," he said.

"Why?"

"You don't trust anybody. You wear black overcoats. You admit you like disguises."

"I don't disguise myself from you."

"No?" He turned toward her, and captured her hand in his. "Then why is your phone number unlisted?"

"Why did you try to find my phone number?" she asked, puzzled. "I only use my cell."

"And why do you disappear all the time?"

"What do you mean, 'disappear'?"

"You don't show up, and I have no idea where you are."

"I don't have to tell you where I am. I'm touring!"

"Where are you touring? Davis Square?"

"I have a career."

"You mean The Chloroforms? That's your career?"

"You don't think programming is my career, do you? I came here to be a performance artist and study physics. You don't think I'm going to start rallying round ISIS and all that."

"I'm sure you were perfectly happy with ISIS when you sold your stock," Orion said, thinking of Sorel's little house.

"Look, I'm the consistent one," said Sorel. "I've always said ISIS is my day job. You're the one obsessed with Jonathan. He loves me. He loves me not. He loves me. You're always looking for affection, even when the relationship is frayed. Even when it's broken."

"Let's leave Molly out of this," said Orion.

"You always do." Sorel pushed her chair back from the table. "ISIS is a case in point. So is Jonathan. You're loyal to everybody. It's a shame, really, that I'm . . ."

"That you're what?" Orion asked.

"So fond of you."

22

Oneness. Jess read the word on the screen displaying Rabbi Helfgott's PowerPoint presentation. He was speaking that evening at the Tree House, at Jess's invitation.

What is Oneness?
Every particle in the universe desires to be One.

- raindrop
- spark
- soul

"It is amazing to think," Rabbi Helfgott told the group of close to thirty Tree Savers, "that all through the world, every *neshamah,* every spirit, whether we know it or not, desires the Oneness that is God. This applies to every living being—animal, plant, insect—trees included. Oneness is our natural state. Our default condition. Unfortunately, too often in our lives, we fall away. The question is: How do we return?"

No one spoke. Some Tree Savers listened closely from where they sat on chairs and couches; others fidgeted, bemused, on the floor, and the rabbi watched them and gazed upon the Jewish faces among them—Jessamine Bach, Noah Levine—as he moved on to the next slide.

- *Tefillah*—Prayer
- *Tshuvah*—Repentance
- *Tzedakah*—Charity

"In our tradition, this is the magic formula," the rabbi said. "This is the answer."

Jess considered the rabbi's three-part solution for reengagement with the eternal. "Does this cover everything a soul can possibly do?"

"Yes!" declared Rabbi Helfgott. "For sure. Yes!"

"What about civil disobedience?" Leon asked.

Now everyone was listening. "That would depend on various factors," the rabbi said diplomatically. "Peaceful or violent? Legal or illegal? Safe or dangerous?"

The Tree Savers hemmed and hummed, debating among themselves, and Daisy said, "I think if you see people interfering with the Oneness of the world, you have to stop them."

"But that's the question," said Jess. "Is stopping them actually some kind of charity? Or prayer? Or does civil disobedience come under the category of repentance? And is it only quiet, peaceful protests that count? Or social justice by any means necessary?"

"Who's more Jewish?" Noah asked. "Mahatma Gandhi? Or Malcolm X?"

In his younger days, Rabbi Helfgott might have felt the discussion slipping away, but he had lived and worked in Berkeley for seventeen years. Magisterially, he raised both hands. "Let me put this on the table. Mahatma Gandhi or Malcolm X? These are very interesting people, but when it comes to more or less Jewish—the answer is simple. Neither was a Jew! However, let's look in depth at our first point: *Tefillah.* Prayer."

"Wait," Jess interrupted once again. "I want to understand whether social action can be a kind of prayer."

Rabbi Helfgott smiled. "No."

"No!" She could not conceal her surprise.

"Social action is original," said Rabbi Helfgott. "But praying is prescribed. In social action we improvise, depending on the situation. However, in the Jewish tradition when we pray, we read words already set down for us. Social action is ad hoc. Prayer is total catastrophic insurance, covering every possibility."

"So you're saying it's better to be spiritually derivative than creative?" Jess asked.

"Absolutely!"

The room was silent. Ha! Helfgott thought. Who was radical now? The Tree Savers? Or their bearded guest speaker in his frock coat? Who was pious now? Students feeling their way on a unique spiritual journey? Or their rabbi who dared suggest that the soul's journey was not unique at all, but scripted?

"This is the gift of our tradition," the rabbi said. "You wish for Oneness—you don't have to reinvent the wheel. The wheel is already there for you. Spinning! You wish to speak to God? You know what to say for every occasion." He lifted up a blue prayer book and watched the Tree Savers' faces: some skeptical, some puzzled. All surprised.

"Therefore social action is not prayer. However, when it comes to charity, this is another story. And the word *tzedakah*, 'charity,' has another meaning. 'Justice'!"

Rabbi Helfgott took a sip from his water bottle, for he did not drink or eat anything in nonkosher houses, not even Tree Houses.

"We look at the problems of the world. The poor, the homeless, the oppressed. We look at the endangered species of the world. We say, 'What can I give? What can I do for those who have so little? For those who are silent?' Prayer is one method. Giving of time and money is another. Are prayer and social action the same? No. Are they connected? Absolutely. *I will lift up mine eyes unto the hills.* Look to the sea. Look to the Earth. Look to the trees. If they aren't God's messengers, they are definitely His witnesses. Look to the world and unite with what is natural around us. I myself have discovered in California more evidence of the Shechinah, the Holy Presence, than I ever saw in my childhood. I myself grew up in an urban environment! One scraggly plant, one asphalt playground. What did I know from the natural world? Until I, who lived in

Crown Heights, began driving my van through the golden hills along 280—what did I know? Until I, who grew up in books, took my family to Point Reyes National Seashore, to see the wildflowers blooming and the waves crash over the rocks—what did I understand? My wife and I saw the immensity of the ocean! Our children saw Tomales Bay. Then I, who never noticed the landscape, came to repent my ignorance. Then I dedicated my heart to the cliffs, the wind, the trees. To the refreshment of our planet speedily in our day."

Silence.

Nervously, Jess scanned the faces around her. Some looked at Helfgott with respect. Others with curiosity. No one spoke. Then suddenly, Arminda said, *"Yeah!"*

Leon applauded, and the others joined in.

"He was great," Leon told Jess that night as they cleaned the kitchen.

Jess twirled her mop happily. "I knew he would be!"

"Clergy are always great. We should have him write an op-ed for us. Something about Wood Rose Glen."

"I don't think he knows anything about Wood Rose Glen," Jess said.

Leon stopped scrubbing the stove. "We could explain what Pacific Lumber is doing and why we need to stop them—and he could put it in his own words."

"Wouldn't that be like using him?" Jess asked.

"Only in the best possible way."

Jess thought about this. "Even if it's for the best, I wouldn't want to. I mean, I couldn't use a rabbi for publicity."

"No, of course not. No more than he wants to use you, taking your invitation to preach."

"Couldn't you imagine a free exchange of ideas?"

"Everyone's got an agenda," Leon said wearily. "Haven't you figured that out yet?"

"If you want him to write an op-ed, then *you* ask him," Jess said.

"I'll be up north."

"Don't go," Jess murmured as she mopped, moistening the tiles at his feet.

"Come with me," Leon said.

"I can't. I have to work. I promised George."

"And what did you promise him, exactly?"

"It's just such a great opportunity."

Leon turned his back on her and finished scrubbing the commercial stove with steel wool. "You keep saying that."

"It's true."

Jess was cataloging the McClintock cookbook collection. Arriving at noon and leaving in the late afternoon, she spent at least five hours every weekday with the books. George was never home in the afternoons. He had given Jess a code of her own for the security system: 1759, the year the first two volumes of *Tristram Shandy* were published, and she came and went as she pleased. Apart from Concepcion, who cleaned three times a week, Jess worked alone.

At first she had felt overwhelmed by the house, its airy symmetry, its silence. Now she was accustomed to the place, but she caught herself wondering, Is this still Berkeley? George's neighborhood felt as far from Telegraph as the hanging gardens of Babylon. You could get a good kebab in Jess's neighborhood, and a Cal T-shirt, and a reproduction NO HIPPIES ALLOWED sign. Where George lived, you could not get anything unless you drove down from the hills. Then you could buy art glass, and temple bells, and burled-wood jewelry boxes, and dresses of hand-painted silk, and you could eat at Chez Panisse, or sip coffee at the authentically grubby French Hotel where your barista took a bent paper clip and drew cats or four-leaf clovers or nudes in your espresso foam. You returned home with organic, free-range groceries, and bouquets of ivory roses and pale green hydrangeas, and you held dinner parties where some guests got lost and arrived late, and others gave up searching for you in the fog. That was George's Berkeley, and even in these environs, his home stood apart, hidden, grand, and rambling; windows set like jewels in their carved frames, gables twined with wisteria of periwinkle and ghostly white.

Jess had the use of one of George's old cars, a Honda Accord, that she drove from the flats to his enchanted hills. Like a pilgrim, she climbed the outdoor staircase, opened the door, and slipped off her shoes. She skated in socks over silken floors to the oak table in the dining room, where George had left her a laptop and a reading light, book cradles, magnifying glass, note cards, sharpened pencils, archival file boxes, Mylar sleeves, references and bibliographies—Bitting, Vicaire, Lowenstein, Maclean, Driver. George had them all. With these tools, she set to work, one book at a time—typing title and publication details into her database, adding descriptive notes: *two cookbooks bound as one, wormholes in section vi.*

Jess had always been the less responsible sister, the whimsical daughter, the girl with the flyaway hair. Openhearted, she had always trusted others, but no one had returned the favor so generously. She was aware, always, of George's faith, his conviction that, working independently, she would not mar these precious volumes, or pocket a small cookbook for herself, or dog-ear pages, or cut out an engraving, as some thieves did, even in great libraries, with staff and guards.

She had never spent time in such beautiful rooms. Lofty ceilings and massive beams, windows glowing with sun and cloud and distant ocean. She had never worked with such material.

She studied each cookbook minutely, turning pages one by one, extracting the collector's drawings, pulling off his paper clips. Removing these artifacts to file, she noted exactly where they occurred, between recipes for pottage, or instructions for preparing trout or carp or pike. She cross-referenced each, as an archaeologist might preserve every tooth and shard of bone.

Who are you? she asked silently, as she laid away the collector's quotations, his drawings, his scraps of famous poetry: *Come live with me and be my love* . . . interleaved with menus: *oysters, fish stew, tortoise in its shell, bread from the oven, honey from the honeycomb.* The books were unsplattered but much fingered, their pages soft with turning and re-turning, like collections of old fairy tales. Often Jess thought of Rapunzel and golden apples and enchanted gardens. She thought of Ovid, and Dante, and Cervantes, and the Pre-Raphaelites, for sometimes McClintock pictured his beloved eating, and sometimes sleeping in fields of poppies, and once throned like Persephone, with strawberry vines entwined in her long hair.

Whom did you love? she wondered to herself, but she found no name for the mysterious woman, and no description. Only the ink drawings, beautifully detailed, and McClintock's fantastic menus, culled from recipes that read like poetry.

To make a tarte of strawberyes, wrote Margaret Parker in 1551, *take and strayne theym with the yolkes of four egges, and a little whyte breade grated, then season it up with suger and swete butter and so bake it.* And Jess, who had spent the past year struggling with Kant's Critiques, now luxuriated in language so concrete. Tudor cookbooks did not theorize, nor did they provide separate ingredient lists, or scientific cooking times or temperatures. Recipes were called receipts, and tallied materials and techniques together. Art and alchemy were their themes, instinct and invention. The grandest performed occult transformations: flora into fauna, where, for example, cooks crushed blanched almonds and beat them with sugar, milk, and rose water into a paste to *cast Rabbets, Pigeons, or any other little bird or beast.* Or flour into gold, gilding *marchpane* and festive tarts. Or mutton into venison, or fish to meat, or pig to fawn, one species prepared to stand in for another.

Cooks turned pigeons out of pies, plumped veal with tongue and truffle, stuffed bustard with goose, with pheasant, with chicken, with duck, with guinea fowl, with teal, with woodcock, with partridge, with plover, with lapwing, with quail, with thrush, with lark, with garden warbler, so that each bird contained the next, each body enveloping one more delicate in mystic sequence, until at last the cook stuffed the warbler with a single olive, as though revelers might finally taste music, arriving at this round placeholder for breath and open voice. Edible decibels. Savory olive for sweet song.

Modern recipes were clean and bloodless by comparison, suppressing violence between cook and cooked. Not so here. *Truss them . . . , lard them, boil them quick and white.* This, Jess read, was how to prepare rabbits. *Cut your woodcocks in four quarters and put them in a sauce-pan; but remember to save the Entrails. . . .* Incantatory, hortatory. All verbs in the imperative: Raise the skin; tie up the necks; parboil them; roast them. Adjectives sparing, nouns succulent and rich, bespeaking bacon, and crisp skin curling from roast fowl.

Jess herself had not eaten fowl or roast or even fish in years, but the books awakened memories of turkey and thick gravy, and crab cakes, and rib-eye roasts. Redolent of smoke and flame, the recipes repelled and also reminded her of pink and tender meat, and breaking open lobster dripping with sweet butter, and sucking marrow out of bones.

Hunger drew her into George's garden, where she devoured the food she'd brought along, her sprouts and avocado sandwich, her carob muffin. Cold pastoral. She returned to epic tales of fish and wild boar, every course a canto, every feast a bestiary. And all these interleaved with the collector's private fantasies, no longer strange to Jess, but familiar, even comforting. Scribbled lines from Jonson seemed the right response to instructions for whole pike and suckling pig, and swans dressed for the table. A reclining nude with grapes was really not so out of place. The food in these cookbooks not at all moral or metaphysical, but dug from the earth, plucked from the garden, slain in the woods. Animals still quivered with life, and required cleaning after slaughter. Red deer ran with blood, broths seethed.

Jess knew some French, but little German and no Dutch. Those works were more mysterious, and also less distracting to catalog. The English cookbooks with their joints and forced meat, their *Bacon stuck with Cloves,* read like Jacobean tragedies. Jess devoured them, scarcely looking up, until Concepcion's vacuum startled her. Then she realized the afternoon was gone, the sky was deepening, and she was hungry once again.

She began to bring more food, a second snack for the end of the day. Rice cakes and a thermos full of miso soup. She ate snap peas and bags of almonds on George's sunny kitchen deck, and bent to sniff the herbs his gardener cultivated in pots. She closed her eyes and smelled basil, thyme and rosemary, spearmint, peppermint, chocolate mint, dill, parsley, lemon grass. Thus fortified, she shouldered her backpack and drove home to the Tree House, where she lived her other life.

In July Leon came to the Tree House for several days to work and reprovision. He assumed that she would drive north with him, and when she told him she needed more time with the books he said, "Jess!" almost like Emily.

"What?" she asked him.

"What are you doing?"

"I'm working," she said once again. "I know you think cookbooks are trivial."

He nodded. "Completely."

"You think rare books are frivolous—but actually when you sit down with them . . ."

"When you sit down with them or when you sit down with him?"

"Don't be rude!" she said, half-laughing. He was already dressed. She had just come from the shower.

"This job is a total setup."

Bending over, drying her thick hair, she told him about the Brandenburg cookbook. "It's got a clasp like a locket. It's a jewel," she told him. "And wait, when you open it and you look at the frontispiece—can I tell you . . . ?"

"Can I tell you about Wood Rose Glen?" he countered. "We've got rangers up there every day, and loggers with megaphones harassing everyone who tries to defend."

She dressed in silence, chastened. "I'll come up in two weeks."

"Come because you want to come. Come because you need to come," said Leon. "Don't do me any favors."

"I do want to. It's just . . ."

"Just what?"

How could she explain to him what she could scarcely articulate to herself? The cookbooks weren't trivial at all. They were, in and of themselves, an entirely new world. She had never felt this way. She dreamed about the books at night. Their collector haunted her. She lived in suspense, speculating about his life, his love, his strange dark handwriting. Sometimes she could hardly bear it—the edge of discovery. "To have a chance to work with a collection like this—" she began.

Leon cut her off. "Watch out or you'll end up in the collection too."

"You're jealous!"

"No," Leon told her coolly. "You can have him."

"Have who? Have George? But I don't *want* him."

"Maybe you don't, but he wants you."

Jess thought of the exquisite, empty house. "He's never even there."

"Don't be stupid." Leon's anger was never desperate or uncontrolled, but he was angry. Cold as liquid nitrogen, he burned.

They heard footsteps overhead, and talking in the hall. When they fought, the other Tree Savers could overhear. She kept her voice down. "You have no right to speak to me that way, when you always leave me here alone."

"I don't leave you here. You choose to stay."

"I want to climb with you," she said, "but I can't."

"That's bullshit, Jess, and you know it. You told me six months ago you were going to climb—and every time, you decide at the last minute that you can't. The truth is that you can, Jess. You can. But you won't. You have an irrational—"

"I know it's irrational. I know it's an irrational fear."

"Well, if you know it's irrational, then why don't you do something about it?"

"Just because something is irrational doesn't mean it isn't real," Jess said.

"Call it whatever you want, it's childish."

"Why are you so nasty?" Jess asked him.

He didn't answer.

"You're nasty, and accusatory, and paranoid."

"I'm not paranoid," Leon said.

"Oh, so you admit to nasty and accusatory." She almost laughed, but he did not.

"Irrational or not, it's your choice, so don't whine about getting left behind."

Whenever she defended herself, or called him on something, Leon said don't be stupid, or accused her of whining. She took a breath. "I'm pointing out that my job is real too."

"And your so-called job is to work for your patron in his house."

"You have patrons! You have that guy from Juniper Systems, and that woman, that actress with the house in the city. You just wish that George were funding you."

"Right, if he were funding us that would be different."

"You're jealous. You really are."

He turned away slightly.

"Don't you think for once you might possibly be wrong?"

"Wrong about your rich friend? I'm not wrong about him," said Leon.

"You don't know him," said Jess.

"Yes, I do."

"I'm not going to argue with you," Jess said.

Leon answered, "Just tell me what happens when he comes home."

That afternoon, while working in George's dining room, she felt something new, a strange apprehension. She jumped to hear the house settle, and started at Concepcion's key in the lock, but George did not burst in on her that day, nor did he visit her the next. He never came home early. While Jess talked to him on occasion, when she stopped in at Yorick's, she never saw him at the house. She left him notes. *Still working on the Salzburg.* Also, *McClintock lists three recipes for swan.*

He rarely wrote in reply, or if he did, he simply scribbled, *Good.* Or *Back up the index as you go.* He could follow her progress on the laptop, where she was creating the annotated bibliography. She knew that he was reading it, because he used the Track Changes tool, and sometimes added to her descriptions of the books, inserting details in red. Occasionally he left books out for her in their foam cradles. Weighted strings held them open to reveal a beautiful engraving, or some particular recipe he had noticed.

Once he left the Haywood out for her with a page number on a scrap of paper, and she opened the book to recipes for "Distillation." Jess laughed at the page George had found for her. There, between instructions to make rose water and clove water, were instructions *to make jessamine water: Take eight ounces of the jessamine flowers, clean picked from their stalks, three quarts of spirit of wine, and two quarts of water: put the whole into an alembic, and draw off three quarts. Then take a pound of sugar dissolved in two quarts of water, and mix it with the distilled liquor.* George left no comment on the recipe, but she read, and read it over, aware that he was thinking of her.

Still, he did not come home, and as weeks passed she relaxed again, for despite Leon's warning, she saw only the housekeeper cleaning the already-clean rooms, rubbing the glowing wood furniture, more, Jess imagined, to warm the chairs, than to polish them. Concepcion kept the house as one might wind a watch, or tune and play stringed instruments to prevent them from cracking with disuse.

The place was lightly lived in. Jess was sure she was the only one who used the first-floor bathroom with its cool stone tiles, and the kitchen looked almost entirely unused as well, although she assumed George ate at home occasionally like everybody else. He kept a wicker basket of onions under one counter, and another basket of potatoes, a can of olive oil near the stove, a braid of garlic heads hanging from a hook, along with a bunch of dried red chili peppers. But she never found a dish left out. Not so much as a coffee mug.

Therefore, she was doubly surprised, the first day of August, to see a piece of fruit lying on the pristine kitchen table. A peach, slightly unbalanced, so that it listed to one side, its hue the color of an early sunrise. Had George remembered their conversation at the party and left the peach for her to eat? Strange. For a moment she thought it might be a trompe l'oeil work of art, some fantastic piece of glass. She leaned over and sniffed. The blooming perfume was unmistakable. She touched it with the tip of her finger. The peach was not quite ripe, but it was real.

The next day, she checked the kitchen as soon as she arrived. The peach lay there still, blushing deeper in the window light. She bent to smell, and the perfume was headier than before, a scent of meadows and summers home from school. Still unripe. Was George waiting to eat this beauty? On a note card she penciled: *Is this a proprietary peach?* She placed the card on the table, but changed her mind immediately, folding her stiff query into quarters and then eighths and finally sixteenths, and then stuffing it into her backpack in the dining room. There she returned to her apportioned books.

This is just to say, she wrote in her notebook, *I've been eying the peach you left on the table and were probably saving for breakfast. Forgive me. It looks delicious. . . .* She gave up on her Williams imitation and continued: *If you did leave it for me, that was . . .* She tore out the page, crumpled, and tossed it in the recycling bin without writing the next word: *sweet.*

On the third day, she smelled the fruit as soon as she came in. She followed the scent to the kitchen, and the peach was radiant, dusky rose and gold, its skin so plush she thought her fingertip might bruise it. This was the day, the very hour to eat—and she had come prepared, but she didn't want Concepcion to see her. She waited until the housekeeper shouldered her leather-handled canvas bag and left.

Then Jess unwrapped the organic peach she'd bought that morning. Slightly smaller, slightly harder, but decently rosy, the peach listed left—just the right direction—when she set it on the table.

Leaving this changeling for George, she washed his ripe fruit, and bit and broke the skin. An intense tang, the underside of velvet. Then flesh dissolved in a rush of nectar. Juice drenched her hand and wet the inside of her wrist. She had forgotten, if she'd ever known, that what was sweet could also be so complicated, that fruit could have a nap, like fabric, soft one way, sleek the other. She licked the juice dripping down her arm.

"Jess."

When had he arrived? How had she not heard him? "What are you doing here?" she blurted out.

"Well, I live here," George said, standing in the kitchen doorway.

"True," she said.

He looked, bemused, from the peach in her hand to the peach on the table. "You brought me a replacement? Jessamine," he chided, picking up the substitute. "This is rock hard."

"Well . . . ," she began.

"Did you think I wouldn't notice?"

She gave up and laughed at herself, even as she stood, holding the beautifully ripe fruit.

"Go ahead," he said. "Finish it."

She tried to bite, and then she turned the peach and tried again. "You're making me nervous."

Suppressing a smile, he walked into the living room, and she quickly devoured what was left.

Eaten in haste, the fruit tasted different, juicy, but not quite so luscious, cut-velvet, but no longer so luxurious. Unsure whether George composted, she set the peach pit on the counter, washed her hands and wrist and arm, and called out, "Do you have a kitchen towel?"

He returned and took a striped towel from a drawer. As she dried herself, she asked, "Why did you come home so early?"

"It's not so early," he told her. "You stayed late."

"Oh, so you weren't planning to run into me."

"No," he said. "Not exactly."

He was at least three steps away, but he looked at her so intently that he seemed much nearer. He'd cut his long hair so that it was not quite shoulder length, and he wasn't wearing glasses, as he did in the store. "Was it good?"

"The most delicious meal I have ever eaten," she told him honestly.

"A peach is not a meal." He couldn't help glancing at his oven and his knife drawer. Thinking of his grill on the deck and how he might roast chicken or lamb or even fish, along with pearl onions and vine-ripened tomatoes.

"It tasted like a meal."

"That was hunger."

"It's the cookbooks," she confessed.

"Occupational hazard." He leaned back against the edge of the kitchen table. Her eyes were greener than he'd ever seen them. Her shirt button was broken, third from the top. "Are you still hungry?"

She thought of Leon. *Tell me what happens when he comes home.* "Not really," she lied.

"Let me cook you dinner."

She shook her head.

"No?" George asked softly, as he took the kitchen towel from her hands.

He was wearing jeans and a faded blue T-shirt, and she saw the scar traveling from the back of his hand up the inside of his forearm. "Tell me what happened," she said.

"Someone tried to fillet me."

Forestalling her next question, he opened what she had assumed to be a bank of cabinets.

"Ohh." She gazed inside a pristine refrigerator with glassy shelves and perfectly arranged vegetables, packages wrapped in white paper, fresh lemons lined up in a row.

"What can't you eat?"

For just a moment, she could not remember. Then he closed the door.

"No meat, of course," she began earnestly. "No poultry, no fish, no living creature of any kind, and no product of any living creature, so no milk, no cheese, no butter, no eggs, nothing dairy, and no refined sugar, no white flour, no white rice—nothing white . . ."

"How about white wine?"

He went to his butler's pantry and brought back two glasses and a bottle, ever so slightly chilled. "This is a Kistler Chardonnay. See that?" He poured out what looked like liquid gold. "It's known for its color." He handed her a glass half full and watched her take the tiniest of sips. He could see she didn't drink, and even the Chard was strong for her, and curious to her tongue. But she liked it, and quickly sipped again.

"Yum."

"Yum?"

"It's good," she said.

"Do you taste citrus?" he asked her. "Mineral?"

"No," she admitted cheerfully. The wine was light and tickling, not heavy or too sweet like others she had tried. Sun poured through the kitchen's tall windows and played across the floor so that the room felt warmer. George himself seemed different, slimmer than she remembered, and more fluid in his movements. A fish in water, she thought, as he took out pans and tongs and a cutting board.

"All right, this is what I have. Dungeness crab. Fresh salmon—by which I mean, caught yesterday. And asparagus."

"I guess I could have that," she said.

"Crab and salmon and asparagus?"

"The asparagus."

"Good, we'll have asparagus—with salmon on the side." He set a pan on the stove for the fish, and began washing and trimming the asparagus. He spread the stalks in a roasting pan, drizzled them with olive oil, and popped the pan in the oven. Then he unwrapped the pink salmon. "This is so fresh, you can almost eat it just like this. Sashimi." He smiled to see Jess back away. "We'll melt butter in the pan and sear the fish and then we'll eat it with a squeeze of lemon—or at least I will. Did you finish that already?" He poured her more.

She'd drunk two glasses by the time they sat down at the kitchen table, and she felt springy, a little bouncy in her chair as she nibbled her emerald-green asparagus, and he served himself the salmon.

"I like this way of roasting," she said.

"Just remember to sprinkle kosher salt when you take them out of the oven."

"*Salt sings,*" said Jess. The collector had copied that from Neruda. "Have you seen McClintock's asparagus drawings?"

"Show me."

"Not while we're eating!"

"Right." He poured out the last of the wine.

"Have you noticed his thing for asparagus?"

"And cabbages," said George.

"Yes! He's got heads of cabbage and cross sections and there's a drawing of this veined cabbage leaf. I think it must have been his botanical training." Jess was talking faster than usual, but then, she never had a chance to discuss the cookbooks, and she was brimming with impressions. "He draws asparagus and cabbages, but he's obsessed with artichokes. He draws them more than any other vegetable. Why artichokes?"

George drained his glass. "The artichoke is a sexy beast. Thorns to cut you, leaves to peel, lighter and lighter as you strip away the outer layers, until you reach the soft heart's core."

Jess laughed and finished her third glass.

"Try this." George offered her a bit of salmon on his fork.

The laughter stopped. "No."

"Why not?"

"I don't eat other creatures."

"This creature is already dead. You're not hurting him. Let's say he died for me. I'll take the blame. I bought him so I killed him. Now you can have a taste."

She shook her head.

"But it's so good." George offered her the flaky pink fish on his fork. "It tastes so good."

"I'm not eating that poor forked animal."

"Just try," George cajoled, scooting his chair around the corner to her side of the table. "Just one bite." He held the fork almost to her lips.

"George," she said, "don't you have certain things you would never do—on principle?"

"Arbitrary rules?"

"Any rules. Not necessarily arbitrary ones."

"I have beliefs," he said. "I have values. I think rules are overrated."

"Is that, like, a sixties thing?" She looked at him questioningly, as though she were gazing back at him through the mists of time.

"Someday you'll get asked about the Reagan years," he said.

"You should try rules," she pressed. "Then your beliefs would have practical applications, and you wouldn't have to drift from one meal to the next. Instead of being so ad hoc, you could rely on a consistent system. Instead of making up your life as you go along, you'd have a set path. You wouldn't have to reinvent the wheel. I think actually structure might be the key to oneness."

"I think you're a little drunk," said George.

"I think you're trying to impeach me."

He laughed even as he protested. "That's not true."

"Well, I'm not drunk at all," she warned him.

"And I'm not trying at all," he retorted playfully.

"Hmm." Her expression was both tender and reproachful. Her delicate hands rested on the table.

"Are you worried?" With his index finger George drew a question mark on her palm.

Almost imperceptibly she shook her head.

The light was shifting, the sky in the windows no longer bright, but watery, sea blue. They were close now, but the change was like nightfall. Neither knew exactly when it happened. They had been sitting apart, and now they found themselves in chairs pushed together. They had been talking, and now they touched instead, fingertips to wrists, and George could feel Jess's quick pulse, and she could feel his.

"Are you in love with him?" George said.

She didn't answer.

"Are you?"

"Why do you ask?"

"For the obvious reason."

"Which is?"

"That I want to know."

Lightly her fingertip glided over the back of his hand, tracing his scar up his arm.

"You're tickling me." He took her hand again.

"Did it hurt?" she asked him.

"Yes, it hurt," he said.

"Who did that to you?"

"An old girlfriend."

"You must have been nasty to her."

"Why do you assume it was my fault?" he asked gently. "Even if it was—who goes after her lover with a paring knife? She was completely unbalanced. She did teach me how to cook."

"Maybe you were such a slow learner she got frustrated."

"I wasn't a slow learner."

"No?" she teased. Her eyes were much darker in the evening light.

"I'm a quick study," he informed her. "I'm an excellent cook, but you'll never know, because you don't eat anything."

"I eat lots of things," she said.

"Judging from the peach, I'd say you eat a few things very well."

"You were watching me?"

"Yes."

"Why were you?"

His thumb stroked the inside of her wrist. "Because I wanted to."

"That's the only reason?"

"And because I never see you," he added.

"You can see me whenever you like," she told him. "You stay away."

"Did you wish I would come home?"

She didn't answer.

"Did you ever look around the house? Did you go upstairs?"

"No," she said, although she had thought about it. Concepcion's presence had prevented her. "I would never wander through your house without an invitation."

"Come." He took her hand.

She remembered climbing the stairs at the Tree House for the first time. "I think I *am* a little drunk."

"We'll go slow," he promised as he led her up the stairs. "These are my nautical charts and surveyors' plans." He turned on the lights in the stairwell, and she saw the antique charts, the hand-drawn schemes of San Francisco Bay. "You can see I have plenty of maps. This is original stained glass here on the landing. You can't tell at night, but I had it cleaned and restored. This place was a mess when I bought it. We copied these stair treads and spindles. This is my office." He showed her a spacious room with a great desk in the center, and a computer and a photocopier. "These are guest rooms." He opened one door after another.

"How many do you have?"

"Three. This is my room." He switched on the lights, and when she blinked in the sudden glare, he turned them down again. His room was huge, with great windows above the bed, stacks of books on the smooth floor, a low music stand and chair, a cello in an open case.

Find someone musical, Jess thought. "Will you play for me?"

"Of course." He sat down in his chair, but he did not reach for his cello. He held out his arms for Jess instead.

She sat on his lap and tucked up her legs, and he felt her weight, and her warmth, and he held still; he nearly held his breath, as she relaxed into his arms.

"My mother wrote about music," Jess said.

"Was she a critic?"

"I can hear your heartbeat," she whispered, resting her head on his chest.

"Was she a musician?" he asked her, as he stroked her hair.

"I think she might have been, if she'd had the chance," Jess said. "Or maybe not. She was an amazing baker too. That's what everybody says."

"You only know from hearsay? Don't tell me you were vegan even then."

"I wasn't vegan. I was too young to remember."

George's hand stopped for a moment, resting lightly on her head.

"When will you play for me?" she asked him.

"Soon."

"Did you learn as a child?"

"Mm-hmm." His lips brushed her ear.

"I wish I'd kept playing the piano. Everybody says that, but of course you imagine you'd play well. You don't imagine . . ."

"Do you miss her?"

"No." She looked up at him quickly, as if to gauge his response. "I'll tell you something terrible," she whispered. "I'll tell you a secret. I don't even think about her. I'm sure Emily thinks about her all the time, but I don't. I just . . ."

"Just what?"

"Don't have her," said Jess, muffled, burying her head again.

He continued stroking her long hair. She kept her head down, and listened to his steady heart.

"Jess?" he said at last.

"What?"

"Are you crying?"

"No." She looked up at him and her eyes were bright, but no tears stained her face. "Don't worry. I'm very cheerful." She sat up straight to make the point. "I'm not a weepy person. I wouldn't cry, even after too much wine."

"You can cry. I don't have rules. You can do anything you want."

"Anything?"

"Almost anything."

"So you have *some* rules."

"I said 'almost' so you'd think I was less of an ancient libertine," he said.

"Libertine? You mean old hippie."

"I was never a hippie."

"Right. You're just a libertine from the ancien régime."

He couldn't help laughing at the playful way she turned on him.

"Am I so funny?" she asked, laughing with him. She rubbed her nose against his. "Am I?"

"Come here, you." He pulled her closer.

"I'm here now," she said, and her voice was so warm and low that for a moment he closed his eyes. "I'm here already."

She caressed his cheek, and touched the tender skin under his eyes. His lips brushed her chin, her nose, her forehead, and finally her soft mouth, as they began to kiss.

PART SIX

Risk

~

August 2001

23

Emily sensed that Jess was keeping something from her. She could tell by the way her sister hid behind her hair.

"Is your cell still working?" Emily asked her.

"I think so."

"Then why don't you use it?"

"I do. Sometimes." Her hair fell like a curtain over her face.

They were sitting in Emily's white condo, in the living room, and they were sharing a vegan chocolate cake Jess had brought for Emily's thirtieth birthday. The big celebration was going to be with Jonathan that weekend at Lake Tahoe, but Jess had come for the actual day, August 8, and she was sitting cross-legged on the floor with the collection of Gillian's birthday letters, hers and Emily's together, in her lap.

For your eleventh birthday . . . For your twelfth birthday . . . For your twentieth birthday . . . I would like to see you at twenty. I think that you'll be tall, and I want to know if I am right.

"What you should do," said Jess, "is print these out on archival stock and make a scrapbook. This isn't good paper, and this ink"—she pointed to the dot matrix printing—"see, it's already fading."

I do miss knowing you at twenty, Emily. Sometimes I'm quite sad about it, and then at other times I think I should be grateful for knowing you as long as

I have. I'm greedy, like everybody else. I want to dot all the i's and cross all the t's. It's never enough, is it? It's not enough to have children. We want to see birthdays, and weddings, and grandchildren as well. I'd like to see them all. Of course there are other children I might have had, or other lives I might have lived, but I don't dwell on those. Why, then, should I mourn this one? Because this is the life I know, and you and your sister are the daughters I love. All the rest slips into the background—the realm of the unborn. That's another way to look at death, isn't it? Simply the part of life that's unexpressed. The might-haves and could-have-beens . . .

"Jess," said Emily, "what's going on with you?"

Jess looked up, startled. "Nothing," she lied.

"You seem . . ."

"What?"

"Evasive."

"Who, me?"

"Why are you so quiet?"

"Because I'm reading," said Jess.

"You never liked to read her letters before."

Jess thought about this for a moment. "But they're more interesting now."

She was spending the night at Emily's place, and long after her sister went to sleep, Jess stayed up reading and rereading her mother's letters. What was it about them? What was it she had overlooked before? Their secrecy. The obliqueness of the language drew her in, where before it had confused and bored her. *I might have been someone else,* her mother wrote. *I might have married someone else. I might have lived a different way, but I chose this life, and I chose you.*

The might-haves and could-have-beens, undescribed and unexplained. How had Jess missed them? She had been curious enough at twelve to read Gillian's letters all at once, devouring those messages to her older self, but she had always looked for information. Her mother was guarded about her illness, and her feelings, and her past, all the things that Jess wanted to find out, and after reading the letters one after another, Jess had turned away in disappointment. It was Gillian's reserve that made the letters interesting now. Those sentences Jess had always

read as generalities looked different. *I might have lived a different way.*
What did Gillian mean? *I might have married someone else.* Who would
that have been? Perhaps after weeks with the cookbooks, Jess was overly
sensitive. After so many hours pondering the collector's notes, she saw
subtexts and secrets everywhere. Even so, she began to read her mother's
words as coded messages. *Dear Emily, at sweet sixteen. Never been kissed?*
Wished you'd been kissed? Wonder if you might have been? I didn't wonder
about kissing when I was your age, although I would later. I didn't like to think
about the future when I had one, and now that my future is running out, I
think about it all the time.

"Gillian!" Jess whispered in surprise. She stared at the picture her
mother had enclosed, a color photo of a laughing freckled woman in a
sundress and a floppy yellow hat. An outdoor picture, a lawn chair in the
background, her mother holding out a piece of chocolate cake. And as
she looked, it occurred to her that she had never seen an earlier image of
her mother. There were no black-and-white photos in the albums in her
father's house. No baby pictures or childhood-recital photos. Hadn't
Gillian performed in piano recitals for her teacher? And didn't anybody
take pictures? There were none. There was only the story Richard told,
which was that Gillian never got along with her parents in London. That
they had been so angry when she'd married a non-Jew that they cut her
off completely. Therefore, Jess and Emily had never met their Jewish
grandparents, or anyone from that side of the family. Gillian's parents
never spoke to her again, and she never spoke of them—or wrote about
them either. And yet she said in her letters to Emily, *I know from my own*
experience that some memories are indelible. This comforts me, because, of
course, I should like to be indelible for you.

But what were these indelible memories? Gillian didn't say. They lived
between the lines, and underneath the letters, in that realm of secrets Jess
could not ferret out. And Jess wondered, poetically, whether there had
been some great love in her mother's life—some other man she might
have married (for she could not imagine her own father as a figure of romance). And she wondered whether there had been a secret hurt, a sad
end to all of Gillian's might-have-beens. Perhaps her parents forbade her
to become a concert pianist, and this was why Gillian played Chopin

Waltzes, in requiem. Late at night, in her pajamas, Jess was open to every dramatic possibility, for she had never felt a kinship with her mother before. She had never thought of Gillian as yearning or secretive. Her mother had died young, but now Jess saw that her mother had *been* young, and that was a different matter altogether. Her letters were no longer prescriptive, but searching, far more powerful now that Jess had a secret of her own.

She lived in the Tree House as before, and did her chores—cooking, cleaning, leafleting, supplying the tree-sitters in the Grove. She attended Rabbi Helfgott's mysticism classes with Mrs. Gibbs, and typed the minutes for Tree House meetings, where she was official scribe. She slept in Leon's bed, but he was away in Humboldt County, climbing, demonstrating, organizing, and who knew what else. He did call and ask her when she would come, but he did not call often, nor did he return to get Jess, and the longer Leon stayed away, the easier it became to slip into the collector's world.

On weekday afternoons, she sat with the cookbooks at George's table, and she lost herself in recipes for marzipan, illustrations of assorted ices, lists of berries for plucking in each season. She read the cookbooks along with their collector, noting where he paused to draw or quote or simply copy some delicious detail. *Take your Angelica when young and tender, which will be about the beginning of May. . . .* She worked with Tom McClintock's ghost, and where he sighed, she sighed, and where he seemed to smile—*Syrup of Maiden-hair!!*—she smiled. And she examined each line drawing of the woman he adored, a lady with wide-set eyes, long wavy hair, small feet, and pointed toes. Jess was beginning to dream about this woman; she felt she knew her; she thought she almost knew her name.

She glided through the house, and ate the plums George left. She cut melons in the kitchen, and ate the dripping slices, cold and sweet. *Be careful with this knife,* he wrote on one of her note cards. Carefully, she slid George's steel knife into round cantaloupe and honeydew and galia melons. And if she waited long enough, he came home. She listened for him now, and met him at the door. She stood on his feet so she could reach, and wrapped her arms around his broad shoulders, and if he came from running, she licked his salt skin, and they kissed until he took her hand and led her upstairs. But they didn't plan to see each other. They talked of everything else and kept their time a secret even from themselves; the food they shared, the wine they drank, the Bach he played for her, music rough and smooth.

He took her to Point Reyes, and they drove through fields of tall grass and wildflowers. Along the coast they smelled a mix of salt and eucalyptus, and as they sped down Sir Francis Drake Highway, they passed a tavern called the Golden Hind, but they did not stop there. They ate a picnic dinner at a beach called Heart's Desire. At dusk when it was time to go, they lingered, and Jess took off her sandals and walked barefoot in the cove on Tomales Bay. The bay was round, green-gray under the round clear sky. Slick under her feet, sea grass tangled in her toes. She called to George, "It's warm. Come in with me."

He said, "No, it's late. We should drive back."

"Come on," she said. "Just get your feet wet."

She stretched out her arms to him until he unlaced his shoes and took off his socks to come and kiss her in the shallow water.

He took her to Santa Cruz, and to Santa Rosa, and to Half Moon Bay. He took her walking with him deep in Tilden Park, but only where he knew that they would be alone.

They were living in a bubble of their own, and when one of them began to speak of it, the other murmured, "No." They were improbable, and at the same time all too predictable. He did not tell Nick or Raj. She did not confess to Leon, or so much as hint to Emily. They scarcely admitted to each other what they were doing. Even a single word could break the spell, and so they kissed instead of speaking, and drank instead of thinking. They heard the mermaids singing. When human voices woke them, they would drown.

Each had moments of lucidity. *You have to stop,* Jess told herself. *You need to see Leon. You need to go away and think.*

Slow down, George told himself. *This is intoxicating.*

But they did not stop. They only delayed a little. He walked through the door and she said, "I have to show you this," and she pulled him into the dining room to unveil that day's discovery. A recipe for *pecokys,* which

schul ben pyarboyld and lardyd and etyn with gyngenyr. And then she
showed him instructions for broiling larks, and then McClintock's handwritten quotations from Gertrude Stein.

"Sweet sweet sweet sweet sweet tea," she read aloud as George stood behind her. Arms around her waist, he was unbuttoning her shirt. *"When the
ancient light grey is clean it is yellow, it is a silver seller."*

She sat on the table with the slip of paper in her hand. "Doesn't silver
seller make you think of salt?"

"Not really," he murmured, kneeling on the chair, kissing her bare
skin.

"Her poetry wasn't abstract at all." She felt his breath and his rough
tongue. "Don't you think *Tender Buttons* is really about . . . ?"

"Yes."

Working in the August afternoons, she wondered what he would bring
home for dinner, what strange fruit, what curious greens, or salty sea
beans. He brought her plums, and Asian pears, and almonds, and she
showed him her discoveries.

"Look at this," she told George, dancing into his arms.

The volume was so slight that they had missed it in their first assessment. In fact, she found it tucked inside a larger book. Scottish, dated
1736, it was one of those palm-sized cookbooks, a handbook that fit literally in the hand. Its recipes were terse, not terribly poetic, nor was the
book illustrated, except for some decoration on the first page, a little head
of Bacchus, tame enough to be a house pet, surrounded by a couple of
clumsy birds and vines. Why then was this book so stuffed with notes?

He laughed when he saw the title. *Mrs. McLintock's Receipts for Cookery and Pastry-Work.* "You think Tom McClintock felt a kinship?"

"It's rare," she said.

"How rare?"

"It's the first Scottish cookbook by a woman. I e-mailed the University of Aberdeen. There are only two known copies in the world, and
they're both in Glasgow."

This was serious. Silently he began to calculate how much a book like this would be worth to the Schlesinger, to the Getty, to those private collectors who would bid for it.

"No one knows about this one," she told him. "This is now the third!"

"Jess," he said.

"We should call reporters," she declared. "We should write an article."

"You should write the article," he said.

"But first I have to understand it better."

"What do you mean?"

She couldn't quite explain. She wanted to know the cookbook's secret life. For days she studied it. She gazed at Mrs. McLintock's name so long that in her mind the letters rearranged themselves: *lock, lint, clint, clit, cock, clock . . . McClintock. McLintock.* She imagined the two fit together, but she found no clues about McClintock in McLintock, and the collector's love remained a mystery.

"George," she said one evening as she lay in his arms.

"Jessamine." His eyes were soft, his face unguarded, almost boyish in the low light.

"I have to ask you something."

"I have to ask you something too." He was wearing his wristwatch, a vintage Patek Philippe he'd forgotten to take off. She didn't wear a watch, and so she wore nothing at all.

"Okay." She had been lying with her head on his chest, and now she propped her chin up on her arms, a gesture both adorable and suffocating.

"No, you ask first," he said, "because I can't breathe."

"I'm sorry!" She rolled off and she lay on her side, facing him. "I wanted to ask you about the cookbook. I doubt McClintock knew how rare it was. I don't think he understood how much the books were worth, but he had a thing for women cookbook writers, and obviously he fixated on McLintock because of her name. So do you think there was a Mrs. McClintock in his life whom Sandra doesn't know about? Do you think maybe he was married at some point when he was young, when he was buying all these books after the War?"

"No, sweetheart," said George.

"Really?" she asked yearningly, and he couldn't tell whether she was questioning the *no* or the word *sweetheart,* which he had never used before.

He caressed her waist and the curve of her hip with his hand. "He never married her. He never got anywhere with her."

"You always say that, but what evidence do you have?"

"The whole collection, every note he wrote."

"People thought Troy was a myth too," Jess reminded George, "and now those ruins have been found. Don't laugh! I think he knew her. She wasn't somebody that he saw once. He drew her as if he saw her every day."

"We'll never know, will we?"

"Yes, we will. I'm going to find out," said Jess, clear-eyed, pure. She was so lovely. Not just her face, but her faith that there was such a thing as truth, her conviction that there were immutable answers if you took the trouble to find them out.

"Stay here tonight," George whispered.

"That's what you were going to ask?"

"Will you?"

He had said one of the things they did not say. "I thought we weren't doing that."

"You're right," he said. "Sleeping together is one thing, but . . ."

She buried her head in his pillow.

"Talking about it is another."

He didn't want to talk about it either. He wanted to remain in this dream state as long as possible. The outside world was all obstacles and complications. Leon. The Tree Savers. Their missions up to Humboldt County. George could say Leon was dangerous. He could tell Jess that she was wrong to get involved with him. What was he offering in return? A sinecure. A dependency. To be crass, his bed. He could say he loved her. Would he mean it? They enjoyed each other. They were friends, and he desired her. He knew himself well enough to doubt that such feelings would last. He was fully capable of breaking Jess's heart.

As for Jess—she was mixed-up about George. She was at home with him. Calm and happy. She could think aloud. She never felt that way at the Tree House, and yet the people there shared her beliefs about the world. Philosophically, ideologically, she and Leon were a pair. She and George agreed on nothing politically. He had no interest in the environment. He recycled like everybody else, but he cared little for other species, and maligned Tree Savers as eco-terrorists. He was old that way, ill-informed and cynical, preferring books to social change, studying antique maps instead of current battlegrounds of deforestation. Living in the past, he turned his back on the future, and this was a position she deplored.

Then there was his money. She remembered Leon's warning: *You'll end up in his collection too.* She could see it happening. She was entranced by his house, his wine, his cookbooks, his quick smile. Recipe for disaster. She was falling in love with George, and she worked for him too. What would that make her? The young girlfriend. The mistress, the kept woman. She hated the thought.

Abashed, she read Haywood's instructions to maidservants, advice on chastity preceding recipes for pickles, directions for choosing meat, best methods for *making all kinds of English wines.*

If you follow the advice I have already given you, concerning going as frequently as you can to hear sermons, and reading the holy scriptures and other good books, I need not be at the pains to inform you how great the sin is of yielding to any unlawful solicitations: but if you even look no farther than this world—oh, practical Eliza, thought Jess—*you will find enough to deter you from giving the least encouragement to any address of that nature, though accompanied with the most soothing and flatterring pretenses.*

Jess sighed. She knew, in the long term, she and George were philosophically unsuited, financially unequal, generationally mismatched. Only in the short term did they agree. Only when it came to fingertips, and tongues and wrists. When he touched her and then slipped his wet fingers in her mouth and said, "This is how you taste." In their laughter and the food he brought her, the freshest and most delicate of vegetables: watercress, fennel, dandelion greens dressed with champagne vinegar. They shared a private language in the cookbooks, and whispered inside jokes. Even their jokes were gentle. Tender buttons. He was tender with her.

She craved his company. The edges of her life were ragged, her feelings conflicted, her behavior incoherent, probably immoral, and at the same time, she was deeply happy, consuming nectarines, and Asian pears, sliced thin, and the pinot he poured for her.

"Try the wine now," George instructed. Then, a little later, "Try it again," and she tasted a new liquid altogether. Wine that had been tight and taciturn became mellifluous.

"It's like finding a door," she told George as they sat together in his kitchen. "It's like stepping into a new room you never knew existed."

"The pinot?"

"No," she told him. "Everything."

For she was becoming a researcher, tracing gorgeous threads, preparing a catalogue raisonné of the McClintock Collection, corresponding with scholars and librarians at the Schlesinger and the Huntington and at universities around the world. She had begun to study sweets—the sparing use of sugar in early cookbooks, and its ubiquity in eighteenth-century recipes. She checked out books from Bancroft. Deerr's *History of Sugar.* Galway's *The Sugar Cane Industry: An Historical Geography from Its Origins to 1914. Sweetness and Power* by Sidney W. Mintz. She spent days writing notes for an article she was planning on the cookbook as cultural emblem and bellwether for abundance and scarcity. Without an affiliation, outside any academic program, she began to imagine weaving together ecology and economics and material culture, embarking on a new career. Should she go back to school? Find herself a program and an advisor? Oh, but it was delicious to work unsupervised. Who had total access to books like these? And when it came to advisors, how could she do better than Tom McClintock, sensualist and lichenologist, artist, lover, ghost?

On a Friday, at the end of August, just before her twenty-fifth birthday, Jess sat alone in George's dining room and unfolded a menu she had not seen before, one of the collector's fantasies on graph paper. The menu was tucked inside *Le Livre de Cuisine,* but titled "McLintock," and the dishes listed were all in English.

McLINTOCK

July-flower wine
Angelica
Nutmeg cream
Eel-pye
Neats Tongue

A strange, unappetizing bill of fare, wine and dessert, followed by eel pie and sheep's tongue. It's not like you, Jess thought, addressing the collector, to put together such an awkward menu. Elsewhere, McClintock sought out the most exotic and delectable combinations. Kisses to begin, new peas, or *muskmelon,* followed by some tender young thing, lamb or fawn, turtledoves to whet the appetite, and then fish, and a succulent main course like loin of veal. Fruit and cream to finish. *Quaking Pudding.* Candied violets, rose petals, tansies, *curran wine* . . .

Why, then, these awkward dishes out of order, and no vegetable or fish or salad course? She read the menu twice and then a third time, and then she wondered if the words could rearrange themselves into something better. *July-Angelica-Nutmeg-Cream* . . . and as her eyes played with the words, she saw a pattern in the first letters, an acrostic reading down:

July-flower wine
Angelica
Nutmeg cream
Eel-pye
Neats Tongue

A name: Jane. Jane McClintock! Was this Mrs. McClintock? Was she the one? But what to do about *Neats Tongue*? A comment on Mrs. McClintock's tongue? Or did she have a middle initial *N*? Jane N. McClintock? Or was it the *T* the collector referred to in his culinary code? Jane T? Janet!

She picked up George's phone and called Sandra, but no one answered. She ran out and drove to Sandra's house. She rang the bell, and rapped on the window, but no one came to the door. Should she leave a note? Try again tomorrow? No, her question wouldn't keep.

She sat on Sandra's porch in a raggedy wicker chair. Curled up in the window, Geoffrey seemed to recognize her, and wish her ill.

An hour passed before Sandra arrived carrying her groceries. Jess jumped up. "Hi!"

"Jessamine," said Sandra, after a moment.

"I'm sorry," Jess said. "I didn't mean to startle you. Could I help you carry those?"

"No, I don't think so," Sandra told her.

"I've been working on the collection," Jess said. "I've been working almost six months. The books are fabulous."

"I'm glad." Sandra pulled at her keys, which she wore on a plastic bracelet around her wrist.

"I've found some interesting material." Jess followed Sandra to the door.

"Good." Sandra stood on the porch, keys in hand, groceries at her feet, but she did not seem at all inclined to invite Jess inside. "I can't let the cat out," she reminded Jess as she gathered all her bags together to rush the door. "You can come in, but you have to be quick."

"Oh, I understand." Body-blocking Geoffrey, Sandra darted inside, and Jess followed.

"Would you like a glass of juice?" Sandra asked. "Would you like to take a seat? Not that one." She warned Jess away from Geoffrey's dark green couch, and Jess settled on a velvet chair instead.

"Who was Mrs. McClintock?" Jess blurted out.

"What do you mean?"

"Are you sure your uncle never married?"

"He never married."

"Are you sure he didn't marry a Janet McClintock?" Jess asked.

"Of course I'm sure," said Sandra. "Janet McClintock was my mother."

George did not know where Jess had gone. She had left her books out. McLintock lay open on the book cradle. The laptop stood open as well, as though Jess intended to return, but it was past five and she did not come back. He called her on her cell, but she didn't answer.

He poured himself a glass of wine and began to think of all the things he might have said or done to offend her. He remembered that the day before they'd had a little spat about her article. They were sitting in the living room on his couch, a massive low-slung piece with great wood slabs for arms. He said that she should write something quick and accessible with gorgeous illustrations for *Gastronomica*. She insisted that this was selling out, that she was developing an argument far more scholarly, with serious notes and tables. She said she had fifty-one pages already, and he'd laughed and warned her not to get lost in all that material.

Then she'd demanded, "Do I look like someone who gets lost easily?"

"Yes," he'd teased, but she hadn't been in the mood, and had snatched a heavy throw pillow, upholstered green, and smacked him upside the head.

They had laughed at the time, but perhaps she was still angry. Or perhaps Leon had suddenly returned, and Jess had decided she would not see George again. Was there some change of heart? Or some emergency? Should he try to reach her sister?

By the time Jess arrived, he had been waiting almost two hours, and he was in such an anxious state that he was almost in no mood to see her. But there she was, out of breath and streaked with sweat from racing up the stairs. "I've solved it," she cried. "I know who she was."

And she showed George how she had picked out *Janet* from the menu, and told him how she had rushed to tell Sandra. "He was in love with Janet when he was young. I think Janet was McClintock's Laura and his Beatrice, and that's why he drew her over and over and he read her into all his cookbooks."

"What did Sandra say?"

"She was very offended!" Jess exclaimed. "She said her uncle didn't even like to eat. She said that he was extremely thin. She told me her mother was happily married for sixty-two years, and she was perfectly sensible and lucid until the day she died at eighty-three."

George smiled.

But Jess was indignant. "I thought she'd thank me!"

"For inventing an embarrassing story about her mother?"

"I didn't invent it," Jess said. "I know I'm right. Maybe it was an unrequited love, but she was the one."

You're the one, thought George.

"You'd think she'd enjoy knowing," Jess said. "She's convinced she was a Russian princess in a past life. Why can't Janet and Tom have had a past life too? Why is that so shocking?"

"Let me take you out to dinner."

"George," said Jess. "Look at me."

"I am looking at you."

"I'm covered with cat hair."

"Come take a bath."

"I don't have fresh clothes."

"We'll stop at your place and you can change."

Jess ignored this. "Charles Dickens was obsessed with his sister-in-law. He never got over her."

"Yes, and I'm sure the family loved to hear about it."

Jess folded her arms across her chest. "And Tolstoy didn't really model Natasha on his wife."

"You're upset," George murmured.

"It's just so anticlimactic—to put together the pieces of the puzzle and then to be . . ."

"Shh." He kissed her.

"Exactly. To be shushed like that. As though I were arriving on her doorstep to blackmail her or something. As though I had something on her. She says she's upset about her grandchildren. Her daughter still can't get custody."

"That explains it," said George, frowning. "Don't you think she'd be preoccupied?"

"I thought she might be . . ."

"She's not going to be grateful to you for suggesting that her mother had some kind of affair with her husband's brother. You got carried away, Jess."

She didn't answer.

"Come here."

She didn't come.

He took her hand. "You have to be careful not to fall in love with your material."

She relented a little. "Maybe."

"I thought she'd be more imaginative," Jess told George as he ran the water in the bath. She perched on the edge of the tub, which was claw-footed, fathoms deep, and she pulled off one grubby sock and George pulled off the other.

"About her own family?"

Jess wriggled out of her jeans. "Don't fill it all the way." She peeled off her T-shirt and bra. "It's a waste of . . ."

"Get in," George said.

She sat in the water, tucking her knees up to her chest. "If someone told me something about *my* mother, I wouldn't be defensive like that. To me that kind of information would be golden."

"Why?" George climbed in after her.

"Why? Because it's . . . it's contact. It means if you know how to read them, underneath the words there's life."

He sat behind her, soaping her shoulders, her arms, her breasts. "You're going to be a historian," he said.

"I am." With a little splash, she turned over in the water and looked into his dark eyes, and she saw that he wasn't laughing at her. He didn't look bemused, or skeptical. She kissed him. She slipped into his arms, and they were closer than before.

When they stepped inside Greens that night and stood together before the great piece of driftwood at the entrance, when they took their table at the wall-high windows and looked out at the Pacific, they were like travelers arriving in a new city. They were like newlyweds in fancy clothes. His sports jacket, her sleeveless dress; his tie, her mother-of-pearl buttons down the front. He ate fish and she ate polenta and they drank a bottle of '97 Chateau Montelena. "Best year since '94," George told Jess, and they toasted the McClintocks, Tom, and Janet, and Mrs. McLintock too. They sat at the great windows and they watched the seagulls diving between waves and sky, and thought but didn't say how strange it was to go out like other couples.

Jess said, "Do you think *marmalet of apples* actually tasted like something?"

And George said, "You never talk about your father."

"It couldn't have been bitter like real marmalade," Jess said.

"You don't get along with him, do you?" George said.

"No," Jess confessed. "Not really."

"Why not?"

"He doesn't like me very much."

George trapped her legs between his underneath the table. "That can't be true."

"Well," said Jess, "he's all computers. He's all math, and I'm humanities. He's all for financial independence—and I am too! But I'm not . . . really independent yet. He has no time for religion, philosophy, or poetry. Fortunately, he's got Emily."

"You must take after your mother," George said.

"Maybe."

"And he loved her."

"I think so," Jess said. "But who knows? It was such a long time ago."

"When he reads your essay, he'll understand what you can do," George said.

"I don't care whether he reads my essay or not." Jess drained her glass and he saw that her face was flushed. "*You* understand what I can do."

"That's a complicated thing to say."

"No, it's not."

"I can't take his place," George said warily.

Jess slipped off her shoes and rubbed her bare feet against George's ankles until he couldn't help smiling. "I never asked you to."

Giddy with each other and the wine, they strolled outside through the Presidio, the old fort now housing restaurants and galleries. Jess explained that she wanted to devise a matrix for scarcity and abundance, frugality and profligacy. She thought that sweetness represented, and in some periods misrepresented, a sense of surplus and shared pleasure. "I don't think taste is purely biological," she said. "I think it's economically, historically, and culturally constructed as well. Sweetness means different things depending on availability, custom, farming, trade. . . ."

She was shivering, and George took off his jacket. "Here, sweetness." He helped her into it and laughed at the way her hands disappeared inside the sleeves.

"Context is key—so the question is, What carries over? What can we still know about sweet and sour? Bitterness. What persists from generation to generation? Do we taste the same things?"

He kissed her, sucking her lower lip and then her tongue. "I think so," he said. "Yes."

"Wait, I'm not finished."

"Continue," he said. "Please."

Testing herself, pushing back against her fear of heights, she climbed atop the thick two-foot wall edging the Presidio's park, and walked above him, while he held her hand, steadying her from below.

"You see, I'm fine walking on this wall," she declared, even as she gripped his fingers. "You see? I've been practicing, and I can climb very well."

George looked up at her. "You like to tower over me, don't you?"

She did. At that moment she wasn't in the least afraid of towering. She was invincible. And she explained her theory about cloves, and she told him how the word *sweet* meant "unsalted" in English cookbooks. *Sweet* meant "fresh," not "sugared" as one might think. She spoke of candying and conserves, and those mysterious syrups in McLintock. *Syrup of Violets, Syrup of Clove Gelly-Flowers, Syrup of Red Poppies, Syrup of Pale Roses.* How did pale roses taste?

They reached the end of the wall and she kept talking. She grew more and more scholarly, investigative, joyful. Absorbed in her lecture, he didn't expect her to jump down just when she did.

"Give me a little warning!" he exclaimed as he caught her in his arms, but he didn't want a warning, he wanted her, and he wrapped her in his arms, his chin brushing the rough weave of his own jacket.

"What's to become of us?" She laughed.

"I don't know."

"Just as long as we don't really . . . you know . . ." She meant fall in love.

"Too late," George said.

24

Love was all very well, but in the world outside, survival mattered most. Veritech was strapped for cash, ISIS on the brink. Emily felt she had no time to breathe, and Jonathan grew warlike, confident as ever, but edgy from lack of sleep.

"Mel!" Jonathan sang out when Mel returned from lunch. "Exactly the person I wanted to see."

Mel stood at the elevator, and his lower back tightened with the familiar mix of dread and pleasure to be singled out.

"Job fair in L.A. September eleventh."

"I didn't think we were hiring," Mel replied.

"I want the ISIS booth there anyway," said Jonathan. "I want to make our presence known."

People were gathering, waiting for the elevators. Movers wheeled boxes out on handcarts. ISIS was decamping to cheaper, East Cambridge real estate.

"Maybe we should discuss this in your office," Mel suggested.

Jonathan ignored him. "We're going out there."

"I'm not sure what we have to offer at a job fair when we're not hiring."

"This isn't about now," said Jonathan. "It's about six months from now.

I want the booth, the literature, the whole nine yards to extend to any programmers out there."

"But realistically," Mel said, "what do we tell these kids?"

"What do we tell them? We tell them who we are."

"Show the flag?"

"Exactly. I need you to show the flag. I have a meeting in San Diego that week, so I might come out too."

"All right." Mel sighed. "I'll see if I can get someone to—"

"No," Jonathan said, "you."

"Me?" Only Mel's associate directors flew west. That was long established. Mel's back could barely withstand the Boston–New York–D.C. shuttle.

"You," said Jonathan.

"I'll prepare everything on this end," Mel said. "I'll prep Keith and Ashley, and they can go together."

"Sorry, man," said Jonathan. "I had to let them go this morning."

"You did what?"

"Yeah, we're making some cuts."

"But you never—"

"It's a top–down thing," said Jonathan. "But it's all good. Feel free to upgrade to business class. Just a second." Jonathan's phone was ringing. "Hey!" he told Emily. "Could you hold on? I'm just finishing a meeting."

Some meeting, Mel thought, standing in the lobby. "Jonathan, I don't think I can physically—I don't know if I can manage that flight and still function in L.A."

"Mel, you underestimate yourself," said Jonathan. "You always do."

"What if I trained Juliet?"

Now Jonathan grew impatient. "Juliet is your secretary, Mel. You're the HR director. You're the one they need to see." He put his phone to his ear and began walking to the stairs. "What's wrong?" he asked, and even as he listened, he turned and pointed straight at Mel. Like a latter-day Uncle Sam, he mouthed, *You.*

"It's Jess," said Emily. "She's driving up to Arcata. She says a bunch of them are going up together. . . ."

"She's been there before," said Jonathan.

"But this time she's going to climb. She says that she's been practicing."

"Good for her." Jonathan took the stairs two at a time.

"No, you don't understand. It's really dangerous for her."

"How is it more dangerous for her than for anybody else?"

"She doesn't know what she's doing and she's afraid of—"

"She'll be with experienced people."

"Do you think it's rational to try to climb a two-hundred-foot redwood when you're afraid of heights?" Emily demanded.

"I don't know—it sounds like fun. When is she going?"

"September fourth through September eleventh," said Emily.

"That's when I'm coming out for Tech World," said Jonathan. "You can meet me in L.A."

He didn't understand that Jess could hurt herself, and sometimes Emily thought he didn't care. He had never liked her sister. From his point of view, she was always in trouble of one kind or another. Impatient, he did not hear Emily's fear that this time was worse.

"Why do you have to go?" Emily asked Jess on the phone.

Jess said, "I can't be a coward all my life."

Emily sat in her office with her picture of Jonathan on the screen saver in front of her. "You aren't a coward. Why do you say that?"

"I can't keep floating from one thing to the next."

"What is going on with you?"

"I have to grow up sometime," Jess said.

"Growing up is not something you do on a tree-climbing expedition," Emily protested. "Tree climbing is the opposite of growing up!"

"You remember when I made my vow," Jess said.

"That ridiculous thing you said in Muir Woods?"

"It was not ridiculous. It was serious. And I said that in January. That was almost nine months ago. The year is almost up, and I haven't followed through. It's now or never."

"What are you talking about?" Emily demanded. "Are you trying to prove something to Leon? Is that it?"

"No," said Jess. "I'm proving this to myself. It's not about Leon." She added silently, *Or George.*

In truth, she was frightened. Her time with George was so intense. Not just the time with him, but the time away from him. She heard his voice. She saw him in her dreams. She had had a dream that she was flying with him through the trees in winter. They were flying slowly, drifting through the air, and she was wearing a long silk skirt that caught in bare branches. *Don't worry,* said George as he floated down to untangle her. But she did worry. She thought about him constantly. She was sleeping over now, and spending mornings with him, as well as evenings. When he left, she missed him. While she worked, thoughts of George distracted her. She was no longer contemplating rose water. She contemplated him. She was no longer simply archiving the collector's notes. She had *become* the collector, dreaming, doodling. She was altogether infatuated. And she wondered: How did this happen to me? How did I fall in love like this when I'm with someone else? And sometimes she and George seemed overdetermined, destined from the start. At other times, the relationship, if that's what it now was, terrified her, because it wasn't just George, but his things that entranced her, and she could not separate him from his possessions. His gorgeous home, his fresh sheets, his garden, his collections.

At the Tree House, Jess pitched in, like everybody else. The Tree Savers cooked and cleaned together, creating their own sanctuary. At George's house Concepcion took care of everything. Sheets and towels reappeared magically, clean and white. Dishes returned sparkling to their shelves. At the Tree House, Jess was part of a team, but at George's house she worked alone, reading, writing, gorging herself on McClintock's fantasies.

To be with George was pure luxury, and she mourned, Oh, I am more materialistic than I thought. Oh, I am no idealist at all. I just want to be stroked and fed. And she was disgusted with herself. The affair was so obvious and degrading. She had nothing, and he was rich. She slept with him and read his books and drank his wine as though she were a little scholar-geisha, when she should be with Leon at the front, fighting against the Pacific Lumber Company. She was an aesthete, just when she should have been an ascetic and a revolutionary. The fact that she loved talking to George, and kissing him and falling asleep in his arms and waking up with him in the morning made the situation a thousand times worse.

So she resolved to fall out of love, and every day she planned to tell George, but that day passed and then another, until at last, as they ate risotto in the kitchen, George gave her an opening. He said, "Jess, I'm having some friends for dinner on Labor Day." That was all, but she knew instantly what he meant.

"You don't want me here."

"Well . . . ," he hedged, and his hesitation was worse than the exclusion. "Don't be offended."

"I'm not offended. I'm glad," she told him. "I'm relieved." And she really was relieved, as well as hurt. "I'm driving up to Arcata that weekend."

"What do you mean, 'driving up to Arcata'?"

"I'm going to meet Leon and the tree-sitters in Wood Rose Glen."

"You aren't really going to start tree-sitting."

"Why wouldn't I?" Jess demanded. But what she meant was, "How dare you tell me what to do when I can't exist for you in the real world in front of your friends?"

"Don't you think tree-sitting in a twenty-story redwood is risky? And just a little adolescent?"

"Don't start lecturing me."

"I wasn't lecturing," he said. "I was asking."

"That was a rhetorical question," Jess said. "So you weren't asking at all."

"How long are you going for?"

"I don't know," Jess answered dangerously. "As long as I want. Obviously you don't have to pay me for the weeks that I'm away."

"Weeks!"

"I'll go for as long as they need me. Leon says they might stay the month."

"And how are you going to live up there?" George asked her.

"The same way everybody else does. We have supplies. We have food.

It's not like I haven't been before. I was there almost two months in the spring."

He turned away, an expression she recognized, disappointment mixed with anger. "You know it's dangerous."

"Doing nothing is also dangerous."

"People get killed up there."

"People get killed on the ground too."

He stood up to clear the risotto bowls, but walked around behind her instead and placed his hands upon her shoulders, a gesture suddenly irritating. She shook him off and sprang up from the table.

"Don't go," he said.

"Don't go? Is that an order?"

"A request."

"What are you thinking?"

"I'm thinking about your safety," he said. "What if something happens to you?"

"Something has happened to me," said Jess. "I've become your little pet. I've become your latest toy, your newest typewriter, and it's not good, and you know it. You can't introduce me to your friends, and there's a reason for that. The reason is they'll see exactly what you've done. They won't approve, and they'll be right. They'll say, 'George, how much did she cost?'"

"That's spiteful," said George. "And childish."

Tears started in Jess's eyes. "What's childish is pretending we live in our own little world, when the truth is that I'm involved with someone else, and I have a life away from here. And you have your friends and your dealers and your store and Colm and all your projects, and it's not like we have a future together, and it's not like we have much of a past. . . ."

"Do you really think you have a future with Leon?"

"That's none of your business."

"You're angry," he said.

"Don't tell me I'm angry," Jess exploded. "I hate it when you say 'You're angry,' or 'You're upset.' I *know* that I'm angry. I'll tell *you* when I'm angry. And I'll tell you what makes me angry. What makes me angry is that you expect me to stay with you at your pleasure."

"Wait—" George interrupted.

"No, you wait. You want me here when it's good for you, and gone when it's inconvenient for you. You want me when it's fun for you, and then when you get bored—not when I get bored—but when you get tired of me, you'll say you've had enough."

"Don't put words in my mouth."

"Or maybe you'll say it's not working out, or we don't belong together long-term. Which is true. We don't. But if I point this out now, then you're defensive, because you aren't done yet. *That* makes me angry. And I'll tell you something else that makes me angry. I used to have a life. Maybe not what you call a life. Maybe you couldn't see it, but I used to wake up and say, 'What will I do today?' Now I wake up and I know what I'll do. I'll work with your books and count the hours until I see you. I don't talk to anyone else. I don't see anyone else. I'm virtually hiding from my sister—"

"Would you stop and let me say something?" George broke in. "I have never done anything to you. I never imprisoned you here in my house."

"That's true," said Jess. "And that's what makes it so bad. I want to work with the collection; I want to eat with you. I want to sleep with you. You're like a drug. I can't stop thinking about you, and it's exhausting. It's . . ."

"So you don't want to see Leon. You want to get away from me," said George.

"I do want to see him," Jess said stubbornly. "And I want my life to be about something besides you." And she walked into the dining room and began stuffing papers, the notes for her essay, into her backpack.

"Jess," said George, "listen. Don't do something you'll regret. I—"

"Don't say something *you'll* regret," Jess countered. "Don't say something that isn't true."

25

She left him there, just like that, and all night he hoped that she would call. All the next day, he hoped she would return, but she did not call, and she did not return. Surely, he thought, she would come back to finish her essay, if not to catalog the collection. She would not abandon her project, even if she was abandoning him. But the days passed, a week passed, and he heard nothing from her.

He went about his business, running with Nick, buying, trading, selling books at Yorick's. He held his little dinner party, and Jess wasn't there, and he told his friends that his cataloger had run off to Humboldt County, as they all did eventually, and now he had to find someone new. But, of course, he had no interest in finding anyone else. No one could replace Jess. He didn't even look at the cookbooks when she was gone.

"You liked her," Nick intuited as they stretched at Inspiration Point.

George said nothing.

"You talked about her all the time."

"How was I talking about her all the time?" George shot back. "I hardly talked about her at all."

"What was her name? Jessica?"

"Jessamine."

"You had a fight."

"It's complicated," George said.

"Really?" Nick teased gently. "It doesn't sound so complicated to me."

"She's in Arcata with her boyfriend. I think she'll probably stay there."

"You think?"

"Well, she wants to stay there."

"Is that what she told you?" asked Nick. They stood together looking at the electrical towers ruining the view of tawny hills. "She's with someone else?" Nick pressed.

"She needs someone her own age. She can't work for me and be with me at the same time. She can't be my employee and my lover. I would be supporting her and I'd have all the power in the relationship. That doesn't work, if she's going to have a life. I'd be exploiting her. I was exploiting her all along."

"Do you love her?"

George didn't answer.

"Do you want to be with her?"

"A relationship like that never lasts," said George.

"It might last—" said Nick.

"It's just too fraught."

"What's the matter with you, man? You're overthinking everything, as usual."

"I'm thinking. I'm not overthinking. I'm reflecting on the situation. Now that it's too late, I keep thinking about what I could have done differently. How I could have dealt with the inequities . . ."

Nick pushed his old friend's shoulder, hard. "It's called marriage, George. In most of the world, that's how it's done."

He tried to work. He tried to sleep. He returned from running and sat at his kitchen table with the *San Francisco Chronicle*. When his phone rang, he jumped, but it was Raj calling about a rare copy of *Ulysses* he had acquired. "I'm telling you first, in case you want to make a preemptive offer."

"No," George said. "I don't like Joyce."

"George," said Raj, "you're the last Victorian."

"Not true," George said. "Not true at all. I'm just not in a buying mood."

He didn't want to talk to Raj. He didn't want anyone but Jess, and he had no way to reach her.

He poured himself a cup of coffee, and began writing a letter. He wrote with his fountain pen, covering small sheets of paper with blue-black ink.

Dear Jessamine,

I spoke disrespectfully to you. You are not a child. I understand why you were angry. I had no right to ask you to go and then a moment later tell you to stay.

You came freely to work at Yorick's, and you are free to leave as well. Forgive me if I seemed to forget. My concern for your safety is real, and I'm sorry it seemed like a jealous attempt to control you.

My own sister was just a little younger than you when she died. She died at twenty-two. As you say, people get killed on the ground.

I don't pretend to be wiser than you are, but I am older, Jess. I've lived longer, and I have more experience in certain areas—among them, communal living, activism, drugs. If you told me you would give up the Tree House and return to school on condition that I never see you again, I would accept your terms. I am thinking about you, not about myself.

I realize that you don't belong to me. I wish that we belonged to each other. I wish I had met you when I was young, but I did not, and I realize that you have to be young on your own. We stole some time together, and we should leave it at that. Live and let live. Yes, that's a sixties thing to say. Or maybe it's just one of the lies we tell ourselves to get what we want. I wanted you—I admit it. I behaved badly. See above.

Selfishness on my part, except for one thing, which is that I'm in love with you. I love you in the worst possible way, sleeplessly, desperately, jealously. I love you in the best way too. I want every good thing for you. I want you to work, and learn, and grow, and find your place in the world. Therefore I must let you . . .

Here George broke off. I will *not*, he thought. I will *not* let you go. Because he did not love Jess in two ways; he loved her one way: passionately, protectively, selfishly, disinterestedly, all mixed together, and he had to be with her. His collections did nothing for him. His cookbooks meant nothing to him without their imaginative interpreter. Writing reasoned paragraphs did not calm him at all, but angered him. The stillness of his house infuriated him. How long, he thought, will I sit here in my kitchen sipping coffee instead of finding her? How long will I wait before telling her?

He logged on to the computer in his office and found the Save the Trees Web site with its photos of redwoods on death row and the plea: *Help us save Galadriel.* Don't be an idiot, he told himself, but he printed out directions to the Wood Rose Glen Tree-Sit anyway. Don't be a fool. He walked out onto his deck, and then downstairs to his garden shrouded in mist. He packed his car, feeling his way through the thick morning fog. A long-eared fawn startled and ran across the street as George turned his big Mercedes gently, easing down the hill.

He drove north, and the sun burned off the morning mist. He made his ascent up the Golden Gate with its gleaming cables, a bridge rigged like a tall ship, so full of life and wind, and as he sped down again into green Marin, he opened his windows and the wind whipped at his face and stung his eyes. What if she wasn't there? What if she had hiked off site, farther into the forest? How would he find her then? And if he did find her, would she listen, even for a moment?

He drove past tawny hills and then through dark mountains forested with oak and pine. The road narrowed, and trucks crowded him on either side. He lost the signal for NPR and turned off his radio. Raindrops fell, surprisingly cold and heavy. He closed his window and drove into the storm.

Rain was falling in Wood Rose Glen, but the redwoods were always damp, and at first Jess didn't notice. She was crouching on a plywood platform 150 feet up in the branches of Galadriel, the majestic cause célèbre, object of so much love and so much hate, the redwood painted by Pacific Lumber with a blue *X* for execution, a two-thousand-year-old tree occupied in shifts for the past three months by Tree Savers.

When the wind picked up, Galadriel began to creak and sway, but the redwood was always in motion, and Jess had grown accustomed to its rolling movements. A blue plastic tarp sheltered her, and massive branches embraced her. After two days, she could almost pretend she was a bird in a nest, or an explorer on a floating island with its own rich soil, and ferns and huckleberry bushes. To lose Galadriel would mean to lose this floating world as well, a miniature forest with its moss and lichen, its birds and flying squirrels close to the clouds. Therefore, Jess would defend the tree. She would stand guard on high, and for the greater good she would withstand the wind, and the increasing damp, and the dark temptation, almost a death wish, to look down. Leon and the other Tree Savers slept far below at base camp as she fulfilled her vow, serving the arboreal cause, living in the redworld she had known before only as an earthbound spectator.

"I see what you mean," she told Leon the first night on her radio. "It's so beautiful."

"We'll come for you in the morning."

"I want to stay the week," she told him.

"Are you sure?"

"I'm sure."

She zipped her parka and curled up under the tarp and closed her eyes and listened to the wind in the trees, Galadriel and the other giants farther off, their limbs entwined. Arwen and Legolas, Elrond, Haldir, Celeborn. Each spreading a vast canopy like a second rustling sky.

She was alone and she could think. She had outclimbed fear and outrun Emily and Mrs. Gibbs, and even George. She scarcely thought of him. She kept telling herself that. *I'm hardly thinking of him!* Even as she staved off hunger with granola, peanuts, dried fruit. She sipped the water she collected in the folds of her blue tarp, and nested in her sleeping bag with *Walden*: *One day when I went out to my wood-pile, or rather my pile of stumps, I observed two large ants . . . contending with one another. . . .* And she said to herself, This is what people look like from a redwood's point of view. This is what history looks like to a two-thousand-year-old tree. Conflicts seem so petty here.

Her fear of falling did not disappear, but settled deep inside her, losing its sharp edge, rising in great nauseating waves and then subsiding. She kept to her solid platform, and as long as the weather held, she watched light shifting through the green canopy, applauded the trapezing squirrels, touched lichen covering the tree like lace. Had McClintock climbed to study these? Or had he relied on earthbound samples? She wrote these questions in her notebook and felt lively, almost scientific. But as the weather changed, she missed George relentlessly, rhythmically, like the slow, steady rain. She fought against loneliness. No, she told herself, I live without him very well. What I need and what he wants are completely different.

The rain fell harder; her tarp sagged under the weight of water, and she was afraid that if she tried retying, she would lose her blue roof altogether. The temperature dropped, and wet seeped through her clothes. She wrung out her knit hat like a dishrag, and all the while, Galadriel's branches swayed and groaned. Jess's supply bags streamed with water, and she lost radio contact with Leon on the ground.

Then Jess no longer felt like Huck Finn rafting in the trees; she was Ishmael clinging to a fragment of the *Pequod* in the storm. Branches thrashed in the dark above her, and she wondered if they might break and fall.

She had seen fallen redwoods, their massive trunks, their shallow roots upended. The giant trees were not anchored deeply in the soil. When redwoods fell, they took down every tree below. Their weight, their height . . . She knew this tree was healthy. Leon said Galadriel was solid to the core, but when night came, she heard a boom. Thunder? Trees toppling? Huddled in her sleeping bag, she clipped on her battery-powered book light and tried to read. *At a certain season of our life we are accustomed to consider every spot as the possible site of a house.*

She was exhausted, but she could not sleep. Adrenaline kept her alert, although there was nothing she could do to save herself. She could not climb down in this darkness and this weather, nor could she shield herself from lightning.

She tried to concentrate on Thoreau's calm book, his little cabin at Walden Pond—but what did Thoreau know? He'd never been to California. She thought of Leon and his pride in her for climbing, his pleasure that at last she was experiencing what he loved most. But Leon couldn't help her now, and remembering his pleasure made her feel a little sick. No, no, I didn't come here for him, she reminded herself, but that was only partly true.

Common sense rebelled. What were you thinking? she asked herself, as Galadriel groaned and cracked and the branches above her turned to deadly missiles in the wind. She had been thinking she would try to love Leon better. That she would turn her back on rare books and commit herself to something greater. She had not been wrong in this. She had not been wrong to defend the trees. So why was George the one she wished for? His was the face she longed to see. His were the arms that she imagined as she closed her eyes. His, the voice she missed.

It was still raining when she woke, but the wind had died. Her radio buzzed in her hand.

"Are you okay?"

"I'm fine," she told Leon. "I'm wet."

"We're bringing food."

Half an hour later, he radioed from the bottom of the tree, and Tree Savers began hooking the supply bags to the ropes. That was when she heard the crack above her.

"Headache!" she called into her radio, but even as she said the word, the branch whistled past, a weight like a falling car, plunging fifteen stories. She heard the crash, the screams below. "Leon!"

She crept to the edge of the platform and saw a cluster of tiny figures, the Tree Savers in their green sweatshirts. Like a missile, the massive branch pierced the earth. She began to tremble. Her hands shook, and her teeth chattered.

"I'm here," Leon told her on his radio. "Nobody's hurt." He spoke in his cool, calm voice, only slightly broken up with static. "We're ready." He meant ready to send up the supplies.

"I can't," she whispered.

"What?"

She felt that at any moment she would plummet. Like the tree branch, she would whistle through the air, cratering the forest floor. Just as she began to fall, the world would rise to meet her. She would detonate on impact, her brain would splatter. She gasped for air. Strange, she knew that she was having a panic attack. She knew exactly what was happening, but she could not stop it. She couldn't breathe. The earth kept rising up to meet her.

"I can't," she gasped into her radio.

"Your friend is here," Leon said.

"What?" She could barely process this.

"Jess," Leon warned. "You committed to a week. If you bail, someone has to take your place."

"I have to come down."

A long pause on the other end. "Come down then."

But Jess could not take the climbing line in her two hands and make that descent. Fear swallowed her up. She tried to draw strength from the redwood. The storm was over; the winds were gone. She would sit and contemplate the ants, so small and strong and organized, always moving forward, up and over every obstacle. She would marvel at the secret gardens of moss and brambles and new trees in the redwood's crown. She told herself all this, but the crack of falling timber echoed in her ears. "Please, please, please, come get me."

When Leon appeared, climbing nimbly, balanced beautifully on his rope, he found Jess crouching with her head between her knees. He saw exactly how frightened she was, and he looked at her with a mixture of pity and anger. Jess had insisted she could handle climbing, pronounced herself cured, insisted on a full-week shift. Now she cowered like a cat up a tree, a total liability.

He examined her with his clear blue eyes, and looking up at him, she felt his distance. She felt, despairingly, that she had failed a test, and she hated herself for failing, but she hated him more for testing her at all.

"It's not your fault," he said. "I shouldn't have encouraged you. You didn't want to be here," he murmured.

"I did," she said.

"You just wanted to prove to me that you could last."

"No, I wanted to prove it to myself," she said.

"Really? That was . . ." His radio crackled. "It was wrong of me to let you." He gestured for her to stand.

"Why?" She held fast to the boards of the platform.

"Because you weren't prepared."

He remembered a day, a soft, windless day when they'd lain together undressed under the trees. A single pine needle had drifted down. He'd watched it fall on her white skin. "Get up. Come on." As he helped Jess to her feet, he pushed that memory away. "Your friend is waiting for you."

"Oh, God."

"He came up yesterday, lecturing everybody, demanding to see you." The next words were almost taunting. "Now he'll get his wish."

That was the hardest moment. That was when she wanted most to stay up in Galadriel, but her body rebelled. Her heart raced. The crash of the tree limb resounded in her ears. She could not calm herself. She had to find her way down.

Miserable, she stood before Leon as he checked her ropes, her clips, her harness, and she knew what he thought of her. She knew what he suspected, and she saw that he wasn't angry. This was worse than anger. He viewed her coolly, absolving her even as he disengaged from her.

He clipped the steel link of her harness to the secondary rope he'd rigged from the ground. "I'm coming down with you. I won't let anything happen, but you have to listen. Do you understand?"

Her hands were stiff with fear, inflexible. She held the rope too tightly, and her palms began to bleed. She saw the blood but could not feel.

Her ascent to the platform had been giddy, joyful. Clear sky and celebration, a picnic under the trees the night before. Sweet cool air, a calming joint, smoke mingling with the fragrant forest, pine and mulch and bay laurel. Climbing had been an otherworldly magic-carpet ride. The descent was like rappelling into the circles of hell. She saw the Tree Savers standing in their green sweatshirts. Standing silent. Waiting for her. And then she saw George watching for her as well. George, who didn't acknowledge Jess to his friends, had no problem materializing in front of hers.

"Jess!" he called, even before her feet touched the ground. "Are you all right?"

Leon slid down and unclipped his harness and then unclipped hers.

George rushed to her and Jess stepped back.

"What were you doing?" George berated her. "Do you have any idea what might have—"

"Please, please, please, shut up," Jess said. She couldn't bear to talk to him in front of everybody else.

But the others were busy. Leon was helping Daisy with her harness. The Tree Savers gathered around her as she started her ascent. "Free the tree," the Tree Savers chanted joyfully, as Daisy lifted off to take Jess's place. "Free the tree. Free the tree. Free the tree."

The Tree Savers were focused on Daisy. Only George was watching Jess as she knelt on the ground, clutching herself, breathing hard.

"Are you hurt? Are you okay?" George tried to help her to her feet, but she shook him off and stood up on her own.

"Let me see your hands."

"No! Go away."

"You can push me away as much as you want," he said. "It won't make any difference."

Jess looked up at Daisy, suspended in the gloaming, small as a silkworm hanging from a slender thread.

"Tell me you won't go up there again," George said.

"You're embarrassing me!"

"I don't care."

"Of course not!" She started walking, taking the trail to the parking lot.

"Wait, Jess."

She didn't answer.

"Where are you going?"

"None of your business!" she called back.

"I was worried about you." He jogged a little to keep up.

She spoke without looking at him. "You've got quite a double standard driving up here."

In the dirt lot, she found the Honda that George had loaned her. Her hands shook, and George called after her, carrying on that she wasn't safe to drive. She didn't listen. Her ripped hands still shook, and the old car shuddered when she turned the key, but she never hesitated as she drove away.

26

Her hands bled on the steering wheel as she wove from one lane to the next. She drove for miles, and her wet jeans felt like lead. There she'd been, guarding Galadriel, and what did she do? She gave up. No dimpled spider for her. No swinging birches. She drove on, and spots appeared before her eyes, tiny points of light, and visions of Daisy climbing, and George making a scene, crashing the Tree-Sit. What was he thinking? Why was everything about him? But most of all, she remembered Leon's face. All their time together ending in his quick glance, his cold assessment, as commanders consider casualties. She was dead to him, and he wouldn't leave Galadriel unguarded. How fast could he replace Jess once he got her to the ground? *Earth's the place for love. Earth's the place for love.* The words rushed like blood in her ears, even as she looked in the rearview mirror and saw George driving after her. *Earth's the place,* she thought as she accelerated in her anger and her humiliation.

George followed in his Mercedes, keeping Jess in sight. She was right, of course, about the double standard. I wasn't ready. We were too new. In a strange way he believed it. The collector in him believed it: His time with Jess was too new, too sweet to share. But that was selfish. That was unfair. She deserved more than that. She needed more, and he could give her more. He could do better—if she would let him.

But she drove for hours in the rattling old car, and all he could do was trail after her. When he lent Jess the Honda he had never intended her to drive so far. Certainly not at this speed. He thought she would tire and pull over, but she did not. She drove for an hour, two hours, almost three, until she seemed to calm herself, slowing down, keeping to one lane as she cut through ranch land and timbered mountains.

When at last Jess exited, George followed, assuming she needed gas, but she did not drive to a rest stop; she took a winding road lined with colossal trees to a place called Fern Hollow, where she parked in the dirt lot.

He waited, but she did not get out of her car. Cautiously he approached and saw her sitting, staring at the dark tree trunks ahead.

"Jessamine."

She didn't answer.

"Jess." He tapped on the glass until she rolled down the window.

"What?"

"What are you doing to my poor old Accord?"

She didn't answer.

George walked around to the passenger side and let himself in. He sat next to Jess and waited. He was sure that she would speak, but she did not. She kept staring straight ahead.

"Do you want me to apologize?" George asked at last. "I apologize."

She didn't answer.

"I was worried about you."

She turned on him. "You embarrassed me!"

"You scared the hell out of me."

"What are you? My father?"

"Why do you have to be Joan of Arc?"

"Why do you have to be such a cynic?"

"Why do you think that trees have rights?" He saw that she was about to interrupt, and didn't let her. "Do you really think redwoods are sentient beings? If you believe that, then vegetables have rights, and you shouldn't eat anything at all."

"You don't care what kind of Earth your children inherit."

"I don't have children."

"Exactly. That's your problem, among other things."

"Which are?"

"That you prefer objects to people."

"I do not . . . ," George protested.

"Oh, really? I think you do. I think you made all that money, and you had your great expectations, but you got hurt, and now you just hide behind your stuff, because you think your books and your maps and your typewriter collection will last. You think they'll last forever and they'll never leave you. So in your mind you think you're Pip, but actually you're Miss Havisham."

"Miss Havisham?"

"With books instead of clothes."

"You love the books," he reminded her. "You're working with the books."

But she ignored this. "You don't have anything left for trees or animals or the outside world, because you've shut yourself in. You're a shut-in. You're like the curator of your own heart."

Wounded, but too proud to let it show, he spoke lightly. "I see why I resisted therapy all these years. I was waiting for you to explain me to myself. And now that you have, I can reach out to other species. Does Leon count?"

"Don't talk about Leon."

"Why not?"

"Because you don't even know him."

"Oh, I exchanged some words with him. I think I was getting to know him pretty well."

"George, do you think this is some kind of joke?"

"That depends on what 'this' is."

"Then you're just being snide? You're trying to offend me? What exactly are you trying to do?"

"Let me see." He reached for her hands.

"It's just rope burn," she said. "I'll clean them up myself."

"Let's get some water."

She hesitated.

"Oh, come on, Jess."

At last, she got out. She found the park restrooms, and then followed him to his car.

"Q.E.D.," she said when he opened the trunk and she saw his duffel bag, a case of bottled water, a tent, a first-aid kit, a cooler full of food. "You've got all your stuff as usual."

"Is that such a bad thing, under the circumstances?" George handed her a water bottle. "Drink."

There were two other cars in the lot, but no hikers visible. They walked down to a picnic table under the trees, and she let him wash and bandage her hands. He knelt down and removed her soggy old climbing shoes and wet socks. With a clean towel he dried her feet, rubbing them up and down. That was when she began to cry.

"Jess," he whispered. "Darling."

"Darling?" She tried out the word through tears.

"I'm sorry I compared you to Joan of Arc."

"I'm sorry I compared you to Miss Havisham." She paused. "But actually . . ."

"Oh, you're fond of that comparison, aren't you?" George teased softly. "You think that was pretty good, and you don't want to give it up. I know you."

"Well . . ."

"Try these." He slipped a pair of his clean socks on her feet, and then his extra pair of running shoes. The shoes were too big, but the socks were also too big, and they padded the shoes. When George laced them, they felt like ice skates. Experimentally, Jess walked this way and that, stretching, shaking out her cramped arms and legs. She gazed at the silent, forgiving redwoods.

"I'm going for a walk." She slipped into the trees, and once again, George followed her.

The trail was well worn, soft and springy underfoot. Tiny creatures sifted through the leaves—glistening beetles, slick black slugs, quick-stepping centipedes.

"So this is the forest of Arden," George said.

Jess breathed deep. The damp air smelled of cedar and of pine. It was so good to walk upon the ground.

The trail descended, turning gradually like a corkscrew, until they came upon the sheltered hollow for which the park was named. Ferns carpeted the ground, covering every open place between the trees in an undulating sea of green. A redwood lay there in ruins, a natural bridge across a lively stream.

"Watch out," George warned as Jess climbed up. The tree was relatively slender, no more than ten feet in diameter, and George found the bark slippery as he climbed after her.

"Let's walk across," Jess said.

"You're not used to those shoes."

"Stop hovering."

"I can't," he confessed. "I wish I could."

"And stop saving me all the time. It's hackneyed."

"Hackneyed!"

"You're just an overbearing, old-school, hegemonical. . . "

"Forgive me for caring whether you live or die. Forgive me for caring about you at all, because obviously that's suspect."

She faced him on the redwood bridge. "Why can't you leave me alone?" she demanded. "Why is it so hard?"

"Because I'm falling in love with you, that's why!"

Her breath caught. "Still falling? Even now?"

"Yes. Are you?"

She looked down at the rushing water. "When will it end?"

"When we're together."

"Didn't we try that?"

"Not yet."

"We don't agree on anything," Jess reminded him.

"No, you see, you always say that, but that's where we differ. We agree on vegetables—asparagus, for example. We agree on wine. I'm prepared to agree with you about the redwoods."

"You don't understand why they're important."

"Probably not. But it's wonderful to touch something living that's so old, and to feel . . ."

"To feel what?"

He looked at her exhausted face. "That life is long."

"It's not long for everyone."

"Don't be sad," George murmured. "You're so young."

"Oh, I'm tired of being young. Being young gets old."

"Be old with me, then," George told her. "Stay with me. Come home with me. Share my books with me. Cook with me. Marry me."

"You'd let me cook with you?"

He pulled her closer. "That's just like you to evade the question."

"How was that a question?" she challenged lightly. "I'm the only one who asked a question."

"It would be your kitchen too."

"What about your friends?"

"I was wrong before. I didn't know. . . . Forgive me."

"I thought you'd rather be alone."

"No," he said. "I'd rather be alone if not for you. Please, Jess."

"Please?"

"I'll teach you how to cut onions properly."

"Oh, in that case . . . ," Jess said.

"And devote my life to you."

Jess shook her head. "Don't."

"Let me."

"We have to be equal, or it doesn't work."

"Then we'll be equal. We'll share everything."

"And what if I say I don't want everything, I'd rather give all your stuff away?"

He hesitated and then he said, "We'd fight."

"Yes."

"Yes, we'd fight? Or yes, you'll marry me?"

"What do you think?"

"I know we'd fight. We do fight," George said. "But not so often."

"Give us time."

"That's the thing," he said. "We need more time."

"We've had time."

He looked away. "More time together. Not more time waiting."

"How long were you waiting?" she asked gently. "Ten days?"

"Forty-one years."

"You kept busy," she reminded him. "You were out there getting rich and learning to cook and breaking hearts. You fell in love lots of times before me."

Her hair was curlier under the damp trees. He pulled a lock to watch it spring back. "It wasn't lots of times—just for the record."

"Just once or twice?"

"Don't hold it against me that I didn't meet you before."

"I don't," Jess protested. "Not exactly."

"At least I didn't make you watch." He was thinking of Noah and Leon.

"I never made you do anything," Jess said.

"You made me love you."

"Not on purpose."

"That's how you did it. Not on purpose. You just walked in. You filled out the questionnaire, and you said I was the kind of guy who reads *Tristram Shandy* over and over again."

"You were lonely," she pointed out.

George sat on the log, and helped her down as well. "You're missing the point."

"How many times *have* you read *Tristram Shandy*?" Jess asked him.

"Marry me."

"Five times? Six times?"

"Eleven," George said. "Marry me."

She didn't answer.

"Please. Jess. Don't be upset. Listen to me. The things I have, the money I made, the house, the collections, the cookbooks, they're all proxies. The life I've led has been"—he struggled for the word—"acquisitive. I was always chasing quartos, folios, maps. . . ."

"I'm not a quarto or a folio."

"Exactly."

"Maybe a map."

"You know what I mean. You're the one I gave up looking for. I'd live for you and live with you. Say yes. Will you?"

The afternoon was fading. A cool breeze riffled through the ferns below.

"Yes," she whispered.

"Really?" He clasped her hands in his.

"Ow!"

"Sorry!" He kissed her fingertips. "Jess—"

She interrupted. "You made up eleven, didn't you? You just picked any number."

"Ah, you caught me," George said.

Then Jess said, "I love you too."

It was dark when they approached the ranger's cabin near the parking lot, and left fifteen dollars for a permit to spend the night.

Jess went to the campground restrooms, and she showered, and washed and combed her hair. Since she didn't have dry clothes, she wore George's sweats, his T-shirt, his black fleece. They carried the cooler and the tent down to the campsite, a dark hollow, a solemn, mystic place, a conference of redwoods called the Philosophers' Grove.

"Socrates, Plato, Aristotle," George named the three tallest trees.

"No, Descartes, Leibniz, Spinoza," Jess said dreamily. "And that one there . . ." She pointed to a deformed, double-trunked pine. "That's Hegel."

"Why?"

"Because he's convoluted and full of obfuscations and . . ."

"Eat," George said. And he served her apples that he'd brought from home, and figs, and even some comté cheese, which she devoured despite her vegan prohibitions because she was so hungry.

He cleared sticks and branches to pitch his tent with its arching supports. He took a rock and hammered the tent stakes into the ground. When he was done, he spread a fly sheet for rain. He smoothed his open sleeping bag and then a heavy blanket on the nylon floor.

"Come in."

She bent down to enter, and he followed.

"Is it true that they spin fleece from soda bottles?" she asked, as he unzipped her.

"I think so."

"That's alchemy then."

"Are you warm enough?" He pulled off her T-shirt.

"That's a funny thing to ask when you're undressing me."

"Are you warmer now?"

"Maybe," she said. "Yes."

They didn't know under the trees what day it was, or how the market closed, or how the sun rose bright on the East Coast where Jess's father woke early, to run and glower at the McMansion abutting his property. They didn't know it was September 11, but no one else did either.

The McMansion's three-car garage opened, and Mel drove away in his black Lexus, while Barbara stood as usual in her bay window, with her black prayer book in her hands. On Alcott Street, Rabbi Zylberfenig's little boys were dressing, pulling out all the clothes from their shared bureau onto the floor.

In Cambridge, by the Charles, Jonathan went running, even as Orion and Sorel sat together on a bench on the riverbank and talked of Fast-Track. The team was combing every line of code before the October rollout.

"Last night was pretty smooth," Orion said with pride.

And Sorel agreed. "Fast-Track is the Second Coming for this company!"

Breathing deep, Jonathan ran along the river, because he could not fly cross-country without exercise. He kept up his quick pace and thought of the day ahead at Tech World, the night he'd spend with Emily, the news he'd bring her, that ISIS was nearly ready to ship its new product, the surveillance system inspired by electronic fingerprinting. He had waited to tell her, but convinced himself that he was right to wait. He recognized that the conversation might be tricky, given his long silence, but he had to prepare her for the rollout. *Emily*, he told her in his mind, *if we're to-*

gether, then we share success. What you do and what I do are almost the same. Emily, he rehearsed for her, *if we have a life together, then your money and mine, your company and mine, your decisions and mine—we hold them all in common.* Admittedly, he had not kept her secret. Admittedly, he had not confided in her about the flaws in Lockbox that winter night she'd asked. But that had been almost two years ago. Running on the riverbank, he envisioned a life with no barriers or limits. Marriage without borders. He saw the future, as he ran to the Eliot Bridge and back again, under the allée of sycamores with their silvery trunks and their green-gold leaves. Orion and Sorel could not have been farther from his mind. Nor did he consider Mel Millstein, who was driving in from Canaan to Logan Airport, bad back and all, to show the flag for ISIS, and to do his bidding. Jonathan thought about his day, not other peoples'. He meted his own stride.

Mel drove along the river to Logan, and he had no idea how close Jonathan was at that moment, nor did Sorel and Orion. They didn't see Jonathan coming. No one ever did.

"I'm thinking of writing a dot-com opera," Sorel said, leaning against Orion, head on his shoulder.

"How would that work?" he asked.

"It would be sort of *Tommy* meets *Ring of the Nibelung.*"

They heard Jonathan's voice first. "What are you guys doing here?" And then they saw him, bright-eyed, sweaty, jogging in place.

Sorel sat up straight.

"Jonathan," Orion said heartily. "How's it going?"

Jonathan looked at the two of them with his dangerous smile. "Come here often?"

"Bird-watching," Sorel said, gesturing toward the fat black geese waddling and honking on the bank.

"Not much to look at," said Jonathan.

"I'm quite nearsighted," Sorel explained, embracing the absurdity of the situation. "I can't see the smaller species, so we come here for the . . . large-print birds."

Humor helped. Jonathan's smile softened, and he shook his head ever so slightly. Then Orion knew he wouldn't tell. He was never sure which

Jonathan he would meet, but this morning he lucked into his old friend, the joker and the rugby player; the boy, not the tycoon.

Under the redwoods, the early-dawn air was chilly, and George tucked the blanket around Jess. "You were tired, after all."

Jess didn't answer. She was still asleep, even as Leon and the Tree Savers camped in Wood Rose Glen, and Daisy shielded Galadriel, and Emily called Jess's cell phone, which was now lost, forgotten in the tree along with her waterlogged Thoreau. Emily left messages. "You said you were coming home on September 11. I'm just wondering where you are, Jess."

At ISIS, programmers drifted to work with cups of coffee. In Central Square, Molly was arriving home, postcall from Beth Israel Deaconess. She was winded, climbing the stairs. She had no time for the gym. She had no time for anything. She had eaten a blueberry muffin for dinner. Blinking in the bright sun, she thought of babies, because all night she had been assisting in deliveries. She had worked for a day and a night inside the hospital, and now it was morning again, and as she walked, she thought of tiny bodies, eyes opening in surprise, mouths opening to cry, forming perfect little Os.

PART SEVEN

The Bottom Line

September and October 2001

27

Years later, they remembered where they had been. At their desks or in their beds, indoors or out. Driving, walking, working, alert, or half asleep. Each recalled momentary confusion. An airplane hit the World Trade Center. Pilot error? Technical glitch? And then the shock. A second plane. No accident. No mistake. The flames were real, as everyone could see on television. The Twin Towers burning, again and again. Bodies falling, again and again. The same towers, and the same bodies, and the Pentagon in flames. The scenes played constantly, at once heartbreaking and titillating, their repetition necessary, but also cheapening. Who, after all, could believe such a catastrophe after just one viewing? And who, after viewing once, could look away?

Finishing the night shift at Alta Bates Summit Medical Center, Mrs. Gibbs saw the fire on every TV, in every patient's room.

Waking early in Los Altos, Laura found her children staring at the giant television in the den. She stood transfixed with her three little ones in their pajamas, until she began to understand what they were seeing, and snatched the remote control away.

Across the country, Chaya Zylberfenig was running on her treadmill in the bedroom, and she called her husband. "Shimon! Come quick!" even as her feet kept moving under her.

Shimon didn't hear. He was sitting outside with his *New York Times,* reading headlines already out of date. As so often, Chaya would be the one to tell him what had happened. Hands on hips, she watched him watch the planes smash into the towers on TV. With dark fierce eyes, she glared at her quixotic husband, as if to say: I dare you to find the good in this.

At ISIS in his corner office, Dave was meeting with Aldwin, when Amanda ran in. "Look at CNN!" That was when Dave saw the breaking story on his desktop. He watched along with Jonathan's friend as the words *American Airlines Flight 11* flashed across the screen.

"That wasn't Jonathan's flight, was it?" Aldwin asked. *"That wasn't . . ."*

Amanda was covering her mouth with her hand.

"Call the airline!" Dave screamed at her.

She burst into tears as she fled back to her office.

Orion lay in bed, asleep after the all-nighter, and his cell phone started ringing on the floor. When he found the phone and opened it, he heard Sorel crying on the other end.

"What?" Orion said, and his voice was fuzzy with sleep. "What's wrong?"

"Jonathan's flight," she said.

"I can't hear you," Orion told her. "Slow down. Sorel, Sorel . . ."

At that moment Molly rushed in from the kitchen, and he closed the phone.

Molly looked so pale that he thought she'd heard him talking, but she had not heard him murmuring Sorel's name. She'd heard the news, and now they watched the flames on television. They watched together, and he read his e-mail, the ISIS announcement that Mel and Jonathan were on American Flight 11 and presumed dead.

Molly leaned against him, and he wrapped his arm around her as he stared at the inferno on the screen. Of course, Jonathan had been Molly's friend too. The news shook her too. He felt the weight of Molly's head on his shoulder, the softness of her face. Despite their troubles, her long hours, her nagging, their estrangement, they absorbed this shock together.

And yet he had to talk to Sorel. He had to be with her. He knew she needed him as well. They had been the last to see Jonathan, and Jonathan had been the first to see them together.

He remembered Jonathan's smile at the river, his expression mischievous but forgiving, his slight shake of the head, as if to say, *I* won't say anything. He remembered Jonathan's laughter, and his aggression. The way he turned from fun-loving to steely, cold—until he switched back again, once he got his way. *Be very careful,* Jonathan told Orion once, and for a moment Orion had hated his old friend, but Jonathan was impossible to hate for long. Of course Orion pitied Mel, poor guy. He remembered Mel too, but in death, as in life, Jonathan was the one you couldn't shake. He was the world beater, the history maker. He had a force field all his own. He drew you in. Oh, Emily, Orion thought. What are you feeling now? How are you getting through?

She heard on the radio just as she sat down for breakfast. She was sitting at her white table, with her bags already packed for L.A. She was bringing them to Veritech and then going to the airport straight from work. That was the plan, anyway. That had been the plan. . . .

Breaking into Susan's report to give you breaking news from New York City where planes, two *planes, have hit both towers of the World Trade Center in Lower Manhattan—the upper floors of the World Trade Center, a hundred and ten stories high . . .*

That's terrible, she thought, as she sliced a banana into her cereal. *The first plane is said to be a commercial airline, and the second, also thought to be a commercial jet. . . .* Software failure? she wondered, as she began to eat. *The indications are that one of the planes that crashed into the World Trade Center was in fact a hijacked plane. The American Airlines plane from Boston . . .*

From Boston? she asked herself, confused. But that wasn't Jonathan's flight. He'd left already.

All air travel has been grounded. . . .

She glanced at her flight bag by the front door. She couldn't go to L.A., and Jonathan was stuck at Logan. Ironic. Typical. She called him, but he must have turned off his phone.

Her own phone began to vibrate in her hand. That would be Jonathan. But it was not Jonathan. It was Dave.

"Emily," he said.

No one had ever spoken her name with such sadness or such dread.

"We're in shock," Dave said. "I am sitting here unable to . . ."

Today we've had a national tragedy, President Bush announced on the radio.

"Jonathan was on the first plane," Dave said.

"What do you mean?" Emily challenged him, opening her laptop to check his itinerary. American Airlines . . .

"Flight Eleven," said Dave.

She forced herself to swallow. That wasn't really Jonathan's flight. It couldn't be.

American Airlines said that one of the aircraft that crashed into the Trade Center was American Airlines Flight Eleven, hijacked after takeoff from Boston en route to Los Angeles . . .

She was shaking. She was sick, vomiting cereal-banana-milk. She couldn't talk. She couldn't listen. She felt her way into what looked like someone else's kitchen, and she opened drawers, but she had no idea what she was looking for.

On the counter, her answering machine was pulsing, filling up with messages. Laura. Orion. Her own father.

"Emily?" Laura's voice wavered, trailing upward, uncertain, childlike, and she seemed to be standing in a crowded room; she seemed to be speaking very quickly, asking questions.

"Are you there?" her father asked her, and his voice was furred with rust.

"Hey," Orion began, and then he said nothing. She heard him standing there trying to think of something to say.

Shivering, she ran upstairs to her bedroom and huddled under blankets. She piled every blanket she owned onto her bed, burying herself, but she could not get warm. She closed her eyes. Sleep was the only respite from this dream.

The house was quiet when she woke. Her arms ached. Her body knew, but she lay in bed, tracing the woven leaves on her comforter, a pattern difficult to follow because the foliage was white on white. She traced each leaf and stem with her finger, and recalled the day before, the night before, the moment before she turned on the radio. She worked her way backward, from banana slicing to pouring milk, to taking out the cereal box. She was nothing if not disciplined, and she kept to her task, tracing white leaves with her finger, working her way backward through time, as though she could repair the breaking news.

She was patient, deliberate, rational. Therefore, she did not cry as she remembered her last conversation with Jonathan, when they'd fought on the phone, and he'd said, "Don't say you miss me, when you won't come to see me."

"I do come. I just did!" she'd protested.

"You came in March. I'm the one dropping everything to fly out to L.A."

"You don't drop everything. You never drop anything," she said. "You work me in. You schedule me in. I'm the one moving. I'm the one leaving my job to move in with *you*."

"Just don't say you miss me," he told her, "when you won't change your schedule for me."

And those had been his last words. *You won't change your schedule for me.* Words that would have faded, once they were together. An argument painful to remember for many reasons, but primarily because she wished their quarrel had been worse, that their bickering had escalated into a full-scale conflagration and his refusal to meet her in L.A.

Oh, but he had refused, he must have. In the end he had missed the flight on purpose. She could not let go of this idea. Jonathan had not stepped aboard that plane. In fact, she was almost convinced he'd been too angry. She would delete the messages on her machine, the panicked voices. One by one, she would erase them, because they were wrong. She knew the truth. She and Jonathan had fought. He'd skipped Tech World, and he was sulking. He wasn't speaking to her. In fact, he had turned off his phone.

This was her delicate logic. Each idea and contingency fed the next, as in a Rube Goldberg machine. A furious little red ball collided with a green ball, which flew up on a miniature trampoline to land at the top of a chute, where it began traveling down again, gathering speed to push over the first domino in a vast array. The last of these black-and-white dominos tripped a switch, which blew a fan, which extinguished a candle. In this way, Emily put the fires out, and saved Jonathan, and the world as well.

To which end she hid in bed. She did not eat or drink or speak to anyone. Far below, she thought she heard someone at the door, but she did not venture down to answer it. She kept the faith all day, pretending nothing had happened, struggling to protect herself, building new facts by which to breathe and live, but she had competition. Working overtime, her imagination took a guilty turn, and reason followed, where it was afraid to lead.

If she had not delayed the wedding, if she had hurried east the year before to marry Jonathan, then he would not have flown out to L.A. to meet her. If she had not hesitated; if she had simply married him when he'd asked, then she would not be alone. If she had loved him as she should have loved him, without trepidation, without tests, then Jonathan would be alive.

Because he was right after all, in everything he said about her. If she had really missed him, if she'd really wanted him, then she would have come to him before. She'd have shown him, instead of talking and postponing all the time. She would have been with him.

What was wrong with her? Why had she held back? She should have left Veritech long ago. It seemed a paltry sacrifice in retrospect. She might have saved him, if she had been less ambitious.

What did waiting get you in the end? There was no perfect time to marry, no ideal moment to move or leave your job. The only perfect time was now, and now was what she had denied herself. Who said that patience was a virtue? And temperance? And practicality? Who said, "Look before you leap"? With all that wisdom she had murdered Jonathan. These were her thoughts, as the banging on the door below grew louder.

I killed him, she thought, as Jess called, "Emily, let me in!"

I never really loved him, she accused herself.

I've never loved anybody, she thought, and she hoped that was wrong. She hoped she had loved Jonathan—loved him still!

"Emily!" Jess screamed, and the banging came from the back of the house, a thumping so loud that even in her distracted state, Emily remembered that her neighbor worked nights and slept days, and she scrambled to open the kitchen door.

"Shh! Be quiet!" Emily pleaded, barefoot, wild-haired, blinking in the late-afternoon sun, balled-up tissues in the pocket of her plaid pajamas. And then her eyes teared up, and she began to laugh and cry at the same time. For there stood Jess, with her hair pulled back, wearing the Vivienne Tam suit Emily had given her a million years ago. Tweed jacket in brown and rust, caramel silk blouse, tailored skirt, and stockings, actual stockings, and a pair of brown pumps. "You're wearing the suit now? You're getting dressed up *now*? Why now?"

"You know why." Jess took her sister's hands in hers.

"What happened to your hands?"

"It doesn't matter." Jess tried to hug her sister.

No, Emily thought. Don't. She would break into pieces at the slightest touch. She would shatter.

Jess sensed this and stepped back. She stood before Emily in that beautiful suit and said, "I got dressed up so that you'd see . . . so you'd know I've come to take care of you."

28

Ash fell. A fine gray powder covered everything. Ash coated burned-out cars and traffic lights. Ash infiltrated apartments, graying books and dishes, smothering house plants, clouding windowsills. Ash smogged streets and soiled papers, loose and lost, invoices and receipts, canceled checks, business cards, appointment books, memoranda unremembered. Black dust, black ink, black banner headlines in *The New York Times*. Black articles about firefighters, rescue workers, schoolchildren, orphans. Black bordered ads from ExxonMobil, Allstate, Prudential, Home Depot, Oppenheimer-Funds, Fleet, Lufthansa—*to our friends in America,* AOL Time Warner, Merrill Lynch. *Our hearts go out to everyone who's been touched by the tragic events . . . our thoughts and prayers . . . our gratitude for the tireless efforts of the emergency and rescue workers.* Condolences from Israel and Egypt, the city of Berlin, the Iranian-American community—*profoundly saddened,* the Red Cross, the Ministries of New York—*we're here to pray for you.*

Museums opened free of charge. Oases of deep color: Rothkos, Rembrandts, Egyptian tombs, Roman glass, iridescent bottles outlasting their perfume. Amulets, silk gowns, and Grecian urns. Those young girls with parted lips, those haystacks, those stone angels taking flight, those paintings of fruit and full-blown flowers.

Classical-music stations broadcast elegies, and listeners stopped what they were doing to hear Fauré's *Requiem* or Barber's *Adagio for Strings*. To breathe again.

Churches opened doors for candle-lighting, singing, sermons, vigils. In the nave of the National Cathedral, President Bush said, "We are here in the middle hour of our grief . . ." and he told the American people to keep on living, to travel, to attend the theater, to go out and buy. Alas, buying did not appeal. Only American flags sold out. Great flags hung from walls and firehouses. Smaller versions adorned shop windows and front doors. Drivers clipped miniature flags to car antennae where they fluttered in the breeze.

A flag was tangible. Its stars and stripes were real, unlike the dot-com bombs of yesterday. Who remembered those? The upstarts, overhyped and overfunded. When the Nasdaq reopened on September 17, even Cisco hovered at twelve dollars a share. Vaporizing into usefulness, online shopping, e-mail, and instant news, the Internet lost its mystique, and suddenly it was everywhere and nowhere, like the air. A flag had value. A leaf blower made sense. Unprofitable companies with huge growth and huge debt did not. Few bought Veritech at two. Fewer wanted ISIS, even at eighty cents.

None of that mattered to Emily. For the first time since Veritech's IPO, she did not check her company's share price. She didn't look; she didn't care. When Alex called, or Bruno, or Milton, or Laura, she let Jess answer the phone. With each ring, she expected Jonathan. She couldn't talk to other people.

When Dave invited her to Jonathan's memorial service, Emily told Jess to thank him and say no.

"Maybe you should think about it," Jess said when she put down the phone.

"No, I don't want to think about it."

"You don't have to decide right away. You don't have to say anything yet."

"Okay, don't say anything."

For days she did nothing. She didn't even open her computer. She sat at one end of the couch with her legs tucked under her, and then sometimes, for a change of scene, she moved to the other end.

Jess reminded Emily to get dressed in the morning. "You can't wear pajamas in the daytime."

"Why not?"

"Your circadian rhythms will get out of whack. I read an article about it. You shouldn't work in your bedroom, you shouldn't wear pajamas in the daytime, and you shouldn't exercise or eat at night, or work too long in the dark. So put these on." Jess pulled out a shirtdress and a sweater. Obediently, Emily changed into clean clothes.

Laura came bearing Emily's dry cleaning along with a loaf of home-made pumpkin bread. The condo association left a giant fruit basket wrapped in cellophane. Emily's cleaning service, Maid for You, sent her a condolence card and refused to charge her for the week of September 11. Orchids proliferated on the coffee table. She had been in all the papers. *He leaves his fiancée, Veritech cofounder Emily Bach,* and so everybody knew.

Jess shopped and prepared meals: oatmeal, or brown rice with broc-coli, or avocado-and-sprout sandwiches on cracked-wheat bread. Like an old married couple, the sisters completed the *New York Times* crossword puzzle each morning. They played Scrabble, backgammon, cribbage, even checkers, and then sometimes they didn't play anything at all. Emily did nothing, and Jess was the perfect companion, fielding phone calls, nibbling cashews, scribbling on dog-eared papers in red pen.

Waking up was hardest, because each day Emily had to teach herself that Jonathan was gone, and the life she might have had with him was gone, their conversations and their fights. That was the worst part. Her struggle against Jonathan was over, all their arguments and their compet-ing claims for time. The person she had been with him was gone, and the man she'd hoped he would become was lost, and she was left with the words Jonathan had said, and the things he'd actually done. Her ideas for him, and her future with him would never come to pass. She hated him for that, for rending her world, ruining what might have been.

After waking, she was careful to stay still. No sudden movements or long conversations. No newspapers, no radio. Brimful, she was afraid of tipping.

She slept poorly, and once, she woke crying with bad dreams. Then Jess lay down at the foot of the bed.

"I'll stay here," Jess said.

"Are you comfortable?" Emily asked anxiously.

"Mm-hmm."

"Are you going to sleep here all night?"

"Yes."

"Jess?" said Emily.

"Stop waking me up."

"What about the Tree Savers?"

"Don't worry about them."

"What do you mean?"

"They're fine without me."

Emily took this in, and then asked delicately, tentatively, "Are you done with them?"

"Done."

"Oh, good," Emily said, but with sleepless, worried interest, she pressed, "What about Yorick's? Isn't George wondering where you went?"

Jess hesitated. "He knows."

"Did you tell him when you're coming back?"

"I'm not coming back."

"You quit? You just left?"

"Well . . . ," said Jess, "I had to stop."

Emily roused herself a little, as though she wanted to see her sister's face, and Jess was glad that it was dark. "What do you mean?"

Don't tell her now, Jess reminded herself. She mustn't say anything now. "It's not important."

"What happened?"

"Nothing. Nothing happened." Jess meant nothing happened compared to what you're going through. "I got a little bit . . . involved with him."

"Jessie!" Emily sat up in bed.

Jess couldn't help laughing.

"It's not funny!"

"I know," said Jess, wiping her eyes. "But it's so good to hear you sounding like yourself."

"Did you . . . did you really . . . ?"

"Well . . ."

"You slept with him? Jess, how could you?"

Jess confessed, "Actually, it wasn't all that difficult."

"I can't believe you!"

"Please."

"You know that he's too old."

Jess said nothing.

"It would be totally—"

Jess cut her off. "I told him that we can't see each other. I explained to him that I'm going to be with you."

"So that's over too."

Jess hedged, "We're still friends and all."

"You have the strangest idea of friends," said Emily.

"I love my friends," protested Jess.

"That's the problem."

"It doesn't matter. It's not important," Jess reassured her sister. "Don't worry."

"It's over," Emily reassured herself.

She tried out those words, but she did not believe them. Jonathan's absence weighed on her, his disappearance clouded her mind. How could he vanish so completely? She longed for a body, a clue, a sign.

And yet he persisted in the world. Jonathan still worked his will at ISIS, in ways she never guessed. With share prices hovering at thirty-two cents, the executive committee met in secret in Oskar's office in the new cheaper building. They dragged in their swivel chairs to speak of Jonathan's pet project, his magic bullet, the October rollout, the surveillance system based on the secret Emily had told him, the plans she'd whispered for electronic fingerprinting.

"He left us with a revolutionary product," Dave murmured to Orion, Jake, Aldwin, and Oskar. "We got it built. We got it tested. We're ready."

"But is this the time—would anybody notice now?" Orion asked.

"Yes! This is the time," said Aldwin. "Think like Jonathan."

"What do you mean, 'think like Jonathan'?" Orion retorted.

"Think smart," said smart old Oskar.

Dave nodded. "Exactly. If you think like Jonathan, you seize the moment."

Aldwin explained, "Our dot-com customers are folding, but government contracts are huge. With the new antiterrorist initiatives, surveillance is the perfect space for us."

"We've got the goods," Dave said.

"And we've got the name from Marketing," Aldwin announced. Standing at Oskar's whiteboard, he uncapped a green dry-erase marker. "Operational Security and Internet Surveillance." Carefully he lettered the new name: OSIRIS.

Hushed, they stared at the new acronym, their new god.

Jake mused, "Osiris was the brother of Isis, right?"

"Right," said Aldwin. "The brother of Isis and her husband too."

"I love this," Oskar said.

"Fantastic," Dave chimed in.

Orion sat up abruptly, and the back of his swivel chair snapped upright. "Wait."

"We can't," said Aldwin. He was wearing a suit jacket with his tie folded in the pocket. ISIS was holding its memorial service that afternoon.

"Now is the time," Dave said sonorously. "Thanks to you and your team, we've got the firepower we need."

Orion protested, "We never said the surveillance tools were for government apps."

"Oh, come on," Aldwin said.

"What do you mean, 'come on'? Our new customer is the Bush administration? We're supposed to be the eyes and ears of the War on Terror?"

"Exactly," Dave said.

"But you do see what this means. Loss of privacy, loss of civil liberties. . . . The Feds could access e-mail, and search everyone's transactions—and we'd be the instrument! This is not what Jonathan was thinking."

"It's what he *would* be thinking," Aldwin said.

Orion closed his eyes. He saw Jonathan's playful smile at the river.

"Take a breath," Dave advised, and Orion understood what that meant: "We all know you're from Vermont and you went to Quaker schools."

Orion did not take a breath. He blurted, "I built Fast-Track."

"OSIRIS," Jake corrected.

"Whatever. OSIRIS. I don't want to see it co-opted for dubious political . . ."

"Not co-opted. Marketed," Dave told Orion gently.

"This is what Jonathan would have wanted," said Jake. "To take the competition by surprise."

"To make new opportunities where there were none," said Dave.

Orion muttered, "To boldly go where no start-up has gone before."

"Yes!" said Aldwin.

"What about free information?" Orion asked the others. "What about free enterprise? Do you think Jonathan built this company to sell out to government agencies? You're stealing my work for your own mercenary purposes."

"If you believe in free exchange of information, why are you so worried about stealing?" Aldwin asked.

"I'd share my work with anyone. The point is, I don't want you to sell it to the government."

"Selling is what we do," Dave said in his most patient voice.

"Do you really think Jonathan wanted to become part of somebody's counterterrorist agenda?"

"It's an important agenda," Dave said. "It's tracking killers, maybe Jonathan's own."

"No," said Orion. "That's not the way Jonathan thought."

"Of course not. How could he have known?" Dave soothed. "But in our position, sitting here right now . . ."

"If he were here right now, we wouldn't be in this position, would we?" Orion said.

"We all miss him," Aldwin said. "We all want him back."

"We need some time," Dave said, "but we don't have time right now. We're hemorrhaging, and even though we're hurting, we have to act."

"Jonathan would not have done this." Orion spoke definitely, but what he meant was more complex: The Jonathan he loved would not have wanted this. He had been too independent. "He was a researcher at heart."

"Before he was a researcher," Dave pointed out, "he was a Marine."

"This is my project," Orion reminded the others, "and I say no."

Dave looked at him steadily. His steely eyes softened. "We want you to be ready, but if you're not, we understand."

We? Orion looked at the others surrounding him, and he understood that they were all against him.

"Look, this is very, very difficult," said Dave. "We're all grappling with this thing. We're all emotional. We have the . . . the memorial service this afternoon. It's a terrible time, the worst possible time, and Orion, you have your issues, and I understand that, so we're leaving this up to you, whether you want to participate in this initiative or not."

"It's amazing to me," Orion said slowly, "how my leadership becomes conditional, and my team becomes collective property, and Jonathan's memory"—his voice broke—"even his memorial service becomes something you can use for your agenda, which is now and has always been solely about money."

"This is not art we're making here," Aldwin shot back indignantly.

"This is my friend you're talking about," Orion said. "Don't tell me what he would have wanted."

"Orion," Dave chided, "we loved him too."

He would say this at the memorial service as well. Orion knew exactly what Dave would say that afternoon. We loved him. We all loved him. Oh, and Mel too. We all loved Mel too.

He was so angry, he didn't want to go, but his father was on the program. Orion had lobbied hard for Lou to come down to read. What better voice for a memorial? Craggy, irreligious, oddly deep. And who but Lou might have anything to offer Emily? From childhood she had admired his work. Naturally Dave worried that the service would run too long, but Orion won him over, promising his father's brief elegy "Where Are the Bees?"

Now, driving to South Station to meet the train, he hoped his father had canceled at the last minute. He had canceled readings before. He was old and shaky. A seventy-seven-year-old man descending from the mountains with his visionary cri de coeur. Jonathan deserved the tribute, but ISIS was hardly worth it.

Orion drove to Boston, and he was late, and Lou didn't own a cell phone. Aggravated, Orion barely glanced at the white sailboats on the river, the dark choppy water, the deep-blue October sky. He arrived at the station to find his father slightly crumpled in a brown corduroy sports jacket, dark trousers, and his old fly-fishing hat. As soon as he saw Orion, pleasure lit up Lou's dark eyes, and for an instant he was young again.

"I'm sorry, Dad."

"Never apologize, never explain," said Lou.

"How are you?" Orion picked up his father's flea-market briefcase, an old-fashioned doctor's bag.

Lou shrugged. "I'm doing about as well as can be expected, given that Dick Cheney and the Bushies have ceded our government to a military-industrial complex which is bombing the Afghan people back to the Stone Age—as if that's going to solve our problems."

"Let me take that." Lou's bag was surprisingly heavy. "Do you want something to eat or drink?"

"I had a drink." Lou laughed at Orion's quick glance.

"Shmancy," Lou said as Orion unlocked the BMW. He caressed the seat when he sat down. "What is this, leather?" He sniffed the upholstery.

"Do you want to rest?" Orion began driving back to Cambridge. "We have plenty of time. Do you want to take a nap?"

"Nah."

"You have the poem?"

Lou gasped. "Oh, *the poem!*"

"Dad!"

"I'm kidding," Lou said. "What's wrong with you?"

"Everything," Orion muttered as an SUV cut him off.

"Drive to the river," Lou told his son.

"What's at the river? I'm going over the river. See? We're driving to the bridge now."

"Closer," said Lou.

Orion parked on Memorial Drive, and he and Lou stepped out. "Watch the traffic, Dad. Careful!" Orion held Lou back as cars whizzed past, and then guided him across the road to the grassy bank.

"Hmm." Lou approached the river and peered down into the murky water.

Orion had a sudden vision. His father in waders and a fly-fishing vest, the green canvas fisherman's hat with a flip-down magnifying glass clipped to the brim. Orion had often watched Lou fishing waist-deep in rushing water. Whenever Orion was too short to stand, Lou would lift him onto a rock on the bank, and then Orion watched his dad casting, his lines floating beautifully, scribbling the surface with a delicately tied caddis or a little midge or mayfly. Sometimes a sleek otter would swim past, a stealthy creature, only its nose showing, its long body submerged, gliding just under the surface of the stream. Orion knew better than to shout this out. No talking and no splashing were the rules, but Orion kept still because Lou held him in suspense, casting and casting with no luck, and then suddenly a trout, bending his wand to water, tripping line with a zzzzzz. Splashing, leaping, a huge brown fish Lou wrestled with his hands and looked in the eye, before he let it go. This casting, this deft motion of the arm and wrist, this balancing in currents with legs apart, had always seemed to Orion the center of his father's life, the source of his art.

When he was ten, Orion had to create a family coat of arms for school. With markers on poster board, he outlined a shield and then divided it on the diagonal. On one side of the divide he drew a pen, an apple, and a rose to represent his mother—the writer, teacher, gardener. On the other side, he drew a big-eyed fish for Lou. On the surface his parents were still together. They didn't divorce for another three years, but Lou was already gone many weekends, and in summers, and odd times in between.

"Is there a motto for the Steiners?" Orion had asked his mother.

"'Catch and release,'" Diane had told him, and Orion hadn't heard the irony at all. The words sounded poetic and sportsmanlike, and he wrote them out in yellow marker, the color closest in the box to gold.

"You aren't going to find much here," Lou said. "Maybe a pike. Possibly a bass."

"The Charles isn't known for fishing," Orion said.

They were standing close to the BU Boathouse, east of the place Orion and Sorel walked in the mornings. No one was rowing, the shells were all locked up inside. A lone rowboat floated gently, tethered to the dock.

Lou said, "Let's take that boat out for a paddle."

"Take the boat? We can't take the boat."

"Why not? We'll bring it back," Lou told him.

"But it's not ours."

"Oh, don't be such a skirt."

"I'm sorry," Orion said, with some heat. "Not everyone can live like you. I wish I did, actually. I'd rather be a painter or a poet, and work for myself and do whatever the hell I wanted without dealing with people, and all their meetings and their games. You have no idea what it's like to fight and play politics and—"

"Hold on, hold on," Lou interrupted. "Let me disabuse you, kid. For sheer backstabbing and jealousy, the politics of poetry are second to none. I guarantee that, compared to poetry in America, anything you've experienced at ISIS is child's play."

"Yeah, right." Orion kicked a tuft of grass. He did not see his father's tender face. He did not realize that Lou had visions too, that he turned to Orion and saw the boy who asked questions like, "Is it true that if you eat enough poppy seeds you fall asleep?"

"Look, it turns out nothing is easy," Lou murmured. "We're all dodging bullets of one kind or another—death or disappointment. Whatcha gonna do?"

"You should have warned me earlier," Orion said. "I would have lowered my expectations."

Lou grinned. "True story. A woman and her lovely young daughter are sitting on the beach. An enormous wave comes crashing down and sweeps the daughter away.

"The mother is hysterical. Weeping, she stands at the water's edge. *If there's a God in heaven,* she screams, *please bring back my child!*

"Lo and behold the wave returns and washes up the lovely daughter, alive and well.

"*Thank you, merciful God!* the mother cries. Then she looks around her. She looks all around, and at last she calls up to heaven once more. She cries out, *There was also a hat?*"

They laughed together, and for a moment Orion felt like himself. He wished he could really talk to Lou, and tell him how he hated ISIS. He wished above all that he could tell him about Sorel.

"We should go," Orion said instead. "We should get there early to check the microphone. You brought your reading glasses, right?"

Lou overrode the question with his own. "How's Molly?"

Orion helped his father up the riverbank. "She's good."

"Is that all?" Lou asked. "That's a shame."

"How is 'good' a shame, Dad?"

"Oh, because goodness is necessary but insufficient."

"She's working very hard. She's totally committed to medicine."

"I never understood that," Lou said.

"What, that Molly is so practical and grounded?"

"I guess I never understood why 'grounded' was such a positive thing," Lou told his son mildly. "Naturally, your mother and I disagreed on this. In your case, I admit, I always pictured you with someone flighty."

Low-slung Kresge Auditorium opened like the wide mouth of a baleen whale. In the glass-walled lobby, professors and administrators milled with students and ISIS employees. Even as Orion opened the door for Lou, he saw the dean of the School of Engineering and the provost standing before a life-sized photograph of Jonathan propped up on an easel. It didn't matter that Jonathan had dropped out of grad school. The university reclaimed him. Another easel supported Mel Millstein, and he had his mourners too, his wife, and her rabbi, listed on the program as Rabbi Shimon Zylberfenig. Suspiciously, Mel's grown children eyed the alien in the black frock coat.

Hundreds upon hundreds were paying their respects, and those who knew Jonathan and Mel the least looked most tragic, mouths turned down, eyes despondent. *Did you see Mel's wife?* they whispered to one an-other. *Did you see Jonathan's parents? They came from Nebraska. Look. Is that his brother? Over there.* And the crowd gazed upon the Millstein and Tilghman families, celebrities in the new hierarchy of grief.

So many gathered that it was difficult to move. Sorel stood sentry by the door, a white usher's flower pinned to her long dark dress.

"Are you okay?" Orion asked her, under cover of the crowd.

Subtly, her hand brushed his, and almost unconsciously his fingers wove through hers. Contact for just the instant the doors opened. The crowd surged forward, and he and Sorel were not touching anymore, but they saw Molly looking at them. What had she seen? Nothing, except the way they stood together. Confused, questioning, Molly turned to Orion, and he might have had to explain himself, if not for the arrival of Emily, and Jess, and Richard, and his wife.

"Emily!" Broken-voiced, Molly embraced her.

"Hello, sweetheart," Lou told Emily. "Remember me?"

"Of course," said Emily, the still center of the storm.

"Emily's read all my books," Lou announced to the assembled. He spoke in his public voice, his poet's voice, fortified with Scotch. "Emily was Orion's first girlfriend," Lou confided to the provost.

"Let's get you inside," Orion said.

Jess wished she could get Emily inside as well. She wanted to spare her sister all the strangers sorry for her loss, but she could not shield Emily entirely. The lesser mourners drew close to Jonathan's fiancée, and looked at her with a mixture of curiosity and awe. They whispered, *I can't imagine what she's going through,* but they wanted to imagine. They wanted to touch her pain, if only to draw back again, as from a flame.

Chaya Zylberfenig was one such stranger, but she observed Emily and Jess with special interest. Chaya remembered Jess perfectly from the Shabbes dinner a year ago in Berkeley. She had thought then that Jess looked familiar. In fact, she looked like one of the Gould cousins. Now, watching Jess standing with Emily, observing the two together, she was sure of the resemblance. It wasn't simply the dark hair, or gray-green eyes, the fair skin, it was something in the manner of these sisters, the way they spoke to each other, the way Emily bent her head to the side, a gesture both gentle and skeptical as she listened to Jess speak. Freyda had that look, as she took in some piece of news.

"Excuse me," Chaya said. "Jessamine? My name is Chaya Zylberfenig. Freyda Helfgott's sister. Do you remember me?"

Jess turned to see a bright-eyed woman in a navy-blue suit with gold buttons, and a sleek wig in pageboy style. The suit was both fancy and fanciful, lending the little rebbetzin a nautical air. "You were at a Friday-night dinner."

"Yes!" said Chaya. "That's right. Is she your sister?"

Jess drew Chaya away from Emily. Richard and Heidi were taking her inside, and Jess delayed Chaya from following.

"*Baruch dayan emet,*" said Chaya, then quickly translating, "'Blessed is the true judge.' Pardon me, may I ask you something? Do you have any relatives with the last name Gould?"

Jess shook her head.

"No one in your family from London?"

"My mother was from London," Jess said, "but that's it."

"Your mother was from London? What was her name?"

"Gillian Bach."

"That was her whole name? What was her maiden name?"

"Gold," said Jess.

"Are you sure?"

Jess hesitated. "I think so. It was either Gold, or Gould."

Oh, but this was all that Chaya needed. "Gould! And her first name. Are you sure that it was Gillian?"

"Yes," said Jess.

"But originally it wasn't Gillian." Chaya's dark eyes widened with discovery. "In Yiddish the name wasn't Gillian, it was Gittel! Your mother was my older sister, Gittel."

Baffled, Jess blurted out, "My mother couldn't be your sister. You're too young to be my aunt."

"I'm the youngest in the family." Now tears filled Chaya's eyes. "I'm the youngest of nine. Gittel was the oldest sister. She ran away when I was a baby, and she left the rest of us behind."

"They're getting started now." Clarence and Umesh, with white flowers pinned to their sweaters, were ushering stragglers into the auditorium, where Bach radiated from a scientific-looking pipe organ, all sawed-off cylinders.

"Jess. Let's go." Richard had returned for her.

"Hold on a second—" Jess began.

"We're sitting with Emily in front." Richard swept past Chaya in her gold buttons and he took Jess by the arm. In his grip, Jess remembered all the slights of childhood, along with larger silences, the relatives he never spoke about, the grandparents who had died, the family in London that Gillian had disowned because they had disowned her.

"We are gathered today," Dave intoned at the lectern, "to celebrate the lives of two very special people."

In their reserved seats in the front row, Jess sat folding and refolding her program in her lap. How could this be? How could her own mother be a Bialystoker? Maybe it wasn't true. Maybe this was just some fairy tale Chaya had made up. When they found out she was Emily's sister, people responded in strange ways, speaking in hushed voices, making odd connections, bringing up an acquaintance of their own who had been killed, or a distant cousin who had gone missing. Jess thought Chaya must be wrong, and yet certain phrases returned to her from Gillian's letters: *I know from my own experience that some memories are indelible.* What memories were those? And why had Gillian kept them to herself?

Jess could not concentrate at all. She could not think about Jonathan. Her own questions interrupted every eulogy. Who was Gillian? And if Chaya was right about her, why had Gillian kept such a secret from her children?

How self-centered the imagination was. The living thought about the living, even when they had gathered to speak about the dead. Orion sensed Molly staring at him, considering him, possibly judging him, maybe even dangerously, expensively forgiving him. Rabbi Zylberfenig stroked his beard and rehearsed his remarks silently, while Lou produced his reading glasses and shuffled the typed pages of his poem. Orion's father had his game face on. Lou understood that he was also clergy.

"Mel Millstein hired me at ISIS. He gave me my chance. . . ." Sorel leaned over as she spoke, and her white usher's-flower weighed down her décolletage. "He always looked after me. . . ."

Lou told Orion, "I'll bet he did."

At the lectern Dave recalled, "The first time I met Jonathan, I thought, 'Is this guy for real?' Let me rephrase that. I thought, 'Is this *kid* for real?' I said to him, 'What are your goals for ISIS?' and he said, 'World domination.' I said, 'You're joking, right?' He said, 'I'm not joking at all.'

"It's one thing to have confidence when the going is great. It's another thing to feel that way when the going gets tough. That's the mark of a leader, a hero if you will." Dave coughed. "I don't use the word *hero* lightly, but I'm not . . . I'm not exaggerating when I say that this young man was a hero to me.

"The last time I saw Jonathan, we were in a meeting and I felt, as I sometimes did, that I had to rein him in. I said, 'The climate is challenging right now.' He said: 'The climate's history. The point is where we're going.' He was already thinking ahead. Six months ago, even nine months ago, he thought his way into a new space. He came to us with that gleam in his eye. He stood at the whiteboard and he wasn't moaning, he wasn't whining—he never whined about anything. He was like a kid in a candy store. 'I have a new paradigm. I have a new plan. . . .' He had no idea then how important his new plan would be—a new system for data tracking."

Dave's words overflowed with feeling, and in the audience tears flowed freely. Even Lou almost forgot his own performance. Only Emily sat up, dry-eyed. Others heard a tribute to Jonathan's indomitable spirit. Emily understood that he had stolen her information, appropriated and built a version of electronic fingerprinting.

"He would never let us down," Dave said. "He would never say die. He led as he lived, fearless, imaginative, excited about the future. How could we lose someone who loved life so much?"

But Emily thought, Jonathan, how could you betray me? All those conversations where you accused me of putting Veritech first. All those times you said I was inflexible. Had you sold me out already? Six months ago. Nine months ago. Had you already betrayed me then?

She heard the other speakers in a dream. She heard them all from far away. Rabbi Zylberfenig spoke of angels. "Our sages teach that for each of us on Earth, there is an angel. This is very interesting to think about. We are each one of a matching pair. Therefore in the universe, we are not alone. . . ."

A baby wailed.

Aldwin read from Kahlil Gibran. *"When you part from your friend, you grieve not; / for that which you love most in him may be clearer in his absence. . . ."*

Sorel sat on a stool and sang Leonard Cohen's "Hallelujah," accompanying herself on her guitar. *"Now I've heard there was a secret chord . . ."*

Until, like the main event he was, Lou Steiner took the stage. Shuffling his papers, clearing his throat, he seemed to have lost his place somehow. Emily stared at him, but she didn't see him. Orion glared at Lou, and he thought, My God, he's drunk. But he underestimated his father. Lou knew his poem by heart, and the poem he recited was not the one promised. Not "Where Are the Bees?" but something else entirely, one of his old sixties flower poems.

> *When truth dies*
> *No one comes.*
> *Truth passes without ceremony.*
> *Her friends can't afford a proper burial.*
> *Truth's enemies write her epitaph*
> *And build her tomb.*
> *As for truth's relatives,*
> *They're estranged.*

How? Emily asked Jonathan. How could you?

> *When peace dies*
> *Everybody comes.*
> *Peace plunges to her death*
> *With fireworks and flags.*
> *Full military honors.*

Her friends hang their heads.
Her enemies say they'll bring her back.
She was so beautiful
And much too young.

This was not the villanelle printed in the program, not at all the short sweet poem Dave and the memorial committee had expected. Subtly, almost imperceptibly, Dave leaned forward to look at Orion.

Orion shook his head and smiled. With a grim satisfaction, he thought, Fuck you. Even you can't tell my father what to do. He didn't see Emily's face, so pale, or hear her panicked thoughts: How could you? How could you?

Visit truth and peace together.
They share a plot.
In lieu of flowers
Please send bodies
To the war.
In lieu of roses
Please send
Your Self-Addressed Stamped Sons. . . .

The audience squirmed and whispered as Lou shifted into higher gear. What did this have to do with Mel and Jonathan? Wasn't he talking about Vietnam? Even in Cambridge, this was almost embarrassing. The poem was almost—well, it was sort of on the nose for a memorial service, wasn't it? And it went on and on. Such was the case with Lou's antiwar poetry, predating his late, great pared-down lyrics, the new minimalism which charmed before it stung.

Even as Lou recited, Emily rose from her seat and hurried down the aisle. Whispers rustled under Lou's clarion voice. *Look. That's the fiancée. It's too much for her . . . too much for her.* Softly they whispered as she exited the auditorium, and watched her as she closed the door.

Jess and Richard looked at each other past Heidi who sat between them, and their eyes said: Should I go after her? No, let me. I will.

In lieu of lilies
Please send
Lies.
In lieu of freesia
Please send
Funds.

Had Emily overheard Chaya Zylberfenig talking? What had Emily heard? Jess rushed to the lobby, where she found her sister standing still and pale.

"What happened?" Jess pleaded.

"Nothing."

"Do you want to go? Was it something Lou said?"

"No." Emily pushed open the glass lobby doors. "I just want to be alone, okay?"

"You were right, you shouldn't have come," Jess fretted.

"I'm glad I came," Emily said grimly.

Then for the first time, Jess was afraid Emily would wander off and hurt herself. "Where are you going? Don't go out there by yourself."

Close-lipped, Emily smiled at the idea that Jess could come along, that anyone could travel with her to this new hell. The pain was entirely new, when she reconsidered all that went before. Where there had been no body, she'd held fast to Jonathan's spirit. And now?

He had given her an enormously expensive ring, but she had given him information worth more than any diamond. She remembered his silence as they lay together in the dark and she told him about fingerprinting. He'd tried to stop her. He was overwhelmed, moved, shocked that she would say so much. Was that because he knew he could not resist making electronic fingerprinting his? Did he already know he would steal her idea?

But the idea had not been hers to tell. If she was accusing Jonathan, she should indict herself as well. Fingerprinting had belonged to Alex. Indeed, it belonged to Alex now. Even now, at Veritech, Alex continued to research fingerprinting for a project his team was developing to check for spyware: a project Emily herself had named Verify. What would Alex do when he heard what Jonathan had done? You were right, Jonathan, she told herself. You were right all along. You win. I'm just like you. You betrayed me, but I betrayed Alex first. She stood on the plaza in front of Kresge, and these ideas spread like poison through her body, numbing her fingers and toes, darkening her vision, blackening the sun.

29

That night, Richard sat with Jess at the kitchen table and he said, "Your sister's been through enough."

"She has to find out sometime," Jess said, and unconsciously Richard glanced up at the ceiling, thinking of Emily upstairs. "Were you really planning to keep us in the dark forever?"

"You treat this as some life-changing revelation," Richard said. "It's not. It doesn't change anything about you."

"Yes, it does! This means that I have Jewish aunts! Chaya Zylberfenig and Freyda Helfgott. And Rabbi Helfgott is my uncle! Why didn't you tell us?"

Heidi poured three mugs of herbal tea.

"You shouldn't have kept a secret like that," Jess accused her father.

Richard met her angry gaze. "It wasn't my secret. Your mother didn't want you or your sister to have any contact with those people."

"Those people are our family," said Jess. "Even if they're religious mystics and they look different and act different from you and me."

Then Richard struggled a little with himself. He tried to speak and stopped. Heidi stood behind his chair and kneaded his shoulders with her small hands until he put his hands up onto hers. "When they found out your mother had married a non-Jew, they sat in mourning for seven days. When she chose to marry me, they declared her dead."

"And Mom took that name—Gillian? And she went by Gold instead of Gould?"

"She wanted a free life," said Richard. "She wanted to choose her own husband. She wanted a musical career."

"Yes, but—"

"She associated those people with pain."

"But you could have told *us*," Jess said. "You could have told Emily and me."

"I did what she asked," Richard said. "She felt that they were dangerous, and I agreed with her."

Upstairs, Emily stirred in her twin bed in the guest room. She heard the voices below and opened her eyes in the half-light shining through the open door.

She heard her father's voice: "Your mother and I . . ." and . . . "Yes, these Bialystokers are open and welcoming to everyone outside, but they have another attitude toward those within the fold, and that attitude is repressive to the—"

"Dad."

"I would not violate your mother's last wish—"

"Her last wish!" Jess raised her voice. "Her last wish was, 'Don't tell my daughters who I really am'?"

"No, you don't understand. She knew exactly who she was. All she asked was that I conceal who she'd been."

"But who you were fits inside of who you are. Can't you see that?" Jess cried out.

Then Heidi said, "You'll wake the children."

But the little girls slept on upstairs. Only Emily lay awake, heart pounding in the dark.

Catharsis was for strangers. Those who knew Jonathan and Mel least went to sleep that night chastened, but cleansed, blessed to come home to their own families and lie down in their own beds. Those who knew Jonathan and Mel best left the memorial service uncomforted. The memorial was something they suffered for the sake of others. They themselves felt queasy at Sorel's "Hallelujah." A service in October was too soon. A service next October might be too soon.

Barbara slept. Whenever possible, she slept upstairs, escaping her relatives from Philly, her divorced younger sister with her autistic foster child, a sweet ten-year-old named Dominique who whooped more often than she spoke, and wouldn't sit in chairs. Barbara outslept her dearest friends, the ones who brought My Grandma's of New England Coffee Cakes and wept in her kitchen, declaring that Mel never hurt anyone, realizing that the world was unfair.

She appreciated Rabbi Zylberfenig's approach, proactive from his first visit in September, when he had arrived with a roll of blue duct tape. All that morning he had taped sheets over the numerous mirrors in Barbara's bathrooms. "This is traditional in a Jewish home of mourning," he had explained.

After the memorial service, even as Barbara was finishing breakfast, the rabbi drove over to study sacred texts with Barbara and whichever relatives and friends showed up.

"Mom," Annie whispered when she spied Zylberfenig through the kitchen window. "Does he have to come here every day?"

"You know Dad thought the Zylberfenigs were creepy," Sam reminded her.

Barbara could not deny this.

"He thought Bialystokers were a cult. That's what he told me," Annie said. Barbara saw her daughter take a breath and turn pale behind her freckles. "We think that Dad wouldn't want them in the house."

Barbara placed her coffee cup gently on the granite kitchen counter. She had been a devoted stay-at-home mother, an involved parent—overinvolved, Mel used to say, when she drove hours every weekend for soccer league, stayed up all night sewing costumes, troubleshooting projects for the science fair. She had been a weeper, crying at every milestone and graduation. Even after the kids had left home, she'd longed for them, rejoicing intensely in their triumphs, hurting and worrying for them when they stumbled. In a real sense she'd lived for them. And now? Grief changed her perspective. Trauma provided sudden distance. Now Barbara looked at Annie and saw a young woman needing a haircut, and probably a new young man as well, someone who might find a way to fly east for his girlfriend's father's memorial.

"We were just thinking of what Dad would want," said Annie.

Oh, really, young lady, Barbara thought. You have a lot of nerve. Did you and your brother get together and figure out what to say? Not very sensitive. Not very thoughtful. Not very bright! But she said none of this. She told Annie mildly, "Your father would want me to do whatever helps."

Do what you have to do. Whatever works. Whatever helps. People said this, Orion mused, but they didn't mean it literally. They didn't mean, for example, go out and get high, or buy a gun and shoot someone. They were thinking more along the lines of go ahead and eat ice cream for dinner, carve a pumpkin, drive to western Mass. for apple picking. None of which appealed.

His anger did not subside. The pain only increased. Losing Jonathan, he had lost a year's work as well. His friend, mentor, and rival dead, his tools repurposed for millennial cyberwars, Orion left the memorial service in such a fury, he didn't know where to go or what to do. He took his father to the train station.

"Take it easy," Lou told him as they hugged good-bye.

"I can't," Orion said.

He sped back to Boston, but he didn't get a ticket. His wheels screeched as he turned off Memorial Drive onto Vassar Street. He hit a pothole that nearly sent his car flying, but he didn't spin out of control. He pulled over and parked illegally in MIT's West Annex Lot. Train tracks ran behind the fence. Every night at nine-thirty a train shuffled past.

He paced the lot, waiting. An hour passed. Two hours passed. At last he heard the horns and jingling bells at the railway crossing a block away, and then the steady shuffling engine.

He sprinted through the parking lot to the cyclone fence that ran along the tracks, and pounced, clawing metal, cutting his right hand, as the train barreled past. *Ringling Bros. Barnum & Bailey circus.* The circus had come to town. He watched the long silver train snake past. What did those cars contain? Tents and tigers, ponies, acrobats, sequined costumes, feather plumes. His father had written a circus poem. "The Circus Animals Return after Successful Contract Negotiations." How did it go? *The troupe returns / Those shopworn joys* . . . His mother had taken him to the circus once, and he had learned to juggle. He had gone through a juggling phase as a child. In high school he got pretty good. He used to irritate his mother while she was cooking. He'd juggle a grapefruit and an avocado and a lemon. Sometimes a cantaloupe. Persimmons tended to explode.

He ran to the Store 24 in Central Square and looked for fruit. Store 24 was excellent because the fruit was so hard. None of it was ripe.

"Anything else?" the salesgirl asked, as she rang up four apples and a preternaturally orange orange.

At first he didn't recognize her. He thought she was a new cashier. Then he saw that she was the same dark-eyed girl who always worked there. The same girl with one difference. She wasn't wearing her head scarf anymore. Her hair was reddish-brown, bobbed to the chin. Couldn't be, he told himself. But she was wearing her barrette with the tiny rhinestone diamond, fastened in her hair just above the ear.

She eyed him nervously. "Would you like a bag?"

He shook his head. He looked at the orange and the apples on the counter, and he didn't want them. He had no desire to juggle anymore.

He walked out into the night, and he thought, Why not? Why not leave the store and the city with its muddy river and its squares of college students? He would leave. He would leave them all behind. His apartment with its splintering roof deck, his convenience store, his frightened cashier, his future in-laws who were already planning for Thanksgiving, his so-called friends who'd cut him loose. The so-called ISIS family. The so-called ISIS team. The company had never been his family, and he'd

never understood the rules if, indeed, there were any. *Think like Jonathan.*
He knew exactly how Jonathan thought: How do I raise hell today?

"I'm leaving ISIS," he told Molly when he got home.

"I know." She was sitting in the living room watching the news.

He took the remote and turned off the television.

"Really leaving."

"You say that every day."

"I can't be there anymore. I can't work there anymore."

Wearily, Molly turned to look at him. "You can't do anything," she
said. "You can't cook. You can't clean. You can't move. You can't grow up.
What is the matter with you?"

Orion didn't answer.

"You barely live here anymore."

"You should talk," Orion shot back.

"I'm working!"

"And I've been working too."

"Right, and now you want to stop. What's your plan, Orion?"

"I don't have a plan," he said. "I don't want a plan. That's the difference
between us. You're the planner. Your parents are the planners. Not me."

"It is eleven o'clock at night," Molly said.

"So?"

"So it's been five hours since the memorial service ended. Where have
you been?"

"Nowhere," said Orion.

"Nowhere? Do you think you might have called me?"

"I might have," said Orion.

"You knew I was home tonight. You knew that I'd be here." She got
off the couch and began brushing crumbs off the cushions onto the floor.
"I am so tired of waiting for you. I'm always waiting for you. For six years,
I've been working and training and waiting for you, and you don't care,
you don't want to be with me, you don't . . ." Tears started in Molly's eyes.
"We were best friends, weren't we? We used to tell each other everything.
When I was upset I could come to you. When you had problems you
would confide in me. But now you don't want to talk to me, you don't
even want to look at me. All you want to do is run away."

"If I'd wanted to run, I would have run already," Orion said.

"Would have? You did! You already have. You run away from me every day."

You make it easy, Orion thought.

Molly rubbed the tears from her eyes. "What if the whole world were like you? What if everybody ran away? What if all the doctors said, 'I can't treat you because I'm afraid of blood'? And the Army said, 'We can't fight to defend you, because somebody could die'?

"Wake up, Orion. Life is messy! The world is messy. And I'm sorry, but people get killed. Even people you and I know. And you can keep on working and try to make things right, or you can give up and make some random tragedy into an excuse for following your original plan—which was to do as little as possible."

He heard his mother in Molly's voice. He heard his mother's anguished pragmatism. *Please don't sit around. Don't sleep the day away. You're wasting light.* Molly's words were angry, but also heartfelt, and he heard their truth.

The truth was not nearly enough. His mother's admonitions were not enough. The old goat, his father, stirred within him. Don't stay, his father whispered. Leave now. Don't ground yourself with Molly, fly away.

"I'm leaving ISIS," Orion said again.

This time Molly heard him differently. He saw the knowledge in her face, which seemed to swell with pain: He's not just leaving ISIS. He's leaving me.

"I'm sorry," Orion told her. "I don't deserve you—obviously."

He was sorry, but that last qualifier carried a sullen little sting.

"You're in love with her, aren't you?" Molly said wonderingly. "You're in love with that girl. The one in the lobby."

"No."

"You're sleeping with her, aren't you?"

"No!" Orion answered truthfully.

"You are such a coward," she gasped. "Standing there like you're having some kind of existential crisis! You're totally involved with her."

"I'm not," Orion lied.

"You were afraid I would find out, and you got scared."

"I'm not scared at all," Orion said.

Before dawn, he knocked on the door of Sorel's house. When she didn't answer, he dialed her number, and her phone rang, but all he got was voice mail.

He stood on the porch and tapped on the window. Then he banged on the door until he heard her sleepy voice on the other side. "For God's sakes."

"Sorel," he said, "it's me. Open up."

"No," she groaned on the other side of the door. "I'm too tired. I'm too sleepy. I'm drunk."

"It's an emergency," he said.

"Then why didn't you call me?"

"Sorel, please."

She opened the door and stepped outside, shivering. She was wearing woolly socks, and a long Phish T-shirt with a sweater over it.

"I missed you."

"Is that an emergency?"

"I'm going away."

"Where?"

"Don't know. I'm leaving ISIS."

"And Molly?"

"Yes."

For a moment she didn't speak. Then she asked, "Are you sure?"

"Oh, yeah. Everybody's sure."

"I'm sorry."

"Really?"

She nodded very slightly and she kept her eyes fixed on him, so that even without her white robes and wings and paint, she looked like the angel in the square. "You're at sea," she said.

"I'm not," he told her. "I'm not at sea at all. Not when I'm with you."

"I like living alone," she said. "And I like traveling. I'm planning an opera! And I'm spending the weekend working on a film in Somerville. A bunch of us from MIT are putting it together. I'm a twelve-foot bride."

"I'd support you in all that," he said, and he was totally serious.

"I have stilts," she said, matching his earnest tone. "I don't need support."

He laughed and folded his arms around her.

"It's a silent movie," she told him. "I wrote the script. It's sort of a feminist *Perils of Pauline,* so when she's angry, she grows really, really tall. We're filming in Union Square."

"Do you have a permit?"

"No! Of course not. Do you think we have that kind of money?"

"So when the cops come you . . . what?"

"Run away."

"On stilts?"

"I'm quite fast," she said.

"Wait, let me get this straight . . . ," he began.

She pulled him toward her and kissed him freely, joyously. "What was the question?"

"I don't have a question." He sighed. "This is so much better than the stairwell."

"You liked stairwells."

"I did, but—"

She interrupted him. "Come in."

30

While the family slept, Emily tiptoed out of the guest room she shared with Jess, down the hall past her father and Heidi's bedroom door, past Maya's, past Lily's. Softly, she glided down the stairs to the glassed-in sunroom where she wrapped herself in the pink and purple afghan on the couch. There she sat and gazed at her sisters' plastic groceries, their books piled on the floor: *Princess Stories, My Body, The Book of Me*. She looked at Lily's miniature dinette, her pink and white play kitchen. She had heard every word of her father's conversation with Jess.

Jonathan had concealed his plans for the future, and Gillian had concealed her past. She had loved them both, and this news made her feel entirely alone.

Or had she loved them? She had loved aspects of Jonathan, and tested him; adored her idea of Gillian, and studied her. She doubted now that she had known either. In the end, she was not a good judge of character— least of all, her own. How strange that people had looked up to her. She was supposed to be the sage one, the stable one. Emily had always told Jess what to do.

She turned and turned her sparkling diamond ring. She could not quite bring herself to take it off. What proof would she have, then, what physical evidence, that what she and Jonathan had was real?

She thought of her mother's ring clinking against the bowl as she kneaded dough. Emily had been the conservator of her mother's memory, keeping the birthday letters on her computer. Reading and rereading them. In the end what did those letters say? *My hope for you and Jessie is that you go on to live your lives happy, independent, unafraid.* Well, what did that mean? Isn't that what everybody wanted? *Guilt and regret are a waste of time. Think about the future.* Tears started in Emily's eyes. Think about the future? Her mother was telling her to play a game with only half the pieces.

Emily had assumed a transparency in people, expected it of everyone, even herself. But why? What basis did she have for such assumptions? She saw in her own case that they were ungrounded. She herself, supposedly so careful and straightforward, so reasonable, had betrayed Veritech's secrets to Jonathan, made a gift of them, a token of love mixed with hope mixed with doubt. In the end her motives were hardly rational, hardly clear. That realization frightened her, but she was reflective, rigorous in her thinking, and she tried to think her way out of this morass. Bewildered, adrift in her father's house, she tried to find a way forward. She was her father's daughter, and she thought like an engineer.

First thing in the morning, she resigned from Veritech. She sent an e-mail to Milton, Alex, and Bruno: *Today, after much thought, I have decided to resign as CEO. My time with you has been challenging, rewarding, and above all, interesting. As you know, I had been planning to step down in January. However, after the events of—*she paused here, and then typed—*the past month, I cannot continue to work at Veritech. I will miss your company, and I will miss the company we have built together, but I realize that now is the time to leave, to think about the future, and spend time with my family. . . .*

No excuses, and no confessions either. Emily's sense of responsibility was strong, but her need for privacy was stronger. She sent the message from her laptop, and then proceeded to the next order of business— helping Heidi prepare breakfast for the children. The nanny arrived.

Heidi took the train to Providence to teach, and Emily took a walk with Jess and Richard.

It seemed to Emily that the leaves had changed overnight. Suddenly, trees of ordinary green were scarlet, gold, spectacular. When she'd arrived in Canaan, she must have been too distraught to notice.

"I heard everything you said," she told Richard, as they walked down Pleasant Street.

Jess took her hand.

"Now I want to know the whole story," Emily told her father.

Richard didn't answer.

"You have to tell us, Dad," said Jess.

Richard kept moving, eyes fixed on the sidewalk ahead. "Well, what do you want to know?"

"I want you to start at the beginning," said Emily.

"Your mother and I met at Cambridge," Richard said. "I was on a Fulbright, and she was a choral scholar."

"We knew that before," said Emily. "I want you to begin at the beginning, with her mother and her father."

But Gillian's parents were not the beginning for Richard. Those dark-costumed people were not the story of his wife. Gillian began with him at Cambridge, where he bicycled with her through golden autumn fields and listened to her sing in the Girton College Chapel Choir. She had applied to college without her parents' knowledge, and when she got her choral scholarship she broke from childhood, choosing music as her religion.

Emily and Jess pressed him, but they didn't understand. Their mother's life began when she came up to Cambridge on her own. "It's like a fairyland here," she used to say, when they walked through the ancient cloisters. She was a quiet rebel, buying a Liberty-dress pattern and sewing her own gown for the Emmanuel College ball, dancing until dawn, and then slipping barefoot onto the velvet lawns reserved for Fellows. As a soprano she sang for services and feasts. As an adventurer, she tried champagne for the first time and pork loin and frog's legs. In summers she and Richard punted on the river Cam. On vacations she stayed in his apartment, and when he got the job at MIT, she married him. Her Hasidic family had nothing to do with it. They would not even meet Richard, much less look at their runaway daughter. She came to America, and took Richard's family for her own.

Emily shook her head. "But don't you see, Dad? That's not good enough. Those are our relatives too. You can't pretend they don't exist."

"How productive is this line of inquiry right now?" Richard asked her. "How will these questions help with what you're going through?"

"Come with us to the Zylberfenigs' house," said Emily.

Richard's jaw tightened. "Absolutely not."

Undeterred, Emily took Jess that very afternoon to Alcott Street. Laptop in hand, she rang the bell. Then she knocked on the door. Seconds later, Chaya Zylberfenig welcomed the sisters with open arms.

"I knew I was right!" Chaya cried. "Come in, come in! The doorbell's broken. Come sit!" She ushered Emily and Jess into her living room filled with bookcases of tall Hebrew books. She seated the young women on her slip-covered couch, under her picture of the Rebbe. Brushing tears from her eyes, Chaya said, "Welcome, nieces."

"Is it really possible you're our aunt?" Jess asked. "It's so strange."

"Ah." Chaya smiled. "My husband always quotes the Rebbe. There are no coincidences."

"You're so young," Emily said shyly.

Once again Chaya explained. "There were nine of us. Your mother, Gittel, *oleha shalom,* was the oldest. I was the ninth, and so I was *much* younger. She left home when Freyda and I were babies."

Emily could not hide her disappointment. "So you didn't know her."

Chaya shook her head, "We were told unfortunately that she had died—even before her real death."

"Don't you think that was wrong?" Jess couldn't help interjecting.

Emily touched her arm in warning.

"It was many years ago," Chaya said diplomatically. "What she did and what our parents did is all said and done. But I can tell you all about the family. Your grandfather Leib, *zichron l'bracha,* was a jeweler."

"A jeweler!"

Jess watched, amazed, as Emily whipped out her laptop and began typing. "How do you spell 'Leib'?"

Two hours later, Emily was still bent over her keyboard, typing. She'd stopped only to plug her power cord into the wall behind the couch as she continued to pepper Chaya with questions. "How did he die?" And, "Where are those children now?" With a kind of manic energy, she added to her family record, while Chaya talked and Jess sat back and watched, overwhelmed by this sudden cousinage in London. Jess knew that there were stages of grief. Was this one of them? The genealogical stage? The note-taking, fact-finding, photo-album stage?

"This is the house where we grew up." Chaya opened her crimson, leather-bound album to a picture of a tall brick town house. "This is my older sister Beyla, who raised us and who lives there now. She knew your mother well. These are my middle brothers, Menachem and Reuven . . . or maybe not." She squinted at the picture. "Maybe that's not Reuven. That could be Cousin Mendy."

Emily studied the pictures. "We need to scan these in. If we digitize everything, then we can share the files." Turning to Jess, she asked, "Did you see the picture of the house?"

"Uh-huh," Jess said weakly from the corner of the couch.

"You'll stay for lunch?" Chaya asked them. They adjourned to the kitchen, and the children gathered, blowing through in a little storm of elbows, arms, and knees. Chaya served cold cuts, which Jess didn't eat. The boys tried to touch their noses with their tongues. These are my cousins, Jess thought. These are Rabbi Helfgott's nephews, and his nieces, just like me. Emily kept typing, her face aglow.

"You in particular look like a Gould," Chaya told Emily. "You have the Gould eyes."

"Hazel?" Emily asked.

"Determined," said Chaya. "This is very much a Gould trait."

"Very much so!" Shimon agreed as he came in from the garage.

"Shimon, meet our nieces, Emily and Jessamine," Chaya said.

"*Baruch Hashem.* Here you are!" said Shimon and he did not look in the least surprised.

"Clear your places!" Chaya called after her boys as they ran off. They doubled back again and threw their paper plates into the trash.

"Life is strange," Jess murmured, looking at her uncle in his black frock coat.

"Life is very, very beautiful." Shimon washed his hands and said a blessing, after which he sat down and fixed himself a sandwich. His blue eyes sparkled as if with news he couldn't tell. Two new nieces, two beautiful souls in his own kitchen in Canaan, and one of them— He didn't think of Emily as rich. He never used that word, even to himself, but she had means. She had capacity to illuminate everything around her. Like Barbara, Emily had much to give.

"Will you join me for my class?" he asked Jess and Emily. "My brother-in-law Rabbi Helfgott tells me that you, Jessamine, are one of his best students. Very philosophical."

"Oh, I'm not," Jess demurred. She didn't feel philosophical at all.

All day and night, Emily continued in her hectic phase. Thoughts of her mother's true identity had unleashed in her a million schemes and plans. She was sending e-mails to Aunt Freyda in Berkeley and Aunt Beyla in London. She was already telling Jess that evening that they should fly to London. The sisters sat on their twin beds in the guest room and Emily said, "We'll go to Golders Green and see the house. We'll see the house where she grew up and meet the family."

"We could," Jess said.

"There might be some of Gittel's papers there, or school reports. Or maybe we can find a diary."

Gently, Jess suggested, "From what Dad and Chaya say, I'm not sure you're going to find any diaries or mementos."

"You never know," said Emily.

She had a new idea to pursue, and she held fast to it. She would not let go. Richard sat with Emily in the living room as she searched for fares to London.

"I don't think this is a good idea," Richard said.

"You knew your grandparents, and you knew your mother," Emily said calmly. "If you hadn't known them and suddenly you got a chance— wouldn't you go?" She seemed strangely happy, and also feverish, downloading Family Tree software and finding it wanting. "The interfaces are terrible," she told her father.

In her first weeks of bereavement, Emily had been quiet and small, almost childlike, retreating into herself. She had tried to contain what she felt, to keep calm, and whenever possible, comfort her own comforters. Now she asserted herself, brooking no dissent, dismissing her father's concerns about "those people" as he called them.

"Look, they're controlling," Richard told her. "They're manipulative."

Emily raised an eyebrow and tilted her head ever so slightly, as if to say, You weren't controlling? You didn't manipulate my sister and me?

"You have a lot of money," Richard reminded Emily.

"Is that what you're worried about?" Emily asked, irritated.

"You're rich," he said. "They're poor. They have to provide for dozens of children, and you need to keep your eyes open."

"How dare you tell me to keep my eyes open," Emily said. "When all these years you kept me in the dark."

Jess had never heard her sister and her father fight before. Jess and Richard had been fire and water, and of course he always won. Emily and Richard were like an ice storm, sparkling, deadly.

"You're in a vulnerable position," Richard said.

"A position you created."

Suddenly something broke in Richard. Emily froze. Jess looked up, horrified to see her father crying. She had never seen her father cry before, and now his eyes were red and he was sobbing. He couldn't stop himself. "I'm afraid for you, Emily!"

Heidi rushed into the room, and she seemed almost as surprised as Emily and Jess. She wrapped her arms around Richard, and he buried his head in her sweater and cried and cried.

"Dad, I'm sorry you're upset . . . ," Emily began. "I'm sorry!" But now that he was crying, Richard could not stop.

Jess couldn't watch. She slipped out the back door and tried to catch her breath. Hugging herself, she sat on Lily's big-girl swing. It was getting cold, but she didn't want to return for her jacket. She stayed out, swinging gently, trying to calm herself, listening to the squeaking chains.

At last she took out her new cell phone and called George.

"Hey," she said softly.

"Jess. How are you?"

"Where are you?" she asked at the same time.

"In my kitchen," he told her. "Missing you. Where are you?"

"On the swing set in the yard."

"Missing me?"

"What do you think?"

Her voice was muffled, weary, terribly sad. "What's wrong now?" George asked. "What happened?"

"I have to go to London."

"No! No, you don't. If your sister wants to go and see all those relatives, then you go ahead and let her. She's a grown woman."

"I have to go," Jess said. "She's in a bad way. I can't let her go alone."

"Why not? Why can't you? You've been with her almost a month. Come home."

"I can't," said Jess. "I can't."

"You keep saying that."

"I'm helping her. She needs me."

"I know," George said. "But what about you?"

Jess demanded, "Can't you look at this from Emily's point of view?"

Then George was honest, much too honest. He knew even as he said the words that they would anger Jess, but he missed her so much that he could not help himself. "I'm not interested in her point of view."

Silence.

"Jess? Are you there?"

"You're very good at that," Jess said.

"Good at what?"

"Triaging. You're first, and I'm second, and everybody else is a distant third."

"You're overwrought," George said. "This situation is poisonous for you."

"Maybe it is," said Jess. "But I'm the only one she has."

"What about your father?"

"You don't understand. He's half the problem." Jess glanced back at the house. "I'm the one who has to go."

All that night and the next day, Emily worked busily. She drew up charts and lists and plans. She asked Laura to FedEx her passport. Then she took Jess for pictures and ordered her a passport as well. Emily was more than pleased. This new discovery satisfied her investigative soul, turning her heart toward social connections which were intricate but calculable, concrete, and fixed. Even as Jess watched, Emily returned to life, e-mailing, organizing, buying guidebooks and new clothes.

She and Jess drove to the Canaan mall and Emily bought Jess a puffy down jacket, and chenille sweaters, and good warm socks, and waterproof boots, and a pair of Indian gold earrings for good measure.

"Does it help?" Jess asked.

"Does what help?"

"Shopping."

"Let's get Dad something at Home Depot." Emily strode across the parking lot to the great brick edifice dedicated to home improvement. "Look at these snowblowers. They've already got snowblowers out and it's not even Halloween."

"Emily?" said Jess.

"What do you think the difference is between Turbo Power Plus and the Turbo Power Max?" Emily murmured.

"Will London make you happy?"

Emily touched her sister's shoulder. "We have a family there. It's just such a gift."

What was wrong with Jess, then? Presented with this gift, she felt utterly alone and empty. George was frustrated with her for staying with Emily for so long, and Emily expected Jess to accompany her. She not only expected Jess to go; she assumed Jess shared her excitement.

Suddenly among the shiny red snowblowers Jess understood how Sandra McClintock must have felt, hearing that her mother was the object of her uncle's affections. She realized how disconcerted Sandra must have been. Information wasn't always such a gift; it was also a loss, the end of possibility. To tell the truth, when it came to her mother, Jess preferred mystery. She preferred to make up her own stories. It was painful to think that Gillian was someone real. Maybe Emily took a macabre satisfaction in diving into the wreck to reclaim this relic and that. Wasn't she missing the point? The storm at sea? The end of all their mother's hopes, ideas, and memories?

"Is that your phone?" Emily asked.

Jess glanced quickly at the number and didn't answer. She didn't want to talk to George.

While Emily hunted down a salesman, Jess slipped away through aisles of locks, power drills, carpet rolls, kitchen sinks, doors with fanlights, bathtubs, vanities. Piled high with storm windows, a beeping forklift backed toward her, even as she scrolled through her telephone's address book and dialed.

"Sandra?" she said.

"Who is this?"

"This is Jessamine Bach. May I speak to Sandra?"

"Oh, Jess!" Sandra exclaimed. "How are you?"

The cheerful voice sounded nothing like the Sandra Jess knew.

"I called to apologize," said Jess as she walked down an aisle of white wire closet organizers.

"What do you mean?" Sandra asked.

"I ambushed you with information about your mother and your uncle. I saw their connection in the McLintock cookbook and I got a little carried away." Pausing, Jess glanced at the shelves. "I was so proud of myself. I never really considered the effect it might have had on you."

"Oh," said Sandra. "Well."

"I'm sorry," Jess whispered. "I didn't understand. I wanted to say that I do understand now. I'm very, very sorry."

"Stop! That's ridiculous," said Sandra. "I'm fine, and everybody's fine. I haven't thought about any of that in weeks. Your discovery was worth a lot to me, as I'm sure you know."

Jess stood before an array of paint chips. "No, I don't know. I've been away. I'm out of town."

"That's right, you aren't working for him anymore. I thought he might have told you. George reassessed the cookbooks after you found the McLintock, and he doubled his payment."

"George?" Jess was shocked. "He paid you double?"

"He did," said Sandra. "My daughter got a new lawyer because of that, and she's settling with her ex for joint custody. We're getting summers and every-other-weekend visitation."

Jess plucked out paint samples in shades of blue: *Chartered Voyage, Summer Dragonfly, Rushing Stream.* "He never told me that."

"Well," Sandra said, "he felt that he'd undervalued the collection. He wanted to give me even more, but I was afraid my uncle would not have liked it. We agreed on donating to the Redwood League instead, toward the purchase of the Dillonwood Grove. Have you heard of it?"

"Yes."

"The league is buying that tract to add to Sequoia National Park, and we're making the donation in honor of Tom McClintock's work on lungwort in the canopy. He was a very important lichenologist, you know."

"I don't think . . . I'm sure George never did anything like that before."

Sandra answered with some pride, "He said he had never seen cookbooks like mine."

Emily found Jess outside, crying among the terra-cotta flowerpots. "They're actually plastic," Jess said. She lifted a giant faux-stone urn. "Look how light they are."

"Jess? What's wrong?" Emily rushed over. "I've been looking everywhere for you. What happened?"

"I didn't know," Jess said.

"How could you have known? Dad wouldn't tell us who she really was. He tried to prevent us from finding out."

Jess shook her head. "That's not what I meant."

"I'm angry at him too," said Emily. "I'm disappointed, but the point is to think about her."

"I can't think about her."

Emily wrapped her arms around her sister. "It's a shock, but it's really better to know. We have to know—even if it's painful. I know you miss her. . . ."

"No. I mean, yes, but it's not that. I miss George," Jess confessed.

"George!" Emily dropped her arms, and suddenly her hands were on her hips. "Oh, Jess, don't tell me that—"

"Please don't say, 'Oh, Jess.' Please don't be that way."

"You said it was over. You said that you're just friends," Emily scolded. "Why did you lie to me?"

"I didn't lie."

"Well, what would you call it then?"

Jess quailed a little before her sister. "Understatement?"

Emily shook her head. "You're amazing. You go from one totally inappropriate guy to the next. Just one after another."

"It's not what you think," said Jess. "It's not some motherless daughter thing."

"Of course it is. How old is he? He's twenty years older than you, isn't he?"

"Sixteen years older," said Jess. "It doesn't matter."

"So he's a very young middle-aged guy? Is that supposed to be endearing? You have no common sense, Jessamine."

Jess turned on her sister. "Aren't you the one flying to London to look up long-lost Hasidic relatives?"

"That's real. That's our family. What you are talking about is yet another of your infatuations."

"No," said Jess. "You're the one infatuated with Gillian's memory. Not me. You're the one chasing a dream. Not me."

For a moment Emily could not speak.

"You don't know him, but George is actually wonderful, and funny. He's musical. He's . . . secretly philanthropic."

"That's the problem," said Emily. "You're part of his philanthropy."

"No, Emily. No. Not really. He understands me. He reads me. I'm in love with him," Jess whispered.

Emily sighed at her legible sister.

"I'm sorry I've cried wolf so many times. This time I mean it."

Emily spun around and took her receipt to Security where the Turbo Max snowblower was waiting for pickup.

"Please believe me." Jess hurried after her.

"If you love him so much, why are you here with me?" Emily asked her.

"Because you need me more right now. You come first."

"If I come first, why can't you confide in me?"

Jess was so startled that she couldn't answer right away. "It . . . it wasn't the time!"

"If you love him, then why is it a secret?" Emily asked. "And if you need him, then you shouldn't be apart."

"You can love someone even if you're separated," Jess answered slowly.

"For how long?" Emily asked.

"Is this some kind of test? For as long as it takes."

"No," Emily said.

"What do you mean?"

When Emily answered, her voice was serious and low. "You can't be apart indefinitely. You can't keep postponing and expect everything to stay the same. If you keep deferring, everything gets old. Even love, eventually."

31

George closed Yorick's at five. He closed the register, and Colm pulled down the metal grille over the front window. No one had come in all afternoon, except for Raj, who had driven over to show off his pristine first-edition *Ulysses*. "It isn't signed," Raj admitted, "and it's been read . . ."

"Oh, too bad," George said drily.

"But it's very beautiful." Raj opened a box, and lifted the cloth-bound novel as gently as a newborn puppy.

"Ooh." Colm raked his fingers through his thick wavy hair.

"You don't have a first-edition *Ulysses*, do you?" Raj asked George.

"I've already told you no, and I'm not buying this one, if that's what you're asking."

"I'm not asking," said Raj, cradling the book. "It's not for sale."

"If it's not for reading, and it's not for selling, what's it for then?" George inquired.

Later when Colm had gone to work in the back room, George whispered to Raj, "If you like him, why don't you just ask him out?"

"It's complicated," Raj said airily.

He began to explain, but George said, "I don't want to know."

He couldn't stand another set of complications. He felt so worn, tired, cranky, old. When he drove home that evening, up Marin Avenue, he thought his transmission was going. When he parked, the young deer devouring his daylilies barely looked up.

He collected the mail, climbed the steps, unlocked his door, and only then did he notice a pair of battered running shoes inside on the mat. His heart pounded as he ran into the dining room.

"Jess!"

"Just a sec," she told him, holding up her hand to stop him.

She was sitting cross-legged at the head of the table with cookbooks stacked up all around her, the reference manuals, the laptop, the note cards, as of old. "What do you think of this? *By 1736, McLintock includes sugar in over half her recipes. Generally she uses a pound of sugar for cake or biscuits. What was scarce is now a staple in the home cook's pantry. The luxurious is now ubiquitous and sugar's smoother, lighter, facile sweetness is not only desired but expected at the table. Desire shifts to expectation, and expectation creates desire. This dynamic applies to everyday mass consumption in the kitchen, and feeds new theories of supply and demand, hunger and satisfaction. Indeed, in 1739, just three years after McLintock published her* Receipts for Cookery and Pastry-Work, *her countryman David Hume diagrams the cycle of desire in his* Treatise of Human Nature: *'Any satisfaction, which we lately enjoy'd, and of which the memory is fresh and recent, operates on the will with more violence, than another of which the traces are decayed. . . .' (Section VI)."*

"Not bad," said George. "Who wrote that?"

"You know I did! I'm still working on the transition to Hume. I know what I want to say, but I still have to . . ."

"Keep reading," he said, but she shook her head and opened up her arms for him.

He knelt at her feet and rested his head in her lap. She ran her fingers through his hair. "That's as far as I got," she said. "If I read you any more, I'll have to back up and start from the beginning."

"I thought you went to London."

"Emily talked me out of it," said Jess. "With a lot of lecturing."

He lifted his head. "I can't believe you're here."

"She says I'm too young for you, and you're too old for me, and we're at different stages. She warned me that we'll become a cliché."

"So what?" He took her by the hand and led her up the stairs.

PART EIGHT

Closely Held

May 2002

32

By spring, fewer troopers with dogs and submachine guns stood guard at the airports. Obituaries and memorial services had tapered off, and flags were smaller where they still flew. Magazines showcased 9/11 widows and their families, especially the babies their husbands would never know, but those same publications featured recipes for easy, breezy outdoor fun, tips for praising children the right way, and full-page photographs of fruit cobblers, no-bake desserts, no-sew craft projects, closet makeovers, and illustrations of simple exercises for those mornings when there was no time to run. Death never died, but the idea of death receded, as it must.

The new reality was clear-eyed. Start-ups scaled back on spending, hiring, and hype. Google was still closely held, its culture whimsical as its search engine was bold. Its founders talked about managing finances carefully and refused to set a date for their IPO. Such were the lessons learned from the prior generation, those high fliers from two years before: Reap what you sow, and look before you reap. Transactions speak louder than words. *Festina lente.*

The new reality was all about repentance: no razzle-dazzle, just hard-earned profits; no more analyst exuberance, just sober assessments. Venture capitalists threw money at fewer start-ups, and demanded even more access to the businesses they funded. No one talked about going public in a year. People took the long view: three years, five years, even more.

Books were written about the old new economy. Memoirs, dissertations. Harvard Business School students studied the successful evolution of the ISIS business model from a focus on Internet security to Internet surveillance, and its shift from servicing small businesses to winning government contracts. Professors lectured on Veritech as well, tracing the rise and fall of the high-flying start-up: a company peaking at $342 a share, falling to under fifty cents, and at last returning to its roots as a much smaller venture, when its remaining principals, Alex, Bruno, and Milton bought back stock. No one knew the secret history of electronic fingerprinting. The germ of the idea remained mysterious, upstaged by larger historical and economic forces. The lightning-quick response by ISIS and other companies that could shift priorities with the shifting times showed up cautious Veritech as a young dinosaur. Once upon a time Xerox had developed the first graphical user interface, but Microsoft had capitalized on the idea with Windows. So now, Veritech had researched electronic fingerprinting, but ISIS cashed in with OSIRIS. ISIS thrived, and Veritech faded into footnotes.

Those who held onto their tech shares lost the most. The market punished true believers, so that Veritech's cook, Charlie, lost his restaurant and drove a taxi. Laura and Kevin ran out of money renovating, and sold the house in Los Altos at a loss. They rented a condo in Mountain View, while Laura kept working and Kevin contemplated going back to school. Sometimes sadder, sometimes wiser, laid-off programmers returned to graduate school to finish their degrees, or joined the Peace Corps, or scrambled for money to start new companies, as seedlings grow in rings around a redwood struck by lightning.

The few who sold stock early traveled, or started nonprofits, or volunteered in soup kitchens, or began analysis, or wrote poetry, or bought land in Oregon and planted lavender. They hosted fund-raisers for Hillary Clinton and invested in innovative ventures, and sat on boards where they drew upon their own experience to deliver sage advice. Jake returned to school, and Oskar settled back into his chair at MIT. The ones who got out early did what they wanted. Jonathan had set up a trust for his younger brothers—a fund which would help and hinder them for the rest of their lives. Apart from that, he'd held on to all his stock, and left no cash. His legacy was still tied up in ISIS. Mel Millstein, on the other hand, had been a financial genius. Who knew? Because he'd sold all his stock at thirty-three dollars a share in October 2000, he'd netted enough money for Barbara to live in comfort for the rest of her life.

So it was on Mother's Day that Barbara Millstein angered her children, and pleased herself, presiding at the dedication of the Melvin H. Millstein Center for Jewish Life. The mayor of Canaan attended the ribbon cutting at Barbara's former mansion, now home to Rabbi Zylberfenig and his wife, Chaya, and their seven children.

"How could you give them your house?" Annie asked Barbara on the phone from California. "And how could you name the center for Dad, when you know how he felt about religion?"

Barbara smiled to think of the little Zylberfenigs racing up the stairs, and Chaya cooking in the grand country kitchen, and the rabbi leading services in the great room, and teaching mysticism in the paneled library, where a portrait of the Rebbe hung in space built for a flat-screen TV.

"I wanted to name something for your father," she said, "and actually, I don't think he minds."

"How can you say that?"

"He wants me to be happy," Barbara declared, knowing full well that she spooked her children when she used the present tense. Did she care if she scared people? Not at all. "He would want to do the thing that makes me happiest."

"You always say that," Annie said. "How do you know?"

"I know," Barbara said simply, "because when he was alive, I did a lot for him."

The center was for everybody, not just Bialystoker Jews. There were plans for a preschool and a little summer camp on the grounds. All the children of Canaan were invited to the dedication, and Barbara herself had organized the entertainment: jugglers, clowns, a trampoline surrounded by a protective net. Even pony rides. She had arranged for face painting, finger painting, sticker art, spin art, a make-your-own-sundae table, and a decorate-your-own-cupcake station. Water tables with plastic boats, and most popular of all, trays of sudsy water for giant-bubble blowing. Dip a bent coat hanger in liquid, then wave gently through the air to look out at the world through the bending, bobbling sheen.

"Dear friends, thank you for coming today," Rabbi Zylberfenig announced from his position on the back deck, overlooking the lawn. "Thank you, Mayor. Thank you, Barbara. Above all, thanks to God for this world and its spirits. Our rabbis teach that a divine spark resides in every one of us, and joy as well, even when you least expect it. At our lowest point and in the darkest hour, we may find within ourselves a source of light. . . ."

"No back flips on the trampoline," Chaya scolded her boys on the other side of the garden. "You heard the rules."

A soft breeze blew, and few listened to the rabbi speak of joy and time, because the weather was so lovely. The children were busy. The mayor told Barbara that, although he had not known her husband personally, he was very moved.

Others embraced Barbara. Neighbors, old friends, teachers from Canaan High School. A gaunt and gray-eyed man stood somewhat apart, a stranger and a loner in the crowd. When he shook Barbara's hand, the two town policemen kept an eye on him. "Bobby," he introduced himself. "Mel's Alexander teacher."

"You did come!" she exclaimed. "Thank you! You did so much for Mel—realigning him."

Bobby looked grim. "I'm sorry."

Barbara pressed his hand in hers. "Thank you. I appreciate it."

She was turning away when Bobby blurted out, "I told him to go to L.A. He came to my office in a panic for realignment. He was all out of kilter and he said, *I don't want to go.* I said, *Don't worry about the flight. Your only fear is fear itself. Your back can take it.*"

Tears started in Barbara's eyes, but she saw she had an opportunity. She realized she had a chance to do a mitzvah. As the Third Bialystoker Rabbi, the Dreamer, said, *How often in this life do we have the opportunity to do something good?*

"Don't blame yourself," she said. "It's not your fault."

"I feel it is," insisted Mel's Alexander teacher. "He got so upset. I always told him, *Mind over matter, Mel, mind over matter.* But in the end it wasn't mind over matter at all."

Barbara sighed. It was such a lot of work to comfort everyone. "Please believe me. Mel's death is not your fault. Your job is backs. Not realigning history."

"I'm sorry to interrupt," Barbara's party planner interrupted. "The ponies are on a break. Do you want the mime now, or do you want to wait? It's your call."

"It is a very interesting fact," Rabbi Zylberfenig was saying, "that few things happen by chance. Look carefully and also look with some distance, and you will see connections and designs in everything."

He knew he was right. Even Chaya admitted he had a point. She saw sad designs in the world as well, terrible coincidences, not just joyous ones, but she told him, "In some ways, maybe you are right." Certainly on that day, at the dedication, she saw Shimon's point of view. Even apart from their own good fortune, at that very hour, their niece Jessamine was marrying George Friedman, a Jewish man dedicated to learning, a scholar and a person of great means, a collector, she was told, of ancient books. Chaya's own brother-in-law was performing the ceremony at the famous Rose Garden of Berkeley, California.

The roses bloomed, thousands of them in a floral amphitheater, blossoms shading from gold and coral at the top of the garden to scarlet and deep pink on tiers below. At the bottom, in the center of the rosy congregation, the palest apricots and ivories perfumed the air.

The wedding was small, just forty friends and family standing in the garden. The roses were all the ornament Jess and George needed, under the blue sky, but Rabbi Helfgott brought a canopy as well, four tall poles and voluminous white cloth. He tied the corners of the cloth to the poles. "This is your *huppah*," he had explained to George and Jess when he met with them some weeks before the ceremony. "You can guess what it stands for."

"Marriage," Jess said.

"Even more specifically than that. What do they say? Think locally."

"Our house?"

The rabbi corrected cheerfully. "Your bed."

Now Nick held one pole, Raj another, Mrs. Gibbs the third, and Freyda held the fourth. The musicians began to play guitar and flute, and George took his place under the huppah on one of the garden's upper tiers. Did he look pale in his dark suit? Could his friends hear his pounding heart? Nick reached over and clapped him on the shoulder, and George was grateful for the contact; he needed to know that this was not a dream—that, in fact, Jess was walking toward him. Her father and her sister were giving her away, escorting her up the tiered steps.

Oh, look at the three of them, whispered Jess's New Jersey aunts. *Look at them together.*

Look at Emily, such a beautiful girl, thought Aunt Freyda. *We have to find someone for her.*

George saw only Jess. Her silk dress was sleeveless, delicate, sea green. Her long hair flowed down her back. She carried a bouquet of leaves and trailing jasmine, and when she reached the huppah she gave the flowers to Emily, and whispered, "Keep them."

As Jess walked toward him, George wanted the moment to last, and at the same time, he couldn't wait for the ceremony to be over.

"Are you ready?"

Rabbi Helfgott's question startled George. He had not expected anything unscripted. He'd prepared for the traditional ceremony, the seven blessings, the marriage contract, and the ring. Jess felt him tense at her side, and she slipped her fingers into his. Her eyes were green, her expression sweet and just slightly satirical. He couldn't help kissing her hand.

"All right, so I see you're more than ready," Rabbi Helfgott said, and those nearest George and Jess laughed, while other relatives farther back turned to each other: *What did he say? I can't hear a thing.*

When Rabbi Helfgott began the welcoming blessing, chanting in Hebrew, Jess tried to recall the translations she had studied, but she could not remember the words. She stood with George and took one sip from the wine the rabbi offered. How strange she felt, standing with him there, all their guests arrayed below, her little sisters dressed as flower girls, her stepmother holding them still, one hand on each.

Jess wanted to remember everything. The cloudless sky, her exuberant uncle's bearded face, her father on his best behavior withstanding the religious onslaught, Mrs.Gibbs in a navy suit and a straw boater. Emily, at Jess's elbow, Emily the true philosopher, braver than anyone Jess knew.

At her side, George looked alert and nervous, unusually shy, knowing no Hebrew, not even a few words. Don't worry, Jess told him silently. Don't think of these as ancient blessings; imagine that they're roses, think of them as scents. She was standing with him on a precipice. She felt fluttery, breathless, but she was not afraid of these heights. She had a high threshold for happiness, a straightforward, trusting nature when it came to joy.

This gladness was what Rabbi Helfgott had recognized in Jess so long ago. He had seen the joy in her then, and that was why he had decided to invest in her, writing the check for eighteen hundred dollars, that mystic multiple of *chai*, the number symbolizing life. The day the rabbi had met George and Jess to discuss their wedding, the bride, his lovely niece, had slipped him a check for eighteen thousand as a donation to the Bialystok Center, returning his investment tenfold! As it was written, there was a time to plant and a time to reap, a time to mourn and a time to dance. Naturally, reaping was preferable! Dancing was more pleasurable.

"King Solomon was a very great man," the rabbi told the assembled. "You have perhaps heard of his gardens, his palaces, above all his Temple built with the best the world had to offer—olive wood, and gold, the finest linen, cedar from Lebanon. This man loved beautiful things! He enjoyed life! However, he also asked, 'What profit is it to own so many things, to stroll in gardens and enjoy precious jewels, to eat such food and drink such wine? In the end, what good is it to collect such riches? Every wall will crumble. The beautiful will wither and decay.'"

"True," murmured Sandra, who stood with the other guests among the roses.

"In the end, nothing lasts. Even *wisdom* will not last—this is what wise Solomon said. What, then, has lasting value? Where should we turn for the eternal?"

"To the good Lord," said Mrs. Gibbs.

The rabbi nodded, but he amended, "Where do we find Hashem when He is so great, transcending our comprehension? Where do we look for Him?"

George looked at Jess.

"We find Him in each other."

Ah, thought Raj, very good. He himself had a soft spot for religious rhetoric. His own mother in Calcutta was a very religious woman.

A perfectly calibrated crowd-pleasing little sermon, mused Richard. The Bialystoker presents himself as a humanist in Hasidic clothing.

"We find Him in each other," Helfgott repeated, gazing at George and Jess, the *chassen* and *kalleh,* in front of him. "And this is why love is sweeter than wine, finer than gold, rarer than the rarest spices. *However,* since we are human, and not entirely angels at this moment in time, we need a record and a proof of what we feel. Therefore, we write up a marriage contract, our *ketubah*." He turned to Nick, who handed him the calligraphed *ketubah* that George and Jess had commissioned. The Hebrew words were scribed in thorny black on vellum, the border illuminated with flowering vines. "And we have a pure, unadorned ring," said Helfgott. "The ring . . . ," he repeated gently to George, who hurriedly reached into his pocket.

"Place it on her forefinger and repeat after me. . . ." Helfgott smiled as George instinctively slipped the gold band onto Jess's ring finger. "Her other forefinger. *Harei at mekudeshet li . . .*"

George repeated the words. As in a dream, he spoke his first words in Hebrew, announcing that he took Jess to be his wife. The blessings afterward were flowing and melodious. He heard them in the distance, as gentle waves against the sand, or soft wind in the trees. Almost imperceptibly, Jess leaned toward him, and although the rabbi seemed to be telling him to wait, George's arm twined around her waist.

"One last thing, one final act, the breaking of the glass." The rabbi turned to Freyda, who produced a gleaming orb from her purse.

"That's not a glass, that's a lightbulb," George whispered, even as Helfgott wrapped the bulb in a cloth napkin.

"It is our tradition to use a lightbulb," the rabbi whispered back, "because in my experience, nine times out of ten, glass goblets are very hard to break."

"Try me," said George.

"I don't think we have a glass," said Helfgott who had used silver cups for the ceremonial wine.

"It doesn't matter," Jess murmured, but quick-thinking Emily hurried to the caterer waiting with champagne and strawberries at the bottom of the garden and returned with a champagne flute, which the rabbi wrapped, and George crushed the glass, stamping it to smithereens.

"Mazel tov!" cried Rabbi Helfgott, and all the guests. Music began again, no longer classical, but klezmer, as George and Jess laughed and kissed.

Everyone descended to the lower garden for refreshments and then repaired to the house on Wildwood for a wedding breakfast of eggs (poached to order in the kitchen), kippered herring, smoked mackerel, cured salmon, scones melting in the mouth to tender crumbs. Rabbi Helfgott beamed, although he would not partake.

Lily and Maya ran through the rooms with fistfuls of anise cookies and madeleines. They showed their mother marzipans of miniature books with gilt-edged pages, and they tried candied ginger, and they ate chocolate lace.

"We got the menu from your uncle," George explained to Sandra.

Jess added, "But we left out the meat."

"And the smoked fish?" Raj asked playfully. "I assume they took their own lives in the wild?"

"Fat aged carps that run into thy net," Colm quoted Jonson. *"And pikes, now weary their own kind to eat, . . ."*

"As loath the second draught or cast to stay," Raj continued without missing a beat. *"Officiously at first themselves betray; . . ."*

"You have a beautiful daughter," Mrs. Gibbs told Richard.

"I have four beautiful daughters." Richard finished his second glass of champagne. "It's very good, isn't it?" he told Heidi.

"It really is." She sighed with relief. Lily and Maya were playing in the garden. As of yet, Richard had said nothing sarcastic. She had spoken to him seriously about this the night before.

"Whatever you think about the rabbi or religion in general, this is your daughter's wedding," Heidi had admonished him.

"I know, I know," he told her. "It's just that George is not what I expected."

"Well," said Heidi, "now you know how my parents felt when I married you."

Jess slipped off her green shoes and glided everywhere at once, kissing Theresa and Roland, her old roommates.

"I told you this would happen," Theresa reminded her. "I told you Mrs. Gibbs would convert you and you would end up . . ."

"Barefoot in the kitchen," said Jess. "Did you try the cake?"

There were three wedding cakes, curious and historical but tasty, each labeled with a calligraphed card:

"Plumb Cake" with currants, nutmeg, mace, cinnamon, salt, citron, orange peel candied, flour, eggs, yeast, wine, cream, raisins. Adapted from Mrs. Simmons, American Cookery, 1796.

"Curran-cake" with sugar, eggs, butter, flour, currans, brandy. Adapted from Mrs. McLintock, Receipts for Cookery and Pastry-Work, 1736.

"Chocolate Honeycake" with oil, unsweetened cocoa and baking chocolate, honey, eggs, vanilla, flour, salt, baking powder. Adapted from Mollie Katzen, The Enchanted Broccoli Forest, 1982.

"Our new company is called Geno.type," Emily told Nick in the living room. "We're working on developing online communities, so you can constantly contact and update everyone in your family on news, birthdays, long-lost relatives."

"So is this a new Web site? Or a service company?" Nick asked.

"What we're really trying to do is move into the social-networking space." Her eyes were shining, alight with her new venture. As of yet, she had just four programmers, but Laura was still working for Emily as executive assistant, and together they were looking for someone in marketing, and they were interviewing Web-site designers. Geno.type filled Emily's days, and she dreamed about her business plan at night. She was not dating, but starting the company was very much like falling in love, turning her head, entrancing her. The world opened up, and it seemed to her as it had once before, that she was living on the cusp of a new era. Internet technology was that exciting. Her entrepreneurial spirit was that strong.

In London she had stayed in her mother's cluttered childhood home. She had met her relatives and their little children, attended the dark synagogue where women sat removed from men in a separate room. She'd sat at long tables for Friday-night dinners and listened to long rounds of song. She'd watched the men all dressed in black as they strolled together down the street. She'd played with babies who teethed on her fingers, and talked to women in the kitchen, helping them cook their heavy meals—their lentil soup with shank bones, their *cholent* with beef, potatoes, parsnips, carrots, beans; watching them bake *mandelbrot* and poppy-seed cake, *babkas, ruggelach*. She had listened to her cousins speak of weddings and births and holidays and met more cousins, and cousins of cousins, until at last she had decided to come home. She had returned without great discoveries about her mother, without a newfound religious faith, without a new identity or an adopted Hebrew name. What she brought back was a business plan. She would leverage the Internet to reconnect long-lost friends and relatives.

"You *look* the same," Jess had said at Christmastime, when she met Emily at the airport. "Except for the ring."

They were standing at the baggage claim, waiting for Emily's suitcases, and Jess couldn't help staring at her sister's bare hand.

"I gave it away," said Emily.

"Where?"

"Susan G. Komen Breast Cancer Foundation."

Even Jess looked a little shocked as she remembered the spectacular trio of white diamonds. "They take rings?"

"It's not a ring anymore," said Emily. "It's the Gillian Gould Bach Research Fund."

Now, at the reception, as Emily told Nick about her company, she nibbled a tiny lemon tart, and she was not perfectly happy. She did not have what Jess had, or what Orion and Sorel had, but she dreamed as George did once, that love was possible.

After the last guests left, after the caterers had packed up the leftovers to give away, George walked down to the garden and sank into the new hammock, a gift from Richard and Heidi. "God, I'm exhausted."

"I'm not," said Jess.

"Come here." George opened his arms. "Ouch!" Of course she would dive on top of him. "Careful," he murmured, caressing her through the silk. "You'll rip your dress."

"I thought McLintock's cake was best," she said. "What did you think?"

"I didn't try it," George admitted.

"Didn't you eat anything?"

"No," he said.

"Not even the strawberries?"

"Not one."

"But you were drinking champagne. I saw you. And I can taste it. I can still taste the bubbles."

"Really?"

"Well . . . metaphorically."

He kissed her. "What do metaphorical bubbles taste like?"

She rested her head on his chest, and tried to describe the champagne bubbles she imagined on his lips, but she could not, so they lay together in the hammock and talked and laughed about the day in dappled light. The house was quiet. Their friends had gone. The scent of roses, wedding music, and laughter faded away. The hammock swayed under them, and George and Jess floated together, although nothing lasted. They held each other, although nothing stayed.

Acknowledgments

I am grateful to the Radcliffe Institute for Advanced Study where I began researching and writing this book during my fellowship year. At the Schlesinger Library, Nancy Cott encouraged me, and her superb staff helped me navigate one of the finest cookbook collections in the world. It was Nancy who introduced me to the extraordinary Barbara Wheaton, a rare scholar who spoke to me at length about cookbooks, domestic history, and the art of collecting. I will never forget our conversations. Nach Waxman of Kitchen Arts & Letters took the time to share his insights and lively enthusiasm for cookbook collecting, trading, and selling. Allen and Grita Kamin told me much about the flora and fauna of Berkeley. Eighteenth-century scholar and oenophile John Bender advised me on French and Californian wines. Each of these eloquent experts taught me and inspired me.

ABOUT THE TYPE

This book was set in Caslon, a typeface first designed in 1722 by William Caslon. Its widespread use by most English printers in the early eighteenth century soon supplanted the Dutch typefaces that had formerly prevailed. The roman is considered a "workhorse" typeface due to its pleasant, open appearance, while the italic is exceedingly decorative.